Room Number 3 & Other Detective Stories by Anna Katharine Green

Anna Katharine Green was born in Brooklyn, New York on November 11th, 1846.

Anna's initial ambition was to be a poet. However that path failed to ignite any significant interest and she turned to fiction writing. She published her first—and most famous work in 1878—'The Leavenworth Case'. Wilkie Collins praised it and it sold extremely well.

It led to Anna writing 40 novels and to becoming known as 'the mother of the detective novel.'

In helping to shape the genre she brought many other innovations including a series detective: her main character was detective Ebenezer Gryce of the New York Metropolitan Police Force, but in three novels he is assisted by the nosy society spinster Amelia Butterworth, another innovation and a prototype for Miss Marple, Miss Silver and others.

She also invented the 'girl detective': in the character of Violet Strange, a debutante with a secret life as a sleuth. Anna's other innovations included the now familiar dead bodies in libraries, newspaper clippings as "clews," the coroner's inquest, and expert witnesses. Yale Law School once used her books to demonstrate how damaging it can be to rely on circumstantial evidence.

Her career was now well advanced and she was much admired.

On November 25, 1884, Green married the actor and stove designer, and later noted furniture maker, Charles Rohlfs, who was seven years her junior. They had three children; Rosamund, Roland and Sterling.

Although Anna was a progressive she did not approve of many of her feminist contemporaries, and was opposed to women's suffrage.

On November 25, 1884, Anna married the actor and noted furniture maker, Charles Rohlfs, who was seven years her junior. They had three children; Rosamund, Roland and Sterling.

Anna Katharine Green died on April 11, 1935 in Buffalo, New York, at the age of 88.

Index of Contents

ROOM NUMBER 3

I

"What door is that? You've opened all the others; why do you pass that one by?"

"Oh, that! That's only Number 3. A mere closet, gentlemen," responded the landlord in a pleasant voice. "To be sure, we sometimes use it as a sleeping-room when we are hard pushed. Jake, the clerk you saw below, used it last night. But it's not on our regular list. Do you want a peep at it?"

"Most assuredly. As you know, it's our duty to see every room in this house, whether it is on your regular list or not."

"All right. I haven't the key of this one with me. But—yes, I have. There, gentlemen!" he cried, unlocking the door and holding it open for them to look inside. "You see it no more answers the young lady's description than the others do. And I haven't another to show you. You have seen all those in front, and this is the last one in the rear. You'll have to believe our story. The old lady never put foot in this tavern."

The two men he addressed peered into the shadowy recesses before them, and one of them, a tall and uncommonly good-looking young man of stalwart build and unusually earnest manner, stepped softly inside. He was a gentleman farmer living near, recently appointed deputy sheriff on account of a recent outbreak of horse-stealing in the neighbourhood.

"I observe," he remarked, after a hurried glance about him, "that the paper on these walls is not at all like that she describes. She was very particular about the paper; said that it was of a muddy pink colour and had big scrolls on it which seemed to move and crawl about in whirls as you looked at it. This paper is blue and striped. Otherwise—"

"Let's go below," suggested his companion, who, from the deference with which his most casual word was received, was evidently a man of some authority. "It's cold here, and there are several new questions I should like to put to the young lady. Mr. Quimby,"—this to the landlord, "I've no doubt you are right, but we'll give this poor girl another chance. I believe in giving every one the utmost chance possible."

"My reputation is in your hands, Coroner Golden," was the quiet reply. Then, as they both turned, "my reputation against the word of an obviously demented girl."

The words made their own echo. As the third man moved to follow the other two into the hall, he seemed to catch this echo, for he involuntarily cast another look behind him as if expectant of some contradiction reaching him from the bare and melancholy walls he was leaving. But no such contradiction came. Instead, he appeared to read confirmation there of the landlord's plain and unembittered statement. The dull blue paper with its old-fashioned and uninteresting stripes seemed to have disfigured the walls for years. It was not only grimy with age, but showed here and there huge discoloured spots, especially around the stovepipe-hole high up on the left-hand side. Certainly he was a dreamer to doubt such plain evidences as these. Yet—

Here his eye encountered Quimby's, and pulling himself up short, he hastily fell into the wake of his comrade now hastening down the narrow passage to the wider hall in front. Had it occurred to him to turn again before rounding the corner—but no, I doubt if he would have learned anything even then. The closing of a door by a careful hand—the slipping up behind him of an eager and noiseless step— what is there in these to re-awaken curiosity and fix suspicion? Nothing, when the man concerned is Jacob Quimby; nothing. Better that he failed to look back; it left his judgment freer for the question confronting him in the room below.

Three Forks Tavern has been long forgotten, but at the time of which I write it was a well-known but little-frequented house, situated just back of the highway on the verge of the forest lying between the two towns of Chester and Danton in southern Ohio. It was of ancient build, and had all the picturesquesness of age and the English traditions of its original builder. Though so near two thriving towns, it retained its own quality of apparent remoteness from city life and city ways. This in a measure was made possible by the nearness of the woods which almost enveloped it; but the character of the man who ran it had still more to do with it, his sympathies being entirely with the old, and not at all with the new, as witness the old-style glazing still retained in its ancient doorway. This, while it appealed to a certain class of summer boarders, did not so much meet the wants of the casual traveller, so that while the house might from some reason or other be overfilled one night, it was just as likely to be almost empty the next, save for the faithful few who loved the woods and the ancient ways of the easy-mannered host and his attentive, soft-stepping help. The building itself was of wooden construction, high in front and low in the rear, with gables toward the highway, projecting here and there above a strip of rude old-fashioned carving. These gables were new, that is, they were only a century old; the portion now called the extension, in the passages of which we first found the men we have introduced to you, was the original house. Then it may have enjoyed the sunshine and air of the valley it overlooked, but now it was so hemmed in by yards and outbuildings as to be considered the most undesirable part of the house, and Number 3 the most undesirable of its rooms; which certainly does not speak well for it.

But we are getting away from our new friends and their mysterious errand. As I have already intimated, this tavern with the curious name (a name totally unsuggestive, by the way, of its location on a perfectly straight road) had for its southern aspect the road and a broad expanse beyond of varied landscape which made the front rooms cheerful even on a cloudy day; but it was otherwise with those in the rear and on the north end. They were never cheerful, and especially toward night were frequently so dark that artificial light was resorted to as early as three o'clock in the afternoon. It was so to-day in the remote parlour which these three now entered. A lamp had been lit, though the daylight still struggled feebly in, and it was in this conflicting light that there rose up before them the vision of a woman, who seen at any time and in any place would have drawn, if not held, the eye, but seen in her present attitude and at such a moment of question and suspense, struck the imagination with a force likely to fix her image forever in the mind, if not in the heart, of a sympathetic observer.

I should like to picture her as she stood there, because the impression she made at this instant determined the future action of the man I have introduced to you as not quite satisfied with the appearances he had observed above. Young, slender but vigorous, with a face whose details you missed in the fire of her eye and the wonderful red of her young, fresh but determined mouth, she stood, on guard as it were, before a shrouded form on a couch at the far end of the room. An imperative Keep back! spoke in her look, her attitude, and the silent gesture of one outspread hand, but it was the Keep back! of love, not of fear, the command of an outraged soul, conscious of its rights and instinctively alert to maintain them.

The landlord at sight of the rebuke thus given to their intrusion, stepped forward with a conciliatory bow.

"I beg pardon," said he, "but these gentlemen, Doctor Golden, the coroner from Chester, and Mr. Hammersmith, wish to ask you a few more questions about your mother's death. You will answer them, I am sure."

Slowly her eyes moved till they met those of the speaker.

"I am anxious to do so," said she, in a voice rich with many emotions. But seeing the open compassion in the landlord's face, the colour left her cheeks, almost her lips, and drawing back the hand which she had continued to hold outstretched, she threw a glance of helpless inquiry about her which touched the younger man's heart and induced him to say:

"The truth should not be hard to find in a case like this. I'm sure the young lady can explain. Doctor Golden, are you ready for her story?"

The coroner, who had been silent up till now, probably from sheer surprise at the beauty and simple, natural elegance of the woman caught, as he believed, in a net of dreadful tragedy, roused himself at this direct question, and bowing with an assumption of dignity far from encouraging to the man and woman anxiously watching him, replied:

"We will hear what she has to say, of course, but the facts are well known. The woman she calls mother was found early this morning lying on her face in the adjoining woods quite dead. She had fallen over a half-concealed root, and with such force that she never moved again. If her daughter was with her at the time, then that daughter fled without attempting to raise her. The condition and position of the wound on the dead woman's forehead, together with such corroborative facts as have since come to light, preclude all argument on this point. But we'll listen to the young woman, notwithstanding; she has a right to speak, and she shall speak. Did not your mother die in the woods? No hocus-pocus, miss, but the plain unvarnished truth."

"Sirs,"—the term was general, but her appeal appeared to be directed solely to the one sympathetic figure before her, "if my mother died in the wood—and, for all I can say, she may have done so—it was not till after she had been in this house. She arrived in my company, and was given a room. I saw the room and I saw her in it. I cannot be deceived in this. If I am, then my mind has suddenly failed me;— something which I find it hard to believe."

"Mr. Quimby, did Mrs. Demarest come to the house with Miss Demarest?" inquired Mr. Hammersmith of the silent landlord.

"She says so," was the reply, accompanied by a compassionate shrug which spoke volumes. "And I am quite sure she means it," he added, with kindly emphasis. "But ask Jake, who was in the office all the evening. Ask my wife, who saw the young lady to her room. Ask anybody and everybody who was around the tavern last night. I'm not the only one to say that Miss Demarest came in alone. All will tell you that she arrived here without escort of any kind; declined supper, but wanted a room, and when I hesitated to give it to her, said by way of explanation of her lack of a companion that she had had trouble in Chester and had left town very hurriedly for her home. That her mother was coming to meet her and would probably arrive here very soon. That when this occurred I was to notify her; but if a gentleman called instead, I was to be very careful not to admit that any such person as herself was in the house. Indeed, to avoid any such possibility she prayed that her name might be left off the register— a favour which I was slow in granting her, but which I finally did, as you can see for yourselves."

"Oh!" came in indignant exclamation from the young woman before them. "I understand my position now. This man has a bad conscience. He has something to hide, or he would not take to lying about little things like that. I never asked him to allow me to leave my name off the register. On the contrary I wrote my name in it and my mother's name, too. Let him bring the book here and you will see."

"We have seen," responded the coroner. "We looked in the register ourselves. Your names are not there."

The flush of indignation which had crimsoned her cheeks faded till she looked as startling and individual in her pallor as she had the moment before in her passionate bloom.

"Not there?" fell from her lips in a frozen monotone as her eyes grew fixed upon the faces before her and her hand went groping around for some support.

Mr. Hammersmith approached with a chair.

"Sit," he whispered. Then, as she sank slowly into an attitude of repose, he added gently, "You shall have every consideration. Only tell the truth, the exact truth without any heightening from your imagination, and, above all, don't be frightened."

She may have heard his words, but she gave no sign of comprehending them. She was following the movements of the landlord, who had slipped out to procure the register, and now stood holding it out toward the coroner.

"Let her see for herself," he suggested, with a bland, almost fatherly, air.

Doctor Golden took the book and approached Miss Demarest.

"Here is a name very unlike yours," he pointed out, as her eye fell on the page he had opened to. "Annette Colvin, Lansing, Michigan."

"That is not my name or writing," said she.

"There is room below it for your name and that of your mother, but the space is blank, do you see?"

"Yes, yes, I see," she admitted. "Yet I wrote my name in the book! Or is it all a monstrous dream!"

The coroner returned the book to the landlord.

"Is this your only book?" he asked.

"The only book."

Miss Demarest's eyes flashed. Hammersmith, who had watched this scene with intense interest, saw, or believed that he saw, in this flash the natural indignation of a candid mind face to face with arrant knavery. But when he forced himself to consider the complacent Quimby he did not know what to think. His aspect of self-confidence equalled hers. Indeed, he showed the greater poise. Yet her tones rang true as she cried:

"You made up one plausible story, and you may well make up another. I demand the privilege of relating the whole occurrence as I remember it," she continued with an appealing look in the one sympathetic direction. "Then you can listen to him."

"We desire nothing better," returned the coroner.

"I shall have to mention a circumstance very mortifying to myself," she proceeded, with a sudden effort at self-control, which commanded the admiration even of the coroner. "My one adviser is dead," here her eyes flashed for a moment toward the silent form behind her. "If I make mistakes, if I seem unwomanly—but you have asked for the truth and you shall have it, all of it. I have no father. Since early this morning I have had no mother. But when I had, I found it my duty to work for her as well as for myself, that she might have the comforts she had been used to and could no longer afford. For this purpose I sought a situation in Chester, and found one in a family I had rather not name." A momentary tremor, quickly suppressed, betrayed the agitation which this allusion cost her. "My mother lived in Danton (the next town to the left). Anybody there will tell you what a good woman she was. I had wished her to live in Chester (that is, at first; later, I—I was glad she didn't), but she had been born in Danton, and could not accustom herself to strange surroundings. Once a week I went home, and once a week, usually on a Wednesday, she would come and meet me on the highroad, for a little visit. Once we met here, but this is a circumstance no one seems to remember. I was very fond of my mother and she of me. Had I loved no one else, I should have been happy still, and not been obliged to face strangers over her body and bare the secrets of my heart to preserve my good name. There is a man, he seems a thousand miles away from me now, so much have I lived since yesterday. He—he lived in the house where I did—was one of the family—always at table—always before my eyes. He fancied me. I—I might have fancied him had he been a better man. But he was far from being of the sort my mother approved, and when he urged his suit too far, I grew frightened and finally ran away. It was not so much that I could not trust him," she bravely added after a moment of silent confusion, "but that I could not trust myself. He had an unfortunate influence over me, which I hated while I half yielded to it."

"You ran away. When was this?"

"Yesterday afternoon at about six. He had vowed that he would see me again before the evening was over, and I took that way to prevent a meeting. There was no other so simple,—or such was my thought at the time. I did not dream that sorrows awaited me in this quiet tavern, and perplexities so much greater than any which could have followed a meeting with him that I feel my reason fail when I contemplate them."

"Go on," urged the coroner, after a moment of uneasy silence. "Let us hear what happened after you left your home in Chester."

"I went straight to the nearest telegraph office, and sent a message to my mother. I told her I was coming home, and for her to meet me on the road near this tavern. Then I went to Hudson's and had supper, for I had not eaten before leaving my employer's. The sun had set when I finally started, and I walked fast so as to reach Three Forks before dark. If my mother had got the telegram at once, which I calculated on her doing, as she lived next door to the telegraph office in Danton, she would be very near this place on my arrival here. So I began to look for her as soon as I entered the woods. But I did not see her. I came as far as the tavern door, and still I did not see her. But farther on, just where the road turns to cross the railroad-track, I spied her coming, and ran to meet her. She was glad to see me, but asked a good many questions which I had some difficulty in answering. She saw this, and held me to the matter till I had satisfied her. When this was done it was late and cold, and we decided to come to the tavern for the night. And we came! Nothing shall ever make me deny so positive a fact. We came, and this man received us."

With her final repetition of this assertion, she rose and now stood upright, with her finger pointing straight at Quimby. Had he cringed or let his eyes waver from hers by so much as a hair's breadth, her accusation would have stood and her cause been won. But not a flicker disturbed the steady patience of his look, and Hammersmith, who had made no effort to hide his anxiety to believe her story, showed his disappointment with equal frankness as he asked:

"Who else was in the office? Surely Mr. Quimby was not there alone?"

She reseated herself before answering. Hammersmith could see the effort she made to recall that simple scene. He found himself trying to recall it, too—the old-fashioned, smoke-begrimed office, with its one long window toward the road and the glass-paned door leading into the hall of entrance. They had come in by that door and crossed to the bar, which was also the desk in this curious old hostelry. He could see them standing there in the light of possibly a solitary lamp, the rest of the room in shadow unless a game of checkers were on, which evidently was not so on this night. Had she turned her head to peer into those shadows? It was not likely. She was supported by her mother's presence, and this she was going to say. By some strange telepathy that he would have laughed at a few hours before, he feels confident of her words before she speaks. Yet he listens intently as she finally looks up and answers:

"There was a man, I am sure there was a man somewhere at the other end of the office. But I paid no attention to him. I was bargaining for two rooms and registering my name and that of my mother."

"Two rooms; why two? You are not a fashionable young lady to require a room alone."

"Gentlemen, I was tired. I had been through a wearing half-hour. I knew that if we occupied the same room or even adjoining ones that nothing could keep us from a night of useless and depressing conversation. I did not feel equal to it, so I asked for two rooms a short distance apart."

An explanation which could at least be accepted. Mr. Hammersmith felt an increase of courage and scarcely winced as his colder-blooded companion continued this unofficial examination by asking:

"Where were you standing when making these arrangements with Mr. Quimby?"

"Right before the desk."

"And your mother?"

"She was at my left and a little behind me. She was a shy woman. I usually took the lead when we were together."

"Was she veiled?" the coroner continued quietly.

"I think so. She had been crying—" The bereaved daughter paused.

"But don't you know?"

"My impression is that her veil was down when we came into the room. She may have lifted it as she stood there. I know that it was lifted as we went upstairs. I remember feeling glad that the lamps gave so poor a light, she looked so distressed."

"Physically, do you mean, or mentally?"

Mr. Hammersmith asked this question. It seemed to rouse some new train of thought in the girl's mind. For a minute she looked intently at the speaker, then she replied in a disturbed tone:

"Both. I wonder—" Here her thought wavered and she ceased.

"Go on," ordered the coroner impatiently. "Tell your story. It contradicts that of the landlord in almost every point, but we've promised to hear it out, and we will."

Rousing, she hastened to obey him.

"Mr. Quimby told the truth when he said that he asked me if I would have supper, also when he repeated what I said about a gentleman, but not when he declared that I wished to be told if my mother should come and ask for me. My mother was at my side all the time we stood there talking, and I did not need to make any requests concerning her. When we went to our rooms a woman accompanied us. He says she is his wife. I should like to see that woman."

"I am here, miss," spoke up a voice from a murky corner no one had thought of looking in till now.

Miss Demarest at once rose, waiting for the woman to come forward. This she did with a quick, natural step which insensibly prepared the mind for the brisk, assertive woman who now presented herself. Mr. Hammersmith, at sight of her open, not unpleasing face, understood for the first time the decided attitude of the coroner. If this woman corroborated her husband's account, the poor young girl, with her incongruous beauty and emotional temperament, would not have much show. He looked to see her quailing now. But instead of that she stood firm, determined, and feverishly beautiful.

"Let her tell you what took place upstairs," she cried. "She showed us the rooms and carried water afterward to the one my mother occupied."

"I am sorry to contradict the young lady," came in even tones from the unembarrassed, motherly-looking woman thus appealed to. "She thinks that her mother was with her and that I conducted this mother to another room after showing her to her own. I don't doubt in the least that she has worked herself up to the point of absolutely believing this. But the facts are these: She came alone and went to her room unattended by any one but myself. And what is more, she seemed entirely composed at the time, and I never thought of suspecting the least thing wrong. Yet her mother lay all that time in the wood—"

"Silence!"

This word was shot at her by Miss Demarest, who had risen to her full height and now fairly flamed upon them all in her passionate indignation. "I will not listen to such words till I have finished all I have to say and put these liars to the blush. My mother was with me, and this woman witnessed our good-night embrace, and then showed my mother to her own room. I watched them going. They went down the hall to the left and around a certain corner. I stood looking after them till they turned this corner, then I closed my door and began to take off my hat. But I wasn't quite satisfied with the good-night which had passed between my poor mother and myself, and presently I opened my door and ran down the hall and around the corner on a chance of finding her room. I don't remember very well how that hall looked. I passed several doors seemingly shut for the night, and should have turned back, confused, if at that moment I had not spied the landlady's figure, your figure, madam, coming out of one room on your way to another. You were carrying a pitcher, and I made haste and ran after you and reached the door just before you turned to shut it. Can you deny that, or that you stepped aside while I ran in and gave my mother another hug? If you can and do, then you are a dangerous and lying woman, or I—But I won't admit that I'm not all right. It is you, base and untruthful woman, who for some end I cannot fathom persist in denying facts on which my honour, if not my life, depends. Why, gentlemen, you, one of you at least, have heard me describe the very room in which I saw my mother. It is imprinted on my mind. I didn't know at the time that I took especial notice of it, but hardly a detail escaped me. The paper on the wall—"

"We have been looking through the rooms," interpolated the coroner. "We do not find any papered with the muddy pink you talk about."

She stared, drew back from them all, and finally sank into a chair. "You do not find—But you have not been shown them all."

"I think so."

"You have not. There is such a room. I could not have dreamed it."

Silence met this suggestion.

Throwing up her hands like one who realises for the first time that the battle is for life, she let an expression of her despair and desolation rush in frenzy from her lips:

"It's a conspiracy. The whole thing is a conspiracy. If my mother had had money on her or had worn valuable jewelry, I should believe her to have been a victim of this lying man and woman. As it is, I don't trust them. They say that my poor mother was found lying ready dressed and quite dead in the wood. That may be true, for I saw men bringing her in. But if so, what warrant have we that she was not lured there, slaughtered, and made to seem the victim of accident by this unscrupulous man and woman? Such things have been done; but for a daughter to fabricate such a plot as they impute to me is past belief, out of Nature and impossible. With all their wiles, they cannot prove it. I dare them to do so; I dare any one to do so."

Then she begged to be allowed to search the house for the room she so well remembered. "When I show you that," she cried, with ringing assurance, "you will believe the rest of my story."

"Shall I take the young lady up myself?" asked Mr. Quimby. "Or will it be enough if my wife accompanies her?"

"We will all accompany her," said the coroner.

"Very good," came in hearty acquiescence.

"It's the only way to quiet her," he whispered in Mr. Hammersmith's ear.

The latter turned on him suddenly.

"None of your insinuations," he cried. "She's as far from insane as I am myself. We shall find the room."

"You, too," fell softly from the other's lips as he stepped back into the coroner's wake. Mr. Hammersmith gave his arm to Miss Demarest, and the landlady brought up the rear.

"Upstairs," ordered the trembling girl. "We will go first to the room I occupied."

As they reached the door, she motioned them all back, and started away from them down the hall. Quickly they followed. "It was around a corner," she muttered broodingly, halting at the first turning. "That is all I remember. But we'll visit every room."

"We have already," objected the coroner, but meeting Mr. Hammersmith's warning look, he desisted from further interference.

"I remember its appearance perfectly. I remember it as if it were my own," she persisted, as door after door was thrown back and as quickly shut again at a shake of her head. "Isn't there another hall? Might I not have turned some other corner?"

"Yes, there is another hall," acquiesced the landlord, leading the way into the passage communicating with the extension.

"Oh!" she murmured, as she noted the increased interest in both the coroner and his companion; "we shall find it here."

"Do you recognise the hall?" asked the coroner as they stepped through a narrow opening into the old part.

"No, but I shall recognise the room."

"Wait!" It was Hammersmith who called her back as she was starting forward. "I should like you to repeat just how much furniture this room contained and where it stood."

She stopped, startled, and then said:

"It was awfully bare; a bed was on the left—"

"On the left?"

"She said the left," quoth the landlord, "though I don't see that it matters; it's all fancy with her."

"Go on," kindly urged Hammersmith.

"There was a window. I saw the dismal panes and my mother standing between them and me. I can't describe the little things."

"Possibly because there were none to describe," whispered Hammersmith in his superior's ear.

Meanwhile the landlord and his wife awaited their advance with studied patience. As Miss Demarest joined him, he handed her a bunch of keys, with the remark:

"None of these rooms are occupied to-day, so you can open them without hesitation."

She stared at him and ran quickly forward. Mr. Hammersmith followed speedily after. Suddenly both paused. She had lost the thread of her intention before opening a single door.

"I thought I could go straight to it," she declared. "I shall have to open all the doors, as we did in the other hall."

"Let me help you," proffered Mr. Hammersmith. She accepted his aid, and the search recommenced with the same results as before. Hope sank to disappointment as each door was passed. The vigour of her step was gone, and as she paused heartsick before the last and only remaining door, it was with an ashy face she watched Mr. Hammersmith stoop to insert the key.

He, on his part, as the door fell back, watched her for some token of awakened interest. But he watched in vain. The smallness of the room, its bareness, its one window, the absence of all furniture save the solitary cot drawn up on the right (not on the left, as she had said), seemed to make little or no impression on her.

"The last! the last! and I have not found it. Oh, sir," she moaned, catching at Mr. Hammersmith's arm, "am I then mad? Was it a dream? Or is this a dream? I feel that I no longer know." Then, as the landlady officiously stepped up, she clung with increased frenzy to Mr. Hammersmith, crying, with positive wildness, "This is the dream! The room I remember is a real one and my story is real. Prove it, or my reason will leave me. I feel it going—going—"

"Hush!" It was Hammersmith who sought thus to calm her. "Your story is real and I will prove it so. Meanwhile trust your reason. It will not fail you."

He had observed the corners of the landlord's hitherto restrained lips settle into a slightly sarcastic curl as the door of this room closed for the second time.

"The girl's beauty has imposed on you."

"I don't think so. I should be sorry to think myself so weak. I simply credit her story more than I do that of Quimby."

"But his is supported by several witnesses. Hers has no support at all."

"That is what strikes me as so significant. This man Quimby understands himself. Who are his witnesses? His wife and his head man. There is nobody else. In the half-hour which has just passed I have searched diligently for some disinterested testimony supporting his assertion, but I have found none. No one knows anything. Of the three persons occupying rooms in the extension last night, two were asleep and the third overcome with drink. The maids won't talk. They seem uneasy, and I detected a sly look pass from the one to the other at some question I asked, but they won't talk. There's a conspiracy somewhere. I'm as sure of it as that I am standing here."

"Nonsense! What should there be a conspiracy about? You would make this old woman an important character. Now we know that she wasn't. Look at the matter as it presents itself to an unprejudiced mind. A young and susceptible girl falls in love with a man, who is at once a gentleman and a scamp. She may have tried to resist her feelings, and she may not have. Your judgment and mine would probably differ on this point. What she does not do is to let her mother into her confidence. She sees the man—runs upon him, if you will, in places or under circumstances she cannot avoid—till her judgment leaves her and the point of catastrophe is reached. Then, possibly, she awakens, or what is more probable, seeks to protect herself from the penetration and opposition of his friends by meetings less open than those in which they had lately indulged. She says that she left the house to escape seeing him again last night. But this is not true. On the contrary, she must have given him to understand where she was going, for she had an interview with him in the woods before she came upon her mother. He acknowledges to the interview. I have just had a talk with him over the telephone."

"Then you know his name?"

"Yes, of course, she had to tell me. It's young Maxwell. I suspected it from the first."

"Maxwell!" Mr. Hammersmith's cheek showed an indignant colour. Or was it a reflection from the setting sun? "You called him a scamp a few minutes ago. A scamp's word isn't worth much."

"No, but it's evidence when on oath, and I fancy he will swear to the interview."

"Well, well, say there was an interview."

"It changes things, Mr. Hammersmith. It changes things. It makes possible a certain theory of mine which accounts for all the facts."

"It does!"

"Yes. I don't think this girl is really responsible. I don't believe she struck her mother or is deliberately telling a tissue of lies to cover up some dreadful crime. I consider her the victim of a mental hallucination, the result of some great shock. Now what was the shock? I'll tell you. This is how I see it, how Mr. Quimby sees it, and such others in the house as have ventured an opinion. She was having this conversation with her lover in the woods below here when her mother came in sight. Surprised, for she had evidently not expected her mother to be so prompt, she hustled her lover off and hastened to meet the approaching figure. But it was too late. The mother had seen the man, and in the excitement of the discovery and the altercation which undoubtedly followed, made such a sudden move, possibly of indignant departure, that her foot was caught by one of the roots protruding at this point and she fell her whole length and with such violence as to cause immediate death. Now, Mr. Hammersmith, stop a minute and grasp the situation. If, as I believe at this point in the inquiry, Miss Demarest had encountered a passionate opposition to her desires from this upright and thoughtful mother, the spectacle of this mother lying dead before her, with all opposition gone and the way cleared in an instant to her wishes, but cleared in a manner which must haunt her to her own dying day, was enough to turn a brain already heated with contending emotions. Fancies took the place of facts, and by the time she reached this house had so woven themselves into a concrete form that no word she now utters can be relied on. This is how I see it, Mr. Hammersmith, and it is on this basis I shall act."

Hammersmith made an effort and, nodding slightly, said in a restrained tone:

"Perhaps you are justified. I have no wish to force my own ideas upon you; they are much too vague at present. I will only suggest that this is not the first time the attention of the police has been drawn to this house by some mysterious occurrence. You remember the Stevens case? There must have been notes to the amount of seven thousand dollars in the pile he declared had been taken from him some time during the day and night he lodged here."

"Stevens! I remember something about it. But they couldn't locate the theft here. The fellow had been to the fair in Chester all day and couldn't swear that he had seen his notes after leaving the grounds."

"I know. But he always looked on Quimby as the man. Then there is the adventure of little Miss Thistlewaite."

"I don't remember that."

"It didn't get into the papers; but it was talked about in the neighbourhood. She is a quaint one, full of her crotchets, but clear—clear as a bell where her interests are involved. She took a notion to spend a summer here—in this house, I mean. She had a room in one of the corners overlooking the woods, and professing to prefer Nature to everything else, was happy enough till she began to miss things—rings, pins, a bracelet and, finally, a really valuable chain. She didn't complain at first—the objects were trivial, and she herself somewhat to blame for leaving them lying around in her room, often without locking the door. But when the chain went, the matter became serious, and she called Mr. Quimby's attention to her losses. He advised her to lock her door, which she was careful to do after that, but not with the expected result. She continued to miss things, mostly jewelry of which she had a ridiculous store. Various domestics were dismissed, and finally one of the permanent boarders was requested to leave, but still the thefts went on till, her patience being exhausted, she notified the police and a detective was sent: I have always wished I had been that detective. The case ended in what was always considered a joke. Another object disappeared while he was there, and it having been conclusively proved to him that it could not have been taken by way of the door, he turned his attention to the window which it was one of her freaks always to keep wide open. The result was curious. One day he spied from a hiding-place he had made in the bushes a bird flying out from that window, and following the creature till she alighted in her nest he climbed the tree and searched that nest. It was encrusted with jewels. The bird was a magpie and had followed its usual habits, but—the chain was not there, nor one or two other articles of decided value. Nor were they ever found. The bird bore the blame; the objects missing were all heavy and might have been dropped in its flight, but I have always thought that the bird had an accomplice, a knowing fellow who understood what's what and how to pick out his share."

The coroner smiled. There was little conviction and much sarcasm in that smile. Hammersmith turned away. "Have you any instructions for me?" he said.

"Yes, you had better stay here. I will return in the morning with my jury. It won't take long after that to see this thing through."

The look he received in reply was happily hidden from him.

III

"Yes, I'm going to stay here to-night. As it's a mere formality, I shall want a room to sit in, and if you have no objection I'll take Number 3 on the rear corridor."

"I'm sorry, but Number 3 is totally unfit for use, as you've already seen."

"Oh, I'm not particular. Put a table in and a good light, and I'll get along with the rest. I have something to do. Number 3 will answer."

The landlord shifted his feet, cast a quick scrutinising look at the other's composed face, and threw back his head with a quick laugh.

"As you will. I can't make you comfortable on such short notice, but that's your lookout. I've several other rooms vacant."

"I fancy that room," was all the reply he got.

Mr. Quimby at once gave his orders. They were received by Jake with surprise.

Fifteen minutes later Hammersmith prepared to install himself in these desolate quarters. But before doing so he walked straight to the small parlour where he had last seen Miss Demarest and, knocking, asked for the privilege of a word with her. It was not her figure, however, which appeared in the doorway, but that of the landlady.

"Miss Demarest is not here," announced that buxom and smooth-tongued woman. "She was like to faint after you gentlemen left the room, and I just took her upstairs to a quiet place by herself."

"On the rear corridor?"

"Oh, no, sir; a nice front room; we don't consider money in a case like this."

"Will you give me its number?"

Her suave and steady look changed to one of indignation.

"You're asking a good deal, aren't you? I doubt if the young lady—"

"The number, if you please," he quietly put in.

"Thirty-two," she snapped out. "She will have every care," she hastened to assure him as he turned away.

"I've no doubt. I do not intend to sleep to to-night; if the young lady is worse, you will communicate the fact to me. You will find me in Number 3."

He had turned back to make this reply, and was looking straight at her as the number dropped from his lips. It did not disturb her set smile, but in some inscrutable way all meaning seemed to leave that smile, and she forgot to drop her hand which had been stretched out in an attempted gesture.

"Number 3," he repeated. "Don't forget, madam."

The injunction seemed superfluous. She had not dropped her hand when he wheeled around once more in taking the turn at the foot of the staircase.

Jake and a very sleepy maid were on the floor above when he reached it. He paid no attention to Jake, but he eyed the girl somewhat curiously. She was comparatively a new domestic in the tavern, having been an inmate there for only three weeks. He had held a few minutes' conversation with her during the half-hour of secret inquiry in which he had previously indulged and he remembered some of her careful answers, also the air of fascination with which she had watched him all the time they were together. He had made nothing of her then, but the impression had remained that she was the one hopeful source of knowledge in the house. Now she looked dull and moved about in Jake's wake like an automaton. Yet Hammersmith made up his mind to speak to her as soon as the least opportunity offered.

"Where is 32?" he asked as he moved away from them in the opposite direction from the course they were taking.

"I thought you were to have room Number 3," blurted out Jake.

"I am. But where is 32?"

"Round there," said she. "A lady's in there now. The one—"

"Come on," urged Jake. "Huldah, you may go now. I'll show the gentleman his room."

Huldah dropped her head, and began to move off, but not before Hammersmith had caught her eye.

"Thirty-two," he formed with his lips, showing her a scrap of paper which he held in his hand.

He thought she nodded, but he could not be sure. Nevertheless, he ventured to lay the scrap down on a small table he was passing, and when he again looked back, saw that it was gone and Huldah with it. But whither, he could not be quite sure. There was always a risk in these attempts, and he only half trusted the girl. She might carry it to 32, and she might carry it to Quimby. In the first case, Miss Demarest would know that she had an active and watchful friend in the house; in the other, the dubious landlord would but receive an open instead of veiled intimation that the young deputy had his eye on him and was not to be fooled by appearances and the lack of evidence to support his honest convictions.

They had done little more than he had suggested to make Number 3 habitable. As the door swung open under Jake's impatient hand, the half-lighted hollow of the almost empty room gaped uninvitingly before them, with just a wooden-bottomed chair and a rickety table added to the small cot-bed which had been almost its sole furnishing when he saw it last. The walls, bare as his hand, stretched without relief from baseboard to ceiling, and the floor from door to window showed an unbroken expanse of unpainted boards, save for the narrow space between chair and table, where a small rug had been laid. A cheerless outlook for a tired man, but it seemed to please Hammersmith. There was paper and ink on the table, and the lamp which he took care to examine held oil enough to last till morning. With a tray of eatables, this ought to suffice, or so his manner conveyed, and Jake, who had already supplied the eatables, was backing slowly out when his eye, which seemingly against his will had been travelling curiously up and down the walls, was caught by that of Hammersmith, and he plunged from the room, with a flush visible even in that half light.

It was a trivial circumstance, but it fitted in with Hammersmith's trend of thought at the moment, and when the man was gone he stood for several minutes with his own eye travelling up and down those dusky walls in an inquiry which this distant inspection did not seem thoroughly to satisfy, for in another instant he had lifted a glass of water from the tray and, going to the nearest wall, began to moisten the paper at one of the edges. When it was quite wet, he took out his penknife, but before using it, he looked behind him, first at the door, and then at the window. The door was shut; the window seemingly guarded by an outside blind; but the former was not locked, and the latter showed, upon closer inspection, a space between the slats which he did not like. Crossing to the door, he carefully turned the key, then proceeding to the window, he endeavoured to throw up the sash in order to close the blinds more effectually. But he found himself balked in the attempt. The cord had been cut and the sash refused to move under his hand.

Casting a glance of mingled threat and sarcasm out into the night, he walked back to the wall and, dashing more water over the spot he had already moistened, began to pick at the loosened edges of the paper which were slowly falling away. The result was a disappointment; how great a disappointment he presently realised, as his knife-point encountered only plaster under the peeling edges of the paper. He had hoped to find other paper under the blue—the paper which Miss Demarest remembered—and not finding it, was conscious of a sinking of the heart which had never attended any of his miscalculations before. Were his own feelings involved in this matter? It would certainly seem so.

Astonished at his own sensations, he crossed back to the table, and sinking into the chair beside it, endeavoured to call up his common sense, or at least shake himself free from the glamour which had seized him. But this especial sort of glamour is not so easily shaken off. Minutes passed—an hour, and little else filled his thoughts than the position of this bewitching girl and the claims she had on his sense of justice. If he listened, it was to hear her voice raised in appeal at his door. If he closed his eyes, it was to see her image more plainly on the background of his consciousness. The stillness into which the house had sunk aided this absorption and made his battle a losing one. There was naught to distract his mind, and when he dozed, as he did for a while after midnight, it was to fall under the conjuring effect of dreams in which her form dominated with all the force of an unfettered fancy. The pictures which his imagination thus brought before him were startling and never to be forgotten. The first was that of an angry sea in the blue light of an arctic winter. Stars flecked the zenith and shed a pale lustre on the moving ice-floes hurrying toward a horizon of skurrying clouds and rising waves. On one of those floes stood a woman alone, with face set toward her death.

The scene changed. A desert stretched out before him. Limitless, with the blazing colours of the arid sand topped by a cloudless sky, it revealed but one suggestion of life in its herbless, waterless, shadowless solitude. She stood in the midst of this desert, and as he had seen her sway on the ice-floe, so he saw her now stretching unavailing arms to the brazen heavens and sink—No! it was not a desert, it was not a sea, ice-bound or torrid, it was a toppling city, massed against impenetrable night one moment, then shown to its awful full the next by the sudden tearing through of lightning-flashes. He saw it all—houses, churches, towers, erect and with steadfast line, a silhouette of quiet rest awaiting dawn; then at a flash, the doom, the quake, the breaking down of outline, the caving in of walls, followed by the sickening collapse in which life, wealth, and innumerable beating human hearts went down into the unseen and unknowable. He saw and he heard, but his eyes clung to but one point, his ears listened for but one cry. There at the extremity of a cornice, clinging to a bending beam, was the figure again—the woman of the ice-floe and the desert. She seemed nearer now. He could see the straining muscles of her arm, the white despair of her set features. He wished to call aloud to her not to look down—then, as the sudden darkness yielded to another illuminating gleam, his mind changed and he would fain have begged her to look, slip, and end all, for subtly, quietly, ominously somewhere below her feet, he had caught the glimpsing of a feathery line of smoke curling up from the lower débris. Flame was there; a creeping devil which soon—

Horror! it was no dream! He was awake, he, Hammersmith, in this small solitary hotel in Ohio, and there was fire, real fire in the air, and in his ears the echo of a shriek such as a man hears but few times in his life, even if his lot casts him continually among the reckless and the suffering. Was it hers? Had these dreams been forerunners of some menacing danger? He was on his feet, his eyes staring at the floor beneath him, through the cracks of which wisps of smoke were forcing their way up. The tavern was not only on fire, but on fire directly under him. This discovery woke him effectually. He bounded to the door; it would not open. He wrenched at the key; but it would not turn, it was hampered in the lock. Drawing back, he threw his whole weight against the panels, uttering loud cries for help. The effort was useless. No yielding in the door, no rush to his assistance from without. Aroused now to his danger—reading the signs of the broken cord and hampered lock only too well—he desisted from his vain attempts and turned desperately toward the window. Though it might be impossible to hold up the sash and crawl under it at the same time, his only hope of exit lay there, as well as his only means of surviving the inroad of smoke which was fast becoming unendurable. He would break the sash and seek escape that way. They had doomed him to death, but he could climb roofs like a cat and feared nothing when once relieved from this smoke. Catching up the chair, he advanced toward the window.

But before reaching it he paused. It was not only he they sought to destroy, but the room. There was evidence of crime in the room. In that moment of keenly aroused intelligence he felt sure of it. What was to be done? How could he save the room, and, by these means, save himself and her? A single glance about assured him that he could not save it. The boards under his feet were hot. Glints of yellow light streaking through the shutters showed that the lower storey had already burst into flame. The room must go and with it every clue to the problem which was agitating him. Meanwhile, his eyeballs were smarting, his head growing dizzy. No longer sure of his feet, he staggered over to the wall and was about to make use of its support in his effort to reach the window, when his eyes fell on the spot from which he had peeled the paper, and he came to a sudden standstill. A bit of pink was showing under one edge of the blue.

Dropping the chair which he still held, he fumbled for his knife, found it, made a dash at that wall, and for a few frenzied moments worked at the plaster till he had hacked off a piece which he thrust into his pocket. Then seizing the chair again, he made for the window and threw it with all his force against the panes. They crashed and the air came rushing in, reviving him enough for the second attempt. This not only smashed the pane, but loosened the shutters, and in one instant two sights burst upon his view—the face of a man in an upper window of the adjoining barn and the sudden swooping up from below of a column of deadly smoke which seemed to cut off all hope of his saving himself by the means he had calculated on. Yet no other way offered. It would be folly to try the door again. This was the only road, threatening as it looked, to possible safety for himself and her. He would take it, and if he succumbed in the effort, it should be with a final thought of her who was fast becoming an integral part of his own being.

Meanwhile he had mounted to the sill and taken another outward look. This room, as I have already intimated, was in the rear of an extension running back from the centre of the main building. It consisted of only two stories, surmounted by a long, slightly-peaked roof. As the ceilings were low in this portion of the house, the gutter of this roof was very near the top of the window. To reach it was not a difficult feat for one of his strength and agility, and if only the smoke would blow aside—Ah, it is doing so! A sudden change of wind had come to his rescue, and for the moment the way is clear for him to work himself out and up on to the ledge above. But once there, horror makes him weak again. A window, high up in the main building overlooking the extension, had come in sight, and in it sways a frantic woman ready to throw herself out. She screamed as he measured with his eye the height of that window from the sloping roof and thence to the ground, and he recognised the voice. It was the same he had heard before, but it was not hers. She would not be up so high, besides the shape and attitude, shown fitfully by the light of the now leaping flames, were those of a heavier, and less-refined woman. It was one of the maids—it was the maid Huldah, the one from whom he had hoped to win some light on this affair. Was she locked in, too? Her frenzy and mad looking behind and below her seemed to argue that she was. What deviltry! and, ah! what a confession of guilt on the part of the vile man who had planned this abominable end for the two persons whose evidence he dreaded. Helpless with horror, he became a man again in his indignation. Such villainy should not succeed. He would fight not only for his own life, but for this woman's. Miss Demarest was doubtless safe. Yet he wished he were sure of it; he could work with so much better heart. Her window was not visible from where he crouched. It was on the other side of the house. If she screamed, he would not be able to hear her. He must trust her to Providence. But his dream! his dream! The power of it was still upon him; a forerunner of fate, a picture possibly of her doom. The hesitation which this awful thought caused him warned him that not in this way could he make himself effective. The woman he saw stood in need of his help, and to her he must make his way. The bustle which now took place in the yards beneath, the sudden shouts and the hurried throwing up of windows all over the house showed that the alarm had now become general. Another moment, and the appalling cry—the most appalling which leaves human lips—of fire! fire! rang from end to end of the threatened building. It was followed by women's shrieks and men's curses and then—by flames.

"She will hear, she will wake now," he thought, with his whole heart pulling him her way. But he did not desist from his intention to drop his eyes from the distraught figure entrapped between a locked door and a fall of thirty feet. He could reach her if he kept his nerve. A slow but steady hitch along the gutter was bringing him nearer every instant. Would she see him and take courage? No! her eyes were on the flames which were so bright now that he could actually see them glassed in her eyeballs. Would a shout attract her? The air was full of cries as the yards filled with escaping figures, but he would attempt it at the first lull—now—while her head was turned his way. Did she hear him? Yes. She is looking at him.

"Don't jump," he cried. "Tie your sheet to the bedpost. Tie it strong and fasten the other one to it and throw down the end. I will be here to catch it. Then you must come down hand over hand."

She threw up her arms, staring down at him in mortal terror; then, as the whole air grew lurid, nodded and tottered back. With incredible anxiety he watched for her reappearance. His post was becoming perilous. The fire had not yet reached the roof, but it was rapidly undermining its supports, and the heat was unendurable. Would he have to jump to the ground in his own despite? Was it his duty to wait for this girl, possibly already overcome by her fears and lying insensible? Yes; so long as he could hold out against the heat, it was his duty, but—Ah! what was that? Some one was shouting to him. He had been seen at last, and men, half-clad but eager, were rushing up the yard with a ladder. He could see their faces. How they glared in the red light. Help and determination were there, and perhaps when she saw the promise of this support, it would give nerve to her fingers and—

But it was not to be. As he watched their eager approach, he saw them stop, look back, swerve and rush around the corner of the house. Some one had directed them elsewhere. He could see the pointing hand, the baleful face. Quimby had realised his own danger in this prospect of Hammersmith's escape, and had intervened to prevent it. It was a murderer's natural impulse, and did not surprise him, but it added another element of danger to his position, and if this woman delayed much longer—but she is coming; a blanket is thrown out, then a dangling end of cloth appears above the sill. It descends. Another moment he has crawled up the roof to the ridge and grasped it.

"Slowly now!" he shouts. "Take time and hold on tight. I will guide you." He feels the frail support stiffen. She has drawn it into her hands; now she is on the sill, and is working herself off. He clutched his end firmly, steadying himself as best he might by bestriding the ridge of the roof. The strain becomes greater, he feels her weight, she is slipping down, down. Her hands strike a knot; the jerk almost throws him off his balance. He utters a word of caution, lost in the growing roar of the flames whose hungry tongues have begun to leap above the gutter. She looks down, sees the approaching peril, and hastens her descent. He is all astrain, with heart and hand nerved for the awful possibilities of the coming moments when—ping! Something goes whistling by his ear, which for the instant sets his hair bristling on his head, and almost paralyses every muscle. A bullet! The flame is not threatening enough! Some one is shooting at him from the dark.

IV

Well! death which comes one way cannot come another, and a bullet is more merciful than flame. The thought steadies Hammersmith; besides he has nothing to do with what is taking place behind his back. His duty is here, to guide and support this rapidly-descending figure now almost within his reach. And he fulfils this duty, though that deadly "ping" is followed by another, and his starting eyes behold the hole made by the missile in the clap-board just before him.

She is down. They stand toppling together on the slippery ridge with no support but the rapidly heating wall down which she had come. He looks one way, then another. Ten feet either way to the gutter! On one side leap the flames; beneath the other crouches their secret enemy. They cannot meet the first and live; needs must they face the latter. Bullets do not always strike the mark, as witness the two they had escaped. Besides, there are friends as well as enemies in the yard on this side. He can hear their encouraging cries. He will toss down the blanket; perhaps there will be hands to hold it and so break her fall, if not his.

With a courage which drew strength from her weakness, he carried out this plan and saw her land in safety amid half a dozen upstretched arms. Then he prepared to follow her, but felt his courage fail and his strength ooze without knowing the cause. Had a bullet struck him? He did not feel it. He was conscious of the heat, but of no other suffering; yet his limbs lacked life, and it no longer seemed possible for him to twist himself about so as to fall easily from the gutter.

"Come on! Come on!" rose in yells from below, but there was no movement in him.

"We can't wait. The wall will fall," rose affrightedly from below. But he simply clung and the doom of flame and collapsing timbers was rushing mercilessly upon him when, in the glare which lit up the whole dreadful scenery, there rose before his fainting eyes the sight of Miss Demarest's face turned his way from the crowd below, with all the terror of a woman's bleeding heart behind it. The joy which this recognition brought cleared his brain and gave him strength to struggle with his lethargy. Raising himself on one elbow, he slid his feet over the gutter, and with a frantic catch at its frail support, hung for one instant suspended, then dropped softly into the blanket which a dozen eager hands held out for him.

As he did so, a single gasping cry went up from the hushed throng. He knew the voice. His rescue had relieved one heart. His own beat tumultuously and the blood throbbed in his veins as he realised this.

The next thing he remembered was standing far from the collapsing building, with a dozen men and boys grouped about him. A woman at his feet was clasping his knees in thankfulness, another sinking in a faint at the edge of the shadow, but he saw neither, for the blood was streaming over his eyes from a wound not yet accounted for, and as he felt the burning flow, he realised a fresh duty.

"Where is Quimby?" he demanded loudly. "He made this hole in my forehead. He's a murderer and a thief, and I order you all in the name of the law to assist me in arresting him."

With the confused cry of many voices, the circle widened. Brushing the blood from his brow, he caught at the nearest man, and with one glance toward the tottering building, pointed to the wall where he and the girl Huldah had clung.

"Look!" he shouted, "do you see that black spot? Wait till the smoke blows aside. There! now! the spot just below the dangling sheet. It's a bullet-hole. It was made while I crouched there. Quimby held the gun. He had his reasons for hindering our escape. The girl can tell you—"

"Yes, yes," rose up from the ground at his feet. "Quimby is a wicked man. He knew that I knew it and he locked my door when he saw the flames coming. I'm willing to tell now. I was afraid before."

They stared at her with all the wonder of uncomprehending minds as she rose with a resolute air to confront them; but as the full meaning of her words penetrated their benumbed brains, slowly, man by man, they crept away to peer about in the barns, and among the clustering shadows for the man who had been thus denounced. Hammersmith followed them, and for a few minutes nothing but chase was in any man's mind. That part of the building in which lay hidden the room of shadows shook, tottered, and fell, loading the heavens with sparks and lighting up the pursuit now become as wild and reckless as the scene itself. To Miss Demarest's eyes, just struggling back to sight and hearing from the nethermost depths of unconsciousness, it looked like the swirling flight of spirits lost in the vortex of hell. For one wild moment she thought that she herself had passed the gates of life and was one of those unhappy souls whirling over a gulf of flame. The next moment she realised her mistake. A kindly voice was in her ear, a kindly hand was pressing a half-burned blanket about her.

"Don't stare so," the voice said. "It is only people routing out Quimby. They say he set fire to the tavern himself, to hide his crime and do away with the one man who knew about it. I know that he locked me in because I—Oh, see! they've got him! they've got him! and with a gun in his hand!"

The friendly hand fell; both women started upright panting with terror and excitement. Then one of them drew back, crying in a tone of sudden anguish, "Why, no! It's Jake, Jake!"

Daybreak! and with it Doctor Golden, who at the first alarm had ridden out post-haste without waiting to collect his jury. As he stepped to the ground before the hollow shell and smoking pile which were all that remained to mark the scene of yesterday's events, he looked about among the half-clad, shivering men and women peering from the barns and stables where they had taken refuge, till his eyes rested on Hammersmith standing like a sentinel before one of the doors.

"What's this? what's this?" he cried, as the other quickly approached. "Fire, with a man like you in the house?"

"Fire because I was in the house. They evidently felt obliged to get rid of me somehow. It's been a night of great experiences for me. When they found I was not likely to perish in the flames they resorted to shooting. I believe that my forehead shows where one bullet passed. Jake's aim might be improved. Not that I am anxious for it."

"Jake? Do you mean the clerk? Did he fire at you?"

"Yes, while I was on the roof engaged in rescuing one of the women."

"The miserable cur! You arrested him, of course, as soon as you could lay your hands on him?"

"Yes. He's back of me in this outhouse."

"And Quimby? What about Quimby?"

"He's missing."

"And Mrs. Quimby?"

"Missing, too. They are the only persons unaccounted for."

"Lost in the fire?"

"We don't think so. He was the incendiary and she, undoubtedly, his accomplice. They would certainly look out for themselves. Doctor Golden, it was not for insurance money they fired the place; it was to cover up a crime."

The coroner, more or less prepared for this statement by what Hammersmith had already told him, showed but little additional excitement as he dubiously remarked:

"So you still hold to that idea."

Hammersmith glanced about him and, catching more than one curious eye turned their way from the crowd now rapidly collecting in all directions, drew the coroner aside and in a few graphic words related the night's occurrences and the conclusions these had forced upon him. Doctor Golden listened and seemed impressed at last, especially by one point.

"You saw Quimby," he repeated; "saw his face distinctly looking toward your room from one of the stable windows?"

"I can swear to it. I even caught his expression. It was malignant in the extreme, quite unlike that he usually turns upon his guests."

"Which window was it?"

Hammersmith pointed it out.

"You have been there? Searched the room and the stable?"

"Thoroughly, just as soon as it was light enough to see."

"And found—"

"Nothing; not even a clue."

"The man is lying dead in that heap. She, too, perhaps. We'll have to put the screws on Jake. A conspiracy like this must be unearthed. Show me the rascal."

"He's in a most careless mood. He doesn't think his master and mistress perished in the fire."

"Careless, eh? Well, we'll see. I know that sort."

But when a few minutes later he came to confront the clerk he saw that his task was not likely to prove quite so easy as his former experience had led him to expect. Save for a slight nervous trembling of limb and shoulder—surely not unnatural after such a night—Jake bore himself with very much the same indifferent ease he had shown the day before.

Doctor Golden surveyed him with becoming sternness.

"At what time did this fire start?" he asked.

Jake had a harsh voice, but he mellowed it wonderfully as he replied:

"Somewhere about one. I don't carry a watch, so I don't know the exact time."

"The exact time isn't necessary. Near one answers well enough. How came you to be completely dressed at near one in a country tavern like this?"

"I was on watch. There was death in the house."

"Then you were in the house?"

"Yes." His tongue faltered, but not his gaze; that was as direct as ever. "I was in the house, but not at the moment the fire started. I had gone to the stable to get a newspaper. My room is in the stable, the little one high in the cock-loft. I did not find the paper at once and when I did I stopped to read a few lines. I'm a slow reader, and by the time I was ready to cross back to the house, smoke was pouring out of the rear windows, and I stopped short, horrified! I'm mortally afraid of fire."

"You have shown it. I have not heard that you raised the least alarm."

"I'm afraid you're right. I lost my head like a fool. You see, I've never lived anywhere else for the last ten years, and to see my home on fire was more than I could stand. You wouldn't think me so weak to look at these muscles."

Baring his arm, he stared down at it with a forlorn shake of his head. The coroner glanced at Hammersmith. What sort of fellow was this! A giant with the air of a child, a rascal with the smile of a humourist. Delicate business, this; or were they both deceived and the man just a good-humoured silly?

Hammersmith answered the appeal by a nod toward an inner door. The coroner understood and turned back to Jake with the seemingly irrelevant inquiry:

"Where did you leave Mr. Quimby when you went to the cock-loft?"

"In the house?"

"Asleep?"

"No, he was making up his accounts."

"In the office?"

"Yes."

"And that was where you left him?"

"Yes, it was."

"Then, how came he to be looking out of your window just before the fire broke out?"

"He?" Jake's jaw fell and his enormous shoulders drooped; but only for a moment. With something between a hitch and a shrug, he drew himself upright and with some slight display of temper cried out, "Who says he was there?"

The coroner answered him. "The man behind you. He saw him."

Jake's hand closed in a nervous grip. Had the trigger been against his finger at that moment it would doubtless have been snapped with some satisfaction, so the barrel had been pointing at Hammersmith.

"Saw him distinctly," the coroner repeated. "Mr. Quimby's face is not to be mistaken."

"If he saw him," retorted Jake, with unexpected cunning, "then the flames had got a start. One don't see in the dark. They hadn't got much of a start when I left. So he must have gone up to my room after I came down."

"It was before the alarm was given; before Mr. Hammersmith here had crawled out of his room window."

"I can't help that, sir. It was after I left the stable. You can't mix me up with Quimby's doings."

"Can't we? Jake, you're no lawyer and you don't know how to manage a lie. Make a clean breast of it. It may help you and it won't hurt Quimby. Begin with the old lady's coming. What turned Quimby against her? What's the plot?"

"I don't know of any plot. What Quimby told you Is true. You needn't expect me to contradict it!"

A leaden doggedness had taken the place of his whilom good nature. Nothing is more difficult to contend with. Nothing is more dreaded by the inquisitor. Hammersmith realised the difficulties of the situation and repeated the gesture he had previously made toward the door leading into an adjoining compartment. The coroner nodded as before and changed the tone of his inquiry.

"Jake," he declared, "you are in a more serious position than you realise. You may be devoted to Quimby, but there are others who are not. A night such as you have been through quickens the conscience of women if it does not that of men. One has been near death. The story of such a woman is apt to be truthful. Do you want to hear it? I have no objections to your doing so."

"What story? I don't know of any story. Women have easy tongues; they talk even when they have nothing to say."

"This woman has something to say, or why should she have asked to be confronted with you? Have her in, Mr. Hammersmith. I imagine that a sight of this man will make her voluble."

A sneer from Jake; but when Hammersmith, crossing to the door I've just mentioned, opened it and let in Huldah, this token of bravado gave way to a very different expression and he exclaimed half ironically, half caressingly:

"Why, she's my sweetheart! What can she have to say except that she was mighty fortunate not to have been burned up in the fire last night?"

Doctor Golden and the detective crossed looks in some anxiety. They had not been told of this relation between the two, either by the girl herself or by the others. Gifted with a mighty close mouth, she had nevertheless confided to Hammersmith that she could tell things and would, if he brought her face to face with the man who tried to shoot him while he was helping her down from the roof. Would her indignation hold out under the insinuating smile with which the artful rascal awaited her words? It gave every evidence of doing so, for her eye flashed threateningly and her whole body showed the tension of extreme feeling as she came hastily forward, and pausing just beyond the reach of his arm, cried out:

"You had a hand in locking me in. You're tired of me. If you're not, why did you fire those bullets my way? I was escaping and—"

Jake thrust in a quick word. "That was Quimby's move—locking your door. He had some game up. I don't know what it was. I had nothing to do with it."

This denial seemed to influence her. She looked at him and her breast heaved. He was good to look at; he must have been more than that to one of her restricted experience. Hammersmith trembled for the success of their venture. Would this blond young giant's sturdy figure and provoking smile prevail against the good sense which must tell her that he was criminal to the core, and that neither his principle nor his love were to be depended on? No, not yet. With a deepening flush, she flashed out:

"You hadn't? You didn't want me dead? Why, then, those bullets? You might have killed me as well as Mr. Hammersmith when you fired!"

"Huldah!" Astonishment and reproach in the tone and something more than either in the look which accompanied it. Both were very artful and betrayed resources not to be expected from one of his ordinarily careless and good-humoured aspect. "You haven't heard what I've said about that?"

"What could you say?"

"Why, the truth, Huldah. I saw you on the roof. The fire was near. I thought that neither you nor the man helping you could escape. A death of that kind is horrible. I loved you too well to see you suffer. My gun was behind the barn door. I got it and fired out of mercy."

She gasped. So, in a way, did the two officials. The plea was so specious, and its likely effect upon her so evident.

"Jake, can I believe you?" she murmured.

For answer, he fumbled in his pocket and drew out a small object which he held up before her between his fat forefinger and thumb. It was a ring, a thin, plain hoop of gold worth possibly a couple of dollars, but which in her eyes seemed to possess an incalculable value, for she had no sooner seen it than her whole face flushed and a look of positive delight supplanted the passionately aggrieved one with which she had hitherto faced him.

"You had bought that?"

He smiled and returned it to his pocket.

"For you," he simply said.

The joy and pride with which she regarded him, despite the protesting murmur of the discomfited Hammersmith, proved that the wily Jake had been too much for them.

"You see!" This to Hammersmith, "Jake didn't mean any harm, only kindness to us both. If you will let him go, I'll be more thankful than when you helped me down off the roof. We're wanting to be married. Didn't you see him show me the ring?"

It was for the coroner to answer.

"We'll let him go when we're assured that he means all that he says. I haven't as good an opinion of him as you have. I think he's deceiving you and that you are a very foolish girl to trust him. Men don't fire on the women they love, for any reason. You'd better tell me what you have against him."

"I haven't anything against him now."

"But you were going to tell us something—"

"I guess I was fooling."

"People are not apt to fool who have just been in terror of their lives."

Her eyes sought the ground. "I'm just a hardworking girl," she muttered almost sullenly. "What should I know about that man Quimby's dreadful doings?"

"Dreadful? You call them dreadful?" It was Doctor Golden who spoke.

"He locked me in my room," she violently declared. "That wasn't done for fun."

"And is that all you can tell us? Don't look at Jake. Look at me."

"But I don't know what to say. I don't even know what you want."

"I'll tell you. Your work in the house has been upstairs work, hasn't it?"

"Yes, sir. I did up the rooms—some of them," she added cautiously.

"What rooms? Front rooms, rear rooms, or both?"

"Rooms in front; those on the third floor."

"But you sometimes went into the extension?"

"I've been down the hall."

"Haven't you been in any of the rooms there,—Number 3, for instance?"

"No, sir; my work didn't take me there."

"But you've heard of the room?"

"Yes, sir. The girls sometimes spoke of it. It had a bad name, and wasn't often used. No girl liked to go there. A man was found dead in it once. They said he killed his own self."

"Have you ever heard any one describe this room?"

"No, sir."

"Tell what paper was on the wall?"

"No, sir."

"Perhaps Jake here can help us. He's been in the room often."

"The paper was blue; you know that; you saw it yourselves yesterday," blurted forth the man thus appealed to.

"Always blue? Never any other colour that you remember?"

"No; but I've been in the house only ten years."

"Oh, is that all! And do you mean to say that this room has not been redecorated in ten years?"

"How can I tell? I can't remember every time a room is repapered."

"You ought to remember this one."

"Why?"

"Because of a very curious circumstance connected with it."

"I don't know of any circumstance."

"You heard what Miss Demarest had to say about a room whose walls were covered with muddy pink scrolls."

"Oh, she!" His shrug was very expressive. Huldah continued to look down.

"Miss Demarest seemed to know what she was talking about," pursued the coroner in direct contradiction of the tone he had taken the day before. "Her description was quite vivid. It would be strange now if those walls had once been covered with just such paper as she described."

An ironic stare, followed by an incredulous smile from Jake; dead silence and immobility on the part of Huldah.

"Was it?" shot from Doctor Golden's lips with all the vehemence of conscious authority.

There was an instant's pause, during which Huldah's breast ceased its regular rise and fall; then the clerk laughed sharply and cried with the apparent lightness of a happy-go-lucky temperament:

"I should like to know if it was. I'd think it a very curious quin—quin—What's the word? quincedence, or something like that."

"The deepest fellow I know," grumbled the baffled coroner into Hammersmith's ear, as the latter stepped his way, "or just the most simple." Then added aloud: "Lift up my coat there, please."

Hammersmith did so. The garment mentioned lay across a small table which formed the sole furnishing of the place, and when Hammersmith raised it, there appeared lying underneath several small pieces of plaster which Doctor Golden immediately pointed out to Jake.

"Do you see these bits from a papered wall?" he asked. "They were torn from that of Number 3, between the breaking out of the fire and Mr. Hammersmith's escape from the room. Come closer; you may look at them, but keep your fingers off. You see that the coincidence you mentioned holds."

Jake laughed again loudly, in a way he probably meant to express derision; then he stood silent, gazing curiously down at the pieces before him. The blue paper peeling away from the pink made it impossible for him to deny that just such paper as Miss Demarest described had been on the wall prior to the one they had all seen and remembered.[A]

[A: Hammersmith's first attempt to settle this fact must have failed from his having chosen a spot for his experiment where the old paper had been stripped away before the new was put on.]

"Well, I vum!" Jake finally broke out, turning and looking from one face to another with a very obvious attempt to carry off the matter jovially. "She must have a great eye; a—a—(another hard word! What is it now?) Well! no matter. One of the kind what sees through the outside of things to what's underneath. I always thought her queer, but not so queer as that. I'd like to have that sort of power myself. Wouldn't you, Huldah?"

The girl, whose eye, as Hammersmith was careful to note, had hardly dwelt for an instant on these bits, not so long by any means as a woman's natural curiosity would seem to prompt, started as attention was thus drawn to herself and attempted a sickly smile.

But the coroner had small appreciation for this attempted display of humour, and motioning to Hammersmith to take her away, he subjected the clerk to a second examination which, though much more searching and rigorous than the first, resulted in the single discovery that for all his specious love-making he cared no more for the girl than for one of his old hats. This the coroner confided to Hammersmith when he came in looking disconsolate at his own failure to elicit anything further from the resolute Huldah.

"But you can't make her believe that now," whispered Hammersmith.

"Then we must trick him into showing her his real feelings."

"How would you set to work? He's warned, she's warned, and life if not love is at stake."

"It don't look very promising," muttered Doctor Golden, "but—"

He was interrupted by a sudden sound of hubbub without.

"It's Quimby, Quimby!" declared Hammersmith in his sudden excitement.

But again he was mistaken. It was not the landlord, but his wife, wild-eyed, dishevelled, with bits of straw in her hair from some sheltering hayrick and in her hand a heavy gold chain which, as the morning sun shone across it, showed sparkles of liquid clearness at short intervals along its whole length.

Diamonds! Miss Thistlewaite's diamonds, and the woman who held them was gibbering like an idiot!

The effect on Jake was remarkable. Uttering a piteous cry, he bounded from their hands and fell at the woman's feet.

"Mother Quimby!" he moaned. "Mother Quimby!" and sought to kiss her hand and wake some intelligence in her eye.

Meanwhile the coroner and Hammersmith looked on, astonished at these evidences of real feeling. Then their eyes stole behind them, and simultaneously both started back for the outhouse they had just left. Huldah was standing in the doorway, surveying the group before her with trembling, half-parted lips.

"Jealous!" muttered Hammersmith. "Providence has done our little trick for us. She will talk now. Look! She's beckoning to us."

V

"Speak quickly. You'll never regret it, Huldah. He's no mate for you, and you ought to know it. You have seen this paper covered with the pink scrolls before?"

The coroner had again drawn aside his coat from the bits of plaster.

"Yes," she gasped, with quick glances at her lover through the open doorway. "He never shed tears for me!" she exclaimed bitterly. "I didn't know he could for anybody. Oh, I'll tell what I've kept quiet here," and she struck her breast violently. "I wouldn't keep the truth back now if the minister was waiting to marry us. He loves that old woman and he doesn't love me. Hear him call her 'mother.' Are mothers dearer than sweethearts? Oh, I'll tell! I don't know anything about the old lady, but I do know that room 3 was repapered the night before last, and secretly, by him. I didn't see him do it, nobody did, but this is how I know: Some weeks ago I was hunting for something in the attic, when I stumbled upon some rolls of old wall-paper lying in a little cubby-hole under the eaves. The end of one of the rolls was torn and lay across the floor. I couldn't help seeing it or remembering its colour. It was like this, blue and striped. Exactly like it," she repeated, "just as shabby and old-looking. The rain had poured in on it, and it was all mouldy and stained. It smelt musty. I didn't give two thoughts to it then, but when after the old lady's death I heard one of the girls say something in the kitchen about a room being blue now which only a little while ago was pink, I stole up into the attic to see if those rolls were still there and found them every one gone. Oh, what is happening now?"

"One of the men is trying to take the diamonds from the woman and she won't let him. Her wits are evidently gone—frightened away by the horrors of the night—or she wouldn't try to cling to what has branded her at once as a thief."

The word seemed to pierce the girl. She stared out at her former mistress, who was again being soothed by the clerk, and murmured hoarsely:

"A thief! and he don't seem to mind, but is just as good to her! Oh, oh, I once served a term myself for—for a smaller thing than that and I thought that was why—Oh, sir, oh, sir, there's no mistake about the paper. For I went looking about in the barrels and where they throw the refuse, for bits to prove that this papering had been done in the night. It seemed so wonderful to me that any one, even Jake, who is the smartest man you ever saw, could do such a job as that and no one know. And though I found nothing in the barrels, I did in the laundry stove. It was full of burned paper, and some of it showed colour, and it was just that musty old blue I had seen in the attic."

She paused with a terrified gasp; Jake was looking at her from the open door.

"Oh, Jake!" she wailed out, "why weren't you true to me? Why did you pretend to love me when you didn't?"

He gave her a look, then turned on his heel. He was very much subdued in aspect and did not think to brush away the tear still glistening on his cheek.

"I've said my last word to you," he quietly declared, then stood silent a moment, with slowly labouring chest and an air of deepest gloom. But, as his eye stole outside again, they saw the spirit melt within him and simple human grief take the place of icy resolution. "She was like a mother to me," he murmured. "And now they say she'll never be herself again as long as she lives." Suddenly his head rose and he faced the coroner.

"You're right," said he. "It's all up with me. No home, no sweetheart, no missus. She [there was no doubt as to whom he meant by that tremulous she] was the only one I've ever cared for and she's just shown herself a thief. I'm no better. This is our story."

I will not give it in his words, but in my own. It will be shorter and possibly more intelligible.

The gang, if you may call it so, consisted of Quimby and these two, with a servant or so in addition. Robbery was its aim; a discreet and none too frequent spoliation of such of their patrons as lent themselves to their schemes. Quimby was the head, his wife the soul of this business, and Jake their devoted tool. The undermining of the latter's character had been begun early; a very dangerous undermining, because it had for one of its elements good humour and affectionate suggestion. At fourteen he was ready for any crime, but he was mercifully kept out of the worst till he was a full-grown man. Then he did his part. The affair of the old woman was an unpremeditated one. It happened in this wise: Miss Demarest's story had been true in every particular. Her mother was with her when she came to the house, and he, Jake, was the person sitting far back in the shadows at the time the young lady registered. There was nothing peculiar in the occurrence or in their behaviour except the decided demand which Miss Demarest made for separate rooms. This attracted his attention, for the house was pretty full and only one room was available in the portion reserved for transients. What would Quimby do? He couldn't send two women away, and he was entirely too conciliatory and smooth to refuse a request made so peremptorily. Quimby did nothing. He hemmed, hawed, and looked about for his wife. She was in the inner office back of him, and, attracted by his uneasy movements, showed herself. A whispered consultation followed, during which she cast a glance Jake's way. He understood her instantly and lounged carelessly forward. "Let them have Number 3," he said. "It's all fixed for the night. I can sleep anywhere, on the settle here or even on the floor of the inner office."

He had whispered these words, for the offer meant more than appeared. Number 3 was never given to guests. It was little more than a closet and was not even furnished. A cot had been put in that very afternoon, but only to meet a special emergency. A long-impending conference was going to be held between him and his employers subsequent to closing up time, and he had planned this impromptu refuge to save himself a late walk to the stable. At his offer to pass the same over to the Demarests, the difficulty of the moment vanished. Miss Demarest was shown to the one empty room in front, and the mother—as being the one less likely to be governed by superstitious fears if it so happened that some rumour of the undesirability of the haunted Number 3 should have reached them—to the small closet so hastily prepared for the clerk. Mrs. Quimby accompanied her, and afterward visited her again for the purpose of carrying her a bowl and some water. It was then she encountered Miss Demarest, who, anxious for a second and more affectionate good-night from her mother, had been wandering the halls in a search for her room. There was nothing to note in this simple occurrence, and Mrs. Quimby might have forgotten all about it if Miss Demarest had not made a certain remark on leaving the room. The bareness and inhospitable aspect of the place may have struck her, for she stopped in the doorway and, looking back, exclaimed: "What ugly paper! Magenta, too, the one colour my mother hates." This Mrs. Quimby remembered, for she also hated magenta, and never went into this room if she could help it.

The business which kept them all up that night was one totally disconnected with the Demarests or any one else in the house. A large outstanding obligation was coming due which Quimby lacked the money to meet. Something must be done with the stolen notes and jewelry which they had accumulated in times past and had never found the will or courage to dispose of. A choice must be made of what was salable. But what choice? It was a question that opened the door to endless controversy and possibly to a great difference of opinion; for in his way Quimby was a miser of the worst type and cared less for what money would do than for the sight and feeling of the money itself, while Mrs. Quimby was even more tenacious in her passion for the trinkets and gems which she looked upon as her part of the booty. Jake, on the contrary, cared little for anything but the good of the couple to whom he had attached himself. He wished Quimby to be satisfied, but not at Mrs. Quimby's expense. He was really fond of the woman and he was resolved that she should have no cause to grieve, even if he had to break with the old man. Little did any of them foresee what the night really held for them, or on what a jagged and unsuspected rock their frail bark was about to split.

Shutting-up time came, and with it the usual midnight quiet. All the doors had been locked and the curtains drawn over the windows and across the glass doors of the office. They were determined to do what they had never done before, lay out the loot and make a division. Quimby was resolved to see the diamonds which his wife had kept hidden for so long, and she, the securities, concerning the value of which he had contradicted himself so often. Jake's presence would keep the peace; they had no reason to fear any undue urging of his claims. All this he knew, and he was not therefore surprised, only greatly excited, when, after a last quiet look and some listening at the foot of the stairs, Mr. Quimby beckoned him into the office and, telling him to lock the door behind him, stepped around the bar to summon his wife. Jake never knew how it happened. He flung the door to and locked it, as he thought, but he must have turned the key too quickly, for the bolt of the lock did not enter the jamb, as they afterward found. Meanwhile they felt perfectly secure. The jewels were brought out of Mrs. Quimby's bedroom and laid on the desk. The securities were soon laid beside them. They had been concealed behind a movable brick at the side of the fireplace. Then the discussion began, involving more or less heat and excitement.

How long this lasted no one ever knew. At half-past eleven no change of attitude had taken place either in Quimby or his wife. At twelve the only difference marked by Jake was the removal of the securities to Quimby's breast pocket, and of the diamond-studded chain to Mrs. Quimby's neck. The former were too large for the pocket, the latter too brilliant for the dark calico background they blazed against. Jake, who was no fool, noted both facts, but had no words for the situation. He was absorbed, and he saw that Quimby was absorbed, in watching her broad hand creeping over those diamonds and huddling them up in a burning heap against her heart. There was fear in the action, fierce and overmastering fear, and so there was in her eyes which, fixed and glassy, stared over their shoulders at the wall behind, as though something had reached out from that wall and struck at the very root of her being. What did it mean? There was nothing in the room to affright her. Had she gone daft? Or—

Suddenly they both felt the blood congeal in their own veins; each turned to each a horrified face, then slowly and as if drawn by a power supernatural and quite outside of their own will, their two heads turned in the direction she was looking, and they beheld standing in their midst a spectre—no, it was the figure of a living, breathing woman, with eyes fastened on those jewels,—those well-known, much-advertised jewels! So much they saw in that instant flash, then nothing! For Quimby, in a frenzy of unreasoning fear, had taken the chair from under him and had swung it at the figure. A lamp had stood on the bar top. It was caught by the backward swing of the chair, overturned and quenched. The splintering of glass mingled its small sound with an ominous thud in the thick darkness. It was the end of all things; the falling of an impenetrable curtain over a horror half sensed, yet all the greater for its mystery.

The silence—the terror—the unspeakable sense of doom which gripped them all was not broken by a heart-beat. All listened for a stir, a movement where they could see nothing. But the stillness remained unbroken. The silence was absolute. The figure which they had believed themselves to have seen had been a dream, an imagination of their overwrought minds. It could not be otherwise. The door had been locked, entrance was impossible; yet doubt held them powerless. The moments were making years of themselves. To each came in a flash a review of every earthly incident they had experienced, every wicked deed, every unholy aspiration. Quimby gritted his teeth. It was the first sound which had followed that thud and, slight as it was, it released them somewhat from their awful tension. Jake felt that he could move now, and was about to let forth his imprisoned breath when he felt the touch of icy fingers trailing over his cheek, and started back with a curse. It was Mrs. Quimby feeling about for him in the impenetrable darkness, and in another moment he could hear her smothered whisper:

"Are you there, Jake?"

"Yes; where are you?"

"Here," said the woman, with an effort to keep her teeth from striking together.

"For God's sake, a light!" came from the hollow darkness beyond.

It was Quimby's voice at last. Jake answered:

"No light for me. I'll stay where I am till daybreak."

"Get a light, you fool!" commanded Quimby, but not without a tremble in his usually mild tone.

Hard breathing from Jake, but no other response, Quimby seemed to take a step nearer, for his voice was almost at their ears now.

"Jake, you can have anything I've got so as you get a light now."

"There ain't nothing to light here. You broke the lamp."

Quiet for a moment, then Quimby muttered hoarsely:

"If you ain't scared out of your seven senses, you can go down cellar and bring up that bit of candle 'longside the ale-barrels."

Into the cellar! Not Jake. The moving of the rickety table which his fat hand had found and rested on spoke for him.

Another curse from Quimby. Then the woman, though with some hesitation, said with more self-control than could be expected:

"I'll get it," and they heard her move away from it toward the trap-door behind the bar.

The two men made no objection. To her that cold, black cellar might seem a refuge from the unseen horror centred here. It had not struck them so. It had its own possibilities, and Jake wondered at her courage, as he caught the sound of her groping advance and the sudden clatter and clink of bottles as the door came up and struck the edge of the bar. There was life and a suggestion of home in that clatter and clink, and all breathed easier for a moment, but only for a moment. The something lying there behind them, or was it almost under their feet, soon got its hold again upon their fears, and Jake found himself standing stock-still, listening both ways for that dreaded, or would it be welcome, movement on the floor behind, and to the dragging sound of Mrs. Quimby's skirt and petticoat as she made her first step down those cellar-stairs. What an endless time it took! He could rush down there in a minute, but she—she could not have reached the third step yet, for that always creaked. Now it did creak. Then there was no sound for some time, unless it was the panting of Quimby's breath somewhere over by the bar. Then the stair creaked again. She must be nearly up.

"Here's matches and the candle," came in a hollow voice from the trap-stairs.

A faint streak appeared for an instant against the dark, then disappeared. Another; but no lasting light. The matches were too damp to burn.

"Jake, ain't you got a match?" appealed the voice of Quimby in half-choked accents.

After a bit of fumbling a small blaze shot up from where Jake stood. Its sulphurous smell may have suggested to all, as it did to one, the immeasurable distance of heaven at that moment, and the awful nearness of hell. They could see now, but not one of them looked in the direction where all their thoughts lay. Instead of that, they rolled their eyes on each other, while the match burned slowly out: Mrs. Quimby from the trap, her husband from the bar, and Jake. Suddenly he found words, and his cry rang through the room:

"The candle! the candle! this is my only match. Where is the candle?"

Quimby leaped forward and with shaking hand held the worn bit of candle to the flame. It failed to ignite. The horrible, dreaded darkness was about to close upon them again before—before—But another hand had seized the candle. Mrs. Quimby has come forward, and as the match sends up its last flicker, thrusts the wick against the flame and the candle flares up. It is lighted.

Over it they give each other one final appealing stare. There's no help for it now; they must look. Jake's head turned first, then Mrs. Quimby, and then that of the real aggressor.

A simultaneous gasp from them all betrays the worst. It had been no phantom called into being by their overtaxed nerves. A woman lay before them, face downward on the hard floor. A woman dressed in black, with hat on head and a little satchel clutched in one stiff, outstretched hand. Miss Demarest's mother! The little old lady who had come into the place four hours before!

With a muttered execration, Jake stepped over to her side and endeavoured to raise her; but he instantly desisted, and looking up at Quimby and his wife, moved his lips with the one fatal word which ends all hope:

"Dead!"

They listened appalled, "Dead?" echoed the now terrified Quimby.

"Dead?" repeated his no less agitated wife.

Jake was the least overcome of the three. With another glance at the motionless figure, he rose, and walking around the body, crossed to the door and seeing what he had done to make entrance possible, cursed himself and locked it properly. Meanwhile, Mrs. Quimby, with her eyes on her husband, had backed slowly away till she had reached the desk, against which she now stood with fierce and furious eyes, still clutching at her chain.

Quimby watched her fascinated. He had never seen her look like this before. What did it portend? They were soon to know.

"Coward!" fell from her lips, as she stared with unrelenting hate at her husband. "An old woman who was not even conscious of what she saw! I'll not stand for this killing, Jacob. You may count me out of this and the chain, too. If you don't—" a threatening gesture finished the sentence and the two men looking at her knew that they had come up against a wall.

"Susan!" Was that Quimby speaking? "Susan, are you going back on me now?"

She pointed at the motionless figure lying in its shrouding black like an ineffaceable blot on the office floor, then at the securities showing above the edge of his pocket.

"Were we not close enough to discovery, without drawing the attention of the police by such an unnecessary murder? She was walking in her sleep. I remember her eyes as she advanced toward me; there was no sight in them."

"You lie!" It was the only word which Quimby found to ease the shock which this simple statement caused him. But Jake saw from the nature of the glance he shot at his poor old victim that her words had struck home. His wife saw it, too, but it did not disturb the set line of her determined mouth.

"You'll let me keep the chain," she said, "and you'll use your wits, now that you have used your hand, to save yourself and myself from the charge of murder."

Quimby, who was a man of great intelligence when his faculties were undisturbed by anger or shock, knelt and turned his victim carefully over so that her face was uppermost.

"It was not murder," he uttered in an indescribable tone after a few minutes of cautious scrutiny. "The old lady fell and struck her forehead. See! the bruise is scarcely perceptible. Had she been younger—"

"A sudden death from any cause in this house at just this time is full of danger for us," coldly broke in his wife.

The landlord rose to his feet, walked away to the window, dropped his head, thought for a minute, and then slowly came back, glanced at the woman again, at her dress, her gloved hands, and her little satchel.

"She didn't die in this house," fell from his lips in his most oily accents. "She fell in the woods; the path is full of bared roots, and there she must be found to-morrow morning. Jake, are you up to the little game?"

Jake, who was drawing his first full breath, answered with a calm enough nod, whereupon Quimby bade his wife to take a look outside and see if the way was clear for them to carry the body out.

She did not move. He fell into a rage; an unusual thing for him.

"Bestir yourself! do as I bid you," he muttered.

Her eyes held his; her face took on the look he had learned to dread. Finally she spoke:

"And the daughter! What about the daughter?"

Quimby stood silent; then with a sidelong leer, and in a tone smooth as oil, but freighted with purpose, "The mother first; we'll look after the daughter later."

Mrs. Quimby shivered; then as her hand spread itself over the precious chain sparkling with the sinister gleam of serpent's eyes on her broad bosom, she grimly muttered:

"How? I'm for no more risks, I tell you."

Jake took a step forward. He thought his master was about to rush upon her. But he was only gathering up his faculties to meet the new problem she had flung at him.

"The girl's a mere child; we shall have no difficulty with her," he muttered broodingly. "Who saw these two come in?"

Then it came out that no one but themselves had been present at their arrival. Further consultation developed that the use to which Number 3 had been put was known to but one of the maids, who could easily be silenced. Whereupon Quimby told his scheme. Mrs. Quimby was satisfied, and he and Jake prepared to carry it out.

The sensations of the next half-hour, as told by Jake, would make your flesh creep. They did not dare to carry a lamp to light the gruesome task, and well as they knew the way, the possibilities of a stumble or a fall against some one of the many trees they had to pass filled them with constant terror. They did stumble once, and the low cry Jake uttered caused them new fears. Was that a window they heard flying up? No; but something moved in the bushes. They were sure of this and guiltily shook in their shoes; but nothing advanced out of the shadows, and they went on.

But the worst was when they had to turn their backs upon the body left lying face downward in the cold, damp woods. Men of no compassion, unreached by ordinary sympathies, they felt the furtive skulking back, step by step, along ways commonplace enough in the daytime, but begirt with terrors now and full of demoniac suggestion.

The sight of a single thread of light marking the door left ajar for them by Mrs. Quimby was a beacon of hope which was not even disturbed by the sight of her wild figure walking in a circle round and round the office, the stump of candle dripping unheeded over her fingers, and her eyes almost as sightless as those of the form left in the woods.

"Susan!" exclaimed her husband, laying hand on her.

She paused at once. The presence of the two men had restored her self-possession.

But all was not well yet. Jake drew Quimby's attention to the register where the two names of mother and daughter could be seen in plain black and white.

"Oh, that's nothing!" exclaimed the landlord, and, taking out his knife, he ripped the leaf out, together with the corresponding one in the back. "The devil's on our side all right, or why did she pass over the space at the bottom of the page and write their two names at the top of the next one?"

He started, for his wife had clutched his arm.

"Yes, the devil's on our side thus far," said she, "but here he stops. I have just remembered something that will upset our whole plan and possibly hang us. Miss Demarest visited her mother in Number 3 and noticed the room well, and particularly the paper. Now if she is able to describe that paper, it might not be so easy for us to have our story believed."

For a minute all stood aghast, then Jake quietly remarked: "It is now one by the clock. If you can find me some of that old blue paper I once chucked under the eaves in the front attic, I will engage to have it on those four walls before daylight. Bring the raggedest rolls you can find. If it shouldn't be dry to the touch when they come to see it to-morrow, it must look so stained and old that no one will think of laying hand on it. I'll go make the paste."

As Jake was one of the quickest and most precise of workers at anything he understood, this astonishing offer struck the other two as quite feasible. The paper was procured, the furniture moved back, and a transformation made in the room in question which astonished even those concerned in it. Dawn rose upon the completed work and, the self-possession of all three having been restored with the burning up of such scraps as remained after the four walls were covered, they each went to their several beds for a half-hour of possible rest. Jake's was in Number 3. He has never said what that half-hour was to him!

The rest we know. The scheme did not fully succeed, owing to the interest awakened in one man's mind by the beauty and seeming truth of Miss Demarest. Investigation followed which roused the landlord to the danger threatening them from the curiosity of Hammersmith, and it being neck or nothing with him, he planned the deeper crime of burning up room and occupant before further discoveries could be made. What became of him in the turmoil which followed, no one could tell, not even Jake. They had been together in Jake's room before the latter ran out with his gun, but beyond that the clerk knew nothing. Of Mrs. Quimby he could tell more. She had not been taken into their confidence regarding the fire, some small grains of humanity remaining in her which they feared might upset their scheme. She had only been given some pretext for locking Huldah in her room, and it was undoubtedly her horror at her own deed when she saw to what it had committed her which unsettled her brain and made her a gibbering idiot for life.

Or was it some secret knowledge of her husband's fate, unknown to others? We cannot tell, for no sign nor word of Jacob Quimby ever came to dispel the mystery of his disappearance.

And this is the story of Three Forks Tavern and the room numbered 3.

MIDNIGHT IN BEAUCHAMP ROW

It was the last house in Beauchamp Row, and it stood several rods away from its nearest neighbour. It was a pretty house in the daytime, but owing to its deep, sloping roof and small bediamonded windows it had a lonesome look at night, notwithstanding the crimson hall-light which shone through the leaves of its vine-covered doorway.

Ned Chivers lived in it with his six months' married bride, and as he was both a busy fellow and a gay one there were many evenings when pretty Letty Chivers sat alone until near midnight.

She was of an uncomplaining spirit, however, and said little, though there were times when both the day and evening seemed very long and married life not altogether the paradise she had expected.

On this evening—a memorable evening for her, the 24th of December, 1911—she had expected her husband to remain with her, for it was not only Christmas eve, but the night when, as manager of a large manufacturing concern, he brought up from New York the money with which to pay off the men on the next working day, and he never left her when there was any unusual amount of money in the house. But with the first glimpse she had of his figure coming up the road she saw that for some reason it was not to be thus to-night, and, indignant, alarmed almost, at the prospect of a lonesome evening under such circumstances, she ran hastily down to the gate to meet him, crying:

"Oh, Ned, you look so troubled I know you have only come home for a hurried supper. But you cannot leave me to-night. Tennie" (their only maid) "has gone for a holiday, and I never can stay in this house alone with all that." She pointed to the small bag he carried, which, as she knew, was filled to bursting with bank notes.

He certainly looked troubled. It is hard to resist the entreaty in a young bride's uplifted face. But this time he could not help himself, and he said:

"I am dreadfully sorry, but I must ride over to Fairbanks to-night. Mr. Pierson has given me an imperative order to conclude a matter of business there, and it is very important that it should be done. I should lose my position if I neglected the matter, and no one but Hasbrouck and Suffern knows that we keep the money in the house. I have always given out that I intrusted it to Hale's safe over night."

"But I cannot stand it," she persisted. "You have never left me on these nights. That is why I let Tennie go. I will spend the evening at The Larches, or, better still, call in Mr. and Mrs. Talcott to keep me company."

But her husband did not approve of her going out or of her having company. The Larches was too far away, and as for Mr. and Mrs. Talcott, they were meddlesome people, whom he had never liked; besides, Mrs. Talcott was delicate, and the night threatened storm. Let her go to bed like a good girl, and think nothing about the money, which he would take care to put away in a very safe place.

"Or," said he, kissing her downcast face, "perhaps you would rather hide it yourself; women always have curious ideas about such things."

"Yes, let me hide it," she entreated. "The money, I mean, not the bag. Every one knows the bag. I should never dare to leave it in that." And begging him to unlock it, she began to empty it with a feverish haste that rather alarmed him, for he surveyed her anxiously and shook his head as if he dreaded the effects of this excitement upon her.

But as he saw no way out of the difficulty, he confined himself to using such soothing words as were at his command, and then, humouring her weakness, helped her to arrange the bills in the place she had chosen, and restuffing the bag with old receipts till it acquired its former dimensions, he put a few bills on top to make the whole look natural, and, laughing at her white face, relocked the bag and put the key back in his pocket.

"There, dear; a notable scheme and one that should relieve your mind entirely!" he cried. "If any one should attempt burglary in my absence and should succeed in getting into a house as safely locked as this will be when I leave it, then trust to their being satisfied when they see this booty, which I shall hide where I always hide it—in the cupboard over my desk."

"And when will you be back?" she questioned, trembling in spite of herself at these preparations.

"By one o'clock if possible. Certainly by two."

"And our neighbours go to bed at ten," she murmured. But the words were low, and she was glad he did not hear them, for if it was his duty to obey the orders he had received, then it was her duty to meet the position in which it left her as bravely as she could.

At supper she was so natural that his face rapidly brightened, and it was with quite an air of cheerfulness that he rose at last to lock up the house and make such preparations as were necessary for his dismal ride over the mountains to Fairbanks. She had the supper dishes to wash up in Tennie's absence, and as she was a busy little housewife she found herself singing a snatch of song as she passed back and forth from dining-room to kitchen. He heard it, too, and smiled to himself as he bolted the windows on the ground floor and examined the locks of the three lower doors, and when he finally came into the kitchen with his greatcoat on to give her his final kiss, he had but one parting injunction to urge, and this was for her to lock and bolt the front door after him and then forget the whole matter till she heard his double knock at midnight.

She smiled and held up her ingenuous face.

"Be careful of yourself," she begged of him. "I hate this dark ride for you, and on such a night too." And she ran with him to the door to look out.

"It is certainly very dark," he responded, "but I'm to have one of Brown's safest horses. Do not worry about me. I shall do well enough, and so will you, too, or you are not the plucky little woman I have always thought you."

She laughed, but there was a choking sound in her voice that made him look at her again. But at sight of his anxiety she recovered herself, and pointing to the clouds said earnestly:

"It's going to snow. Be careful as you ride by the gorge, Ned; it is very deceptive there in a snowstorm."

But he vowed that it would not snow before morning and giving her one final embrace he dashed down the path toward Brown's livery stable. "Oh, what is the matter with me?" she murmured to herself as his steps died out in the distance. "I never knew I was such a coward." And she paused for a moment, looking up and down the road, as if in despite of her husband's command she had the desperate idea of running away to some neighbour.

But she was too loyal for that, and smothering a sigh she retreated into the house. As she did so the first flakes fell of the storm that was not to have come till morning.

It took her an hour to get her kitchen in order, and nine o'clock struck before she was ready to sit down. She had been so busy she had not noticed how the wind had increased or how rapidly the snow was falling. But when she went to the front door for another glance up and down the road she started back, appalled at the fierceness of the gale and at the great pile of snow that had already accumulated on the doorstep.

Too delicate to breast such a wind, she saw herself robbed of her last hope of any companionship, and sighing heavily she locked and bolted the door for the night and went back into her little sitting-room, where a great fire was burning. Here she sat down, and determined, since she must pass the evening alone, to do it as cheerfully as possible, she began to sew. "Oh, what a Christmas eve!" she thought, as a picture of other homes rose before her eyes,—homes in which husbands sat by wives and brothers by sisters; and a great wave of regret poured over her and a longing for something, she hardly dared say what, lest her unhappiness should acquire a sting that would leave traces beyond the passing moment.

The room in which she sat was the only one on the ground floor except the dining-room and kitchen. It therefore was used both as parlour and sitting-room, and held not only her piano, but her husband's desk.

Communicating with it was the tiny dining-room. Between the two, however, was an entry leading to a side entrance. A lamp was in this entry, and she had left it burning, as well as the one in the kitchen, that the house might look cheerful and as if the whole family were at home.

She was looking toward this entry and wondering what made it seem so dismally dark to her, when there came a faint sound from the door at its further end.

Knowing that her husband must have taken peculiar pains with the fastenings of this door, as it was the one toward the woods and therefore most accessible to wayfarers, she sat where she was, with all her faculties strained to listen. But no further sound came from that direction, and after a few minutes of silent terror she was allowing herself to believe that she had been deceived by her fears when she suddenly heard the same sound at the kitchen door, followed by a muffled knock.

Frightened now in good earnest, but still alive to the fact that the intruder was as likely to be a friend as foe, she stepped to the door, and with her hand on the lock stooped and asked boldly enough who was there. But she received no answer, and more affected by this unexpected silence than by the knock she had heard, she recoiled farther and farther till not only the width of the kitchen, but the dining-room also, lay between her and the scene of her alarm, when to her utter confusion the noise shifted again to the side of the house, and the door she thought so securely fastened, swung violently open as if blown in by a fierce gust, and she saw precipitated into the entry the burly figure of a man covered with snow and shaking with the violence of the storm that seemed at once to fill the house.

Her first thought was that it was her husband come back, but before she could clear her eyes from the snow which had rushed tumultuously in, he had thrown off his outer covering and she found herself face to face with a man in whose powerful frame and cynical visage she saw little to comfort her and much to surprise and alarm.

"Ugh!" was his coarse and rather familiar greeting. "A hard night, missus! Enough to drive any man indoors. Pardon the liberty, but I couldn't wait for you to lift the latch; the wind drove me right in."

"Was—was not the door locked?" she feebly asked, thinking he must have staved it in with his foot, which was certainly well fitted for such a task.

"Not much," he chuckled. "I s'pose you're too hospitable for that." And his eyes passed from her face to the comfortable firelight shining through the sitting-room.

"Is it refuge you want?" she demanded, suppressing as much as possible all signs of fear.

"Sure, missus—what else! A man can't live in a gale like that, specially after a tramp of twenty miles or more. Shall I shut the door for you?" he asked, with a mixture of bravado and good nature that frightened her more and more.

"I will shut it," she replied, with a half notion of escaping this sinister stranger by a flight through the night.

But one glance into the swirling snowstorm deterred her, and making the best of the alarming situation, she closed the door, but did not lock it, being now more afraid of what was inside the house than of anything left lingering without.

The man, whose clothes were dripping with water, watched her with a cynical smile, and then, without any invitation, entered the dining-room, crossed it, and moved toward the kitchen fire.

"Ugh! ugh! But it is warm here!" he cried, his nostrils dilating with an animal-like enjoyment, that in itself was repugnant to her womanly delicacy. "Do you know, missus, I shall have to stay here all night? Can't go out in that gale again; not such a fool." Then with a sly look at her trembling form and white face he insinuatingly added, "All alone, missus?"

The suddenness with which this was put, together with the leer that accompanied it, made her start. Alone? Yes, but should she acknowledge it? Would it not be better to say that her husband was upstairs? The man evidently saw the struggle going on in her mind, for he chuckled to himself and called out quite boldly:

"Never mind, missus; it's all right. Just give me a bit of cold meat and a cup of tea or something, and we'll be very comfortable together. You're a slender slip of a woman to be minding a house like this. I'll keep you company if you don't mind, leastwise until the storm lets up a bit, which ain't likely for some hours to come. Rough night, missus, rough night."

"I expect my husband home at any time," she hastened to say. And thinking she saw a change in the man's countenance at this she put on quite an air of sudden satisfaction and bounded toward the front of the house. "There! I think I hear him now," she cried.

Her motive was to gain time, and if possible to obtain the opportunity of shifting the money from the place where she had first put it into another and safer one. "I want to be able," she thought, "to swear that I have no money with me in this house. If I can only get it into my apron I will drop it outside the door into the snowbank. It will be as safe there as in the vaults it came from." And dashing into the sitting-room she made a feint of dragging down a shawl from a screen, while she secretly filled her skirt with the bills which had been put between some old pamphlets on the bookshelves.

She could hear the man grumbling in the kitchen, but he did not follow her front, and taking advantage of the moment's respite from his none too encouraging presence she unbarred the door and cheerfully called out her husband's name.

The ruse was successful. She was enabled to fling the notes where the falling flakes would soon cover them from sight, and feeling more courageous, now that the money was out of the house, she went slowly back, saying she had made a mistake, and that it was the wind she had heard.

The man gave a gruff but knowing guffaw and then resumed his watch over her, following her steps as she proceeded to set him out a meal, with a persistency that reminded her of a tiger just on the point of springing. But the inviting look of the viands with which she was rapidly setting the table soon distracted his attention, and allowing himself one grunt of satisfaction, he drew up a chair and set himself down to what to him was evidently a most savoury repast.

"No beer? No ale? Nothing o' that sort, eh? Don't keep a bar?" he growled, as his teeth closed on a huge hunk of bread.

She shook her head, wishing she had a little cold poison bottled up in a tight-looking jug.

"Nothing but tea," she smiled, astonished at her own ease of manner in the presence of this alarming guest.

"Then let's have that," he grumbled, taking the bowl she handed him, with an odd look that made her glad to retreat to the other side of the room.

"Jest listen to the howling wind," he went on between the huge mouthfuls of bread and cheese with which he was gorging himself. "But we're very comfortable, we two! We don't mind the storm, do we?"

Shocked by his familiarity and still more moved by the look of mingled inquiry and curiosity with which his eyes now began to wander over the walls and cupboards, she hurried to the window overlooking her nearest neighbour, and, lifting the shade, peered out. A swirl of snowflakes alone confronted her. She could neither see her neighbours, nor could she be seen by them. A shout from her to them would not be heard. She was as completely isolated as if the house stood in the centre of a desolate western plain.

"I have no trust but in God," she murmured as she came from the window. And, nerved to meet her fate, she crossed to the kitchen.

It was now half-past ten. Two hours and a half must elapse before her husband could possibly arrive.

She set her teeth at the thought and walked resolutely into the room.

"Are you done?" she asked.

"I am, ma'am," he leered. "Do you want me to wash the dishes? I kin, and I will." And he actually carried his plate and cup to the sink, where he turned the water upon them with another loud guffaw.

"If only his fancy would take him into the pantry," she thought, "I could shut and lock the door upon him and hold him prisoner till Ned gets back."

But his fancy ended its flight at the sink, and before her hopes had fully subsided he was standing on the threshold of the sitting-room door.

"It's pretty here," he exclaimed, allowing his eye to rove again over every hiding-place within sight. "I wonder now—" He stopped. His glance had fallen on the cupboard over her husband's desk.

"Well?" she asked, anxious to break the thread of his thought, which was only too plainly mirrored in his eager countenance.

He started, dropped his eyes, and, turning, surveyed her with a momentary fierceness. But, as she did not let her own glance quail, but continued to meet his gaze with what she meant for an ingratiating smile, he subdued this outward manifestation of passion, and, chuckling to hide his embarrassment, began backing into the entry, leering in evident enjoyment of the fears he caused.

However, once in the hall, he hesitated for a long time; then slowly made for the garment he had dropped on entering, and stooping, drew from underneath its folds a wicked-looking stick. Giving a kick to the coat, which sent it into a remote corner, he bestowed upon her another smile, and still carrying the stick, went slowly and reluctantly away into the kitchen.

"Oh, God Almighty, help me!" was her prayer.

There was nothing left for her now but to endure, so throwing herself into a chair, she tried to calm the beating of her heart and summon up courage for the struggle which she felt was before her. That he had come to rob and only waited to take her off her guard she now felt certain, and rapidly running over in her mind all the expedients of self-defence possible to one in her situation, she suddenly remembered the pistol which Ned kept in his desk.

Oh, why had she not thought of it before! Why had she let herself grow mad with terror when here, within reach of her hand, lay such a means of self-defence? With a feeling of joy (she had always hated pistols before and scolded Ned when he bought this one) she started to her feet and slid her hand into the drawer. But it came back empty. Ned had taken the weapon away with him.

For a moment, a surge of the bitterest feeling she had ever experienced passed over her; then she called reason to her aid and was obliged to acknowledge that the act was but natural, and that from his standpoint he was much more likely to need it than herself. But the disappointment, coming so soon after hope, unnerved her, and she sank back in her chair, giving herself up for lost.

How long she sat there with her eyes on the door through which she momentarily expected her assailant to reappear, she never knew. She was conscious only of a sort of apathy that made movement difficult and even breathing a task. In vain she tried to change her thoughts. In vain she tried to follow her husband in fancy over the snow-covered roads and into the gorge of the mountains. Imagination failed her at this point. Do what she would, all was misty to her mind's eye, and she could not see that wandering image. There was blankness between his form and her, and no life or movement anywhere but here in the scene of her terror.

Her eyes were on a strip of rug covering the entry floor, and so strange was the condition of her mind that she found herself mechanically counting the tassels finishing off its edge, growing wroth over one that was worn, till she hated that sixth tassel and mentally determined that if she ever outlived this night she would strip them all off and be done with them.

The wind had lessened, but the air had grown cooler and the snow made a sharp sound where it struck the panes. She felt it falling, though she had cut off all view of it. It seemed to her that a pall was settling over the world and that she would soon be smothered under its folds.

Meanwhile no sound came from the kitchen. A dreadful sense of doom was creeping upon her—a sense growing in intensity till she found herself watching for the shadow of that lifted stick on the wall of the entry and almost imagined she saw the tip of it appearing.

But it was the door which again blew in, admitting another man of so threatening an aspect that she succumbed instantly before him and forgot all her former fears in this new terror.

The second intruder was a negro of powerful frame and lowering aspect, and as he came forward and stood in the doorway there was observable in his fierce and desperate countenance no attempt at the insinuation of the other, only a fearful resolution that made her feel like a puppet before him, and drove her, almost without her volition, to her knees.

"Money? Is it money you want?" was her desperate greeting. "If so, here's my purse and here are my rings and watch. Take them and go."

But the stolid wretch did not even stretch out his hands. His eyes went beyond her, and the mingled anxiety and resolve which he displayed would have cowed a stouter heart than that of this poor woman.

"Keep de trash," he growled. "I want de company's money. You've got it—two thousand dollars. Show me where it is, that's all, and I won't trouble you long after I close on it."

"But it's not in the house," she cried. "I swear it is not in the house. Do you think Mr. Chivers would leave me here alone with two thousand dollars to guard?"

But the negro, swearing that she lied, leaped into the room, and tearing open the cupboard above her husband's desk, seized the bag from the corner where they had put it.

"He brought it in this," he muttered, and tried to force the bag open, but finding this impossible he took out a heavy knife and cut a big hole in its side. Instantly there fell out the pile of old receipts with which they had stuffed it, and seeing these he stamped with rage, and flinging them at her in one great handful, rushed to the drawers below, emptied them, and, finding nothing, attacked the bookcase.

"The money is somewhere here. You can't fool me," he yelled. "I saw the spot your eyes lit on when I first came into the room. Is it behind these books?" he growled, pulling them out and throwing them helter-skelter over the floor. "Women is smart in the hiding business. Is it behind these books, I say?"

They had been, or rather had been placed between the books, but she had taken them away, as we know, and he soon began to realise that his search was bringing him nothing. Leaving the bookcase he gave the books one kick, and seizing her by the arm, shook her with a murderous glare on his strange and distorted features.

"Where's the money?" he hissed. "Tell me, or you are a goner."

He raised his heavy fist. She crouched and all seemed over, when, with a rush and cry, a figure dashed between them and he fell, struck down by the very stick she had so long been expecting to see fall upon her own head. The man who had been her terror for hours had at the moment of need acted as her protector.

She must have fainted, but if so, her unconsciousness was but momentary, for when she woke again to her surroundings she found the tramp still standing over her adversary.

"I hope you don't mind, ma'am," he said, with an air of humbleness she certainly had not seen in him before, "but I think the man's dead." And he stirred with his foot the heavy figure before him.

"Oh, no, no, no!" she cried. "That would be too fearful. He's shocked, stunned; you cannot have killed him."

But the tramp was persistent. "I'm 'fraid I have," he said. "I done it before. I'm powerful strong in the biceps. But I couldn't see a man of that colour frighten a lady like you. My supper was too warm in me, ma'am. Shall I throw him outside the house?"

"Yes," she said, and then, "No; let us first be sure there is no life in him." And, hardly knowing what she did, she stooped down and peered into the glassy eyes of the prostrate man.

Suddenly she turned pale—no, not pale, but ghastly, and cowering back, shook so that the tramp, into whose features a certain refinement had passed since he had acted as her protector, thought she had discovered life in those set orbs, and was stooping down to make sure that this was so, when he saw her suddenly lean forward and, impetuously plunging her hand into the negro's throat, tear open the shirt and give one look at his bared breast.

It was white.

"O God! O God!" she moaned, and lifting the head in her two hands she gave the motionless features a long and searching look. "Water!" she cried. "Bring water." But before the now obedient tramp could respond, she had torn off the woolly wig disfiguring the dead man's head, and seeing the blond curls beneath had uttered such a shriek that it rose above the gale and was heard by her distant neighbours.

It was the head and hair of her husband.

They found out afterwards that he had contemplated this theft for months; that each and every precaution necessary to the success of this most daring undertaking had been made use of and that but for the unexpected presence in the house of the tramp, he would doubtless not only have extorted the money from his wife, but have so covered up the deed by a plausible alibi as to have retained her confidence and that of his employers.

Whether the tramp killed him out of sympathy for the defenceless woman or in rage at being disappointed in his own plans has never been determined. Mrs. Chivers herself thinks he was actuated by a rude sort of gratitude.

THE RUBY AND THE CALDRON

As there were two good men on duty that night, I did not see why I should remain at my desk, even though there was an unusual stir created in our small town by the grand ball given at The Evergreens.

But just as I was preparing to start for home, an imperative ring called me to the telephone, and I heard:

"Halloo! Is this the police-station?"

"It is."

"Well, then, a detective is wanted at once at The Evergreens. He cannot be too clever or too discreet. A valuable jewel has been lost, which must be found before the guests disperse for home. Large reward if the matter ends successfully."

"May I ask who is speaking to me?"

"Mrs. Ashley."

It was the mistress of The Evergreens and giver of the ball.

"Madam, a man shall be sent at once. Where will you see him?"

"In the butler's pantry at the rear. Let him give his name as Jennings."

"Very good. Good-bye."

"Good-bye."

A pretty piece of work! Should I send Hendricks or should I send Hicks? Hendricks was clever and Hicks discreet, but neither united both qualifications in the measure demanded by the sensible and quietly resolved woman with whom I had just been talking. What alternative remained? But one: I must go myself.

It was not late—not for a ball-night, at least—and as half the town had been invited to the dance, the streets were alive with carriages. I was watching the blink of their lights through the fast-falling snow when my attention was drawn to a fact which struck me as peculiar. These carriages were all coming my way instead of rolling in the direction of The Evergreens. Had they been empty this would have needed no explanation; but, so far as I could see, most of them were full, and that, too, of loudly-talking women and gesticulating men.

Something of a serious nature must have occurred at The Evergreens. Rapidly I paced on, and soon found myself before the great gates.

A crowd of vehicles of all descriptions blocked the entrance. None seemed to be passing up the driveway; all stood clustered at the gates; and as I drew nearer I perceived many an anxious head thrust forth from their quickly-opened doors, and heard many an ejaculation of disappointment as the short interchange of words went on between the drivers of these various turnouts and a man drawn up in quiet resolution before the unexpectedly barred entrance.

Slipping round to this man's side, I listened to what he was saying. It was simple, but very explicit.

"Mrs. Ashley asks everybody's pardon, but the ball can't go on to-night. Something has happened which makes the reception of further guests impossible. To-morrow evening she will be happy to see you all. The dance is simply postponed."

This he had probably repeated forty times, and each time it had probably been received with the same mixture of doubt and curiosity which now held the lengthy procession in check.

Not wishing to attract attention, yet anxious to lose no time, I pressed up still nearer, and, bending towards him from the shadow cast by a convenient post, uttered the one word:

"Jennings."

Instantly he unlocked a small gate at his right. I passed in, and with professional sang-froid proceeded to take my way to the house through the double row of evergreens bordering the semicircular approach.

As these trees stood very close together, and were, besides, heavily laden with fresh-fallen snow, I failed to catch a glimpse of the building itself until I stood in front of it. Then I saw that it was brilliantly lighted, and gave evidence here and there of some festivity; but the guests were too few for the effect to be very exhilarating, and, passing around to the rear, I sought the special entrance to which I had been directed.

A heavy-browed porch, before which stood a caterer's wagon, led me to a door which had every appearance of being the one I sought. Pushing it open, I entered without ceremony, and speedily found myself in the midst of twenty or more coloured waiters and chattering housemaids. To one of the former I addressed the question:

"Where is the butler's pantry? I am told that I shall find the lady of the house there."

"Your name?" was the curt demand.

"Jennings."

"Follow me."

I was taken through narrow passages and across one or two storerooms to a small but well-lighted closet, where I was left, with the assurance that Mrs. Ashley would presently join me. I had never seen this lady, but I had often heard her spoken of as a woman of superior character and admirable discretion.

She did not keep me waiting. In two minutes the door opened, and this fine, well-poised woman was telling her story in the straightforward manner I so much admire.

The article lost was a large ruby of singular beauty and great value, the property of Mrs. Burton, the Senator's wife, in whose honour this ball was being given. It had not been lost in the house, nor had it been originally missed this evening. Mrs. Burton and herself had attended the great football game in the afternoon, and it was on the college campus that Mrs. Burton had first dropped her invaluable jewel. But a reward of five hundred dollars having been at once offered to whomever should find and restore it, a great search had followed, which ended in its being picked up by one of the students, and brought back as far as the driveway in front of The Evergreens, when it had again disappeared, and in a way to rouse conjecture of the strangest and most puzzling character.

The young man who had brought it thus far bore the name of John Deane, and was a member of the senior class. He had been the first to detect its sparkle in the grass, and those who were near enough to see his face at that happy moment say that it expressed the utmost satisfaction at his good luck.

"You see," said Mrs. Ashley, "he has a sweetheart, and five hundred dollars looks like a fortune to a young man just starting life. But he was weak enough to take this girl into his confidence; and on their way here—for both were invited to the ball—he went so far as to pull it out of his pocket and show it to her.

"They were admiring it together, and vaunting its beauties to the young lady friend who had accompanied them, when their carriage turned into the driveway and they saw the lights of the house flashing before them. Hastily restoring the jewel to the little bag he had made for it out of the finger-end of an old glove—a bag in which he assured me he had been careful to keep it safely tied ever since picking it up on the college green—he thrust it back into his pocket and prepared to help the ladies out. But just then a disturbance arose in front. A horse which had been driven up was rearing in a way that threatened to overturn the light buggy to which it was attached. As the occupants of this buggy were ladies, and seemed to have no control over the plunging beast, young Deane naturally sprang to the rescue. Bidding his own ladies alight and make for the porch, he hurriedly ran forward and, pausing in front of the maddened animal, waited for an opportunity to seize him by the rein. He says that as he stood there facing the beast with fixed eye and raised hand, he distinctly felt something strike or touch his breast. But the sensation conveyed no meaning to him in his excitement, and he did not think of it again till, the horse well in hand and the two alarmed occupants of the buggy rescued, he turned to see where his own ladies were, and beheld them looking down at him from the midst of a circle of young people, drawn from the house by the screaming of the women. Instantly a thought of the treasure he carried recurred to his mind, and releasing the now quieted horse, he thrust his hand hastily into his pocket. The jewel was gone. He declares that for a moment he felt as if he had been struck on the head by one of the hoofs of the frantic horse he had just handled. But immediately the importance of his loss and the necessity he felt for instant action restored him to himself, and shouting aloud, "I have dropped Mrs. Burton's ruby!" he begged every one to stand still while he made a search for it.

"This all occurred, as you must know, more than an hour and a half ago, consequently before many of my guests had arrived. My son, who was one of the few spectators gathered on the porch, tells me that there was only one other carriage behind the one in which Mr. Deane had brought his ladies. Both of these had stopped short of the stepping-stone, and as the horse and buggy which had made all this trouble had by this time been driven to the stable, nothing stood in the way of his search but the rapidly accumulating snow, which, if you remember, was falling very thick and fast at the time.

"My son, who had rushed in for his overcoat, came running down the steps to help him. So did some others. But, with an imploring gesture, he begged to be allowed to conduct the search alone, the ground being in such a state that the delicately-mounted jewel ran great risk of being trodden into the snow and thus injured or lost. They humoured him for a moment, then, seeing that his efforts bade fair to be fruitless, my son insisted upon joining him, and the two looked the ground over, inch by inch, from the place where Mr. Deane had set foot to ground in alighting from his carriage to the exact spot where he had stood when he had finally seized hold of the horse. But no ruby. Then Harrison (that is my son's name) sent for a broom and went over the place again, sweeping aside the surface snow and examining carefully the ground beneath, but with no better results than before. No ruby could be found. My son came to me panting. Mrs. Burton and myself stood awaiting him in a state of suspense. Guests and fête were alike forgotten. We had heard that the jewel had been found on the campus by one of the students, and had been brought back as far as the step in front, and then lost again in some unaccountable manner in the snow, and we hoped, nay, expected from moment to moment, that it would be brought in.

"When Harrison finally entered, pale, dishevelled and shaking his head, Mrs. Burton caught me by the hand, and I thought she would faint. For this jewel is of far greater value to her than its mere worth in money, though that is by no means small.

"It is a family jewel, and was given to her by her husband under special circumstances. He prizes it even more than she does, and he is not here to counsel or assist her in this extremity. Besides, she was wearing it in direct opposition to his expressed wishes. This I must tell you, to show how imperative it is for us to recover it; also to account for the large reward she is willing to pay. When he last looked at it he noticed that the fastening was a trifle slack, and, though he handed the trinket back, he told her distinctly that she was not to wear it till it had been either to Tiffany's or Starr's. But she considered it safe enough, and put it on to please the boys, and lost it. Senator Burton is a hard man and—in short, the jewel must be found. I give you just one hour in which to do it."

"But, madam—" I protested.

"I know," she put in, with a quick nod and a glance over her shoulder to see if the door was shut. "I have not finished my story. Hearing what Harrison had to say, I took action at once. I bade him call in the guests, whom curiosity or interest still detained in the porch, and seat them in a certain room which I designated to him. Then, after telling him to send two men to the gates with orders to hold back all further carriages from entering, and two others to shovel up and cart away to the stable every particle of snow for ten feet each side of the front step, I asked to see Mr. Deane. But here my son whispered something into my ear, which it is my duty to repeat. It was to the effect that Mr. Deane believed that the jewel had been taken from him; that he insisted, in fact, that he had felt a hand touch his breast while he stood awaiting an opportunity to seize the horse. 'Very good,' said I, 'we'll remember that too; but first see that my orders are carried out, and that all approaches to the grounds are guarded and no one allowed to come in or go out without permission from me.'

"He left us, and I was turning to encourage Mrs. Burton when my attention was caught by the eager face of a little friend of mine, who, quite unknown to me, was sitting in one of the corners of the room. She was studying my countenance with a subdued anxiety, hardly natural in one so young, and I was about to relieve my mind by questioning her when she made a sudden rush and vanished from the room. Some impulse made me follow her. She is a conscientious little thing, but timid as a hare, and though I saw she had something to say, it was with difficulty I could make her speak. Only after the most solemn assurances that her name should not be mentioned in the matter would she give me the following bit of information, which you may possibly think throws another light upon the affair. It seems that she was looking out of one of the front windows when Mr. Deane's carriage drove up. She had been watching the antics of the horse attached to the buggy, but as soon as she saw Mr. Deane going to the assistance of those in danger, she let her eyes stray back to the ladies whom he had left behind him in the carriage.

"She did not know these ladies, but their looks and gestures interested her, and she watched them quite intently as they leaped to the ground and made their way toward the porch. One went on quickly, and without pause, to the step; but the other—the one who came last—did not do this. She stopped a moment, perhaps to watch the horse in front, perhaps to draw her cloak more closely about her, and when she again moved on it was with a start and a hurried glance at her feet, terminating in a quick turn and a sudden stooping to the ground. When she again stood upright she had something in her hand which she thrust furtively into her breast."

"How was this lady dressed?" I inquired.

"In a white cloak, with an edging of fur. I took pains to learn that too, and it was with some curiosity, I assure you, that I examined the few guests that had now been admitted to the room I had so carefully pointed out to my son. Two of them wore white cloaks, but one of these was Mrs. Dalrymple, and I did not give her or her cloak a second thought. The other was a tall, fine-looking girl, with an air and bearing calculated to rouse admiration if she had not looked so disturbed. But her preoccupation was evident, a circumstance which, had she been Mr. Deane's fiancée, would have needed no explanation; but, as she was only that lady's friend, its cause was not so apparent.

"The floor of the room, as I had happily remembered, was covered with crash, and as I lifted each garment off—I allowed no maid to assist me in this—I shook it well; ostensibly because of the few flakes clinging to it, really to see if anything could be shaken out of it. Of course, I met with no success. I had not expected to, but it is my disposition to be thorough. These wraps I saw all hung in an adjoining closet, the door of which I locked—here is the key—after which I handed my guests over to my son, and went to notify the police."

I bowed, and asked where the young people were now.

"Still in the drawing-room. I have ordered the musicians to play, and consequently there is more or less dancing. But, of course, nothing can remove the wet blanket which has fallen over us all—nothing but the finding of this jewel. Do you see your way to accomplishing this? We are from this very moment at your disposal; only I pray that you will make no more disturbance than is necessary, and, if possible, arouse no suspicions you cannot back up by facts. I dread a scandal almost as much as I do sickness and death, and these young people—well, their lives are all before them, and neither Mrs. Burton nor myself would wish to throw the shadow of a false suspicion over any one of them."

I assured her that I sympathised with her scruples, and would do my best to recover the ruby without inflicting undue annoyance upon the innocent. Then I inquired whether it was known that a detective had been called in. She seemed to think it was suspected by some, if not by all. At which my way seemed a trifle complicated.

We were about to proceed when another thought struck me.

"Madam, you have not said whether the carriage itself was searched."

"I forgot. Yes, the carriage was thoroughly overhauled before the coachman left the box."

"Who did this overhauling?"

"My son. He would not trust any one else in a business of this kind."

"One more question, madam. Was any one seen to approach Mr. Deane on the carriage-drive prior to his assertion that the jewel was lost?"

"No. And there were no tracks in the snow of any such person. My son looked."

And I would look, or so I decided within myself, but I said nothing; and in silence we proceeded toward the drawing-room.

I had left my overcoat behind me, and always being well dressed, I did not present so bad an appearance. Still, I was not in party attire, and naturally could not pass for a guest even if I had wanted to, which I did not. I felt that I must rely on insight in this case, and on a certain power I had always possessed of reading faces. That the case called for just this species of intuition I was positive. Mrs. Burton's ruby was within a hundred yards of us at this very moment, probably within a hundred feet; but to lay hands on it and without scandal—well, that was a problem calculated to rouse the interest of even an old police-officer like myself.

A strain of music—desultory, however, and spiritless, like everything else about the place that night— greeted us as Mrs. Ashley opened the door leading directly into the large front hall.

Immediately a scene meant to be festive, but which was, in fact, desolate, burst upon us. The lights, the flowers, and the brilliant appearance of such ladies as flitted into sight from the almost empty parlours, were all suggestive of the cheer suitable to a great occasion; but, in spite of this, the effect was altogether melancholy, for the hundreds who should have graced this scene, and for whom this illumination had been made and these festoons hung, had been turned away from the gates, and the few who felt they must remain, because their hostess showed no disposition to let them go, wore any but holiday faces, for all their forced smiles and pitiful attempts at nonchalance and gaiety.

I scrutinised these faces carefully. I detected nothing in them but annoyance at a situation which certainly was anything but pleasant.

Turning to Mrs. Ashley, I requested her to be kind enough to point out her son, adding that I should be glad to have a moment's conversation with him before I spoke to Mr. Deane.

"That will give Mr. Deane time to compose himself. He is quite upset. Not even Mrs. Burton can comfort him. My son—oh, there is Harrison!"

A tall, fine-looking young man was crossing the hall. Mrs. Ashley beckoned to him, and in another moment we were standing together in one of the empty parlours. I gave him my name and told him my business. Then I said:

"Your mother has allotted me an hour in which to find the valuable jewel which has just been lost on these premises." Here I smiled. "She evidently has great confidence in my ability. I must see that I do not disappoint her."

All this time I was examining his face. It was not only handsome, but expressive of great candour. The eyes looked straight into mine, and, while showing anxiety, betrayed no deeper emotion than the occasion naturally called for.

"Have you any suggestions to offer? I understand that you were on the ground almost as soon as Mr. Deane discovered his loss."

His eyes changed a trifle, but did not swerve. Of course, he had been informed by his mother of the suspicious action of the young lady who had been a member of that gentleman's party, and shrank, as any one in his position would, from the responsibilities entailed by this knowledge.

"No," said he. "We have done all we can. The next move must come from you."

"I know of one that will settle the matter at once," I assured him, still with my eyes fixed scrutinisingly on his face—"a universal search, not of places, but of persons. But it is a harsh measure."

"A most disagreeable one," he emphasised, flushing. "Such an indignity offered to guests would never be forgotten or forgiven."

"True. But if they offered to submit to this themselves?"

"They? How?"

"If you, the son of the house—their host, we may say—should call them together, and for your own satisfaction empty out your pockets in the sight of every one, don't you think that all the men, and possibly all the women too"—here I let my voice fall suggestively—"would be glad to follow suit? It could be done in apparent joke."

He shook his head with a straightforward air, which set him high in my estimation.

"That would call for little but effrontery on my part," said he. "But think how it would affect these boys who came here for the sole purpose of enjoying themselves. I will not so much as mention the ladies."

"Yet one of the latter—"

"I know," he quietly acknowledged, growing restless for the first time.

I withdrew my eyes from his face. I had learned what I wished. Personally, he did not shrink from search, therefore the jewel was not in his pockets. This left but two persons for suspicion to halt between. But I disclosed nothing of my thoughts; I merely asked pardon for a suggestion that, while pardonable in a man accustomed to handle crime with ungloved hands, could not fail to prove offensive to a gentleman like himself.

"We must move by means less open," I concluded. "It adds to our difficulties, but that cannot be helped. I should now like a glimpse of Mr. Deane."

"Do you not wish to speak to him?"

"I should prefer a sight of his face first."

He led me across the hall and pointed through an open door. In the centre of a small room containing a table and some chairs I perceived a young man sitting, with fallen head and dejected air, staring at vacancy. By his side, with hand laid on his, knelt a young girl, striving in this gentle but speechless way to comfort him. It made a pathetic picture. I drew Ashley away.

"I am disposed to believe in that young man," said I. "If he still has the jewel, he would not try to carry off the situation just this way. He really looks broken-hearted."

"Oh, he is dreadfully cut up! If you could have seen how frantically he searched for the stone, and the depression into which he fell when he realised that it was not to be found, you would not doubt him for an instant. What made you think he might still have the ruby?"

"Oh, we police-officers think of everything. Then the fact that he insists that something or some one touched his breast on the driveway strikes me as a trifle suspicious. Your mother says that no second person could have been there, or the snow would have given evidence of it."

"Yes; I looked expressly. Of course, the drive itself was full of hoof-marks and wheel-tracks, for several carriages had already passed over it. Then there were all of Deane's footsteps, but no other man's, so far as I could see."

"Yet he insists that he was touched or struck."

"Yes."

"With no one there to touch or strike him."

Mr. Ashley was silent.

"Let us step out and take a view of the place," I suggested. "I should prefer doing this to questioning the young man in his present state of mind." Then, as we turned to put on our coats, I asked with suitable precautions: "Do you suppose that he has the same secret suspicions as ourselves, and that it is to hide these he insists upon the jewel's having been taken away from him at a point the ladies are known not to have approached?"

Young Ashley looked more startled than pleased.

"Nothing has been said to him of what Miss Peters saw Miss Glover do. I could not bring myself to mention it. I have not even allowed myself to believe—"

Here a fierce gust, blowing in from the door he had just opened, cut short his words, and neither of us spoke again till we stood on the exact spot in the driveway where the episode we were endeavouring to understand had taken place.

"Oh," I cried, as soon as I could look about me; "the mystery is explained. Look at that bush, or perhaps you call it a shrub. If the wind were blowing as freshly as it is now, and very probably it was, one of those slender branches might easily be switched against his breast, especially if he stood, as you say he did, close against this border."

"Well, I'm a fool. Only the other day I told the gardener that these branches would need trimming in the spring, and yet I never so much as thought of them when Mr. Deane spoke of something striking his breast."

As we turned back I made this remark:

"With this explanation of the one doubtful point in his otherwise plausible account, we can credit his story as being in the main true, which," I calmly added, "places him above suspicion and narrows our inquiry down to one."

We had moved quickly, and were now at the threshold of the door by which we had come out.

"Mr. Ashley," I continued, "I shall have to ask you to add to your former favours that of showing me the young lady in whom, from this moment on, we are especially interested. If you can manage to let me see her first without her seeing me, I shall be infinitely obliged to you."

"I do not know where she is. I shall have to search for her."

"I will wait by the hall door."

In a few minutes he returned to me.

"Come," said he, and led me into what I judged to be the library.

With a gesture towards one of the windows, he backed quickly out, leaving me to face the situation alone. I was rather glad of this. Glancing in the direction he had indicated, and perceiving the figure of a young lady standing with her back to me on the farther side of a flowing lace curtain, I took a few steps toward her, hoping that the movement would cause her to turn. But it entirely failed to produce this effect, nor did she give any sign that she noted the intrusion. This prevented me from catching the glimpse of her face which I so desired, and obliged me to confine myself to a study of her dress and attitude.

The former was very elegant, more elegant than the appearance of her two friends had led me to expect. Though I am far from being an authority on feminine toilets, I yet had experience enough to know that such a gown represented not only the best efforts of the dressmaker's art, but very considerable means on the part of the woman wearing it.

This was a discovery which instantly altered the complexion of my thoughts; for I had presupposed her a girl of humble means, willing to sacrifice certain scruples to obtain a little extra money. This imposing figure might be that of a millionaire's daughter; how, then, could I associate her, even in my own mind, with theft? I decided that I must see her face before giving answer to these doubts.

She did not seem inclined to turn. She had raised the shade from before the wintry panes and was engaged in looking out. Her attitude was not that of one simply enjoying a moment's respite from the dance. It was rather that of an absorbed mind brooding upon what gave little or no pleasure; and as I further gazed and noted the droop of her lovely shoulders and the languor visible in her whole bearing, I saw that a full glimpse of her features was imperative. Moving forward, I came upon her suddenly.

"Excuse me, Miss Smith," I boldly exclaimed; then paused, for she had turned instinctively, and I had seen that for which I had risked this daring move. "Your pardon," I hastily apologised. "I mistook you for another young lady," and drew back with a low bow to let her pass, for I saw that her mind was bent on escape.

And I did not wonder at this, for her eyes were streaming with tears, and her face, which was doubtless a pretty one under ordinary conditions, looked so distorted with distracting emotions that she was no fit subject for any man's eye, let alone that of a hard-hearted officer of the law on the lookout for the guilty hand which had just appropriated a jewel worth anywhere from eight to ten thousand dollars.

Yet I was glad to see her weep, for only first offenders weep, and first offenders are amenable to influence, especially if they have been led into wrong by impulse, and are weak rather than wicked.

Anxious to make no blunder, I resolved, before proceeding further, to learn what I could of the character and antecedents of the suspected one, and this from the only source which offered—Mr. Deane's affianced.

This young lady was a delicate girl, with a face like a flower. Recognising her sensitive nature, I approached her with the utmost gentleness. Not seeking to disguise either the nature of my business or my reasons for being in the house, since all this gave me authority, I modulated my tone to suit her gentle spirit, and, above all, I showed the utmost sympathy for her lover, whose rights in the reward had been taken from him as certainly as the jewel had been taken from Mrs. Burton. In this way I gained her confidence, and she was quite ready to listen when I observed:

"There is a young lady here who seems to be in a state of even greater trouble than Mr. Deane. Why is this? You brought her here. Is her sympathy with Mr. Deane so great as to cause her to weep over his loss?"

"Frances? Oh no. She likes Mr. Deane and she likes me, but not well enough to cry over our misfortunes. I think she has some trouble of her own."

"One that you can tell me?"

Her surprise was manifest.

"Why do you ask that? What interest can a police-officer, called in, as I understand, to recover a stolen jewel, have in Frances Glover's personal difficulties?"

I saw that I must make my position perfectly plain.

"Only this: She was seen to pick up something from the driveway, where no one else had succeeded in finding anything."

"She? When? Who saw her?"

"I cannot answer all these questions at once," I said, smiling. "She was seen to do this—no matter by whom—while you were stepping down from the carriage. As you preceded her, you naturally did not observe this action, which was fortunate, perhaps, as you would scarcely have known what to do or say about it."

"Yes, I should," she retorted with a most unexpected display of spirit. "I should have asked her what she had found, and I should have insisted upon an answer. I love my friends, but I love the man I am to marry better."

Here her voice fell, and a most becoming blush suffused her cheek.

"Quite right," I assented. "Now will you answer my former question? What troubles Miss Glover? Can you tell me?"

"That I cannot. I only know that she has been very silent ever since she left the house. I thought her beautiful new dress would please her, but it does not seem to. She has been unhappy and preoccupied all the evening. She only roused a bit when Mr. Deane showed us the ruby, and said—Oh, I forgot!"

"What's that? What have you forgot?"

"Your remark of a moment ago. I wouldn't add a word—"

"Pardon me," I smilingly interrupted, looking as fatherly as I could, "but you have added this word, and now you must tell me what it means. You were going to speak of the interest she showed in the extraordinary jewel which Mr. Deane took from his pocket, and—"

"In what he said about the reward he expected. That is, she looked eagerly at the ruby, and sighed when he acknowledged that he expected it to bring him five hundred dollars before midnight. But any girl of means no larger than hers might do that. It would not be fair to lay too much stress on a sigh."

"Is not Miss Glover wealthy? She wears a very expensive dress, I observe."

"I know it, and I have wondered a little at it, for her father is not called very well off. But perhaps she bought it with her own money. I know she has some; she is an artist in burnt wood."

I let the subject of Miss Glover's dress drop. I had heard enough to satisfy me that my first theory was correct. This young woman, beautifully dressed, and with a face from which the rounded lines of early girlhood had not yet departed, held in her possession, probably at this very moment, Mrs. Burton's magnificent jewel. But where? On her person or hidden in some of her belongings? I remembered the cloak in the closet, and thought it wise to assure myself that the jewel was not secreted in this garment before I proceeded to extreme measures. Mrs. Ashley, upon being consulted, agreed with me as to the desirability of this, and presently I had this poor girl's cloak in my hands.

Did I find the ruby? No; but I found something else tucked away in an inner pocket which struck me as bearing quite pointedly upon this case. It was the bill—crumpled, soiled, and tear-stained—of the dress whose elegance had so surprised her friends and made me for a short time regard her as the daughter of wealthy parents. An enormous bill, which must have struck dismay to the soul of this self-supporting girl, who probably had no idea of how a French dressmaker can foot up items. Four hundred and fifty dollars, and for one gown! I declare I felt indignant myself, and could quite understand why she heaved that little sigh when Mr. Deane spoke of the five hundred dollars he expected from Mrs. Burton, and, later, when, in following the latter's footsteps up the driveway, she stumbled upon this same jewel, fallen, as it were, from his pocket into her very hands, how she came to succumb to the temptation of endeavouring to secure this sum for herself.

That he would shout aloud his loss, and thus draw the whole household out on the porch, was, naturally, not anticipated by her. Of course, when this occurred, the feasibility of her project was gone, and I only wished that I had been present and able to note her countenance, as, crowded in with others on that windy porch, she watched the progress of the search, which every moment made it not only less impossible for her to attempt the restoration upon which the reward depended, but must have caused her to feel, if she had been as well brought up as all indications showed, that it was a dishonest act of which she had been guilty, and that, willing or not, she must look upon herself as a thief so long as she held the jewel back from Mr. Deane or its rightful owner. But how face the publicity of restoring it now, after so elaborate and painful a search, in which even the son of her hostess had taken part!

That would be to proclaim her guilt, and thus effectually ruin her in the eyes of everybody concerned. No, she would keep the compromising article a little longer, in the hope of finding some opportunity of returning it without risk to her good name. And so she allowed the search to proceed.

I have entered thus elaborately into the supposed condition of this girl's mind on this critical evening that you may understand why I felt a certain sympathy for her, which forbade harsh measures. I was sure, from the glimpse I had caught of her face, that she longed to be relieved from the tension she was under, and that she would gladly rid herself of this valuable jewel if she only knew how. This opportunity I proposed to give her; and this is why, on returning the bill to its place, I assumed such an air of relief on rejoining Mrs. Ashley.

She saw, and drew me aside.

"You have not found it," she said.

"No," I returned; "but I am positive where it is."

"And where is that?"

"Over Miss Glover's uneasy heart."

Mrs. Ashley turned pale.

"Wait," said I. "I have a scheme for getting it back without making her shame public. Listen!" and I whispered a few words in her ear.

She surveyed me in amazement for a moment, then nodded, and her face lighted up.

"You are certainly earning your reward," she declared; and summoning her son, who was never far away from her side, she whispered her wishes. He started, bowed, and hurried from the room.

By this time my business in the house was well known to all, and I could not appear in hall or parlour without a great silence falling upon every one present, followed by a breaking up of the only too small circle of unhappy guests into agitated groups. But I appeared to see nothing of all this till the proper moment, when, turning suddenly upon them all, I cried out cheerfully, but with a certain deference I thought would please them:

"Ladies and gentlemen, I have an interesting fact to announce. The snow which was taken up from the driveway has been put to melt in the great feed caldron over the stable fire. We expect to find the ruby at the bottom, and Mrs. Ashley invites you to be present at its recovery. It has now stopped snowing, and she thought you might enjoy the excitement of watching the water ladled out."

A dozen girls bounded forward.

"Oh yes! What fun! Where are our cloaks—our rubbers?"

Two only stood hesitating. One of these was Mr. Deane's lady-love, and the other her friend, Miss Glover. The former, perhaps, secretly wondered. The latter—but I dared not look long enough or closely enough in her direction to judge rightly of her emotions. Amid the bustle which now ensued I caught sight of Mr. Deane's face peering from an open doorway. It was all alive with hope. I also perceived a lady looking down from the second storey, who I felt sure was Mrs. Burton herself. Evidently my confident tone had produced more effect than the words themselves. Every one looked upon the jewel as already recovered, and regarded my invitation to the stable as a ruse by which I hoped to restore universal good feeling by giving them all a share in my triumph.

All but one! Nothing could make Miss Glover look otherwise than anxious, restless, and unsettled; and though she followed in the wake of the rest, it was with hidden face and lagging step, as if she recognised the whole thing as a farce, and doubted her own power to go through it calmly.

"Ah, ha! my lady," thought I, "only be patient and you will see what I shall do for you." And, indeed, I thought her eye brightened as we all drew up around the huge caldron standing full of water over the stable stove. As pains had already been taken to put out the fire in this stove, the ladies were not afraid of injuring their dresses, and consequently crowded as close as their numbers would permit. Miss Glover especially stood within reach of the brim, and as soon as I noted this, I gave the signal which had been agreed upon between Mr. Ashley and myself. Instantly the electric lights went out, leaving the place in total darkness.

A scream from the girls, a burst of hilarious laughter from their escorts, mingled with loud apologies from their seemingly mischievous host, filled up the interval of darkness which I had insisted should not be too soon curtailed; then the lights flared up as suddenly as they had gone out, and while the glare was fresh on every face, I stole a glance at Miss Glover to see if she had made good use of the opportunity given her for ridding herself of the jewel by dropping it into the caldron. If she had, both her troubles and mine were at an end; if she had not, then I need feel no further scruple in approaching her with the direct question I had hitherto found it so difficult to put.

She stood with both hands grasping her cloak, which she had drawn tightly about the rich folds of her new and expensive dress; but her eyes were fixed straight before her, with a soft light in their depths which made her positively beautiful.

The jewel is in the pot, I inwardly decided, and ordered the two waiting stablemen to step forward with their ladles. Quickly those ladles went in, but before they could be lifted out dripping, half the ladies had scurried back, afraid of injury to their pretty dresses. But they soon sidled forward again, and watched with beaming eyes the slow but sure emptying of the great caldron at whose bottom they anticipated finding the lost jewel.

As the ladles were plunged deeper and deeper, the heads drew closer, and so great was the interest shown that the busiest lips forgot to chatter, and eyes whose only business up till now had been to follow with shy curiosity every motion made by their handsome young host now settled on the murky depths of the great pot whose bottom was almost in sight.

As I heard the ladles strike this bottom, I instinctively withdrew a step in anticipation of the loud hurrah which would naturally hail the first sight of the lost ruby. Conceive, then, my chagrin, my bitter and mortified disappointment, when, after one look at the broad surface of the now exposed bottom, the one shout which rose was: "Nothing!"

I was so thoroughly put out that I did not wait to hear the loud complaints which burst from every lip. Drawing Mr. Ashley aside (who, by the way, seemed as much affected as myself by the turn affairs had taken), I remarked to him that, after this, there was only one course left for me to take.

"And what is that?"

"To ask Miss Glover to show me what she picked up from your driveway."

"And if she refuses?"

"To take her quietly with me to the station, where we have women who can make sure that the ruby is not on her person."

Mr. Ashley made an involuntary gesture of strong repugnance.

"Let us pray that it will not come to that," he objected hoarsely. "Such a fine figure of a girl! Did you notice how bright and happy she looked when the lights sprang up? I declare she struck me as lovely."

"So she did me, and caused me to draw some erroneous conclusions. I shall have to ask you to procure me an interview with her as soon as we return to the house."

"She shall meet you in the library."

But when, a few minutes later, she joined me in the room just designated, I own that my task became suddenly hateful to me. She was not far from my own daughter's age, and, had it not been for her furtive look of care, appeared almost as blooming and bright. Would it ever come to pass that a harsh man of the law should feel it his duty to speak to my Flora as I must now speak to the young girl before me? The thought made me inwardly recoil, and it was in as gentle a manner as possible that I made my bow and began with the following remark:

"I hope you will pardon me, Miss Glover—I am told that is your name. I hate to disturb your pleasure"—this with the tears of alarm and grief rising in her eyes—"but you can tell me something which will greatly simplify my task, and possibly put matters in such shape that you and your friends can be released to your homes."

"I?"

She stood before me with amazed eyes, the colour rising in her cheeks. I had to force my next words, which, out of consideration for her, I made as direct as possible.

"Yes, miss. What was the article you were seen to pick up from the driveway soon after leaving your carriage?"

She started, then stumbled backward, tripping in her long train.

"I pick up?" she murmured. Then with a blush, whether of anger or pride I could not tell, she coldly answered: "Oh, that was something of my own—something I had just dropped. I had rather not tell you what it was."

I scrutinised her closely. She met my eyes squarely, yet not with just the clear light I should, remembering Flora, have been glad to see there.

"I think it would be better for you to be entirely frank," said I. "It was the only article known to have been picked up from the driveway after Mr. Deane's loss of the ruby; and though we do not presume to say that it was the ruby, yet the matter would look clearer to us all if you would frankly state what this object was."

Her whole body seemed to collapse, and she looked as if about to sink.

"Oh, where is Minnie? Where is Mr. Deane?" she moaned, turning and staring at the door, as if she hoped they would fly to her aid. Then, in a burst of indignation which I was fain to believe real, she turned on me with the cry: "It was a bit of paper which I had thrust into the bosom of my gown. It fell out—"

"Your dressmaker's bill?" I intimated.

"She stared, laughed hysterically for a moment, then sank upon a sofa nearby, sobbing spasmodically.

"Yes," she cried, after a moment; "my dressmaker's bill. You seem to know all my affairs." Then suddenly, and with a startling impetuosity, which drew her to her feet: "Are you going to tell everybody that? Are you going to state publicly that Miss Glover brought an unpaid bill to the party, and that because Mr. Deane was unfortunate enough, or careless enough, to drop and lose the jewel he was bringing to Mrs. Burton she is to be looked upon as a thief, because she stooped to pick up this bill which had slipped inadvertently from its hiding-place? I shall die if you do!" she cried. "I shall die if it is already known," she pursued with increasing emotion. "Is it? Is it?"

Her passion was so great, so much greater than any likely to rise in a breast wholly innocent, that I began to feel very sober.

"No one but Mrs. Ashley, and possibly her son, know about the bill," said I, "and no one shall if you will go with that lady to her room, and make plain to her, in the only way you can, that the extremely valuable article which has been lost to-night is not in your possession."

She threw up her arms with a scream. "Oh, what a horror! I cannot! I cannot! Oh, I shall die of shame! My father! My mother!" And she burst from the room like one distraught.

But in another moment she came cringing back.

"I cannot face them," she said. "They all believe it; they will always believe it unless I submit! Oh, why did I ever come to this dreadful place? Why did I order this hateful dress, which I can never pay for, and which, in spite of the misery it has caused me, has failed to bring me the—" She did not continue. She had caught my eye and seen there, perhaps, some evidence of the pity I could not but experience for her. With a sudden change of tone she advanced upon me with the appeal: "Save me from this humiliation. I have not seen the ruby. I am as ignorant of its whereabouts as—as Mr. Ashley himself. Won't you believe me? Won't they be satisfied if I swear—"

I was really sorry for her. I began to think, too, that some dreadful mistake had been made. Her manner seemed too ingenuous for guilt. Yet where could that ruby be, if not with this young girl? Certainly, all other possibilities had been exhausted, and her story of the bill, even if accepted, would never quite exonerate her from secret suspicion while that elusive jewel remained unfound.

"You give me no hope," she moaned. "I must go out before them all, and ask to have it proved that I am no thief. Oh, if God would only have pity—!"

"Or some one should succeed in finding—Halloo, what's that?"

A shout had risen from the hall beyond.

She gasped, and we both plunged forward. Mr. Ashley, still in his overcoat, stood at the other end of the hall, and facing him were ranged the whole line of young people whom I had left scattered about in the various parlours. I thought he appeared to be in a peculiar frame of mind; and when he glanced our way, and saw who was standing with me in the library doorway, his voice took on a tone which made me doubt whether he was about to announce good news or bad.

But his first word settled that question.

"Rejoice with me!" he cried. "The ruby has been found! Do you want to see the culprit, for there is a culprit? We have him at the door. Shall we bring him in?"

"Yes, yes!" cried several voices, among them that of Mr. Deane, who now strode forward with beaming eyes and instinctively lifted hand. But some of the ladies looked frightened, and Mr. Ashley, noting this, glanced for encouragement in our direction.

He seemed to find it in Miss Glover's eyes. She had quivered and nearly fallen at that word found, but had drawn herself up by this time, and was awaiting his further action in a fever of relief and hope, which, perhaps, no one but myself could fully appreciate.

"A vile thief! A most unconscionable rascal!" vociferated Mr. Ashley. "You must see him, mother; you must see him, ladies, else you will not realise our good fortune. Open the door there, and bring in the robber!"

At this command, uttered in ringing tones, the huge leaves of the great front-door swung slowly forward, revealing two sturdy stablemen leading into view—a huge horse.

The scream of astonishment which went up from all sides, united to Mr. Ashley's shout of hilarity, caused the animal, unused, no doubt, to drawing-rooms, to rear to the length of his bridle. At which Mr. Ashley laughed again, and gaily cried:

"Confound the fellow! Look at him, mother! look at him, ladies! Do you not see guilt written on his brow? It is he who has made us all this trouble. First, he must needs take umbrage at the two lights with which we presumed to illuminate our porch; then, envying Mrs. Burton her ruby and Mr. Deane his reward, seek to rob them both by grinding his hoofs all over the snow of the driveway till he came upon the jewel which Mr. Deane had dropped from his pocket, and, taking it up in a ball of snow, secrete it in his left hind shoe—where it might be yet, if Mr. Spencer"—here he bowed to a strange gentleman who at that moment entered—"had not come himself for his daughters and, going first to the stable, found his horse so restless and seemingly lame—there, boys, you may take the wretch away now and harness him, but first hold up that guilty left hind hoof for the ladies to see—that he stooped to examine him, and so came upon this."

Here the young gentleman brought forward his hand. In it was a nondescript little wad, well soaked and shapeless; but once he had untied the kid, such a ray of rosy light burst from his outstretched palm that I doubt if a single woman there noted the clatter of the retiring beast or the heavy clang made by the two front-doors as they shut upon the robber. Eyes and tongues were too busy, and Mr. Ashley, realising, probably, that the interest of all present would remain, for a few minutes at least, with this marvellous jewel so astonishingly recovered, laid it, with many expressions of thankfulness, in Mrs. Burton's now eagerly outstretched palm, and advancing towards us, greeted Miss Glover with a smile.

"Congratulate me," he prayed. "All our troubles are over. Oh, what now?"

The poor young thing, in trying to smile, had turned as white as a sheet. Before either of us could interpose an arm, she had slipped to the floor in a dead faint. With a murmur of pity and possibly of inward contrition, he stooped over her, and together we carried her into the library, where I left her in his care, confident, from certain indications, that my presence would not be greatly missed by either of them.

Whatever hope I may have had of reaping the reward offered by Mrs. Ashley was now lost, but in the satisfaction I experienced at finding this young girl as innocent as my Flora, I did not greatly care.

Well, it all ended even more happily than may here appear. The horse not putting in his claim to the reward, and Mr. Spencer repudiating all right to it, it was paid in full to Mr. Deane, who, accompanied by his two ladies, went home in as buoyant a state of mind as was possible to him after the great anxieties of the preceding two hours. I was told that Mr. Ashley declined to close the carriage door upon them till the whole three had promised to come again the following night.

Anxious to make such amends as I personally could for my share in the mortification to which Miss Glover had been subjected, I visited her in the morning, with the intention of offering a suggestion or two in regard to that little bill. But she met my first advance with a radiant smile and the glad exclamation:

"Oh, I have settled all that! I have just come from Madame Dupré's. I told her that I had never imagined the dress could possibly cost more than a hundred dollars, and I offered her that sum if she would take the garment back. And she did, she did, and I shall never have to wear that dreadful satin again!"

I made a note of this dressmaker's name. She and I may have a bone to pick some day. But I said nothing to Miss Glover. I merely exclaimed:

"And to-night?"

"Oh, I have an old spotted muslin which, with a few natural flowers, will make me look festive enough. One does not need fine clothes when one is—happy."

The dreamy far-off smile with which she finished the sentence was more eloquent than words, and I was not surprised when some time later I read of her engagement to Mr. Ashley.

But it was not till she could sign herself with his name that she told me just what underlay the misery of that night. She had met Harrison Ashley more than once before, and, though she did not say so, had evidently conceived an admiration for him which made her especially desirous of attracting and pleasing him. Not understanding the world very well, certainly having very little knowledge of the tastes and feelings of wealthy people, she conceived that the more brilliantly she was attired the more likely she would be to please this rich young man. So in a moment of weakness she decided to devote all her small savings (a hundred dollars, as we know) to buying a gown such as she felt she could appear in at his house without shame.

It came home—as dresses from French dress-makers are very apt to do—just in time for her to put it on for the party. The bill came with it, and when she saw the amount—it was all itemised, and she could find no fault with anything but the summing up—she was so overwhelmed that she nearly fainted. But she could not give up her ball; so she dressed herself, and, being urged all the time to hurry, hardly stopped to give one look at the new and splendid gown which had cost so much. The bill—the incredible, the enormous bill—was all she could think of, and the figures, which represented nearly her whole year's earnings, danced constantly before her eyes. She could not possibly pay it, nor could she ask her father to do so. She was ruined. But the ball and Mr. Ashley—these still awaited her; so presently she worked herself up to some anticipation of enjoyment, and, having thrown on her cloak, was turning down her light preparatory to departure, when her eye fell on the bill lying open on her dresser.

It would never do to leave it there—never do to leave it anywhere in her room. There were prying eyes in the house, and she was as ashamed of that bill as she might have been of a contemplated theft. So she tucked it into her corsage, and went down to join her friends in the carriage.

The rest we know, with the exception of one small detail which turned to gall whatever enjoyment she was able to get out of the evening. There was a young girl present, dressed in a simple muslin gown. While looking at it, and inwardly contrasting it with her own splendour, Mr. Ashley passed by with another gentleman, and she heard him say:

"How much better young girls look in simple white than in the elaborate silks suited only to their mothers!"

Thoughtless words—possibly forgotten as soon as uttered—they sharply pierced this already sufficiently stricken and uneasy breast, and were the cause of the tears which had aroused my suspicion when I came upon her in the library, standing with her face to the night.

But who can say whether, if the evening had been devoid of these occurrences, and no emotions of contrition and pity had been awakened in her behalf in the breast of her chivalrous host, she would ever have become Mrs. Ashley?

THE LITTLE STEEL COILS

I

"A Lady to see you, sir."

I looked up and was at once impressed by the grace and beauty of the person thus introduced to me.

"Is there anything I can do to serve you?" I asked, rising.

She cast me a childlike look full of trust and candour as she seated herself in the chair I had pointed out.

"I believe so; I hope so," she earnestly assured me. "I—I am in great trouble. I have just lost my husband—but it is not that. It is the slip of paper I found on my dresser, and which—which—"

She was trembling violently and her words were fast becoming incoherent. I calmed her and asked her to relate her story just as it had happened; and after a few minutes of silent struggle she succeeded in collecting herself sufficiently to respond with some degree of connection and self-possession.

"I have been married six months. My name is Lucy Holmes. For the last few weeks my husband and I have been living in an apartment house on Fifty-ninth Street, and, as we had not a care in the world, we were very happy till Mr. Holmes was called away on business to Philadelphia. This was two weeks ago. Five days later I received an affectionate letter from him, in which he promised to come back the next day; and the news so delighted me that I accepted an invitation to the theatre from some intimate friends of ours. The next morning I naturally felt fatigued and rose late; but I was very cheerful, for I expected my husband at noon. And now comes the perplexing mystery. In the course of dressing myself I stepped to my bureau, and seeing a small newspaper slip attached to the cushion by a pin, I drew it off and read it. It was a death notice, and my hair rose and my limbs failed me as I took in its fatal and incredible words.

"'Died this day at the Colonnade, James Forsythe De Witt Holmes. New York papers please copy.'

"James Forsythe De Witt Holmes was my husband, and his last letter, which was at that very moment lying beside the cushion, had been dated from the Colonnade. Was I dreaming or under the spell of some frightful hallucination which led me to misread the name on the slip of paper before me? I could not determine. My head, throat, and chest seemed bound about with iron, so that I could neither speak nor breathe with freedom, and, suffering thus, I stood staring at this demoniacal bit of paper which in an instant had brought the shadow of death upon my happy life. Nor was I at all relieved when a little later

I flew with the notice into a neighbour's apartment, and praying her to read it to me, found that my eyes had not deceived me and that the name was indeed my husband's and the notice one of death.

"Not from my own mind but from hers came the first suggestion of comfort.

"'It cannot be your husband who is meant,' said she; 'but some one of the same name. Your husband wrote to you yesterday, and this person must have been dead at least two days for the printed notice of his decease to have reached New York. Some one has remarked the striking similarity of names, and wishing to startle you, cut the slip out and pinned it on your cushion.'

"I certainly knew of no one inconsiderate enough to do this, but the explanation was so plausible, I at once embraced it and sobbed aloud in my relief. But in the midst of my rejoicing I heard the bell ring in my apartment, and, running thither, encountered a telegraph boy holding in his outstretched hand the yellow envelope which so often bespeaks death or disaster. The sight took my breath away. Summoning my maid, whom I saw hastening toward me from an inner room, I begged her to open the telegram for me. Sir, I saw in her face, before she had read the first line, a confirmation of my very worst fears. My husband was—"

The young widow, choked with her emotions, paused, recovered herself for the second time, and then went on.

"I had better show you the telegram."

Taking it from her pocketbook, she held it toward me. I read it at a glance. It was short, simple, and direct:

"Come at once. Your husband found dead in his room this morning. Doctors say heart disease. Please telegraph."

"You see it says this morning," she explained, placing her delicate finger on the word she so eagerly quoted. "That means a week ago Wednesday, the same day on which the printed slip recording his death was found on my cushion. Do you not see something very strange in this?"

I did; but, before I ventured to express myself on this subject, I desired her to tell me what she had learned in her visit to Philadelphia.

Her answer was simple and straightforward.

"But little more than you find in this telegram. He died in his room. He was found lying on the floor near the bell-button, which he had evidently risen to touch. One hand was clenched on his chest, but his face wore a peaceful look, as if death had come too suddenly to cause him much suffering. His bed was undisturbed; he had died before retiring, possibly in the act of packing his trunk, for it was found nearly ready for the expressman. Indeed, there was every evidence of his intention to leave on an early morning train. He had even desired to be awakened at six o'clock; and it was his failure to respond to the summons of the bellboy which led to so early a discovery of his death. He had never complained of any distress in breathing, and we had always considered him a perfectly healthy man; but there was no reason for assigning any other cause than heart failure to his sudden death, and so the burial certificate was made out to that effect, and I was allowed to bring him home and bury him in our vault at

Woodlawn. But"—and here her earnestness dried up the tears which had been flowing freely during this recital of her husband's lonely death and sad burial—"do you not think an investigation should be made into a death preceded by a false obituary notice? For I found when I was in Philadelphia that no paragraph such as I had found pinned to my cushion had been inserted in any paper there, nor had any other man of the same name ever registered at the Colonnade, much less died there."

"Have you this notice with you?" I asked.

She immediately produced it, and while I was glancing it over remarked:

"Some persons would give a superstitious explanation to the whole matter; think I had received a supernatural warning and been satisfied with what they would call a spiritual manifestation. But I have not a bit of such folly in my composition. Living hands set up the type and printed the words which gave me so deathly a shock; and hands, with a real purpose in them, cut it from the paper and pinned it to my cushion for me to see when I woke on that fatal morning. But whose hands? That is what I want you to discover."

I had caught the fever of her suspicions long before this and now felt justified in showing my interest.

"First, let me ask," said I, "who has access to your rooms besides your maid?"

"No one; absolutely no one."

"And what of her?"

"She is innocence herself. She is no common housemaid, but a girl my mother brought up, who for love of me consents to do such work in the household as my simple needs require."

"I should like to see her."

"There is no objection to your doing so; but you will gain nothing by it. I have already talked the subject over with her a dozen times and she is as much puzzled by it as I am myself. She says she cannot see how any one could have found an entrance to my room during my sleep, as the doors were all locked. Yet, as she very naturally observes, some one must have done so, for she was in my bedroom herself just before I returned from the theatre, and can swear, if necessary, that no such slip of paper was to be seen on my cushion at that time, for her duties led her directly to my bureau and kept her there for full five minutes."

"And you believed her?" I suggested.

"Implicitly."

"In what direction, then, do your suspicions turn?"

"Alas! in no direction. That is the trouble. I don't know whom to mistrust. It was because I was told that you had the credit of seeing light where others can see nothing but darkness that I have sought your aid in this emergency. For the uncertainty surrounding this matter is killing me and will make my sorrow quite unendurable if I cannot obtain relief from it."

"I do not wonder," I began, struck by the note of truth in her tones. "And I shall certainly do what I can for you. But before we go any further, let us examine this scrap of newspaper and see what we can make out of it."

I had already noted two or three points in connection with it to which I now proceeded to direct her attention.

"Have you compared this notice," I pursued, "with such others as you find every day in the papers?"

"No," was her eager answer. "Is it not like them all—"

"Read," was my quiet interruption. "'On this day at the Colonnade'—on what day? The date is usually given in all the bona fide notices I have seen."

"Is it?" she asked, her eyes, moist with unshed tears, opening widely in her astonishment.

"Look in the papers on your return home and see. Then the print. Observe that the type is identical on both sides of this make-believe clipping, while in fact there is always a perceptible difference between that used in the obituary column and that to be found in the columns devoted to other matter. Notice also," I continued, holding up the scrap of paper between her and the light, "that the alignment on one side is not exactly parallel with that on the other; a discrepancy which would not exist if both sides had been printed on a newspaper press. These facts lead me to conclude, first, that the effort to match the type exactly was the mistake of a man who tried to do too much; and, secondly, that one of the sides at least, presumably that containing the obituary notice, was printed on a hand-press, on the blank side of a piece of galley proof picked up in some newspaper office."

"Let me see." And stretching out her hand with the utmost eagerness, she took the slip and turned it over. Instantly a change took place in her countenance. She sank back in her seat and a blush of manifest confusion suffused her cheeks. "Oh!" she exclaimed; "what will you think of me! I brought this scrap of print into the house myself, and it was I who pinned it on the cushion with my own hands! I remember it now. The sight of those words recalls the whole occurrence."

"Then there is one mystery less for us to solve," I remarked, somewhat drily.

"Do you think so?" she protested, with a deprecatory look. "For me the mystery deepens, and becomes every minute more serious. It is true that I brought this scrap of newspaper into the house, and that it had, then as now, the notice of my husband's death upon it, but the time of my bringing it in was Tuesday night, and he was not found dead till Wednesday morning."

"A discrepancy worth noting," I remarked.

"Involving a mystery of some importance," she concluded.

I agreed to that.

"And since we have discovered how the slip came into your room, we can now proceed to the clearing up of this mystery," I observed. "You can, of course, inform me where you procured this clipping which you say you brought into the house?"

"Yes. You may think it strange, but when I alighted from the carriage that night, a man on the sidewalk put this tiny scrap of paper into my hand. It was done so mechanically that it made no more impression on my mind than the thrusting of an advertisement upon me. Indeed, I supposed it was an advertisement, and I only wonder that I retained it in my hand at all. But that I did do so, and that, in a moment of abstraction, I went so far as to pin it to my cushion, is evident from the fact that a vague memory remains in my mind of having read this recipe which you see printed on the reverse side of the paper."

"It was the recipe, then, and not the obituary notice which attracted your attention the night before?"

"Probably, but in pinning it to the cushion, it was the obituary notice that chanced to come uppermost. Oh, why should I not have remembered this till now! Can you understand my forgetting a matter of so much importance?"

"Yes," I allowed, after a momentary consideration of her ingenuous countenance. "The words you read in the morning were so startling that they disconnected themselves from those you had carelessly glanced at the night before."

"That is it," she replied; "and since then I have had eyes for the one side only. How could I think of the other? But who could have printed this thing and who was the man who put it into my hand? He looked like a beggar, but—Oh!" she suddenly exclaimed, her cheeks flushing scarlet and her eyes flashing with a feverish, almost alarming glitter.

"What is it now?" I asked. "Another recollection?"

"Yes." She spoke so low I could hardly hear her. "He coughed and—"

"And what?" I encouragingly suggested, seeing that she was under some new and overwhelming emotion.

"That cough had a familiar sound, now that I think of it. It was like that of a friend who—But no, no; I will not wrong him by any false surmises. He would stoop to much, but not to that; yet—"

The flush on her cheeks had died away, but the two vivid spots which remained showed the depth of her excitement.

"Do you think," she suddenly asked, "that a man out of revenge might plan to frighten me by a false notice of my husband's death, and that God to punish him, made the notice a prophecy?"

"I think a man influenced by the spirit of revenge might do almost anything," I answered, purposely ignoring the latter part of her question.

"But I always considered him a good man. At least I never looked upon him as a wicked one. Every other beggar we meet has a cough; and yet," she added after a moment's pause, "if it was not he who gave me this mortal shock, who was it? He is the only person in the world I ever wronged."

"Had you not better tell me his name?" I suggested.

"No, I am in too great doubt. I should hate to do him a second injury."

"You cannot injure him if he is innocent. My methods are very safe."

"If I could forget his cough! but it had that peculiar catch in it that I remembered so well in the cough of John Graham. I did not pay any especial heed to it at the time. Old days and old troubles were far enough from my thoughts; but now that my suspicions are raised, that low, choking sound comes back to me in a strangely persistent way, and I seem to see a well-remembered form in the stooping figure of this beggar. Oh, I hope the good God will forgive me if I attribute to this disappointed man a wickedness he never committed."

"Who is John Graham?" I urged, "and what was the nature of the wrong you did him?"

She rose, cast me one appealing glance, and perceiving that I meant to have her whole story, turned towards the fire and stood warming her feet before the hearth, with her face turned away from my gaze.

"I was once engaged to marry him," she began. "Not because I loved him, but because we were very poor—I mean my mother and myself—and he had a home and seemed both good and generous. The day came when we were to be married—this was in the West, way out in Kansas—and I was even dressed for the wedding, when a letter came from my uncle here, a rich uncle, very rich, who had never had anything to do with my mother since her marriage, and in it he promised me fortune and everything else desirable in life if I would come to him, unencumbered by any foolish ties. Think of it! And I within half an hour of marriage with a man I had never loved and now suddenly hated. The temptation was overwhelming, and, heartless as my conduct may appear to you, I succumbed to it. Telling my lover that I had changed my mind, I dismissed the minister when he came, and announced my intention of proceeding East as soon as possible. Mr. Graham was simply paralysed by his disappointment, and during the few days which intervened before my departure, I was haunted by his face, which was like that of a man who had died from some overwhelming shock. But when I was once free of the town, especially after I arrived in New York, I forgot alike his misery and himself. Everything I saw was so beautiful! Life was so full of charm, and my uncle so delighted with me and everything I did! Then there was James Holmes, and after I had seen him—But I cannot talk of that. We loved each other, and under the surprise of this new delight how could I be expected to remember the man I had left behind me in that barren region in which I had spent my youth? But he did not forget the misery I had caused him. He followed me to New York; and on the morning I was married found his way into the house, and mixing with the wedding guests, suddenly appeared before me just as I was receiving the congratulations of my friends. At sight of him I experienced all the terror he had calculated upon causing, but remembering our old relations and my new position, I assumed an air of apparent haughtiness. This irritated John Graham. Flushing with anger, and ignoring my imploring look, he cried peremptorily, 'Present me to your husband!' and I felt forced to present him. But his name produced no effect upon Mr. Holmes. I had never told him of my early experience with this man, and John Graham, perceiving this, cast me a bitter glance of disdain and passed on, muttering between his teeth, 'False to me and false to him! Your punishment be upon you!' and I felt as if I had been cursed."

She stopped here, moved by emotions readily to be understood. Then with quick impetuosity she caught up the thread of her story and went on.

"That was six months ago; and again I forgot. My mother died and my husband soon absorbed my every thought. How could I dream that this man, who was little more than a memory to me and scarcely that, was secretly planning mischief against me? Yet this scrap about which we have talked so much may have been the work of his hands; and even my husband's death—"

She did not finish, but her face, which was turned towards me, spoke volumes.

"Your husband's death shall be inquired into," I assured her. And she, exhausted by the excitement of her discoveries, asked that she might be excused from further discussion of the subject at that time.

As I had no wish, myself, to enter any more fully into the matter just then, I readily acceded to her request, and the pretty widow left me.

II

Obviously the first fact to be settled was whether Mr. Holmes had died from purely natural causes. I accordingly busied myself the next few days with the question, and was fortunate enough to so interest the proper authorities that an order was issued for the exhumation and examination of the body.

The result was disappointing. No traces of poison were to be found in the stomach nor was there to be seen on the body any mark of violence with the exception of a minute prick upon one of his thumbs.

This speck was so small that it escaped every eye but my own.

The authorities assuring the widow that the doctor's certificate given her in Philadelphia was correct, the body was again interred. But I was not satisfied; and confident that this death had not been a natural one, I entered upon one of those secret and prolonged investigations which for so many years have constituted the pleasure of my life. First, I visited the Colonnade in Philadelphia, and being allowed to see the room in which Mr. Holmes died, went through it carefully. As it had not been used since that time I had some hopes of coming upon a clue.

But it was a vain hope, and the only result of my journey to this place was the assurance I received that the gentleman had spent the entire evening preceding his death in his own room, where he had been brought several letters and one small package, the latter coming by mail. With this one point gained—if it was a point—I went back to New York.

Calling on Mrs. Holmes, I asked her if, while her husband was away, she had sent him anything besides letters, and upon her replying to the contrary, requested to know if in her visit to Philadelphia she had noted among her husband's effects anything that was new or unfamiliar to her. "For he received a package while there," I explained, "and though its contents may have been perfectly harmless, it is just as well for us to be assured of this before going any further."

"Oh, you think, then, he was really the victim of some secret violence."

"We have no proof of it," I said. "On the contrary, we are assured that he died from natural causes. But the incident of the newspaper slip outweighs, in my mind, the doctor's conclusions, and until the mystery surrounding that obituary notice has been satisfactorily explained by its author I shall hold to the theory that your husband has been made away with in some strange and seemingly unaccountable manner, which it is our duty to bring to light."

"You are right! You are right! Oh, John Graham!"

She was so carried away by this plain expression of my belief that she forgot the question I had put to her.

"You have not said whether or not you found anything among your husband's effects that can explain this mystery," I suggested.

She at once became attentive.

"Nothing," said she; "his trunks were already packed and his bag nearly so. There were a few things lying about the room which I saw thrust into the latter. Would you like to look through them? I have not had the heart to open the bag since I came back."

As this was exactly what I wished, I said as much, and she led me into a small room, against the wall of which stood a trunk with a travelling-bag on top of it. Opening the latter, she spread the contents out on the trunk.

"I know all these things," she sadly murmured, the tears welling in her eyes.

"This?" I inquired, lifting up a bit of coiled wire with two or three rings dangling from it.

"No; why, what is that?"

"It looks like a puzzle of some kind."

"Then it is of no consequence. My husband was forever amusing himself over some such contrivance. All his friends knew how well he liked these toys and frequently sent them to him. This one evidently reached him from Philadelphia."

Meanwhile I was eyeing the bit of wire curiously. It was undoubtedly a puzzle, but it had appendages to it that I did not understand.

"It is more than ordinarily complicated," I observed, moving the rings up and down in a vain endeavour to work them off.

"The better he would like it," she said.

I kept working with the rings. Suddenly I gave a painful start. A little prong in the handle of the toy had started out and pierced me.

"You had better not handle it," said I, and laid it down. But the next moment I took it up again and put it in my pocket. The prick made by this treacherous bit of mechanism was in or near the same place on my thumb as the one I had noticed on the hand of the deceased Mr. Holmes.

There was a fire in the room, and before proceeding further I cauterised that prick with the end of a red-hot poker. Then I made my adieux to Mrs. Holmes and went immediately to a chemist friend of mine.

"Test the end of this bit of steel for me," said I. "I have reason to believe it carries with it a deadly poison."

He took the toy, promising to subject it to every test possible and let me know the result. Then I went home. I felt ill, or imagined I did, which under the circumstances was almost as bad.

Next day, however, I was quite well, with the exception of a certain inconvenience in my thumb. But not till the following week did I receive the chemist's report. It overthrew my whole theory. He found nothing, and returned me the bit of steel.

But I was not convinced.

"I will hunt up this John Graham," thought I, "and study him."

But this was not so easy a task as it may appear. As Mrs. Holmes possessed no clue to the whereabouts of her quondam lover, I had nothing to aid me in my search for him, save her rather vague description of his personal appearance and the fact that he was constantly interrupted in speaking by a low, choking cough. However, my natural perseverance carried me through. After seeing and interviewing a dozen John Grahams without result, I at last lit upon a man of that name who presented a figure of such vivid unrest and showed such a desperate hatred of his fellows, that I began to entertain hopes of his being the person I was in search of. But determined to be sure of this before proceeding further, I confided my suspicions to Mrs. Holmes, and induced her to accompany me down to a certain spot on the "Elevated" from which I had more than once seen this man go by to his usual lounging place in Printing House Square.

She showed great courage in doing this, for she had such a dread of him that she was in a state of nervous excitement from the moment she left her house, feeling sure that she would attract his attention and thus risk a disagreeable encounter. But she might have spared herself these fears. He did not even glance up in passing us, and it was mainly by his walk she recognised him. But she did recognise him; and this nerved me at once to set about the formidable task of fixing upon him a crime which was not even admitted as a fact by the authorities.

He was a man-about-town, living, to all appearances, by his wits. He was to be seen mostly in the downtown portions of the city, standing for hours in front of some newspaper office, gnawing at his finger-ends, and staring at the passers-by with a hungry look alarming to the timid and provoking alms from the benevolent. Needless to say that he rejected the latter expression of sympathy with angry contempt.

His face was long and pallid, his cheek-bones high, and his mouth bitter and resolute in expression. He wore neither beard nor moustache, but made up for their lack by an abundance of light-brown hair, which hung very nearly to his shoulders. He stooped in standing, but as soon as he moved, showed decision and a certain sort of pride which caused him to hold his head high and his body more than usually erect. With all these good points his appearance was decidedly sinister, and I did not wonder that Mrs. Holmes feared him.

My next move was to accost him. Pausing before the doorway in which he stood, I addressed him some trivial question. He answered me with sufficient politeness, but with a grudging attention which betrayed the hold which his own thoughts had upon him. He coughed while speaking, and his eye, which for a moment rested on mine, produced an impression upon me for which I was hardly prepared, great as was my prejudice against him. There was such an icy composure in it; the composure of an envenomed nature conscious of its superiority to all surprises. As I lingered to study him more closely, the many dangerous qualities of the man became more and more apparent to me; and convinced that to proceed further without deep and careful thought would be to court failure where triumph would set me up for life, I gave up all present attempt at enlisting him in conversation and went away in an inquiring and serious mood.

In fact, my position was a peculiar one, and the problem I had set for myself one of unusual difficulty. Only by means of some extraordinary device such as is seldom resorted to by the police of this or any other nation, could I hope to arrive at the secret of this man's conduct, and triumph in a matter which to all appearance was beyond human penetration.

But what device? I knew of none, nor through two days and nights of strenuous thought did I receive the least light on the subject. Indeed, my mind seemed to grow more and more confused the more I urged it into action. I failed to get inspiration indoors or out; and feeling my health suffer from the constant irritation of my recurring disappointment, I resolved to take a day off and carry myself and my perplexities into the country.

I did so. Governed by an impulse which I did not then understand, I went to a small town in New Jersey and entered the first house on which I saw the sign "Room to Let." The result was most fortunate. No sooner had I crossed the threshold of the neat and homely apartment thrown open to my use, than it recalled a room in which I had slept two years before and in which I had read a little book I was only too glad to remember at this moment. Indeed, it seemed as if a veritable inspiration had come to me through this recollection, for though the tale to which I allude was a simple child's story written for moral purposes, it contained an idea which promised to be invaluable to me at this juncture. Indeed, by means of it, I believed myself to have solved the problem that was puzzling me, and, relieved beyond expression, I paid for the night's lodging I had now determined to forego, and returned immediately to New York, having spent just fifteen minutes in the town where I had received this happy inspiration.

My first step on entering the city was to order a dozen steel coils made similar to the one which I still believed answerable for James Holmes's death. My next to learn as far as possible all of John Graham's haunts and habits. At a week's end I had the springs and knew almost as well as he did himself where he was likely to be found at all times of the day and night. I immediately acted upon this knowledge. Assuming a slight disguise, I repeated my former stroll through Printing House Square, looking into each doorway as I passed. John Graham was in one of them, staring in his old way at the passing crowd, but evidently seeing nothing but the images formed by his own disordered brain. A manuscript roll stuck out of his breast-pocket, and from the way his nervous fingers fumbled with it, I began to understand the restless glitter of his eyes, which were as full of wretchedness as any eyes I have ever seen.

Entering the doorway where he stood, I dropped at his feet one of the small steel coils with which I was provided. He did not see it. Stopping near him, I directed his attention to it by saying:

"Pardon me, but did I not see something drop out of your hand?"

He started, glanced at the seemingly inoffensive toy I had pointed out, and altered so suddenly and so vividly that it became instantly apparent that the surprise I had planned for him was fully as keen and searching a one as I had anticipated. Recoiling sharply, he gave me a quick look, then glanced down again at his feet as if half expecting to find the object of his terror gone. But, perceiving it still lying there, he crushed it viciously with his heel, and uttering some incoherent words dashed impetuously from the building.

Confident that he would regret this hasty impulse and return, I withdrew a few steps and waited. And sure enough, in less than five minutes, he came slinking back. Picking up the coil with more than one sly look about, he examined it closely. Suddenly he gave a sharp cry and went staggering out. Had he discovered that the seeming puzzle possessed the same invisible spring which had made the one handled by James Holmes so dangerous?

Certain as to the place he would be found next, I made a short cut to an obscure little saloon in Nassau Street, where I took up my stand in a spot convenient for seeing without being seen. In ten minutes he was standing at the bar asking for a drink.

"Whiskey!" he cried. "Straight."

It was given him, but as he set the empty glass down on the counter he saw lying before him another of the steel springs, and was so confounded by the sight that the proprietor, who had put it there at my instigation, thrust out his hand toward him as if half afraid he would fall.

"Where did that—that thing come from?" stammered John Graham, ignoring the other's gesture and pointing with a trembling hand at the insignificant bit of wire between them.

"Didn't it drop from your coat-pocket?" inquired the proprietor. "It wasn't lying here before you came in."

With a horrible oath the unhappy man turned and fled from the place. I lost sight of him after that for three hours, then I suddenly came upon him again. He was walking uptown with a set purpose in his face that made him look more dangerous than ever. Of course I followed him, expecting him to turn towards Fifty-ninth Street, but at the corner of Madison Avenue and Forty-seventh Street he changed his mind and dashed toward Third Avenue. At Park Avenue he faltered and again turned north, walking for several blocks as if the fiends were behind him. I began to think that he was but attempting to walk off his excitement, when, at a sudden rushing sound in the cut beside us, he stopped and trembled. An express train was shooting by. As it disappeared in the tunnel beyond, he looked about him with a blanched face and wandering eye; but his glance did not turn my way, or, if it did, he failed to attach any meaning to my near presence.

He began to move on again and this time towards the bridge spanning the cut. I followed him very closely. In the centre of it he paused and looked down at the track beneath him. Another train was approaching. As it came near he trembled from head to foot, and, catching at the railing against which he leaned, was about to make a quick move forward when a puff of smoke arose from below and sent him staggering backward, gasping with a terror I could hardly understand till I saw that the smoke had taken the form of a spiral and was sailing away before him in what to his disordered imagination must have looked like a gigantic image of the coil with which twice before on this day he had found himself confronted.

It may have been chance and it may have been providence; but whichever it was it saved him. He could not face that semblance of his haunting thought; and turning away he cowered down on the neighbouring curbstone, where he sat for several minutes, with his head buried in his hands; when he arose again he was his own daring and sinister self. Knowing that he was now too much master of his faculties to ignore me any longer, I walked quickly away and left him. I knew where he would be at six o'clock and had already engaged a table at the same restaurant. It was seven, however, before he put in an appearance, and by this time he was looking more composed. There was a reckless air about him, however, which was perhaps only noticeable to me; for none of the habitués of this especial restaurant were entirely without it; wild eyes and unkempt hair being in the majority.

I let him eat. The dinner he ordered was simple and I had not the heart to interrupt his enjoyment of it.

But when he had finished and came to pay, then I allowed the shock to come. Under the bill which the waiter laid at the side of his plate was the inevitable steel coil; and it produced even more than its usual effect. I own I felt sorry for him.

He did not dash from the place, however, as he had from the liquor saloon. A spirit of resistance had seized him and he demanded to know where this object of his fear had come from. No one could tell him (or would). Whereupon he began to rave and would certainly have done himself or somebody else an injury if he had not been calmed by a man almost as wild-looking as himself. Paying his bill, but vowing he would never enter the place again, he went out, clay white, but with the swaggering air of a man who had just asserted himself.

He drooped, however, as soon as he reached the street, and I had no difficulty in following him to a certain gambling den, where he gained three dollars and lost five. From there he went to his lodgings in West Tenth Street.

I did not follow him. He had passed through many deep and wearing emotions since noon, and I had not the heart to add another to them.

But late the next day I returned to this house and rang the bell. It was already dusk, but there was light enough for me to notice the unrepaired condition of the iron railings on either side of the old stoop and to compare this abode of decayed grandeur with the spacious and elegant apartment in which pretty Mrs. Holmes mourned the loss of her young husband. Had any such comparison ever been made by the unhappy John Graham, as he hurried up these battered steps into the dismal halls beyond?

In answer to my summons there came to the door a young woman to whom I had but to intimate my wish to see Mr. Graham for her to let me in with the short announcement:

"Top floor, back room! Door open, he's out; door shut, he's in."

As an open door meant liberty to enter, I lost no time in following the direction of her finger, and presently found myself in a low attic chamber overlooking an acre of roofs. A fire had been lighted in the open grate, and the flickering red beams danced on ceiling and walls with a cheeriness greatly in contrast to the nature of the business which had led me there. As they also served to light the room, I proceeded to make myself at home; and drawing up a chair, sat down at the fireplace in such a way as to conceal myself from any one entering the door.

In less than half an hour he came in.

He was in a state of high emotion. His face was flushed and his eyes burning. Stepping rapidly forward, he flung his hat on the table in the middle of the room, with a curse that was half cry and half groan. Then he stood silent and I had an opportunity of noting how haggard he had grown in the short time which had elapsed since I had seen him last. But the interval of his inaction was short, and in a moment he flung up his arms with a loud "Curse her!" that rang through the narrow room and betrayed the source of his present frenzy. Then he again stood still, grating his teeth and working his hands in a way terribly suggestive of the murderer's instinct. But not for long. He saw something that attracted his attention on the table, a something upon which my eyes had long before been fixed, and starting forward with a fresh and quite different display of emotion, he caught up what looked like a roll of manuscript and began to tear it open.

"Back again! Always back!" wailed from his lips; and he gave the roll a toss that sent from its midst a small object which he no sooner saw than he became speechless and reeled back. It was another of the steel coils.

"Good God!" fell at last from his stiff and working lips. "Am I mad or has the devil joined in the pursuit against me? I cannot eat, I cannot drink, but this diabolical spring starts up before me. It is here, there, everywhere. The visible sign of my guilt; the—the—" He had stumbled back upon my chair, and turning, saw me.

I was on my feet at once, and noting that he was dazed by the shock of my presence, I slid quietly between him and the door.

The movement roused him. Turning upon me with a sarcastic smile in which was concentrated the bitterness of years, he briefly said:

"So I am caught! Well, there has to be an end to men as well as to things, and I am ready for mine. She turned me away from her door to-day, and after the hell of that moment I don't much fear any other."

"You had better not talk," I admonished him. "All that falls from you now will only tell against you on your trial."

He broke into a harsh laugh. "And do you think I care for that? That having been driven by a woman's perfidy into crime I am going to bridle my tongue and keep down the words which are my only safeguard from insanity? No, no; while my miserable breath lasts I will curse her, and if the halter is to cut short my words, it shall be with her name blistering my lips."

I attempted to speak, but he would not give me an opportunity. The passion of weeks had found vent and he rushed on recklessly:

"I went to her house to-day. I wanted to see her in her widow's weeds; I wanted to see her eyes red with weeping over a grief which owed its bitterness to me. But she would not grant me admittance. She had me thrust from her door, and I shall never know how deeply the iron has sunk into her soul. But"—and here his face showed a sudden change—"I shall see her if I am tried for murder. She will be in the courtroom—on the witness stand—"

"Doubtless," I interjected; but his interruption came quickly and with vehement passion.

"Then I am ready. Welcome trial, conviction, death, even. To confront her eye to eye is all I wish. She shall never forget it, never!"

"Then you do not deny—" I began.

"I deny nothing," he returned, and held out his hands with a grim gesture. "How can I, when there falls from everything I touch the devilish thing which took away the life I hated?"

"Have you anything more to say or do before you leave these rooms?" I asked.

He shook his head, and then, bethinking himself, pointed to the roll of paper which he had flung on the table.

"Burn that!" he cried.

I took up the roll and looked at it. It was the manuscript of a poem in blank verse.

"I have been with it into a dozen newspaper and magazine offices," he explained with great bitterness. "Had I succeeded in getting a publisher for it I might have forgotten my wrongs and tried to build up a new life on the ruins of the old. But they would not have it, none of them; so I say, burn it! that no memory of me may remain in this miserable world."

"Keep to the facts!" I severely retorted. "It was while carrying this poem from one newspaper to another that you secured that bit of print upon the blank side of which yourself printed the obituary notice with which you savoured your revenge upon the woman who had disappointed you."

"You know that? Then you know where I got the poison with which I tipped the silly toy with which that weak man fooled away his life?"

"No," said I, "I do not know where you got it. I merely know it was no common poison bought at a druggist's, or from any ordinary chemist."

"It was woorali; the deadly, secret woorali. I got it from—but that is another man's secret. You will never hear from me anything that will compromise a friend. I got it, that is all. One drop, but it killed my man."

The satisfaction, the delight, which he threw into these words are beyond description. As they left his lips a jet of flame from the neglected fire shot up and threw his figure for one instant into bold relief upon the lowering ceiling; then it died out, and nothing but the twilight dusk remained in the room and on the countenance of this doomed and despairing man.

THE STAIRCASE AT HEART'S DELIGHT

In the spring of 18—, the attention of the New York police was attracted by the many cases of well-known men found drowned in the various waters surrounding the lower portion of our great city. Among these may be mentioned the name of Elwood Henderson, the noted tea merchant, whose remains were washed ashore at Redhook Point; and of Christopher Bigelow, who was picked up off Governor's Island after having been in the water for five days, and of another well-known millionaire whose name I cannot now recall, but who, I remember, was seen to walk towards the East River one March evening, and was not met with again till the 5th of April, when his body floated into one of the docks near Peck's Slip.

As it seemed highly improbable that there should have been a concerted action among so many wealthy and distinguished men to end their lives within a few weeks of each other, and all by the same method of drowning, we soon became suspicious that a more serious verdict than that of suicide should have been rendered in the case of Henderson, Bigelow, and the other gentleman I have mentioned. Yet one fact, common to all these cases, pointed so conclusively to deliberate intention on the part of the sufferers that we hesitated to take action.

This was, that upon the body of each of the above-mentioned persons there were found, not only valuables in the shape of money and jewelry, but papers and memoranda of a nature calculated to fix the identity of the drowned man, in case the water should rob him of his personal characteristics. Consequently, we could not ascribe these deaths to a desire for plunder on the part of some unknown person.

I was a young man in those days, and full of ambition. So, though I said nothing, I did not let this matter drop when the others did, but kept my mind persistently upon it and waited, with odd results as you will hear, for another victim to be reported at police headquarters.

Meantime I sought to discover some bond or connection between the several men who had been found drowned, which would serve to explain their similar fate. But all my efforts in this direction were fruitless. There was no bond between them, and the matter remained for a while an unsolved mystery.

Suddenly one morning a clue was placed, not in my hands, but in those of a superior official who at that time exerted a great influence over the whole force. He was sitting in his private room, when there was ushered into his presence a young man of a dissipated but not unprepossessing appearance, who, after a pause of marked embarrassment, entered upon the following story:

"I don't know whether or no I should offer an excuse for the communication I am about to make; but the matter I have to relate is simply this: Being hard up last night (for though a rich man's son I often lack money), I went to a certain pawnshop in the Bowery where I had been told I could raise money on my prospects. This place—you may see it some time, so I will not enlarge upon it—did not strike me favourably; but, being very anxious for a certain definite sum of money, I wrote my name in a book which was brought to me from some unknown quarter and proceeded to follow the young woman who attended me into what she was pleased to call her good master's private office.

"He may have been a good master, but he was anything but a good man. In short, sir, when he found out who I was, and how much I needed money, he suggested that I should make an appointment with my father at a place he called Groll's in Grand Street, where, said he, 'your little affair will be arranged, and you made a rich man within thirty days. That is,' he slily added, 'unless your father has already made a will, disinheriting you.'

"I was shocked, sir, shocked beyond all my powers of concealment, not so much at his words, which I hardly understood, as at his looks, which had a world of evil suggestion in them; so I raised my fist and would have knocked him down, only that I found two young fellows at my elbows, who held me quiet for five minutes, while the old fellow talked to me. He asked me if I came to him on a fool's errand or really to get money; and when I admitted that I had cherished hopes of obtaining a clear two thousand dollars from him, he coolly replied that he knew of but one way in which I could hope to get such an amount, and that if I was too squeamish to adopt it, I had made a mistake in coming to his shop, which was no missionary institution, etc., etc.

"Not wishing to irritate him, for there was menace in his eye, I asked, with a certain weak show of being sorry for my former heat, whereabouts in Grand Street I should find this Groll.

"The retort was quick. 'Groll is not his name,' said he, 'and Grand Street is not where you are to go to find him. I threw out a bait to see if you would snap at it, but I find you timid, and therefore advise you to drop the matter entirely.'

"I was quite willing to do so, and answered him to this effect; whereupon, with a side glance I did not understand, but which made me more or less uneasy in regard to his intentions towards me, he motioned to the men who held my arms to let go their hold, which they at once did.

"'We have your signature,' growled the old man as I went out. 'If you peach on us or trouble us in any way we will show it to your father and that will put an end to all your hopes of future fortune.' Then raising his voice, he shouted to the girl in the outer office, 'Let the young man see what he has signed.'

"She smiled and again brought forward the book in which I had so recklessly placed my name, and there at the top of the page I read these words: 'For moneys received, I agree to notify Rube Goodman, within the month, of the death of my father, so that he may recover from me, without loss of time, the sum of ten thousand dollars as his part of the amount I am bound to receive as my father's heir.'

"The sight of these lines knocked me hollow. But I am less of a coward morally than physically, and I determined to acquaint my father at once with what I had done, and get his advice as to whether or not I should inform the police of my adventure. He heard me with more consideration than I expected, but insisted that I should immediately make known to you my experience in this Bowery pawnbroker's shop."

The officer, highly interested, took down the young man's statement in writing, and, after getting a more accurate description of the house itself, allowed his visitor to go.

Fortunately for me, I was in the building at the time, and was able to respond when a man was called up to investigate this matter. Thinking that I saw a connection between it and the various mysterious deaths of which I have previously spoken, I entered into the affair with much spirit. But, wishing to be sure that my possibly unwarranted conclusions were correct, I took pains to inquire, before proceeding upon my errand, into the character of the heirs who had inherited the property of Elwood Henderson and Christopher Bigelow, and found that in each case there was one among the rest who was well known for his profligacy and reckless expenditure. It was a significant discovery, and increased, if possible, my interest in running down this nefarious trafficker in the lives of wealthy men.

Knowing that I could hope for no success in my character of detective, I made an arrangement with the father of the young gentleman before alluded to, by which I was to enter the pawnshop as an emissary of the latter. Accordingly, I appeared there, one dull November afternoon, in the garb of a certain Western sporting man, who, for a consideration, allowed me the temporary use of his name and credentials.

Entering beneath the three golden balls, with the swagger and general air of ownership I thought most likely to impose upon the self-satisfied female who presided over the desk, I asked to see her boss.

"On your own business?" she queried, glancing with suspicion at my short coat, which was rather more showy than elegant.

"No," I returned, "not on my own business, but on that of a young gent—"

"Any one whose name is written here?" she interposed, reaching towards me the famous book, over the top of which, however, she was careful to lay her arm.

I glanced down the page she had opened and instantly detected that of the young gentleman on whose behalf I was supposed to be there, and nodded "Yes," with all the assurance of which I was capable.

"Come, then," said she, ushering me without more ado into a den of discomfort where sat a man with a great beard and such heavy overhanging eyebrows that I could hardly detect the twinkle of his eyes, keen and incisive as they were.

Smiling upon him, but not in the same way I had upon the girl, I glanced behind me at the open door, and above me at the partitions, which failed to reach the ceiling. Then I shook my head and drew a step nearer.

"I have come," I insinuatingly whispered, "on behalf of a certain party who left this place in a huff a day or so ago, but who since then has had time to think the matter over, and has sent me with an apology which he hopes"—here I put on a diabolical smile, copied, I declare to you, from the one I saw at that moment on his own lips—"you will accept."

The old wretch regarded me for full two minutes in a way to unmask me had I possessed less confidence in my disguise and in my ability to support it.

"And what is this young gentleman's name?" he finally asked.

For reply, I handed him a slip of paper. He took it and read the few lines written on it, after which he began to rub his palms softly together with an unction eminently in keeping with the stray glints of light that now and then found their way through his bushy eyebrows.

"And so the young gentleman had not the courage to come again himself?" he softly suggested, with just the suspicion of an ironical laugh. "Thought, perhaps, I would exact too much commission; or make him pay too roundly for his impertinent assurance."

I shrugged my shoulders, but vouchsafed no immediate reply, and he saw that he had to open the business himself. He did it warily and with many an incisive question which would have tripped me up if I had not been very much on my guard; but it all ended, as such matters usually do, in mutual understanding, and a promise that if the young gentleman was willing to sign a certain paper, which, by the way, was not shown me, he would in exchange give him an address which, if made proper use of, would lead to my patron finding himself an independent man within a very few days.

As this address was the one thing I was most desirous of obtaining, I professed myself satisfied with the arrangement, and proceeded to hunt up my patron, as he was called. Informing him of the result of my visit, I asked if his interest in ferreting out these criminals was strong enough to lead him to sign the vile document which the pawnbroker would probably have in readiness for him on the morrow; and being told it was, we separated for that day, with the understanding that we were to meet the next morning at the spot chosen by the pawnbroker for the completion of his nefarious bargain.

Being certain that I was being followed in all my movements by the agents of this adept in villainy, I took care, upon leaving Mr. L—, to repair to the hotel of the sporting man I was personifying. Making myself square with the proprietor I took up my quarters in the room of my sporting friend, and the better to deceive any spy who might be lurking about, I received his letters and sent out his telegrams, which, if they did not create confusion in the affairs of "The Plunger," must at least have occasioned him no little work the next day.

Promptly at ten o'clock on the following morning I met my patron at the appointed place of rendezvous; and when I tell you that this was no other than the ancient and now disused cemetery of which a portion is still to be seen off Chatham Square, you will understand the uncanny nature of this whole adventure, and the lurking sense there was in it of brooding death and horror. The scene, which in these days is disturbed by elevated railroad trains and the flapping of long lines of parti-coloured clothes strung high up across the quiet tombstones, was at that time one of peaceful rest, in the midst of a quarter devoted to everything for which that rest is the fitting and desirable end; and as we paused among the mossy stones, we found it hard to realise that in a few minutes there would be standing beside us the concentrated essence of all that was evil and despicable in human nature.

He arrived with a smile on his countenance that completed his ugliness, and would have frightened any honest man from his side at once. Merely glancing my way, he shuffled up to my companion, and leading him aside, drew out a paper which he laid on a flat tombstone with a gesture significant of his desire that the other should affix to it the required signature.

Meantime I stood guard, and while attempting to whistle a light air, was carelessly taking in the surroundings, and conjecturing, as best I might, the reasons which had induced the old ghoul to make use of this spot for his diabolical business, and had about decided that it was because he was a ghoul, and thus felt at home among the symbols of mortality, when I caught sight of two or three young fellows who were lounging on the other side of the fence.

These were so evidently accomplices that I wondered if the two sly boys I had engaged to stand by me through this affair had spotted them, and would know enough to follow them back to their haunts.

A few minutes later, the old rascal came sneaking towards me, with a gleam of satisfaction in his half-closed eyes.

"You are not wanted any longer," he grunted. "The young gentleman told me to say that he could look out for himself now."

"The young gentleman had better pay me the round fifty he promised me," I grumbled in return, with that sudden change from indifference to menace which I thought best calculated to further my plans; and shouldering the miserable wretch aside, I stepped up to my companion, who was still lingering in a state of hesitation among the gravestones.

"Quick! Tell me the number and street which he has given you!" I whispered, in a tone quite out of keeping with the angry and reproachful air I had assumed.

He was about to answer, when the old fellow came sidling up behind us. Instantly the young man before me rose to the occasion, and putting on an air of conciliation, said in a soothing tone:

"There, there, don't bluster. Do one thing more for me, and I will add another fifty to that I promised you. Conjure up an anonymous letter—you know how—and send it to my father, saying that if he wants to know where his son loses his hundreds, he must go to the place on the dock, opposite 5 South Street, some night shortly after nine. It would not work with most men, but it will with my father, and when he has been in and out of that place, and I succeed to the fortune he will leave me, then I will remember you, and—"

"Say, too," a sinister voice here added in my ear, "that if he wishes to effect an entrance into the gambling den which his son haunts, he must take the precaution of tying a bit of blue ribbon in his buttonhole. It is a signal meaning business, and must not be forgotten," chuckled the old fellow, evidently deceived at last into thinking I was really one of his own kind.

I answered by a wink, and taking care to attempt no further communication with my patron, I left the two, as soon as possible, and went back to the hotel, where I dropped "the sport," and assumed a character and dress which enabled me to make my way undetected to the house of my young patron, where for two days I lay low, waiting for a suitable time in which to make my final attempt to penetrate this mystery.

I knew that for the adventure I was now contemplating considerable courage was required. But I did not hesitate. The time had come for me to show my mettle. In the few communications I was enabled to hold with my superiors I told them of my progress and arranged with them my plan of work. As we all agreed that I was about to encounter no common villainy, these plans naturally partook of finesse, as you will see if you follow my narrative to the end.

Early in the evening of a cool November day I sallied forth into the streets, dressed in the habiliments and wearing the guise of the wealthy old gentleman whose secret guest I had been for the last few days. As he was old and portly, and I young and spare, this disguise had cost me no little thought and labour. But assisted as I was by the darkness, I had but little fear of betraying myself to any chance spy who might be upon the watch, especially as Mr. L— had a peculiar walk, which, in my short stay with him, I had learned to imitate perfectly. In the lapel of my overcoat I had tied a tag of blue ribbon, and, though for all I knew this was a signal devoting me to a secret and mysterious death, I walked along in a buoyant condition of mind, attributable, no doubt, to the excitement of the venture and to my desire to test my powers, even at the risk of my life.

It was nine o'clock when I reached South Street. It was no new region to me, nor was I ignorant of the specified drinking den on the dock to which I had been directed. I remembered it as a bright spot in a mass of ship-prows and bow-rigging, and was possessed, besides, of a vague consciousness that there was something odd in connection with it which had aroused my curiosity sufficiently in the past for me to have once formed the resolution of seeing it again under circumstances which would allow me to give it some attention. But I never thought that the circumstances would involve my own life, impossible as it is for a detective to reckon upon the future or to foresee the events into which he will be hurried by the next crime which may be reported at police headquarters.

There were but few persons in the street when I crossed to The Heart's Delight—so named from the heart-shaped opening in the framework of the door, through which shone a light, inviting enough to one chilled by the keen November air and oppressed by the desolate appearance of the almost deserted street. But amongst those persons I thought I recognised more than one familiar form, and felt reassured as to the watch which had been set upon the house.

The night was dark and the river especially so, but in the gloomy space beyond the dock I detected a shadow blacker than the rest, which I took for the police boat they had promised to have in readiness in case I needed rescue from the waterside. Otherwise the surroundings were as usual, and saving the gruff singing of some drunken sailor coming from a narrow side street near by, no sound disturbed the somewhat lugubrious silence of this weird and forsaken spot.

Pausing an instant before entering, I glanced up at the building, which was about three stories high, and endeavoured to see what there was about it which had once arrested my attention, and came to the conclusion that it was its exceptional situation on the dock, and the ghostly effect of the hoisting-beam projecting from the upper story like a gibbet. And yet this beam was common to many a warehouse in the vicinity, though in none of them were there any such signs of life as proceeded from the curious mixture of sail loft, boat shop, and drinking saloon, now before me. Could it be that the ban of criminality was upon the house, and that I had been conscious of this without being able to realise the cause of my interest?

Not stopping to solve my sensations further, I tried the door, and, finding it yield easily to my touch, turned the knob and entered. For a moment I was blinded by the smoky glare of the heated atmosphere into which I stepped, but presently I was able to distinguish the vague outlines of an oyster bar in the distance, and the motionless figures of some half-dozen men, whose movements had been arrested by my sudden entrance. For an instant this picture remained; then the drinking and card playing were resumed, and I stood, as it were, alone, on the sanded floor near the door.

Improving the opportunity for a closer inspection of the place, I was struck by its picturesqueness. It had evidently been once used as a ship chandlery, and on the walls, which were but partly plastered, there still hung old bits of marlin, rusty rings, and such other evidences of former traffic as did not interfere with the present more lucrative business.

Below were the two bars, one at the right of the door, and the other at the lower end of the room near a window, through whose small, square panes I caught a glimpse of the coloured lights of a couple of ferryboats, passing each other in midstream.

At a table near me sat two men, grumbling at each other over a game of cards. They were large and powerful figures in the contracted space of this long and narrow room, and my heart gave a bound of joy as I recognised on them certain marks by which I was to know friend from foe in this possible den of thieves and murderers.

Two sailors at the bar were bona fide habitués of the place and so were the two other waterside characters I could faintly discern in one of the dim corners. Meantime a man was approaching me.

Let me see if I can describe him. He was about thirty, and had the complexion and figure of a consumptive, but his eye shone with the yellow glare of a beast of prey, and in the cadaverous hollows of his ashen cheeks and amid the lines about his thin drawn lips there lay, for all his conciliatory smile, an expression so cold and yet so ferocious that I spotted him at once as the man to whose genius we were indebted for the new scheme of murder which I was jeopardising my life to understand. But I allowed none of the repugnance with which he inspired me to appear in my manner, and, greeting him with half a nod, waited for him to speak. His voice had that smooth quality which betrays the hypocrite.

"Has the gentleman any appointment here?" he asked, letting his glance fall for the merest instant on the lapel of my coat.

I returned a decided affirmative. "Or rather," I went on, with a meaning look he evidently comprehended, "my son has, and I have made up my mind to know just what deviltry he is up to these days. I can make it worth your while to give me the opportunity."

"Oh, I see," he assented with a glance at the pocketbook I had just drawn out. "You want a private room from which you can watch the young scapegrace. I understand, I understand. But the private rooms are above. Gentlemen are not comfortable here."

"I should say not," I murmured, and drew from the pocketbook a bill which I slid quietly into his hand. "Now take me where I shall be safe," I suggested, "and yet in full sight of the room where the young gentlemen play. I wish to catch him at his tricks. Afterwards—"

"All will be well," he finished smoothly, with another glance at my blue ribbon. "You see I do not ask you the young gentleman's name. I take your money and leave all the rest to you. Only don't make a scandal, I pray, for my house has the name of being quiet."

"Yes," thought I, "too quiet!" and for an instant felt my spirits fail me. But it was only for an instant. I had friends about me and a pistol at half-cock in the pocket of my overcoat. Why should I fear any surprise, prepared as I was for every emergency?

"I will show you up in a moment," said he; and left me to put up a heavy board shutter over the window opening on the river. Was this a signal or a precaution? I glanced towards my two friends playing cards, took another note of their broad shoulders and brawny arms, and prepared to follow my host, who now stood bowing at the other end of the room, before a covered staircase which was manifestly the sole means of reaching the floor above.

The staircase was quite a feature in the room. It ran from back to front, and was boarded all the way up to the ceiling. On these boards hung a few useless bits of chain, wire, and knotted ends of tarred ropes, which swung to and fro as the sharp November blast struck the building, giving out a weird and strangely muffled sound. Why did this sound, so easily to be accounted for, ring in my ears like a note of warning? I understand now, but I did not then, full of expectation as I was for developments out of the ordinary.

Crossing the room, I entered upon the staircase, in the wake of my companion. Though the two men at cards did not look up as I passed them, I noticed that they were alert and ready for any signal I might choose to give them. But I was not ready to give one yet. I must see danger before I summoned help, and there was no token of danger yet.

When we were about half-way up the stairs the faint light which had illuminated us from below suddenly vanished, and we found ourselves in total darkness. The door at the foot had been closed by a careful hand, and I felt, rather than heard, the stealthy pushing of a bolt across it.

My first impulse was to forsake my guide and rush back, but I subdued the unworthy impulse and stood quite still, while my companion, exclaiming, "Damn that fellow! What does he mean by shutting the door before we're half-way up!" struck a match and lit a gas jet in the room above, which poured a flood of light upon the staircase.

Drawing my hand from the pocket in which I had put my revolver, I hastened after him into the small landing at the top of the stairs. An open door was before me, in which he stood bowing, with the half-burnt match in his hand. "This is the place, sir," he announced, motioning me in.

I entered and he remained by the door, while I passed quickly about the room, which was bare of every article of furniture save a solitary table and chair. There was not even a window in it, with the exception of one small light situated so high up in the corner made by the jutting staircase that I wondered at its use, and was only relieved of extreme apprehension at the prison-like appearance of the place by the gleam of light which came through this dusty pane, showing that I was not entirely removed from the presence of my foes if I was from that of my friends.

"Ah, you have spied the window," remarked my host, advancing toward me with a countenance he vainly endeavoured to make reassuring and friendly. "That is your post of observation, sir," he whispered, with a great show of mystery. "By mounting on the table you can peer into the room where my young friends sit securely at play."

As it was not part of my scheme to show any special mistrust, I merely smiled a little grimly, and cast a glance at the table on which stood a bottle of brandy and one glass.

"Very good brandy," he whispered; "not such stuff as we give those fellows downstairs."

I shrugged my shoulders and he slowly backed towards the door.

"The young men you bid me watch are very quiet," I suggested, with a careless wave of my hand towards the room he had mentioned.

"Oh, there is no one there yet. They begin to straggle in about ten o'clock."

"Ah," was my quiet rejoinder, "I am likely, then, to have use for your brandy."

He smiled again and made a swift motion towards the door.

"If you want anything," said he, "just step to the foot of the staircase and let me know. The whole establishment is at your service." And with one final grin that remains in my mind as the most threatening and diabolical I have ever witnessed, he laid his hand on the knob of the door and slid quickly out.

It was done with such an air of final farewell that I felt my apprehensions take a positive form. Rushing towards the door through which he had just vanished, I listened and heard, as I thought, his stealthy feet descend the stair. But when I sought to follow, I found myself for the second time overwhelmed by darkness. The gas jet, which had hitherto burned with great brightness in the small room, had been turned off from below, and beyond the faint glimmer which found its way through the small window of which I have spoken, not a ray of light now disturbed the heavy gloom of this gruesome apartment.

I had thought of every contingency but this, and for a few minutes my spirits were dashed. But I soon recovered some remnants of self-possession, and began feeling for the knob I could no longer see. Finding it after a few futile attempts, I was relieved to discover that this door at least was not locked; and, opening it with a careful hand, I listened intently, but could hear nothing save the smothered sound of men talking in the room below.

Should I signal for my companions? No, for the secret was not yet mine as to how men passed from this room into the watery grave which was the evident goal for all wearers of the blue ribbon.

Stepping back into the middle of the room, I carefully pondered my situation, but could get no further than the fact that I was somehow, and in some way, in mortal peril. Would it come in the form of a bullet, or a deadly thrust from an unseen knife? I did not think so. For, to say nothing of the darkness, there was one reassuring fact which recurred constantly to my mind in connection with the murders I was endeavouring to trace to this den of iniquity.

None of the gentlemen who had been found drowned had shown any marks of violence on their bodies, so it was not attack I was to fear, but some mysterious, underhanded treachery which would rob me of consciousness and make the precipitation of my body into the water both safe and easy. Perhaps it was in the bottle of brandy that the peril lay; perhaps—but why speculate further! I would watch till midnight and then, if nothing happened, signal my companions to raid the house.

Meantime a peep into the next room might help me towards solving the mystery. Setting the bottle and glass aside, I dragged the table across the floor, placed it under the lighted window, mounted, and was about to peer through, when the light in that apartment was put out also. Angry and overwhelmed, I leaped down, and, stretching out my hands till they touched the wainscoting, I followed the wall around till I came to the knob of the door, which I frantically clutched. But I did not turn it immediately, I was too anxious to catch these villains at work.

Would I be conscious of the harm they meditated against me, or would I imperceptibly yield to some influence of which I was not yet conscious, and drop to the floor before I could draw my revolver or put to my mouth the whistle upon which I depended for assistance and safety? It was hard to tell, but I determined to cling to my first intention a little longer, and so stood waiting and counting the minutes, while wondering if the captain of the police boat was not getting impatient, and whether I had not more to fear from the anxiety of my friends than the cupidity of my foes.

You see, I had anticipated communicating with the men in this boat by certain signals and tokens which had been arranged between us. But the lack of windows in the room had made all such arrangements futile, so I knew as little of their actions as they did of my sufferings; all of which did not tend to add to the cheerfulness of my position.

However, I held out for a half-hour, listening, waiting, and watching in a darkness which, like that of Egypt, could be felt, and when the suspense grew intolerable I struck a match and let its blue flame flicker for a moment over the face of my watch. But the matches soon gave out and with them my patience, if not my courage, and I determined to end the suspense by knocking at the door beneath.

This resolution taken, I pulled open the door before me and stepped out. Though I could see nothing, I remembered the narrow landing at the top of the stairs, and, stretching out my arms, I felt for the boarding on either hand, guiding myself by it, and began to descend, when something rising, as it were, out of the cavernous darkness before me made me halt and draw back in mingled dread and horror.

But the impression, strong as it was, was only momentary, and, resolved to be done with the matter, I precipitated myself downward, when suddenly, at about the middle of the staircase, my feet slipped and I slid forward, plunging and reaching out with hands whose frenzied grasp found nothing to cling to, down a steep inclined plane—or what to my bewildered senses appeared such—till I struck a yielding surface and passed with one sickening plunge into the icy waters of the river, which in another moment had closed dark and benumbing above my head.

It was all so rapid I did not think of uttering a cry. But happily for me the splash I made told the story, and I was rescued before I could sink a second time.

It was full half an hour before I had sufficiently recovered from the shock to relate my story. But when once I had made it known, you can imagine the gusto with which the police prepared to enter the house and confound the obliging host with a sight of my dripping garments and accusing face. And, indeed, in all my professional experience I have never beheld a more sudden merging of the bully into a coward than was to be seen in this slick villain's face, when I was suddenly pulled from the crowd and placed before him, with the old man's wig gone from my head, and the tag of blue ribbon still clinging to my wet coat.

His game was up, and he saw it; and Ebenezer Gryce's career had begun.

Like all destructive things the device by which I had been run into the river was simple enough when understood. In the first place it had been constructed to serve the purpose of a stairway and chute. The latter was in plain sight when it was used by the sailmakers to run the finished sails into the waiting yawls below. At the time of my adventure, and for some time before, the possibilities of the place had been discovered by mine host, who had ingeniously put a partition up the entire stairway, dividing the steps from the smooth runway. At the upper part of the runway he had built a few steps, wherewith to lure the unwary far enough down to insure a fatal descent. To make sure of his game he had likewise ceiled the upper room all around, including the inclosure of the stairs.

The door to the chute and the door to the stairs were side by side, and being made of the same boards as the wainscoting, were scarcely visible when closed, while the single knob that was used, being transferable from one to the other, naturally gave the impression that there was but one door. When this adroit villain called my attention to the little window around the corner, he no doubt removed the knob from the stairs' door and quickly placed it in the one opening upon the chute. Another door, connecting the two similar landings without, explains how he got from the chute staircase into which he passed on leaving me, to the one communicating with the room below.

The mystery was solved, and my footing on the force secured; but to this day—and I am an old man now—I have not forgotten the horror of the moment when my feet slipped from under me, and I felt myself sliding downward, without hope of rescue, into a pit of heaving waters, where so many men of conspicuous virtue had already ended their valuable lives.

Myriad thoughts flashed through my brain in that brief interval, and among them the whole method of operating this death-trap, together with every detail of evidence that would secure the conviction of the entire gang.

THE AMETHYST BOX

I

THE FLASK WHICH HELD BUT A DROP

It was the night before the wedding. Though Sinclair, and not myself, was the happy man, I had my own causes for excitement, and, finding the heat of the billiard-room insupportable, I sought the veranda for a solitary smoke in sight of the ocean and a full moon.

I was in a condition of rapturous, if unreasoning, delight. That afternoon a little hand had lingered in mine for just an instant longer than the circumstances of the moment strictly required; and small as the favour may seem to those who do not know Dorothy Camerden, to me, who realised fully both her delicacy and pride, it was a sign that my long, if secret, devotion was about to be rewarded, and that at last I was free to cherish hopes whose alternative had once bid fair to wreck the happiness of my life.

I was revelling in the felicity of these anticipations, and contrasting this hour of ardent hope with others of whose dissatisfaction and gloom I was yet mindful, when a sudden shadow fell across the broad band of light issuing from the library window, and Sinclair stepped out.

He had the appearance of being disturbed—very much disturbed, I thought, for a man on the point of marrying the woman for whom he professed to entertain the one profound passion of his life; but remembering his frequent causes of annoyance—causes quite apart from his bride and her personal attributes—I kept on placidly smoking till I felt his hand on my shoulder, and turned to see that the moment was a serious one.

"I have something to say to you," he whispered. "Come where we shall run less risk of being disturbed."

"What's wrong?" I asked, facing him with curiosity, if not with alarm. "I never saw you look like this before. Has the old lady taken this last minute to—"

"Hush!" he prayed, emphasising the word with a curt gesture not to be mistaken. "The little room over the west porch is empty just now. Follow me there."

With a sigh for the cigar I had so lately lighted, I tossed it into the bushes and sauntered in after him. I thought I understood his trouble. The prospective bride was young—a mere slip of a girl indeed—bright, beautiful, and proud, yet with odd little restraints in her manner and language, due probably to her peculiar bringing up, and the surprise, not yet overcome, of finding herself, after an isolated, if not despised, childhood, the idol of society and the recipient of general homage. The fault was not with her. But she had for guardian (alas! my dear girl had the same) an aunt who was a gorgon. This aunt must have been making herself disagreeable to the prospective bridegroom, and he, being quick to take offence—quicker than myself, it was said—had probably retorted in a way to make things unpleasant. As he was a guest in the house, he and all the other members of the bridal party—Mrs. Armstrong having insisted upon opening her magnificent Newport villa for this wedding and its attendant festivities—the matter might well look black to him. Yet I did not feel disposed to take much interest in it, even though his case might be mine some day, with all its accompanying drawbacks.

But once confronted with Sinclair in the well-lighted room above, I perceived that I had better drop all selfish regrets and give my full attention to what he had to say. For his eye, which had flashed with an unusual light at dinner, was clouded now; and his manner, when he strove to speak, betrayed a nervousness I had considered foreign to his nature ever since the day I had seen him rein in his horse so calmly on the extreme edge of a precipice, where a fall would have meant certain death, not only to himself, but also to the two riders who unwittingly were pressing closely behind him.

"Walter," he faltered, "something has happened—something dreadful, something unprecedented! You may think me a fool—God knows, I would be glad to be proved so!—but this thing has frightened me. I"—he paused and pulled himself together—"I will tell you about it, then you can judge for yourself. I am in no condition—"

"Don't beat about the bush! Speak up! What's the matter?"

He gave me an odd look full of gloom—a look I felt the force of, though I could not interpret it; then, coming closer, though there was no one within hearing—possibly no one any nearer than the drawing-room below—he whispered in my ear:

"I have lost a little vial of the deadliest drug ever compounded—a Venetian curiosity, which I was foolish enough to take out and show the ladies, because the little box which holds it is such an exquisite example of jeweller's work. There's death in its taste, almost in its smell; and it's out of my hands, and—"

"Well, I'll tell you how to fix that up," I put in with my usual frank decision. "Order the music stopped; call everybody into the drawing-room, and explain the dangerous nature of this toy. After which, if anything happens, it will not be your fault, but that of the person who has so thoughtlessly appropriated it."

His eyes, which had been resting eagerly on mine, shifted aside in visible embarrassment.

"Impossible! It would only aggravate matters, or, rather, would not relieve my fears at all. The person who took it knew its nature very well, and that person—"

"Oh, then you know who took it!" I broke in in increasing astonishment. "I thought from your manner that—"

"No," he moodily corrected, "I do not know who took it. If I did, I should not be here. That is, I do not know the exact person. Only—" Here he again eyed me with his former singular intentness, and, observing that I was nettled, made a fresh beginning. "When I came here I brought with me a case of rarities chosen from my various collections. In looking over them preparatory to making a present to Gilbertine, I came across the little box I have just mentioned. It is made of a single amethyst, and contains—or so I was assured when I bought it—a tiny flask of old but very deadly poison. How it came to be included with the other precious and beautiful articles I had picked out for her cadeau I cannot say. But there it was; and conceiving that the sight of it would please the ladies, I carried it down into the library, and in an evil hour called three or four of those about me to inspect it. This was while you boys were in the billiard-room, so the ladies could give their entire attention to the little box, which is certainly worth the most careful scrutiny.

"I was holding it out on the palm of my hand, where it burned with a purple light which made more than one feminine eye glitter, when somebody inquired to what use so small and yet so rich a receptacle could be put. The question was such a natural one I never thought of evading it; besides, I enjoy the fearsome delight which women take in the marvellous. Expecting no greater result than lifted eyebrows or flushed cheeks, I answered by pressing a little spring in the filigree-work surrounding the gem. Instantly the tiniest of lids flew back, revealing a crystal flask of such minute proportions that the usual astonishment followed its disclosure.

"'You see!' I cried, 'it was made to hold that!' And moving my hand to and fro under the gas jet, I caused to shine in their eyes the single drop of yellow liquid it still held. 'Poison!' I impressively announced. 'This trinket may have adorned the bosom of a Borgia or flashed from the arm of some great Venetian lady as she flourished her fan between her embittered heart and the object of her wrath or jealousy.'

"The first sentence had come naturally, but the last was spoken at random, and almost unconsciously. For at the utterance of the word 'poison' a quickly suppressed cry had escaped the lips of some one behind me, which, while faint enough to elude the attention of any ear less sensitive than my own, contained such an astonishing, if involuntary, note of self-betrayal that my mind grew numb with horror, and I stood staring at the fearful toy which had called up such a revelation of—what? That is what I am here to ask, first of myself, then of you. For the two women pressing behind me were—"

"Who?" I sharply demanded, partaking in some indefinable way of his excitement and alarm.

"Gilbertine Murray and Dorothy Camerden!"—his prospective bride and the woman I loved and whom he knew I loved, though I had kept my secret quite successfully from every one else!

The look we exchanged neither of us will ever forget.

"Describe the sound," I presently said.

"I cannot," he replied. "I can only give you my impression of it. You, like myself, fought in more than one skirmish in the Cuban War. Did you ever hear the cry made by a wounded man when the cup of cool water for which he has long agonised is brought suddenly before his eyes? Such a sound, with all that goes to make it eloquent, did I hear from one of the two girls who leaned over my shoulder. Can you understand this amazing, this unheard-of circumstance? Can you name the woman—can you name the grief capable of making either of these seemingly happy and innocent girls hail the sight of such a doubtful panacea, with an unconscious ebullition of joy? You would clear my wedding-eve of a great dread if you could, for if this expression of concealed misery came from Gilbertine—"

"Do you mean," I cried in vehement protest, "that you really are in doubt as to which of these two women uttered the cry which so startled you? That you positively cannot tell whether it was Gilbertine or—or—"

"I cannot; as God lives, I cannot! I was too dazed, too confounded by the unexpected circumstance, to turn at once, and when I did, it was to see both pairs of eyes shining, and both faces dimpling with real or affected gaiety. Indeed, if the matter had stopped there, I should have thought myself the victim of some monstrous delusion; but when, a half-hour later, I found this box missing from the cabinet where I had hastily thrust it at the peremptory summons of our hostess, I knew that I had not misunderstood the nature of the cry I had heard; that it was indeed one of secret longing, and that the hand had simply taken what the heart desired. If a death occurs in this house to-night—"

"Sinclair, you are mad!" I exclaimed with great violence. No lesser word would fit either the intensity of my feeling or the confused state of my mind. "Death here! where all are so happy! Remember your bride's ingenuous face! Remember the candid expression of Dorothy's eye—her smile, her noble ways! You exaggerate the situation. You neither understand aright the simple expression of surprise you heard, nor the feminine frolic which led these girls to carry off this romantic specimen of Italian deviltry."

"You are losing time," was his simple comment. "Every minute we allow to pass in inaction only brings the danger nearer."

"What! You imagine—"

"I imagine nothing. I simply know that one of these girls has in her possession the means of terminating life in an instant; that the girl so having it is not happy; and that if anything happens to-night it will be because we rested supine in the face of a very real and possible danger. Now, as Gilbertine has never given me reason to doubt either her affection for myself or her satisfaction in our approaching union, I have allowed myself—"

"To think that the object of your fears is Dorothy," I finished, with a laugh I vainly strove to make sarcastic.

He did not answer, and I stood battling with a dread I could neither conceal nor avow. For, preposterous as his idea was, reason told me that he had some grounds for his doubt.

Dorothy, unlike Gilbertine Murray, was not to be read at a glance, and her trouble—for she certainly had a trouble—was not one she chose to share with any one, even with me. I had flattered myself in days gone by that I understood it well enough, and that any lack of sincerity I might observe in her could be easily explained by the position of dependence she held toward an irascible aunt. But now that I forced myself to consider the matter carefully, I could not but ask if the varying moods by which I had found myself secretly harrowed had not sprung from a very different cause—a cause for which my persistent love was more to blame than the temper of her relative. The aversion she had once shown to my attentions had yielded long ago to a shy but seemingly sincere appreciation of them, and gleams of what I was fain to call real feeling had shown themselves now and then in her softened manner, culminating to-day in that soft pressure of my hand which had awakened my hopes and made me forget all the doubts and caprices of a disturbing courtship.

But, had I interpreted that strong, nervous pressure aright? Had it necessarily meant love? Might it not have sprung from a sudden desperate resolution to accept a devotion which offered her a way out of difficulties especially galling to one of her gentle but lofty spirit? Her expression when she caught my look of joy had little of the demure tenderness of a maiden blushing at her first involuntary avowal. There was shrinking in it, but it was the shrinking of a frightened woman, not of an abashed girl; and when I strove to follow her, the gesture with which she waved me back had that in it which would have alarmed a more exacting lover. Had I mistaken my darling's feelings? Was her heart still cold, her affection unwon? Or—thought insupportable!—had she secretly yielded to another what she had so long denied me, and—?

"Ah!" quoth Sinclair at this juncture, "I see that I have roused you at last." And unconsciously his tone grew lighter and his eye lost the strained look which had made it the eye of a stranger. "You begin to see that a question of the most serious import is before us, and that this question must be answered before we separate for the night."

"I do," said I.

His relief was evident.

"Then, so much is gained. The next point is, how are we to settle our doubts? We cannot approach either of these ladies with questions. A girl wretched enough to contemplate suicide would be especially careful to conceal both her misery and its cause. Neither can we order a search to be made for an object so small that it can be concealed about the person."

"Yet this jewel must be recovered. Listen, Sinclair. I will have a talk with Dorothy, you with Gilbertine. A kind talk, mind you! one that will soothe, not frighten. If a secret lurks in either breast, our tenderness should find it out. Only, as you love me, promise to show me the same frankness I here promise to show you. Dear as Dorothy is to me, I swear to communicate to you the full result of my conversation with her, whatever the cost to myself or even to her."

"And I will be equally fair as regards Gilbertine. But before we proceed to such extreme measures let us make sure that there is no shorter road to the truth. Some one may have seen which of our two dear girls went back to the library after we all came out of it. That would narrow down our inquiry, and save one of them, at least, from unnecessary disturbance."

It was a happy thought, and I told him so, but at the same time bade him look in the glass and see how impossible it would be for him to venture below without creating an alarm which might precipitate the dread event we both feared.

He replied by drawing me to his side before the mirror and pointing to my own face. It was as pale as his own.

Most disagreeably impressed by this self-betrayal, I coloured deeply under Sinclair's eye, and was but little, if any, relieved when I noticed that he coloured under mine. For his feelings were no enigma to me. Naturally, he was glad to discover that I shared his apprehensions, since it gave him leave to hope that the blow he so dreaded was not necessarily directed toward his own affections. Yet, being a generous fellow, he blushed to be detected in his egotism, while I—well, I own that at that moment I should have felt a very unmixed joy at being assured that the foundations of my own love were secure, and that the tiny flask Sinclair had missed had not been taken by the hand of her upon whom I depended for all my earthly happiness.

And my wedding-day was as yet a vague and distant hope, while his was set for the morrow.

"We must carry downstairs very different faces from these," he remarked, "or we shall be stopped before we reach the library."

I made an effort at composure, so did he; and both being determined men, we soon found ourselves in a condition to descend among our friends without attracting any closer attention than was naturally due to him as prospective bridegroom and to myself as best man.

II

BEATON'S DREAM

Mrs. Armstrong, our hostess, was fond of gaiety, and amusements were never lacking. As we stepped down into the great hall we heard music in the drawing-room, and saw that a dance was in progress.

"That is good," observed Sinclair. "We shall run less risk of finding the library occupied."

"Shall I not look and see where the girls are? It would be a great relief to find them both among the dancers."

"Yes," said he; "but don't allow yourself to be inveigled into joining them. I could not stand the suspense."

I nodded, and slipped toward the drawing-room. He remained in the bay-window overlooking the terrace.

A rush of young people greeted me as soon as I showed myself. But I was able to elude them, and catch the one full glimpse I wanted of the great room beyond. It was a magnificent apartment, and so brilliantly lighted that every nook stood revealed. On a divan near the centre was a lady conversing with two gentlemen. Her back was toward me, but I had no difficulty in recognising Miss Murray. Some distance from her, but with her face also turned away, stood Dorothy. She was talking with an unmarried friend, and appeared quite at ease and more than usually cheerful.

Relieved, yet sorry that I had not succeeded in catching a glimpse of their faces, I hastened back to Sinclair, who was watching me with furtive eyes from between the curtains of the window in which he had secreted himself. As I joined him a young man, who was to act as usher, sauntered from behind one of the great pillars forming a colonnade down the hall, and, crossing to where the music-room door stood invitingly open, disappeared behind it with the air of a man perfectly contented with his surroundings.

With a nervous grip Sinclair seized me by the arm.

"Was that Beaton?" he asked.

"Certainly; didn't you recognise him?"

He gave me a very strange look.

"Does the sight of him recall anything?"

"No."

"You were at the breakfast-table yesterday morning?"

"I was."

"Do you remember the dream he related for the delectation of such as would listen?"

Then it was my turn to go white.

"You don't mean—" I began.

"I thought at the time that it sounded more like a veritable adventure than a dream; now I am sure that it was such."

"Sinclair! You do not mean that the young girl he professed himself to have surprised one moonlit night standing on the verge of the cliff, with arms upstretched and a distracted air, was a real person?"

"I do. We laughed at the time; he made it seem so tragic and preposterous. I do not feel like laughing now."

I gazed at Sinclair in horror. The music was throbbing in our ears, and the murmur of gay voices and swiftly-moving feet suggested nothing but joy and hilarity. Which was the dream? This scene of seeming mirth and happy promise, or the fancies he had conjured up to rob us both of peace?

"Beaton mentioned no names," I stubbornly protested. "He did not even call the vision he encountered a woman. It was a wraith, you remember, a dream-maiden, a creature of his own imagination, born of some tragedy he had read."

"Beaton is a gentleman," was Sinclair's cold reply. "He did not wish to injure, but to warn the woman for whose benefit he told his tale."

"Warn?"

"He doubtless reasoned in this way: If he could make this young and probably sensitive girl realise that she had been seen and her intentions recognised, she would beware of such attempts in the future. He is a kind-hearted fellow. Did you notice which end of the table he ignored when relating this dramatic episode?"

"No."

"If you had we might be better able to judge where his thoughts were. Probably you cannot even tell how the ladies took it?"

"No, I never thought of looking. Good God, Sinclair, don't let us harrow up ourselves unnecessarily! I saw them both a moment ago, and nothing in their manner showed that anything was amiss with either of them."

For answer he drew me toward the library.

This room was not frequented by the young people at night. There were two or three elderly people in the party, notably the husband and the brother of the lady of the house, and to their use the room was more or less given up after nightfall. Sinclair wished to show me the cabinet where the box had been.

There was a fire in the grate, for the evenings were now more or less chilly. When the door had closed behind us we found that this fire supplied all the light there was in the room. Both gas jets had been put out, and the rich yet homelike room glowed with ruddy hues, interspersed with great shadows. A solitary scene, yet an enticing one.

Sinclair drew a deep breath. "Mr. Armstrong must have gone elsewhere to read the evening papers," he remarked.

I replied by casting a scrutinising look into the corners. I dreaded finding a pair of lovers hid somewhere in the many nooks made by the jutting bookcases. But I saw no one. However, at the other end of the large room there stood a screen near one of the many lounges, and I was on the point of approaching this place of concealment when Sinclair drew me toward a tall cabinet upon whose glass doors the firelight was shimmering, and, pointing to a shelf far above our heads, cried:

"No woman could reach that unaided. Gilbertine is tall, but not tall enough for that. I purposely put it high."

I looked about for a stool. There was one just behind Sinclair. I drew his attention to it.

He flushed and gave it a kick, then shivered slightly and sat down in a chair nearby. I knew what he was thinking. Gilbertine was taller than Dorothy. This stool might have served Gilbertine, if not Dorothy.

I felt a great sympathy for him. After all, his case was more serious than mine. The Bishop was coming to marry him the next day.

"Sinclair," said I, "the stool means nothing. Dorothy has more inches than you think. With this under her feet, she could reach the shelf by standing tiptoe. Besides, there are the chairs."

"True, true!" and he started up; "there are the chairs! I forgot the chairs. I fear my wits have gone wool-gathering. We shall have to take others into our confidence." Here his voice fell to a whisper. "Somehow or by some means we must find out if either of them was seen to come into this room."

"Leave that to me," said I. "Remember that a word might raise suspicion, and that in a case like this— Halloa, what's that?"

A gentle snore had come from behind the screen.

"We are not alone," I whispered. "Some one is over there on the lounge."

Sinclair had already bounded across the room. I pressed hurriedly behind him, and together we rounded the screen and came upon the recumbent figure of Mr. Armstrong, asleep on the lounge, with his paper fallen from his hand.

"That accounts for the lights being turned out," grumbled Sinclair. "Dutton must have done it."

Dutton was the butler.

I stood contemplating the sleeping figure before me.

"He must have been lying here for some time," I muttered.

Sinclair started.

"Probably some little while before he slept," I pursued. "I have often heard that he dotes on the firelight."

"I have a notion to wake him," suggested Sinclair.

"It will not be necessary," said I, drawing back, as the heavy figure stirred, breathed heavily, and finally sat up.

"I beg pardon," I now entreated, backing politely away. "We thought the room empty."

Mr. Armstrong, who, if slow to receive impressions, is far from lacking intelligence, eyed us with sleepy indifference for a moment, then rose ponderously to his feet, and was on the instant the man of manner and unfailing courtesy we had ever found him.

"What can I do to oblige you?" he asked, his smooth, if hesitating, tones sounding strange to our excited ears.

I made haste to forestall Sinclair, who was racking his brains for words with which to propound the question he dared not put too boldly.

"Pardon me, Mr. Armstrong, we were looking about for a small pin dropped by Miss Camerden." (How hard it was for me to use her name in this connection only my own heart knew.) "She was in here just now, was she not?"

The courteous gentleman bowed, hemmed, and smiled a very polite but unmeaning smile. Evidently he had not the remotest notion whether she had been in or not.

"I am sorry, but I am afraid I lost myself for a moment on that lounge," he admitted. "The firelight always makes me sleepy. But if I can help you," he cried, starting forward, but almost immediately pausing again and giving us rather a curious look. "Some one was in the room. I remember it now. It was just before the warmth and glow of the fire became too much for me. I cannot say that it was Miss Camerden, however. I thought it was some one of quicker movement. She made quite a rattle with the chairs."

I purposely did not look back at Sinclair.

"Miss Murray?" I suggested.

Mr. Armstrong made one of his low, old-fashioned bows. This, I doubt not, was out of deference to the bride-to-be.

"Does Miss Murray wear white to-night?"

"Yes," muttered Sinclair, coming hastily forward.

"Then it may have been she, for as I lay there deciding whether or not to yield to the agreeable somnolence I felt creeping over me, I caught a glimpse of the lady's skirt as she passed out. And that skirt was white—white silk I suppose you call it. It looked very pretty in the firelight."

Sinclair, turning on his heel, stalked in a dazed way toward the door. To cover this show of abruptness, which was quite unusual on his part, I made the effort of my life, and, remarking lightly, "She must have been here looking for the pin her friend has lost," I launched forth into an impromptu dissertation on one of the subjects I knew to be dear to the heart of the bookworm before me—and kept it up, too, till I saw by his brightening eye and suddenly freed manner that he had forgotten the insignificant episode of a minute ago, never in all probability to recall it again. Then I made another effort, and released myself with something like deftness from the long-drawn-out argument I saw impending, and making for the door in my turn, glanced about for Sinclair. So far as I was concerned the question as to who had taken the box from the library was settled.

It was now half-past eight. I made my way from room to room and from group to group looking for Sinclair. At last I returned to my old post near the library door, and was instantly rewarded by the sight of his figure approaching from a small side-passage in company with the butler, Dutton. His face, as he stepped into the full light of the open hall, showed discomposure, but not the extreme distress I had anticipated. Somehow, at sight of it, I found myself seeking the shadow just as he had done a short time before, and it was in one of the recesses made by a row of bay-trees that we came face to face.

He gave me one look, then his eyes dropped.

"Miss Camerden has lost a pin from her hair," he impressively explained to me. Then, turning to Dutton, he nonchalantly remarked: "It must be somewhere in this hall; perhaps you will be good enough to look for it."

"Certainly," replied the man. "I thought she had lost something when I saw her come out of the library a little while ago, holding her hand to her hair."

My heart gave a leap, then sank cold and almost pulseless in my breast. In the hum to which all sounds had sunk, I heard Sinclair's voice rise again in the question with which my own mind was full.

"When was that? After Mr. Armstrong went into the room, or before?"

"Oh, after he fell asleep. I had just come from putting out the gas when I saw Miss Camerden slip in and almost immediately come out again. I will search for the pin very carefully, sir."

So Mr. Armstrong had made a mistake! It was Dorothy, and not Gilbertine, whom he had seen leaving the room. I braced myself up and met Sinclair's eye.

"Dorothy's dress is grey to-night; but Mr. Armstrong's eye may not be very good for colours."

"It is possible that both were in the room," was Sinclair's reply. But I could see that he advanced this theory solely out of consideration for me; that he did not really believe it. "At all events," he went on, "we cannot prove anything this way; we must revert to our original idea. I wonder if Gilbertine will give me the chance to speak to her."

"You will have an easier task than I," was my half-sullen retort. "If Dorothy perceives that I wish to approach her, she has but to lift her eyes to any of the half-dozen fellows here, and the thing becomes impossible."

"There is to be a rehearsal of the ceremony at half-past ten. I might get a word in then; only, this matter must be settled first. I could never go through the farce of standing up before you all at Gilbertine's side, with such a doubt as this in my mind."

"You will see her before then. Insist on a moment's talk. If she refuses—"

"Hush!" he here put in. "We part now to meet in this same place again at ten. Do I look fit to enter among the dancers? I see a whole group of them coming for me."

"You will be in another moment. Approaching matrimony has made you sober, that's all."

It was some time before I had the opportunity, even if I had the courage, to look Dorothy in the face. When the moment came she was flushed with dancing and looked beautiful. Ordinarily she was a little pale, but not even Gilbertine, with her sumptuous colouring, showed a warmer cheek than she, as, resting from the waltz, she leaned against the rose-tinted wall, and let her eyes for the first time rise slowly to where I stood talking mechanically to my partner.

Gentle eyes they were, made for appeal, and eloquent with a subdued heart language. But they were held in check by an infinite discretion. Never have I caught them quite off their guard, and to-night they were wholly unreadable. Yet she was trembling with something more than the fervour of the dance, and the little hand which had touched mine in lingering pressure a few hours before was not quiet for a moment. I could not see it fluttering in and out of the folds of her smoke-coloured dress without a sickening wonder if the little purple box which was the cause of my horror lay somewhere concealed amid the airy puffs and ruffles that rose and fell so rapidly over her heaving breast. Could her eye rest on mine, even in this cold and perfunctory manner, if the drop which could separate us for ever lay concealed over her heart? She knew that I loved her. From the first hour we met in her aunt's forbidding parlour in Thirty-sixth Street she had recognised my passion, however perfectly I had succeeded in concealing it from others. Inexperienced as she was in those days, she had noted as quickly as any society belle the effect produced upon me by her chill prettiness and her air of meek reserve, under which one felt the heart break; and though she would never openly acknowledge my homage, and frowned down every attempt on my part at lover-like speech or attention, I was as sure that she rated my feelings at their real value as that she was the dearest, yet most incomprehensible, mortal my narrow world contained. When, therefore, I encountered her eyes at the end of the dance, I said to myself:

"She may not love me, but she knows that I love her, and, being a woman of sympathetic instincts, would never meet my eyes with so calm a look if she were meditating an act which must infallibly plunge me into misery."

Yet I was not satisfied to go away without a word. So, taking the bull by the horns, I excused myself to my partner, and crossed to Dorothy's side.

"Will you dance the next waltz with me?" I asked.

Her eyes fell from mine directly, and she drew back in a way that suggested flight.

"I shall dance no more to-night," said she, her hand rising in its nervous fashion to her hair.

I made no appeal. I just watched that hand, whereupon she flushed vividly, and seemed more than ever anxious to escape. At which I spoke again.

"Give me a chance, Dorothy. If you will not dance, come out on the veranda and look at the ocean. It is glorious to-night. I will not keep you long. The lights here trouble my eyes; besides, I am most anxious to ask you—"

"No, no," she vehemently objected, very much as if frightened. "I cannot leave the drawing-room—do not ask me! Seek some other partner—do, to-night."

"You wish it?"

"Very much."

She was panting, eager. I felt my heart sink, and dreaded lest I should betray my feelings.

"You do not honour me, then, with your regard," I retorted, bowing ceremoniously as I became assured that we were attracting more attention than I considered desirable.

She was silent. Her hand went again to her hair.

I changed my tone. Quietly, but with an emphasis which moved her in spite of herself, I whispered: "If I leave you now, will you tell me to-morrow why you are so peremptory with me to-night?"

With an eagerness which was anything but encouraging, she answered, almost gaily:

"Yes, yes, after all this excitement is over."

And slipping her hand into that of a friend who was passing, she was soon in the whirl again and dancing—she who had just assured me that she did not mean to dance again that night.

III

A SCREAM IN THE NIGHT

I turned and, hardly conscious of my actions, stumbled from the room. A bevy of young people at once surrounded me. What I said to them I hardly know. I only remember that it was several minutes before I found myself again alone and making for the little room into which Beaton had vanished a half-hour before. It was the one given up to card-playing. Did I expect to find him seated at one of the tables? Possibly; at all events, I approached the doorway, and was about to enter, when a heavy step shook the threshold before me, and I found myself confronted by the advancing figure of an elderly lady, whose portrait it is now time for me to draw. It is no pleasurable task, but one I cannot escape.

Imagine, then, a broad, weighty woman of not much height, with a face whose features were usually forgotten in the impression made by her great cheeks and falling jowls. If the small eyes rested on you, you found them sinister and strange, but if they were turned elsewhere, you asked in what lay the power of the face, and sought in vain amid its long wrinkles and indeterminate lines for the secret of that spiritual and bodily repulsion which the least look into this impassive countenance was calculated to produce. She was a woman of immense means, and an oppressive consciousness of this spoke in every movement of her heavy frame, which always seemed to take up three times as much space as rightfully belonged to any human creature. Add to this that she was seldom seen without a display of diamonds which made her broad bust look like the bejewelled breast of some Eastern idol, and some idea may be formed of this redoubtable woman whom I have hitherto confined myself to speaking of as the gorgon.

The stare she gave me had something venomous and threatening in it. Evidently for the moment I was out of her books, and while I did not understand in what way I had displeased her, for we always had met amicably before, I seized upon this sign of displeasure on her part as explanatory, perhaps, of the curtness and show of contradictory feelings on the part of her dependent niece. Yet why should the old woman frown on me? I had been told more than once that she regarded me with great favour. Had I unwittingly done something to displease her, or had the game of cards she had just left gone against her, ruffling her temper and making it imperative for her to choose some object on which to vent her spite? I entered the room to see. Two men and one woman stood in rather an embarrassed silence about a table on which lay some cards, which had every appearance of having been thrown down by an impatient hand. One of the men was Will Beaton, and it was he who now remarked:

"She has just found out that the young people are enjoying themselves. I wonder upon which of her two unfortunate nieces she will expend her ill-temper to-night."

"Oh, there's no question about that," remarked the lady who stood near him. "Ever since she has had a reasonable prospect of working Gilbertine off her hands, she has devoted herself quite exclusively to her remaining burden. I hear," she impulsively continued, craning her neck to be sure that the object of her remarks was quite out of earshot, "that the south hall was blue to-day with the talk she gave Dorothy Camerden. No one knows what about, for the girl evidently tries to please her. But some women have more than their own proper share of bile; they must expend it on some one." And she in turn threw down her cards, which up till now she had held in her hand.

I gave Beaton a look and stepped out on the veranda. In a minute he followed me, and in the corner facing the ocean, where the vines cluster the thickest, we held our conversation.

I began it, with a directness born of my desperation.

"Beaton," said I, "we have not known each other long, but I recognise a man when I see him, and I am disposed to be frank with you. I am in trouble. My affections are engaged, deeply engaged, in a quarter where I find some mystery. You have helped make it." (Here a gesture escaped him.) "I allude to the story you related the other morning of the young girl you had seen hanging over the verge of the cliff, with every appearance of intending to throw herself over."

"It was as a dream I related that," he gravely remarked.

"That I am aware of. But it was no dream to me, Beaton. I fear I know that young girl; I also fear that I know what drove her into contemplating so rash an act. The conversation just held in the card-room should enlighten you. Beaton, am I wrong?"

The feeling I could not suppress trembled in my tones. He may have been sensitive to it, or he may have been simply good-natured. Whatever the cause, this is what he said in reply:

"It was a dream. Remember that I insist upon its being a dream. But some of its details are very clear in my mind. When I stumbled upon this dream-maiden in the moonlight her face was turned from me toward the ocean, and I did not see her features then or afterwards. Startled by some sound I made, she crouched, drew back, and fled to cover. That cover, I have good reason to believe, was this very house."

I reached out my hand and touched him on the arm.

"This dream-maiden was a woman?" I inquired. "One of the women now in this house?"

He replied reluctantly:

"She was a young woman, and she wore a long cloak. My dream ends there. I cannot even say whether she was fair or dark."

I recognised that he had reached the limit of his explanations, and, wringing his hand, I started for the nearest window, which proved to be that of the music-room. I was about to enter when I saw two women crossing to the opposite doorway, and paused with a full heart to note them, for one was Mrs. Lansing and the other Dorothy. The aunt had evidently come for the niece, and they were leaving the room together. Not amicably, however. Harsh words had passed, or I am no judge of the human countenance. Dorothy especially bore herself like one who finds difficulty in restraining herself from some unhappy outburst, and as she disappeared from my sight in the wake of her formidable companion my attention was again called to her hands, which she held clenched at her sides.

I was stepping into the room when my impulse was again checked. Another person was sitting there, a person I had been most anxious to see ever since my last interview with Sinclair. It was Gilbertine Murray, sitting alone in an attitude of deep, and possibly not altogether happy thought.

I paused to study the sweet face. Truly she was a beautiful woman. I had never before realised how beautiful. Her rich colouring, her noble traits, and the spirited air which gave her such marked distinction, bespoke at once an ardent nature and a pure soul.

I did not wonder that Sinclair had succumbed to charms so pronounced and uncommon, and as I gazed longer and noted the tremulous droop of her ripe lips and the far-away look of eyes which had created a great stir in the social world when they first flashed upon it, I felt that if Sinclair could see her now he would never doubt her again, despite the fact that the attitude into which she had fallen was one of great fatigue, if not despondency.

She held a fan in her hand, and as I stood looking at her she dropped it. As she stooped to pick it up her eyes met mine, and a startling change passed over her. Springing up, she held out her hands in wordless appeal, then let them drop again as if conscious that I would not be likely to understand either herself or her mood. She was very beautiful.

Entering the room, I approached her. Had Sinclair managed to have his little conversation with her? Something must have happened, for never had I seen her in such a state of suppressed excitement, and I had seen her many times, both here and in her aunt's house when I was visiting Dorothy. Her eyes were shining, not with a brilliant, but a soft light, and the smile with which she met my advance had something in it strangely tremulous and expectant.

"I am glad to have a moment in which to speak to you alone," I said. "As Sinclair's oldest and closest friend, I wish to tell you how truly you can rely both on his affection and esteem. He has an infinitely good heart."

She did not answer as brightly and as quickly as I expected. Something seemed to choke her—something which she finally mastered, though only by an effort which left her pale, but self-contained, and even more lovely, if that is possible, than before.

"Thank you," she then said, "my prospects are very happy. No one but myself knows how happy."

And she smiled again, but with an expression which recalled to my mind Sinclair's fears.

I bowed. Some one was calling her name; evidently our interview was to be short.

"I am obliged," she murmured. Then quickly: "I have not seen the moon to-night. Is it beautiful? Can you see it from this veranda?"

But before I could answer she was surrounded and dragged off by a knot of young people, and I was left free to keep my engagement with Sinclair.

I did not find him at his post, nor could any one tell where he had vanished.

It was plain that his conduct was looked upon as strange, and I felt some anxiety lest it should appear more so before the evening was over. I found him at last in his room, sitting with his head buried in his arms. He started up as I entered.

"Well?" he asked sharply.

"I have learned nothing decisive."

"Nor I."

"I exchanged some words with both ladies and I tackled Beaton; but the matter remains just about where it was. It may have been Dorothy who took the box and it may have been Gilbertine. But there seems to be greater reason for suspecting Dorothy. She lives a terrible life with that aunt."

"And Gilbertine is on the point of escaping that bondage. I know; I have thought of that. Walter, you are a generous fellow;" and for a moment Sinclair looked relieved. Before I could speak, however, he was sunk again in his old despondency. "But the doubt," he cried—"the doubt! How can I go through this rehearsal with such a doubt in my mind? I cannot and will not. Go, tell them I am ill, and cannot come down again to-night. God knows you will tell no untruth."

I saw that he was quite beside himself, but ventured upon one remonstrance.

"It will be unwise to rouse comment," I said. "If that box was taken for the death it holds, the one restraint most likely to act upon the young girl who retains it will be the conventionalities of her position and the requirements of the hour. Any break in the settled order of things—anything which would give her a moment by herself—might precipitate the dreadful event we fear. Remember, one turn of the hand, and all is lost. A drop is quickly swallowed."

"Frightful!" he murmured, the perspiration oozing from his forehead. "What a wedding-eve! And they are laughing down there. Listen to them. I even imagine I hear Gilbertine's voice. Is there unconsciousness in it, or just the hilarity of a distracted mind bent on self-destruction? I cannot tell; the sound conveys no meaning to me."

"She has a sweet, true face," I said, "and she wears a very beautiful smile to-night."

He sprang to his feet.

"Yes, yes—a smile that maddens me; a smile that tells me nothing, nothing! Walter, Walter, don't you see that, even if that cursed box remains unopened, and nothing ever comes of its theft, the seeds of distrust are sown thick in my breast, and I must always ask: 'Was there a moment when my young bride shrank from me enough to dream of death?' That is why I cannot go through the mockery of this rehearsal."

"Can you go through the ceremony of marriage?"

"I must—if nothing happens to-night."

"And then?"

I spoke involuntarily. I was thinking not of him, but of myself. But he evidently found in my words an echo of his own thought.

"Yes, it is the then," he murmured. "Well may a man quail before that then."

He did go downstairs, however, and later on went through the rehearsal very much as I had expected him to do—quietly and without any outward show of emotion.

As soon as possible after this the company separated, Sinclair making me an imperceptible gesture as he went upstairs. I knew what it meant, and was in his room as soon as the fellows who accompanied him had left him alone.

"The danger is from now on," he cried, as soon as I had closed the door behind me. "I shall not undress to-night."

"Nor I."

"Happily we both have rooms by ourselves in this great house. I shall put out my light, and then open my door as far as need be. Not a move in the house will escape me."

"I will do the same."

"Gilbertine—God be thanked!—is not alone in her room. Little Miss Lane shares it with her."

"And Dorothy?"

"Oh, she is under the strictest bondage night and day. She sleeps in a little room off her aunt's. Do you know her door?"

I shook my head.

"I will pass down the hall and stop an instant before the two doors we are most interested in. When I pass Gilbertine's I will throw out my right hand."

I stood on the threshold of his room and watched him. When the two doors were well fixed in my mind, I went to my own room and prepared for my self-imposed watch. When quite ready, I put out my light. It was then eleven o'clock.

The house was very quiet. There had been the usual bustle attending the separation of a party of laughing, chattering girls for the night; but this had not lasted long, for the great doings of the morrow called for bright eyes and fresh cheeks, and these can only be gained by sleep. In this stillness twelve o'clock struck, and the first hour of my anxious vigil was at an end. I thought of Sinclair. He had given no token of the watch he was keeping, but I knew he was sitting with his ear to the door, listening for the alarm which must come soon if it came at all.

But would it come at all? Were we not wasting strength and a great deal of emotion on a dread which had no foundation in fact? What were we two sensible and, as a rule, practical men thinking of, that we should ascribe to either of these dainty belles of a conventional and shallow society the wish to commit a deed calling for the vigour and daring of some wilful child of nature? It was not to be thought of in this sober, reasoning hour. We had given ourselves over to a ghastly nightmare, and would yet awake.

Why was I on my feet? Had I heard anything?

Yes, a stir, a very faint stir somewhere down the hall—the slow, cautious opening of a door, then a footfall—or had I imagined the latter? I could hear nothing now.

Pushing open my own door, I looked cautiously out. Only the pale face of Sinclair confronted me. He was peering from the corner of an adjacent passage-way, the moonlight at his back. Advancing, we met in silence. For the moment we seemed to be the only persons awake in the vast house.

"I thought I heard a step," was my cautious whisper after a moment of intense listening.

"Where?"

I pointed toward that portion of the house where the ladies' rooms were situated.

"That is not what I heard," was his murmured protest; "what I heard was a creak in the small stairway running down at the end of the hall where my room is."

"One of the servants," I ventured, and for a moment we stood irresolute. Then we both turned rigid as some sound arose in one of the far-off rooms, only to quickly relax again as that sound resolved itself into a murmur of muffled voices. Where there was talking there could be no danger of the special event we feared. Our relief was so great we both smiled. Next instant his face, and, I have no doubt, my own, turned the colour of clay, and Sinclair went reeling back against the wall.

A scream had risen in this sleeping house—a piercing and insistent scream such as raises the hair and curdles the blood.

IV

This scream seemed to come from the room where we had just heard voices. With a common impulse Sinclair and I both started down the hall, only to find ourselves met by a dozen wild interrogations from behind as many quickly opened doors. Was it fire? Had burglars got in? What was the matter? Who had uttered that dreadful shriek? Alas! that was the question which we of all men were most anxious to hear answered. Who? Gilbertine or Dorothy?

Gilbertine's door was reached first. In it stood a short, slight figure, wrapped in a hastily-donned shawl. The white face looked into ours as we stopped, and we recognised little Miss Lane.

"What has happened?" she gasped. "It must have been an awful cry to waken everybody so!"

We never thought of answering her.

"Where is Gilbertine?" demanded Sinclair, thrusting his hand out as if to put her aside.

She drew herself up with sudden dignity.

"In bed," she replied. "It was she who told me that somebody had shrieked. I didn't wake."

Sinclair uttered a sigh of the greatest relief that ever burst from a man's overcharged breast.

"Tell her we will find out what it means," he answered kindly, drawing me rapidly away.

By this time Mr. and Mrs. Armstrong were aroused, and I could hear the slow and hesitating tones of the former in the passage behind us.

"Let us hasten," whispered Sinclair, "Our eyes must be the first to see what lies behind that partly-opened door."

I shivered. The door he had designated was Dorothy's.

Sinclair reached it first and pushed it open. Pressing up behind him, I cast a fearful look over his shoulder. Only emptiness confronted us. Dorothy was not in the little chamber. With an impulsive gesture Sinclair pointed to the bed—it had not been lain in—then to the gas—it was still burning. The communicating-room, in which Mrs. Lansing slept, was also lighted, but silent as the one in which we stood. This last fact struck us as the most incomprehensible of all. Mrs. Lansing was not the woman to sleep through a disturbance. Where was she, then? And why did we not hear her strident and aggressive tones rising in angry remonstrance at our intrusion? Had she followed her niece from the room? Should we in another minute encounter her ponderous figure in the group of people we could now hear hurrying toward us? I was for retreating and hunting the house over for Dorothy. But Sinclair, with truer instinct, drew me across the threshold of this silent room.

Well was it for us that we entered there together, for I do not know how either of us, weakened as we were by our forebodings and all the alarms of this unprecedented night, could have borne alone the sight that awaited us.

On the bed situated at the right of the doorway lay a form—awful, ghastly, and unspeakably repulsive. The head, which lay high but inert upon the pillow, was surrounded with the grey hairs of age, and the eyes, which seemed to stare into ours, were glassy with reflected light and not with inward intelligence. This glassiness told the tale of the room's grim silence. It was death we looked on, not the death we had anticipated, and for which we were in a measure prepared, but one fully as awful, and having for its victim, not Dorothy Camerden nor even Gilbertine Murray, but the heartless aunt, who had driven them both like slaves, and who now lay facing the reward of her earthly deeds alone.

As a realisation of the awful truth came upon me I stumbled against the bedpost, looking on with almost blind eyes as Sinclair bent over the rapidly whitening face, whose naturally ruddy colour no one had ever before seen disturbed. And I was still standing there when Mr. Armstrong and all the others came pouring in. Nor have I any distinct remembrance of what was said or how I came to be in the antechamber again. All thought, all consciousness even, seemed to forsake me, and I did not really waken to my surroundings till some one near me whispered:

"Apoplexy!"

Then I began to look about me and peer into the faces crowding up on every side for the only one which could give me back my self-possession. But though there were many girlish countenances to be seen in the awestruck groups huddled in every corner, I beheld no Dorothy, and was therefore but little astonished when in another moment I heard the cry go up:

"Where is Dorothy? Where was she when her aunt died?"

Alas! there was no one there to answer, and the looks of those about, which hitherto had expressed little save awe and fright, turned to wonder, and more than one person left the room as if to look for her. I did not join them. I was rooted to the place. Nor did Sinclair stir a foot, though his eye, which had been wandering restlessly over the faces about him, now settled inquiringly on the doorway. For whom was he looking? Gilbertine or Dorothy? Gilbertine, no doubt, for he visibly brightened as her figure presently appeared clad in a négligée, which emphasised her height, and gave to her whole appearance a womanly sobriety unusual to it.

She had evidently been told what had occurred, for she asked no questions, only leaned in still horror against the doorpost, with her eyes fixed on the room within. Sinclair, advancing, held out his arm. She gave no sign of seeing it. Then he spoke. This seemed to rouse her, for she gave him a grateful look, though she did not take his arm.

"There will be no wedding to-morrow," fell from her lips in self-communing murmur.

Only a few minutes had passed since they had started to find Dorothy, but it seemed an age to me. My body remained in the room, but my mind was searching the house for the girl I loved. Where was she hidden? Would she be found huddled but alive in some far-off chamber? Or was another and more dreadful tragedy awaiting us? I wondered that I could not join the search. I wondered that even Gilbertine's presence could keep Sinclair from doing so. Didn't he know what in all probability this missing girl had with her? Didn't he know what I had suffered, was suffering? Ah! what now? She is coming! I can hear them speaking to her. Gilbertine moves from the door, and a young man and woman enter with Dorothy between them.

But what a Dorothy! Years could have made no greater change in her. She looked and she moved like one who is done with life, yet fears the few remaining moments left her. Instinctively we fell back before her; instinctively we followed her with our eyes as, reeling a little at the door, she cast a look of inconceivable shrinking, first at her own bed, then at the group of older people watching her with serious looks from the room beyond. As she did so I noted that she was still clad in her evening dress of grey, and that there was no more colour on cheek or lip than in the neutral tints of her gown.

Was it our consciousness of the relief which Mrs. Lansing's death, horrible as it was, must bring to this unhappy girl, and of the inappropriateness of any display of grief on her part, which caused the silence with which we saw her pass with forced step and dread anticipation into the room where that image of dead virulence awaited her? Impossible to tell. I could not read my own thoughts. How, then, the thoughts of others!

But thoughts, if we had any, all fled when, after one slow turn of her head towards the bed, this trembling young girl gave a choking shriek, and fell, face down, on the floor. Evidently she had not been prepared for the look which made her aunt's still face so horrible. How could she have been? Had it not imprinted itself upon my mind as the one revolting vision of my life? How, then, if this young and tender-hearted girl had been insensible to it! As her form struck the floor Mr. Armstrong rushed forward; I had not the right. But it was not by his arms she was lifted. Sinclair was before him, and it was with a singularly determined look I could not understand, and which made us all fall back, that he raised her and carried her into her own bed, where he laid her gently down. Then, as if not content with this simple attention, he hovered over her for a moment, arranging the pillows and smoothing her dishevelled hair. When at last he left her the women rushed forward.

"Not too many of you," was his final adjuration, as, giving me a look, he slipped out into the hall.

I followed him immediately. He had gained the moon-lighted corridor near his own door, where he stood awaiting me with something in his hand. As I approached, he drew me to the window and showed me what it was. It was the amethyst box, open and empty, and beside it, shining with a yellow instead of a purple light, the little vial void of the one drop which used to sparkle within it.

"I found the vial in the bed with the old woman," said he. "The box I saw glittering among Dorothy's locks before she fell. That was why I lifted her."

V

THREE O'CLOCK IN THE MORNING

As he spoke, youth with its brilliant hopes, illusions, and beliefs, passed from me, never to return in the same measure again. I stared at the glimmering amethyst, I stared at the empty vial, and, as a full realisation of all his words implied seized my benumbed faculties, I felt the icy chill of some grisly horror moving among the roots of my hair, lifting it on my forehead and filling my whole being with shrinking and dismay.

Sinclair, with a quick movement, replaced the tiny flask in its old receptacle, and then, thrusting the whole out of sight, seized my hand and wrung it.

"I am your friend," he whispered. "Remember, under all circumstances and in every exigency, your friend."

"What are you going to do with those?" I demanded, when I regained control of my speech.

"I do not know."

"What are you going to do with—with Dorothy?"

He drooped his head; I could see his fingers working in the moonlight.

"The physicians will soon be here. I heard the telephone going a few minutes ago. When they have pronounced the old woman dead we will give the—the lady you mention an opportunity to explain herself."

Explain herself, she! Simple expectation. Unconsciously I shook my head.

"It is the least we can do," he gently persisted. "Come, we must not be seen with our heads together—not yet. I am sorry that we two were found more or less dressed at the time of the alarm. It may cause comment."

"She was dressed, too," I murmured, as much to myself as to him.

"Unfortunately, yes," was the muttered reply, with which he drew off and hastened into the hall, where the now thoroughly-aroused household stood in a great group about the excited hostess.

Mrs. Armstrong was not the woman for an emergency. With streaming hair and tightly-clutched kimono, she was gesticulating wildly and bemoaning the break in the festivities which this event must necessarily cause. As Sinclair approached, she turned her tirade on him, and as all stood still to listen and add such words of sympathy or disappointment as suggested themselves in the excitement of the moment, I had an opportunity to note that neither of the two girls most interested was within sight. This troubled me. Drawing up to the outside of the circle, I asked Beaton, who was nearest to me, if he knew how Miss Camerden was.

"Better, I hear. Poor girl! it was a great shock to her."

I ventured nothing more. The conventionality of his tone was not to be mistaken. Our conversation on the veranda was to be ignored. I did not know whether to feel relief at this or an added distress. I was in a whirl of emotion which robbed me of all discrimination. As I realised my own condition, I concluded that my wisest move would be to withdraw myself for a time from every eye. Accordingly, and at the risk of offending more than one pretty girl who still had something to say concerning this terrible mischance, I slid away to my room, happy to escape the murmurs and snatches of talk rising on every side. One bitter speech, uttered by I do not know whom, rang in my ears and made all thinking unendurable. It was this:

"Poor woman! she was angry once too often. I heard her scolding Dorothy again after she went to her room. That is why Dorothy is so overcome. She says it was the violence of her aunt's rage which killed her—a rage of which she unfortunately was the cause."

So there were words again between these two after the door closed upon them for the night! Was this what we heard just before that scream went up? It would seem so. Thereupon, quite against my will, I found myself thinking of Dorothy's changed position before the world. Only yesterday a dependent slave; to-day, the owner of millions. Gilbertine would have her share—a large one—but there was enough to make them both wealthy. Intolerable thought! Would that no money had been involved! I hated to think of those diamonds and—

Oh, anything was better than this! Dashing from my room, I joined one of the groups into which the single large circle had now broken up. The house had been lighted from end to end, and some effort had been made at a more respectable appearance by such persons as I now saw; some even were fully dressed. All were engaged in discussing the one great topic. Listening and not listening, I waited for the front-door bell to ring. It sounded while one woman was saying to another:

"The Sinclairs will now be able to take their honeymoon in their own yacht."

I made my way to where I could watch Sinclair while the physicians were in the room. I thought his face looked very noble. The narrowness of his own escape, the sympathy for me which the event, so much worse than either of us anticipated, had wakened in his generous breast, had called out all that was best in his naturally reserved and not-always-to-be-understood nature. A tower of strength he was to me at that hour. I knew that mercy, and mercy only, would influence his conduct. He would be guilty of no rash or inconsiderate act. He would give this young girl a chance.

Therefore, when the physicians had pronounced the case one of apoplexy (a conclusion most natural under the circumstances), and the excitement which had held together the various groups of uneasy guests had begun to subside, it was with perfect confidence I saw him approach and address Gilbertine. She was standing fully dressed at the stair-head, where she had stopped to hold some conversation with the retiring physicians; and the look she gave him in return, and the way she moved off in obedience to his command or suggestion, assured me that he was laying plans for an interview with Dorothy. Consequently, I was quite ready to obey him when he finally stepped up to me and said:

"Go below, and if you find the library empty, as I have no doubt you will, light one gas jet, and see that the door to the conservatory is unlocked. I require a place in which to make Gilbertine comfortable while I have some words with her cousin."

"But how will you be able to influence Miss Camerden to come down?" Somehow, the familiar name of Dorothy would not pass my lips. "Do you think she will recognise your right to summon her to an interview?"

"Yes."

I had never seen his lip take that firm line before, yet I had always known him to be a man of great resolution.

"But how can you reach her? She is shut up in her own room, under the care, I am told, of Mrs. Armstrong's maid."

"I know; but she will escape that dreadful place as soon as her feet will carry her. I shall wait in the hall till I see her come out; then I will urge her to follow me, and she will do so, attended by Gilbertine."

"And I? Do you mean me to be present at an interview so painful—nay, so serious and so threatening? It would cut short every word you hope to hear. I—cannot—"

"I have not asked you to. It is imperative that I should see Miss Camerden alone." (He could not call her Dorothy, either.) "I shall ask Gilbertine to accompany us, so that appearances may be preserved. I want you to be able to inform any one who approaches the door that you saw me go in there with Miss Murray."

"Then I am to stay in the hall?"

"If you will be so kind."

The clock struck three.

"It is very late," I exclaimed. "Why not wait till morning?"

"And have the whole house about our ears? No. Besides, some things will not keep an hour, a moment. I must hear what this young girl has to say in response to my questions. Remember, I am the owner of the flask whose contents killed the old woman!"

"You believe she died from swallowing that drop?"

"Absolutely."

I said no more, but hastened downstairs to do his bidding.

I found the lower hall partly lighted, but none of the rooms.

Entering the library, I lit the gas as Sinclair had requested. Then I tried the conservatory door. It was unlocked. Casting a sharp glance around, I made sure that the lounges were all unoccupied, and that I could safely leave Sinclair to hold his contemplated interview without fear of interruption. Then, dreading a premature arrival on his part, I slid quickly out, and moved down the hall to where the light of the one burning jet failed to penetrate. "I will watch from here," thought I, and entered upon the quick pacing of the floor which my impatience and the overwrought condition of my nerves demanded.

But before I had turned on my steps more than half a dozen times, a brilliant ray coming from some half-open door in the rear caught my eye, and I stepped back to see if any one was sharing my watch. In doing so I came upon the little spiral staircase which, earlier in the evening, Sinclair had heard creak under some unknown footstep. Had this footstep been Dorothy's, and if so, what had brought her into this remote portion of the house? Fear? Anguish? Remorse? A flying from herself or from it? I wished I knew just where she had been found by the two young persons who had brought her back into her aunt's room. No one had volunteered the information, and I had not seen the moment when I felt myself in a position to demand it.

Proceeding further, I stood amazed at my own forgetfulness. The light which had attracted my attention came from the room devoted to the display of Miss Murray's wedding-gifts. This I should have known instantly, having had a hand in their arrangement. But all my faculties were dulled that night, save such as responded to dread and horror. Before going back I paused to look at the detective whose business it was to guard the room. He was sitting very quietly at his post, and if he saw me he did not look up. Strange that I had forgotten this man when keeping my own vigil above. I doubted if Sinclair had remembered him either. Yet he must have been unconsciously sharing our watch from start to finish— must even have heard the cry as only a waking man could hear it. Should I ask him if this was so? No. Perhaps I had not the courage to hear his answer.

Shortly after my return into the main hall I heard steps on the grand staircase. Looking up, I saw the two girls descending, followed by Sinclair. He had been successful, then, in inducing Dorothy to come down. What would be the result? Could I stand the suspense of the impending interview?

As they stepped within the rays of the solitary gas jet already mentioned, I cast one quick look into Gilbertine's face, then a long one into Dorothy's. I could read neither. If it was horror and horror only which rendered both so pale and fixed of feature, then their emotion was similar in character and intensity. But if in either breast the one dominant sentiment was fear—horrible, blood-curdling fear— then was that fear confined to Dorothy; for while Gilbertine advanced bravely, Dorothy's steps lagged, and at the point where she should have turned into the library, she whirled sharply about, and made as if she would fly back upstairs.

But one stare from Gilbertine, one word from Sinclair, recalled her to herself, and she passed in, and the door closed upon the three. I was left to prevent possible intrusion, and to eat out my heart in intolerable suspense.

VI

DOROTHY SPEAKS

I shall not subject you to the ordeal from which I suffered. You shall follow my three friends into the room. According to Sinclair's description, the interview proceeded thus:

As soon as the door had closed upon them, and before either of the girls had a chance to speak, he remarked to Gilbertine:

"I have brought you here because I wish to express to you, in the presence of your cousin, my sympathy for the bereavement which in an instant has robbed you both of a lifelong guardian. I also wish to say, in the light of this sad event, that I am ready, if propriety so exacts, to postpone the ceremony which I hoped would unite our lives to-day. Your wish shall be my wish, Gilbertine; though I would suggest that possibly you never more needed the sympathy and protection which only a husband can give than you do to-day."

He told me afterward that he was so taken up with the effect of this suggestion on Gilbertine that he forgot to look at Dorothy, though the hint he strove to convey of impending trouble was meant as much for her as for his affianced bride. In another moment he regretted this, especially when he saw that Dorothy had changed her attitude, and was now looking away from them both.

"What do you say, Gilbertine?" he asked earnestly, as she sat flushing and paling before him.

"Nothing. I have not thought—it is a question for others to decide—others who know what is right better than I. I appreciate your consideration," she suddenly burst out, "and should be glad to tell you at this moment what to expect. But—give me a little time—let me see you later—in the morning, Mr. Sinclair, after we are all somewhat rested, and when I can see you quite alone."

Dorothy rose.

"Shall I go?" she asked.

Sinclair advanced, and with quiet protest touched her on the shoulder. Quietly she sank back into her seat.

"I want to say a half-dozen words to you, Miss Camerden. Gilbertine will pardon us; it is about matters which must be settled to-night. There are decisions to arrive at and arrangements to be made. Mrs. Armstrong has instructed me to question you in regard to these, as the one best acquainted with Mrs. Lansing's affairs and general tastes. We will not trouble Gilbertine. She has her own decisions to reach. Dear, will you let me make you comfortable in the conservatory while I talk for five minutes with Dorothy?"

He said she met this question with a look so blank and uncomprehending that he just lifted her and carried her in among the palms.

"I must speak to Dorothy," he pleaded, placing her in the chair where he had often seen her sit of her own accord. "Be a good girl; I will not keep you here long."

"But why cannot I go to my room? I do not understand—I am frightened—what have you to say to Dorothy you cannot say to me?"

She seemed so excited that for a minute, just a minute, he faltered in his purpose. Then he took her gravely by the hand.

"I have told you," said he. Then he kissed her softly on the forehead. "Be quiet, dear, and rest. See, here are roses!"

He plucked and flung a handful into her lap. Then he crossed back to the library and shut the conservatory door behind him. I am not surprised that Gilbertine wondered at her peremptory bridegroom.

When Sinclair re-entered the library, he found Dorothy standing with her hand on the knob of the door leading into the hall. Her head was bent thoughtfully forward, as though she were inwardly debating whether to stand her ground or fly. Sinclair gave her no further opportunity for hesitation. Advancing rapidly, he laid his hand gently on hers, and with a gravity which must have impressed her, quietly remarked:

"I must ask you to stay and hear what I have to say. I wished to spare Gilbertine; would that I could spare you! But circumstances forbid. You know and I know that your aunt did not die of apoplexy."

She gave a violent start, and her lips parted. If the hand under his clasp had been cold, it was now icy. He let his own slip from the contact.

"You know!" she echoed, trembling and pallid, her released hand flying instinctively to her hair.

"Yes; you need not feel about for the little box. I took it from its hiding-place when I laid you fainting on the bed. Here it is."

He drew it from his pocket and showed it to her. She hardly glanced at it; her eyes were fixed in terror on his face, and her lips seemed to be trying in vain to formulate some inquiry.

He tried to be merciful.

"I missed it many hours ago from the shelf yonder where you all saw me place it. Had I known that you had taken it, I would have repeated to you how deadly were the contents, and how dangerous it was to handle the vial or to let others handle it, much less to put it to the lips."

She started, and instinctively her form rose to its full height.

"Have you looked in that little box since you took it from my hair?" she asked.

"Yes."

"Then you know it to be empty?"

For answer he pressed the spring, and the little lid flew open.

"It is not empty now, you see." Then more slowly and with infinite meaning: "But the little flask is."

She brought her hands together and faced him with a noble dignity which at once put the interview on a different footing.

"Where was this vial found?" she demanded.

He found it difficult to answer. They seemed to have exchanged positions. When he did speak it was in a low tone, and with less confidence than he had shown before.

"In the bed with the old lady. I saw it there myself. Mr. Worthington was with me. Nobody else knows anything about it. I wish to give you an opportunity to explain. I begin to think you can—but how, God only knows. The box was hidden in your hair from early evening. I saw your hand continually fluttering toward it all the time we were dancing in the parlour."

She did not lose an iota of her dignity or pride.

"You are right," she said. "I put it there as soon as I took it from the cabinet. I could think of no safer hiding-place. Yes, I took it," she acknowledged, as she saw the flush rise to his cheek. "I took it; but with no worse motive than the dishonest one of having for my own an object which bewitched me. I was hardly myself when I snatched it from the shelf and thrust it into my hair."

He stared at her in amazement, her confession and her attitude so completely contradicted each other.

"But I had nothing to do with the vial," she went on. And with this declaration her whole manner, even her voice changed, as if with the utterance of these few words she had satisfied some inner demand of self-respect, and could now enter into the sufferings of those about her. "This I think it right to make plain to you. I supposed the vial to be in the box when I took it, but when I got to my room and had an opportunity to examine the deadly trinket, I found it empty, just as you found it when you took it from my hair. Some one had taken the vial out before my hand had ever touched the box."

Like a man who feels himself suddenly seized by the throat, yet who struggles for the life slowly but inexorably leaving him, Sinclair cast one heart-rending look toward the conservatory, then heavily demanded:

"Why were you out of your room? Why did they have to look for you? And who was the person who uttered that scream?"

She confronted him sadly, but with an earnestness he could not but respect.

"I was not in the room because I was troubled by my discovery. I think I had some idea of returning the box to the shelf from which I had taken it. At all events, I found myself on the little staircase in the rear when that cry rang through the house. I do not know who uttered it; I only know that it did not spring from my lips."

In a rush of renewed hope he seized her by the hand.

"It was your aunt!" he whispered. "It was she who took the vial out of the box; who put it to her own lips; who shrieked when she felt her vitals gripped. Had you stayed you would have known this. Can't you say so? Don't you think so? Why do you look at me with those incredulous eyes?"

"Because you must not believe a lie. Because you are too good a man to be sacrificed. It was a younger throat than my aunt's which gave utterance to that shriek. Mr. Sinclair, be advised; do not be married to-morrow!"

Meanwhile I was pacing the hall without in a delirium of suspense. I tried hard to keep within the bounds of silence. I had turned for the fiftieth time to face that library door, when suddenly I heard a hoarse cry break from within, and saw the door fly open and Dorothy come hurrying out. She shrank when she saw me, but seemed grateful that I did not attempt to stop her, and soon was up the stairs and out of sight. I rushed at once into the library.

I found Sinclair sitting before a table with his head buried in his hands. In an instant I knew that our positions were again reversed, and, without stopping to give heed to my own sensations, I approached him as near as I dared and laid my hand on his shoulder.

He shuddered, but did not look up, and it was minutes before he spoke. Then it all came in a rush.

"Fool! fool that I was! And I saw that she was consumed by fright the moment it became plain that I was intent upon having some conversation with Dorothy. Her fingers where they gripped my arm must have left marks behind them. But I saw only womanly nervousness when a man less blind would have detected guilt. Walter, I wish that the mere scent of this empty flask would kill. Then I should not have to re-enter that conservatory door—or look again in her face, or—"

He had taken out the cursed jewel and was fingering it in a nervous way which went to my heart of hearts. Gently removing it from his hand, I asked with all the calmness possible:

"What is all this mystery? Why have your suspicions returned to Gilbertine? I thought you had entirely dissociated her with this matter, and that you blamed Dorothy, and Dorothy only, for the amethyst's loss?"

"Dorothy had the empty box; but the vial! the vial!—that had been taken by a previous hand. Do you remember the white silk train which Mr. Armstrong saw slipping from this room? I cannot talk, Walter; my duty leads me there."

He pointed towards the conservatory. I drew back and asked if I should take up my watch again outside the door.

He shook his head.

"It makes no difference; nothing makes any difference. But if you want to please me, stay here."

I at once sank into a chair. He made a great effort and advanced to the conservatory door. I studiously looked another way; my heart was breaking with sympathy for him.

But in another instant I was on my feet. I could hear him rushing about among the palms. Presently I heard his voice shout out the wild cry:

"She is gone! I forgot the other door communicating with the hall."

I crossed the floor and entered where he stood gazing down at an empty seat and a trail of scattered roses. Never shall I forget his face. The dimness of the spot could not hide his deep, unspeakable emotions. To him this flight bore but one interpretation—guilt.

I did not advocate Sinclair's pressing the matter further that night. I saw that he was exhausted, and that any further movement would tax him beyond his strength. We therefore separated immediately after leaving the library, and I found my way to my own room alone. It may seem callous in me, but I fell asleep very soon after, and did not wake till roused by a knock at my door. On opening it I confronted Sinclair, looking haggard and unkempt. As he entered, the first clear notes of the breakfast-call could be heard rising from the lower hall.

"I have not slept," he said. "I have been walking the hall all night, listening by spells at her door, and at other times giving what counsel I could to the Armstrongs. God forgive me, but I have said nothing to any one of what has made this affair an awful tragedy to me! Do you think I did wrong? I waited to give Dorothy a chance. Why should I not show the same consideration to Gilbertine?"

"You should." But our eyes did not meet, and neither voice expressed the least hope.

"I shall not go to breakfast," he now declared. "I have written this line to Gilbertine. Will you see that she gets it?"

For reply I held out my hand. He placed the note in it, and I was touched to see that it was unsealed.

"Be sure, when you give it to her, that she will have an opportunity of reading it alone. I shall request the use of one of the little reception-rooms this morning. Let her come there if she is so impelled. She will find a friend as well as a judge."

I endeavoured to express sympathy, urge patience, and suggest hope. But he had no ear for words, though he tried to listen, poor fellow! so I soon stopped, and he presently left the room. I immediately made myself as presentable as a night of unprecedented emotions would allow, and went below to do him such service as opportunity offered and the exigencies of the case permitted.

I found the lower hall alive with eager guests and a few outsiders. News of the sad event was slowly making its way through the avenue, and some of the Armstrongs' nearest neighbours had left their breakfast-tables to express their interest and to hear the particulars. Among these stood the lady of the house; but Mr. Armstrong was nowhere within sight. For him the breakfast waited. Not wishing to be caught in any little swirl of conventional comment, I remained near the staircase waiting for some one to descend who could give me news concerning Miss Murray. For I had small expectation of her braving the eyes of these strangers, and doubted if even Dorothy would be seen at the breakfast-table. But little Miss Lane, if small, was gifted with a great appetite. She would be sure to appear prior to the last summons, and as we were good friends, she would listen to my questions and give me the answer I needed for the carrying out of Sinclair's wishes. But before her light footfall was heard descending I was lured from my plans by an unexpected series of events. Three men came down, one after the other, followed by Mr. Armstrong, looking even more grave and ponderous than usual. Two of them were the physicians who had been called in the night, and whom I myself had seen depart somewhere near three o'clock. The third I did not know, but he looked like a doctor also. Why were they here again so early? Had anything new come to light?

It was a question which seemed to strike others as well as myself. As Mr. Armstrong ushered them down the hall and out of the front-door many were the curious glances which followed them, and it was with difficulty that the courteous host on his return escaped the questions and detaining hands of some of his inquisitive guests. A pleasant word, an amiable smile, he had for all; but I was quite certain, when I saw him disappear into the little room he retained for his own use, that he had told them nothing which could in any way relieve their curiosity.

This filled me with a vague alarm. Something must have occurred—something which Sinclair ought to know. I felt a great anxiety, and was closely watching the door behind which Mr. Armstrong had vanished when it suddenly opened, and I perceived that he had been writing a telegram. As he gave it to one of the servants he made a gesture to the man standing with extended hand by the Chinese gong, and the summons rang out for breakfast. Instantly the hum of voices ceased, and young and old turned toward the dining-room, but the host did not enter with them. Before the younger and more active of his guests could reach his side he had slid into the room which I have before described as set apart for the display of Gilbertine's wedding-presents. Instantly I lost all inclination for breakfast, and lingered about in the hall until every one had passed me, even little Miss Lane, who had come down unperceived while I was watching Mr. Armstrong's door. Not very well pleased with myself for having missed the one opportunity which might have been of service to me, I was asking myself whether I should follow her, and make the best attempt I could at sociability, if not at eating, when Mr. Armstrong approached from the side hall, and, accosting me, inquired if Mr. Sinclair had come down yet.

I assured him that I had not seen him, and did not think he meant to come to breakfast, adding that he had been very much affected by the affairs of the night, and had told me that he was going to shut himself up in his room and rest.

"I am sorry, but there is a question I must ask him immediately. It is about a little Italian trinket which I am told he displayed to the ladies yesterday afternoon."

VII

CONSTRAINT

So our dreadful secret was not confined to ourselves, as we had supposed, but was shared, or at least suspected, by our host.

Thankful that it was I, rather than Sinclair, who was called upon to meet and sustain this shock, I answered with what calmness I could:

"Yes; Sinclair mentioned the matter to me. Indeed, if you have any curiosity on the subject, I think I can enlighten you as fully as he can."

Mr. Armstrong glanced up the stairs, hesitated, then drew me into his private room.

"I find myself in a very uncomfortable position," he began. "A strange and quite unaccountable change has shown itself in the appearance of Mrs. Lansing's body during the last few hours—a change which baffles the physicians and raises in their minds very unfortunate conjectures. What I want to know is whether Mr. Sinclair still has in his possession the box which is said to hold a vial of deadly poison, or whether it has passed into any other hand since he showed it to certain ladies in the library."

We were standing directly in the light of an eastern window. Deception was impossible, even if I had felt like employing it. In Sinclair's interests, if not in my own, I resolved to be as true to our host as our positions demanded, yet, at the same time, to save Gilbertine as much as possible from premature, if not final suspicion.

I therefore replied: "That is a question I can answer as well as Sinclair." (Happy was I to save him this cross-examination.) "While he was showing this toy, Mrs. Armstrong came into the room and proposed a stroll, which drew all of the ladies from the room and called for his attendance as well. With no thought of the danger involved, he placed the trinket on a high shelf in the cabinet, and went out with the rest. When he came back for it, it was gone."

The usually ruddy aspect of my host's face deepened, and he sat down in the great armchair which did duty before his writing-table.

"This is dreadful!" was his comment; "entailing I do not know what unfortunate consequences upon this household and on the unhappy girl—"

"Girl?" I repeated.

He turned upon me with great gravity. "Mr. Worthington, I am sorry to have to admit it, but something strange, something not easily explainable, took place in this house last night. It has only just come to light, otherwise the doctors' conclusions might have been different. You know there is a detective in the house. The presents are valuable, and I thought best to have a man here to look after them."

I nodded; I had no breath for speech.

"This man tells me," continued Mr. Armstrong, "that just a few minutes previous to the time the whole household was aroused last night he heard a step in the hall overhead, then the sound of a light foot descending the little staircase in the servants' hall. Being anxious to find out what this person wanted at an hour so late, he lowered the gas, closed his door, and listened. The steps went by his door. Satisfied that it was a woman he heard, he pulled open the door again and looked out. A young girl was standing not very far from him in a thin streak of moonlight. She was gazing intently at something in her hand, and that something had a purple gleam to it. He is ready to swear to this. Next moment, frightened by some noise she heard, she fled back, and vanished again in the region of the little staircase. It was soon, very soon, after this that the shriek came. Now, Mr. Worthington, what am I to do with this knowledge? I have advised this man to hold his peace till I can make inquiries, but where am I to make them? I cannot think that Miss Camerden—"

The ejaculation which escaped me was involuntary. To hear her name for the second time in this association was more than I could bear.

"Did he say it was Miss Camerden?" I hurriedly inquired, as he looked at me in some surprise. "How should he know Miss Camerden?"

"He described her," was the unanswerable reply. "Besides, we know that she was circulating in the halls at that time. I declare I have never known a worse business," this amiable man bemoaned. "Let me send for Sinclair; he is more interested than any one else in Gilbertine's relatives; or, stay, what if I should send for Miss Camerden herself? She should be able to tell how she came by this box."

I subdued my own instincts, which were all for clearing Dorothy on the spot, and answered as I thought Sinclair would like me to answer.

"It is a serious and very perplexing piece of business," said I; "but if you will wait a short time I do not think you will have to trouble Miss Camerden. I am sure that explanations will be given. Give the lady a chance," I stammered. "Imagine what her feelings would be if questioned on so delicate a topic. It would make a breach which nothing could heal. Later, if she does not speak, it will be only right for you to ask her why."

"She did not come down this morning."

"Naturally not."

"If I could take counsel of my wife! But she is of too nervous a temperament. I am anxious to keep her from knowing this fresh complication as long as possible. Do you think I can look for Miss Camerden to explain herself before the doctors return, or before Mrs. Lansing's physician, for whom I have telegraphed, can arrive from New York?"

"I am sure that three hours will not pass before you hear the truth. Leave me to work out the situation. I promise that if I cannot bring it about to your satisfaction, Sinclair shall be asked to lend his assistance. Only keep the gossips from Miss Camerden's good name. Words can be said in a moment that will not be forgotten in years. I tremble at such a prospect for her."

"No one knows of her having been seen with the box," he protested; and, relieved as much by his manner as by his words, I took my leave of him, and made my way at once to the dining-room. Should I find Miss Lane there? Yes, and what was better still, the fortunes of the day had decreed that the place beside her should be unoccupied.

I was on my way to that place when I was struck by the extreme quiet into which the room had fallen. It had been humming with talk when I first entered, but now not a voice was raised and scarcely an eye. In the hurried glance I cast about the board, not a look met mine in recognition or welcome.

What did it mean? Had they been talking about me? Possibly; and in a way, it would seem, that was not altogether flattering to my vanity.

Unable to hide my sense of the general embarrassment which my presence had called forth, I passed to the seat I have indicated, and let my inquiring look settle on Miss Lane. She was staring, in imitation of the others, straight into her plate; but as I saluted her with a quiet "Good-morning," she looked up and acknowledged my courtesy with a faint, almost sympathetic, smile. At once the whole tableful broke again into chatter, and I could safely put the question with which my mind was full.

"How is Miss Murray?" I asked. "I do not see her here."

"Did you expect to? Poor Gilbertine! This is not the bridal-day she expected." Then, with irresistible naïveté, entirely in keeping with her fairy-like figure and girlish face, she added: "I think it was just horrid in the old woman to die the night before the wedding, don't you?"

"Indeed I do," I emphatically rejoined, humouring her in the hope of learning what I wished to know. "Does Miss Murray still cherish the expectation of being married to-day? No one seems to know."

"Nor do I. I haven't seen her since the middle of the night. She didn't come back to her room. They say she is sobbing out her terror and disappointment in some attic corner. Think of that for Gilbertine Murray! But even that is better than—"

The sentence trailed away into an indistinguishable murmur, the murmur into silence. Was it because of a fresh lull in the conversation about us? I hardly think so, for though the talk was presently resumed, she remained silent, not even giving the least sign of wishing to prolong this particular topic. I finished my coffee as soon as possible and quitted the room, but not before many had preceded me. The hall was consequently as full as before of a gossiping crowd.

I was on the point of bowing myself through the various groups blocking my way to the library door, when I noticed renewed signs of embarrassment on all the faces turned my way. Women who were clustered about the newel-post drew back, and some others sauntered away into side-rooms with an appearance of suddenly wishing to go somewhere. This certainly was very singular, especially as these marks of disapproval did not seem to be directed so much at myself as at some one behind me. Who could this some one be? Turning quickly, I cast a glance up the staircase, before which I stood, and saw the figure of a young girl dressed in black hesitating on the landing. This young girl was Dorothy Camerden, and it took but a moment's contemplation of the scene for me to feel assured that it was against her this feeling of universal constraint had been directed.

VIII

GILBERTINE SPEAKS

Knowing my darling's innocence, I felt the insult shown her in my heart of hearts, and might in the heat of the moment have been betrayed into an unwise utterance of my indignation, if at that moment I had not encountered the eye of Mr. Armstrong fixed on me from the rear hall. In the mingled surprise and distress he displayed, I saw that it was not from any indiscretion of his that this feeling against her had started. He had not betrayed the trust I had placed in him, yet the murmur had gone about which virtually ostracised her, and instead of confronting the eager looks of friends, she found herself met by averted glances and coldly turned backs, and soon by an almost empty hall.

She flushed as she realised the effect of her presence, and cast me an agonised look which, without her expectation, perhaps, roused every instinct of chivalry within me. Advancing, I met her at the foot of the stairs, and with one quick word seemed to restore her to herself.

"Be patient!" I whispered. "To-morrow they will all be around you again. Perhaps sooner. Go into the conservatory and wait."

She gave me a grateful pressure of the hand, while I bounded upstairs, determined that nothing should stop me from finding Gilbertine, and giving her the letter with which Sinclair had entrusted me.

But this was more easily planned than accomplished. When I had reached the third floor (an unaccustomed and strange spot for me to find myself in) I at first found no one who could tell me to which room Miss Murray had retired. Then, when I did come across a stray housemaid, and she, with an extraordinary stare, had pointed out the door, I found it quite impossible to gain any response from within, though I could hear a quick step moving restlessly to and fro, and now and then catch the sound of a smothered sob or low cry. The wretched girl would not heed me, though I told her who I was, and that I had a letter from Mr. Sinclair in my hand. Indeed, she presently became perfectly quiet, and let me knock again and again, till the situation became ridiculous, and I felt obliged to draw off.

Not that I thought of yielding. No, I would stay there till her own fancy drove her to open the door, or till Mr. Armstrong should come up and force it. A woman upon whom so many interests depended would not be allowed to remain shut up the whole morning. Her position as a possible bride forbade it. Guilty or innocent, she must show herself before long. As if in answer to my expectation, a figure appeared at this very moment at the other end of the hall. It was Dutton, the butler, and in his hand he held a telegram. He seemed astonished to see me there, but passed me with a simple bow, and stopped before the door I had so unavailingly assailed a few minutes before.

"A telegram, miss," he shouted, as no answer was made to his knock. "Mr. Armstrong asked me to bring it to you. It is from the Bishop, and calls for an immediate reply."

There was a stir within, but the door did not open. Meanwhile, I had sealed and thrust forth the letter I had held concealed in my breast pocket.

"Give her this, too," I signified, and pointed to the crack under the door.

He took the letter, laid the telegram on it, and pushed them both in. Then he stood up, and eyed the unresponsive panels with the set look of a man who does not easily yield his purpose.

"I will wait for the answer!" he shouted through the keyhole, and, falling back, he took up his stand against the opposite wall.

I could not keep him company there. Withdrawing into a big dormer window, I waited with beating heart to see if her door would open. Apparently not; yet as I still lingered I heard the lock turn, followed by the sound of a measured but hurried step. Dashing from my retreat, I reached the main hall in time to see Miss Murray disappear toward the staircase. This was well, and I was about to follow, when, to my astonishment, I perceived Dutton standing in the doorway she had just left, staring down at the floor with a puzzled look.

"She didn't pick up the letters!" he cried in amazement. "She just walked over them. What shall I do now? It's the strangest thing I ever saw!"

"Take them to the little boudoir over the porch," I suggested. "Mr. Sinclair is there, and if she is not on her way to join him now, she certainly will be soon."

Without a word Dutton caught up the letters and made for the stairs.

Left to await the result, I found myself so worked upon that I wondered how much longer I should be able to endure these shifts of feeling and constantly recurring moments of extreme suspense. To escape the torture of my own thoughts, or, possibly, to get some idea of how Dorothy was sustaining an ordeal which was fast destroying my own self-possession, I prepared to go downstairs. What was my astonishment, in passing the little boudoir on the second floor, to find its door ajar and the place empty. Either the interview between Sinclair and Gilbertine had been very much curtailed, or it had not yet taken place. With a heart heavy with forebodings I no longer sought to analyse, I made my way down, and reached the lower step of the great staircase just as a half-dozen girls, rushing from different quarters of the hall, surrounded the heavy form of Mr. Armstrong coming from his own little room.

Their questions made a small hubbub. With a good-natured gesture he put them all back, and, raising his voice, said to the assembled crowd:

"It has been decided by Miss Murray that, under the circumstances, it will be wiser for her to postpone the celebration of her marriage to some time and place less fraught with mournful suggestions. A telegram has just been sent to the Bishop to that effect, and while we all suffer from this disappointment, I am sure there is no one here who will not see the propriety of her decision."

As he finished, Gilbertine appeared behind him. At the same moment I caught, or thought I did, the flash of Sinclair's eye from the recesses of the room beyond; but I could not stop to make sure of this, for Gilbertine's look and manner were such as to draw my full attention, and it was with a mixture of almost inexplicable emotions that I saw her thread her way among her friends, in a state of high feeling which made her blind to their outstretched hands and deaf to the murmur of interest and sympathy which instinctively followed her. She was making for the stairs, and whatever her thoughts, whatever the state of her mind, she moved superbly, in her pale, yet seemingly radiant abstraction. I watched her, fascinated, yet when she left the last group and began to cross the small square of carpet which alone separated us, I stepped down and aside, feeling that to meet her eye just then without knowing what had passed between her and Sinclair would be cruel to her and well-nigh unbearable to myself.

She saw the movement and seemed to hesitate an instant, then she turned for one brief instant in my direction, and I saw her smile. Great God! it was the smile of innocence. Fleeting as it was, the pride that was in it, the sweet assertion and the joy were unmistakable. I felt like springing to Sinclair's side in the gladness of my relief, but there was no time; another door had opened down the hall, another person had stepped upon the scene, and Miss Murray, as well as myself, recognised by the hush which at once fell upon every one present that something of still more startling import awaited us.

"Mr. Armstrong and ladies!" said this stranger—I knew he was a stranger by the studied formality of the former's bow—"I have made a few inquiries since I came here a short time ago, and I find that there is one young lady in the house who ought to be able to tell me better than any one else under what circumstances Mrs. Lansing breathed her last. I allude to her niece, who slept in the adjoining room. Is that young lady here? Her name, if I remember rightly, is Camerden—Miss Dorothy Camerden."

A movement as of denial passed from group to group down the hall, and, while no one glanced toward the library and some did glance upstairs, I felt the dart of sudden fear—or was it hope—that Dorothy, hearing her name called, would leave the conservatory and proudly confront the speaker in face of this whole suspicious throng. But no Dorothy appeared. On the contrary, it was Gilbertine who turned, and, with an air of authority for which no one was prepared, asked in tones vibrating with feeling:

"Has this gentleman the official right to question who was and who was not with my aunt when she died?"

Mr. Armstrong, who showed his surprise as ingenuously as he did every other emotion, glanced up at the light figure hovering over them from the staircase, and made out to answer:

"This gentleman has every right, Miss Murray. He is the coroner of the town, accustomed to inquire into all cases of sudden death."

"Then," she vehemently rejoined, her pale cheeks breaking out into a scarlet flush, above which her eyes shone with an almost unearthly brilliancy, "do not summon Dorothy Camerden. She is not the witness you want. I am. I am the one who uttered that scream; I am the one who saw our aunt die. Dorothy cannot tell you what took place in her room and at her bedside, for Dorothy was not there; but I can."

Amazed, not as others were, at the assertion itself, but at the manner and publicity of the utterance, I contemplated this surprising girl in ever-increasing wonder. Always beautiful, always spirited and proud, she looked at that moment as if nothing in the shape of fear, or even contumely, could touch her. She faced the astonishment of her best friends with absolute fearlessness, and before the general murmur could break into words, added:

"I feel it my duty to speak thus publicly, because, by keeping silent so long, I have allowed a false impression to go about. Stunned with terror, I found it impossible to speak during that first shock. Besides, I was in a measure to blame for the catastrophe itself, and lacked courage to own it. It was I who took the little crystal flask into my aunt's room. I had been fascinated by it from the first, fascinated enough to long to see it closer, and to hold it in my hand. But I was ashamed of this fascination—ashamed, I mean, to have any one know that I could be moved by such a childish impulse; so, instead of taking the box itself, which might easily be missed, I simply abstracted the tiny vial, and, satisfied with its possession, carried it about till I got to my room. Then, when the house was quiet and my room-mate asleep, I took it out and looked at it, and feeling an irresistible desire to share my amusement with my cousin, I stole to her room by means of the connecting balcony, just as I had done many times before when our aunt was in bed and asleep. But unlike any previous occasion, I found the room empty. Dorothy was not there; but as the light was burning high, I knew she would soon be back, and so ventured to step in.

"Instantly, I heard my aunt's voice. She was awake, and wanted something. She had evidently called before, for her voice was sharp with impatience, and she used some very harsh words. When she heard me in Dorothy's room, she shouted again, and, as I have always been accustomed to obey her commands, I hastened to her side, with the little vial concealed in my hand. As she expected to see Dorothy and not me, she rose up in unreasoning anger, asking where my cousin was, and why I was not in bed. I attempted to answer her, but she would not listen to me, and bade me turn up the gas, which I did.

"Then, with her eyes fixed on mine as though she knew I was trying to conceal something from her, she commanded me to rearrange her hair and make her more comfortable. This I could not do with the tiny flask still in my hand, so with a quick movement, which I hoped would pass unobserved, I slid it behind some bottles standing on a table by the bedside, and bent to do what she required. But to attempt to escape her eyes was useless. She had seen my action, and at once began to feel about for what I had attempted to hide from her. Coming in contact with the tiny flask, she seized it, and, with a smile I shall never forget, held it up between us.

"'What's this?' she cried, showing such astonishment at its minuteness and perfection of shape that it was immediately apparent she had heard nothing of the amethyst box displayed by Mr. Sinclair in the library. 'I never saw a bottle as small as this before. What is in it, and why were you so afraid of my seeing it?'

"As she spoke she attempted to wrench out the stopper. It stuck, so I was in hopes she would fail in the effort, but she was a woman of uncommon strength, and presently it yielded, and I saw the vial open in her hand.

"Aghast with terror, I caught at the table beside me, fearing to drop before her eyes. Instantly her look of curiosity changed to one of suspicion, and repeating, 'What's in it? What's in it?' she raised the flask to her nostrils, and when she found she could make out nothing from the smell, lowered it to her lips, with the intention, I suppose, of determining its contents by tasting them. As I caught sight of this fatal action, and beheld the one drop, which Mr. Sinclair had said was enough to kill a man, slip from its hiding-place of centuries into her open throat, I felt as if the poison had entered my own veins; I could neither speak nor move. But when, an instant later, I met the look which spread suddenly over her face—a look of horror and hatred, accusing horror and unspeakable hatred mingled with what I dimly felt must mean death—an agonised cry burst from my lips, after which, panic-stricken, I flew, as if for life, back by the way I had come, to my own room. This was a great mistake. I should have remained with my aunt and boldly met the results of the tragedy which my folly had brought about. But terror knows no law, and having once yielded to the instinct of concealment, I knew no other course than to continue to maintain an apparent ignorance of what had just occurred. With chattering teeth and an awful numbness at my heart, I tore off my wrapper and slid into bed. Miss Lane had not wakened, but every one else had, and the hall was full of people. This terrified me still more, and for the moment I felt that I could never own the truth and bring down upon myself all this wonder and curiosity. So I allowed a wrong impression of the event to go about, for which act of cowardice I now ask the pardon of every one here, as I have already asked that of Mr. Sinclair and of our kind friend Mr. Armstrong."

She paused, and stood for a moment confronting us all with proud eyes and flaming cheeks, then amid a hubbub which did not seem to affect her in the least, she stepped down, and approaching the man who, she had been told, had a right to her full confidence, she said, loud enough for all who wished to hear her:

"I am ready to give you whatever further information you may require. Shall I step into the drawing-room with you?"

He bowed, and as they disappeared from the great hall the hubbub of voices became tumultuous.

Naturally I should have joined in the universal expressions of surprise and the gossip incident to such an unexpected revelation. But I found myself averse to any kind of talk. Till I could meet Sinclair's eye and discern in it the happy clearing-up of all his doubts, I should not feel free to be my own ordinary and sociable self again. But Sinclair showed every evidence of wishing to keep in the background; and while this was natural enough, so far as people in general were concerned, I thought it odd and very unlike him not to give me an opportunity to express my congratulations at the turn affairs had taken and the frank attitude assumed by Gilbertine. I own I felt much disturbed by this neglect, and as the minutes passed and he failed to appear, I found my satisfaction in her explanations dwindle under the consciousness that they had failed, in some respects, to account for the situation; and before I knew it I was the prey of fresh doubts, which I did my best to smother, not only for the sake of Sinclair, but because I was still too much under the influence of Gilbertine's imposing personality to wish to believe aught but what her burning words conveyed.

She must have spoken the truth, but was it the entire truth? I hated myself for asking the question; hated myself for being more critical with her than I had been with Dorothy, who certainly had not made her own part in this tragedy as clear as one who loved her could wish. Ah, Dorothy! it was time some one told her that Gilbertine had openly vindicated her, and that she could now come forth and face her friends without hesitation and without dread. Was she still in the conservatory? Doubtless. But it would be better, perhaps, for me to make sure.

Approaching the place by the small door connecting it with the hallway in which I stood, I took a hurried look within, and, seeing no one, stepped boldly down between the palms to the little nook where lovers of this quiet spot were accustomed to sit. It was empty, and so was the library beyond. Coming back, I accosted Dutton, whom I found superintending the removal of the potted plants which encumbered the passages, and asked him if he knew where Miss Camerden was? He answered without hesitation that she had stood in the rear hall a little while before, listening to Miss Murray; that she had then gone upstairs by the spiral staircase, leaving word with him that if anybody wanted her she would be found in the small boudoir over the porch.

I thanked him, and was on my way to join her when Mr. Armstrong called me. He must have kept me a half-hour in his room discussing every aspect of the affair and apologising for the necessity which he now felt of bidding farewell to most of his guests, among whom, he was careful to state, he did not include me. Then, when I thought this topic exhausted, he began to talk about his wife, and what this dreadful occurrence was to her, and how he despaired of ever reconciling her to the fact that it had been considered necessary to call in a coroner. Then he spoke of Sinclair, but with some constraint and a more careful choice of words, at which, realising that I was to reap nothing from this interview, only suffer strong and continued irritation at a delay which was costing me the inestimable privilege of being the first to tell Dorothy of her re-establishment in every one's good opinion, I exerted myself for release, and to such good purpose that I presently found myself again in the hall, where the first person I ran against was Sinclair.

He started, and so did I, at this unexpected encounter. Then we stood still, and I stared at him in amazement, for everything about the man was changed, and—inexplicable fact!—in nothing was this change more marked than in his attitude toward myself. Yet he tried to be friendly and meet me on the old footing, and observed as soon as we found ourselves beyond the hearing of others:

"You heard what Gilbertine said. There is no reason for doubting her words. I do not doubt them, and you will show yourself my friend by not doubting them either." Then, with some impetuosity and a gleam in his eye quite foreign to its natural expression, he pursued, with a pitiful effort to speak dispassionately: "Our wedding is postponed—indefinitely. There are reasons why this seemed best to Miss Murray. To you I will say that postponed nuptials seldom culminate in marriage. In fact, I have just released Miss Murray from all obligations to myself."

The stare of utter astonishment I gave him provoked the first and only sneer I have ever seen on his face. What was I to say—what could I say, in response to such a declaration, following so immediately upon his warm assertion of her innocence? Nothing. With that indefinable chill between us, which had come I know not how, I felt tongue-tied.

He saw my embarrassment, possibly my emotion, for he smiled somewhat bitterly, and put a step or so between us before he remarked:

"Miss Murray has my good wishes. Out of respect to her position, I shall show her a friend's attention while we remain in this house. That is all I have to say, Walter. You and I have held our last conversation on this subject."

He was gone before I had sufficiently recovered to realise that in this conversation I had had no part, neither had it contained any explanation of the very facts which had once formed our greatest grounds for doubt—namely, Beaton's dream; the smothered cry uttered behind Sinclair's shoulder when he first made known the deadly qualities of the little vial; and, lastly, the strange desire acknowledged to by both these young ladies, to touch and hold an object calculated rather to repel than to attract the normal feminine heart.

At every previous stage of this ever-shifting drama my instinct had been to set my wits against the facts, and, if I could, puzzle out the mystery. But I felt no such temptation now. My one desire was to act, and that immediately. Dorothy, for all Gilbertine's intimation to the contrary, held in her own breast the key to the enigma. Otherwise she would not have ventured upon the surprising and necessarily unpalatable advice to Sinclair—an advice he seemed to have followed—not to marry Gilbertine Murray at the time proposed. Nothing short of a secret acquaintanceship with facts unknown as yet to the rest of us could have nerved her to such an act.

My one hope, then, of understanding the matter lay with her. To seek her at once in the place where I had been told she awaited me seemed the only course to take. If any real gratitude underlay the look of trust which she had given me at the termination of our last interview, she would reward my confidence by unbosoming herself to me.

I was at the door of the boudoir immediately upon forming this resolution. Finding it ajar, I pushed it softly open, and as softly entered. To my astonishment the place was very dark. Not only had the shades been drawn down, but the shutters had been closed, so that it was with difficulty I detected the slight, black-robed figure which lay face down among the cushions of a lounge. She had evidently not heard my entrance, for she did not move; and, struck by her pathetic attitude, I advanced in a whirl of feeling, which made me forget all conventionalities, and everything else, in fact, but that I loved her, and had the utmost confidence in her power to make me happy. Laying my hand softly on her head, I tenderly whispered:

"Look up, dear. Whatever barrier may have intervened between us has fallen. Look up and hear how I love you."

She thrilled as a woman only thrills when her secret soul is moved, and, rising with a certain grand movement, turned her face upon me, glorious with a feeling that not even the dimness of the room could hide.

Why, then, did my brain whirl and my heart collapse?

It was Gilbertine and not Dorothy who stood before me.

Never had a suspicion crossed my mind of any such explanation of our secret troubles. I had seen as much of one cousin as the other in my visits to Mrs. Lansing's house, but Gilbertine being from the first day of our acquaintance engaged to my friend Sinclair, I naturally did not presume to study her face for any signs of interest in myself, even if my sudden and uncontrollable passion for Dorothy had left me the heart to do so. Yet now, in the light of her unmistakable smile, of her beaming eyes, from which all troublous thoughts seemed to have fled for ever, a thousand recollections forced themselves upon my attention, which not only made me bewail my own blindness, but which served to explain the peculiar attitude always maintained towards me by Dorothy, and many other things which a moment before had seemed fraught with impenetrable mystery.

All this in the twinkling of an eye. Meanwhile, misled by my words, Gilbertine drew back a step, and, with her face still bright with the radiance I have mentioned, murmured in low, but full-toned accents:

"Not just yet; it is too soon. Let me simply enjoy the fact that I am free, and that the courage to win my release came from my own suddenly acquired trust in Mr. Sinclair's goodness. Last night"—and she shuddered—"I saw only another way—a way the horrors of which I hardly realised. But God saved me from so dreadful, yea, so unnecessary a crime, and this morning—"

It was cruel to let her go on—cruel to stand there and allow this ardent, if mistaken, nature to unfold itself so ingenuously, while I, with ear half turned toward the door, listened for the step of her whom I had never so much loved as at that moment, possibly because I had only just come to understand the cause of her seeming vacillations. My instincts were so imperative, my duty and the obligations of my position so unmistakable, that I made a move as Gilbertine reached this point, which caused her first to hesitate, then to stop. How should I fill up this gap of silence? How tell her of the great, the grievous mistake she had made? The task was one to try the courage of stouter souls than mine. But the thought of Dorothy nerved me; perhaps also my real friendship and commiseration for Sinclair.

"Gilbertine," I began, "I will make no pretence of misunderstanding you. The situation is too serious, the honour which you do me too great; only, I am not free to accept that honour. The words which I uttered were meant for your cousin Dorothy. I expected to find her in this room. I have long loved your cousin— in secrecy, I own, but honestly and with every hope of some day making her my wife. I—I—"

There was no need for me to finish. The warm hand turning to ice in my clasp, the wide-open blind-struck eyes, the recoil, the maiden flush rising, deepening, covering cheek and chin and forehead, then fading out again till the whole face was white as marble and seemingly as cold—told me that the blow had gone home, and that Gilbertine Murray, the unequalled beauty, the petted darling of a society ready to recognise every charm she possessed save her ardent nature and great heart, had reached the height of her many miseries, and that it was I who had placed her there.

Overcome with pity, but conscious also of a profound respect, I endeavoured to utter some futile words, which she at once put an end to by an appealing gesture.

"You can say nothing," she began. "I have made an awful mistake, the worst a woman can make, I think." Then, with long pauses, as though her tongue were clogged by shame—perhaps by some deeper if less apparent feeling: "You love Dorothy. Does Dorothy love you?"

My answer was an honest one.

"I have dared to hope so, despite the little opportunity she has given me to express my feelings. She has always held me back, and that very decidedly, or my devotion would have been apparent to everybody."

"Oh, Dorothy!"

Regret, sorrow, infinite tenderness, all were audible in that cry. Indeed, it seemed as if for the moment her thoughts were more taken up with her cousin's unhappiness than with her own.

"How I must have made her suffer! I have been a curse to those who loved me. But I am humbled now, and very rightly."

I began to experience a certain awe of this great nature. There was grandeur even in her contrition, and as I took in the expression of her colourless features, sweet with almost an unearthly sweetness in spite of the anguish consuming her, I suddenly realised what Sinclair's love for her must be. I also as suddenly realised the depth and extent of his suffering. To call such a woman his, to lead her almost to the foot of the altar, and then to see her turn aside and leave him! Surely his lot was an intolerable one, and though the interference I had unconsciously made in his wishes had been involuntary, I felt like cursing myself for not having been more open in my attentions to the girl I really loved.

Gilbertine seemed to divine my thoughts, for, pausing at the door she had unconsciously approached, she stood with the knob in her hand, and, with averted brow, remarked gravely:

"I am going out of your life. Before I do so, however, I should like to say a few words in palliation of my conduct. I have never known a mother. I early fell under my aunt's charge, who, detesting children, sent me away to school, where I was well enough treated, but never loved. I was a plain child, and felt my plainness. This gave an awkwardness to my actions, and as my aunt had caused it to be distinctly understood that her sole intention in sending me to the Academy was to have me educated for a teacher, my position awakened little interest, and few hearts, if any, warmed toward me. Meanwhile, my breast was filled with but one thought, one absorbing wish. I longed to love passionately, and be passionately loved in return. Had I found a mate—but I never did. I was not destined for any such happiness.

"Years passed. I was a woman, but neither my happiness nor my self-confidence had kept pace with my growth. Girls who once passed me with a bare nod now stopped to stare, sometimes to whisper comments behind my back. I did not understand this change, and withdrew more and more into myself and the fairy-land made for me by books. Romance was my life, and I had fallen into the dangerous habit of brooding over the pleasures and excitements which would have been mine had I been born beautiful and wealthy, when my aunt suddenly visited the school, saw me, and at once took me away and placed me in the most fashionable school in New York City. From there I was launched, without any word of motherly counsel, into the gay society you know so well. Almost with my coming out I found the world at my feet, and though my aunt showed me no love, she evinced a certain pride in my success, and cast about to procure for me a great match. Mr. Sinclair was the victim. He visited me, took me to theatres, and eventually proposed. My aunt was in ecstasies. I, who felt helpless before her will, was glad that the husband she had chosen for me was at least a gentleman, and, to all appearances, respectable in his living and nice in his tastes. But he was not the man I had dwelt on in my dreams; and while I accepted him (it was not possible to do anything else, with my aunt controlling every action, if not every thought), I cared so little for Mr. Sinclair himself that I forgot to ask if his many attentions were the result of any real feeling on his part, or only such as he considered due to the woman he expected to make his wife. You see what girls are. How I despise myself now for this miserable frivolity!

"All this time I knew that I was not my aunt's only niece; that Dorothy Camerden, whom I had never met, was as closely related to her as myself. True to her heartless code, my aunt had placed us in separate schools, and not till she found that I was to leave her, and that soon there would be nobody to see that her dresses were bought with discretion, and her person attended to with something like care, did she send for Dorothy. I shall never forget my first impression of her. I had been told that I need not expect much in the way of beauty and style, but from my first glimpse of her dear face I saw that my soul's friend had come, and that, marriage or no marriage, I need never be solitary again.

"I do not think I made as favourable an impression on my cousin as she did on me. Dorothy was new to elaborate dressing and to all the follies of fashionable life, and her look had more of awe than expectation in it. But I gave her a hearty kiss, and in a week she was as brilliantly equipped as myself.

"I loved her, but, from blindness of eye or an overwhelming egotism which God has certainly punished, I did not consider her beautiful. This I must acknowledge to you, if only to complete my humiliation. I never imagined for a moment, even after I became the daily witness of your many attentions to her, that it was on her account you visited the house so often. I had been so petted and spoiled since entering society that I thought you were kind to her simply because honour forbade you to be too kind to me; and under this delusion I confided my folly to Dorothy.

"You will have many a talk with her in the future, and some day she may succeed in proving to you that it was vanity and not badness of heart which led me to misunderstand your feelings. Having repressed my own impulses so long, I saw in your reticence the evidences of a like struggle; and when, immediately upon my break with Mr. Sinclair, you entered here and said the words you did—Well, we have finished with this subject for ever.

"The explanations which I gave below of the part I played in my aunt's death were true. I only omitted one detail, which you may consider a very important one. The fact which paralysed my hand and voice when I saw her lift the drop of death to her lips was this: I had meant to die by this drop myself, in Dorothy's room, and with Dorothy's arms about me. This was my secret—a secret which no one can blame me for keeping as long as I could, and one which I should hardly have the courage to disclose to you now if I had not already parted with it to the coroner, who would not credit my story till I had told him the whole truth."

"Gilbertine," I urged, for I saw her fingers closing upon the knob she had held lightly till now, "do not go till I have said this. A young girl does not always know the demands of her own nature. The heart you have ignored is one in a thousand. Do not let it slip from you. God never gives a woman such a love twice."

"I know it," she murmured, and turned the knob.

I thought she was gone, and let the sigh which had been labouring at my breast have vent, when I caught one last word whispered from the threshold:

"Throw back the shutters and let in the light. Dorothy is coming. I am going now to call her."

An hour had passed, the hour of hours for me, for in it the sun of my happiness rose full-orbed, and Dorothy and I came to understand each other. We were sitting hand in hand in this blessed little boudoir, when suddenly she turned her sweet face toward me and gently remarked:

"This seems like selfishness on our part; but Gilbertine insisted. Do you know what she is doing now? Helping old Mrs. Cummings and holding Mrs. Barnstable's baby while her maid packs. She will work like that all day, and with a smile, too. Oh, it is a rich nature, an ideal nature. I think we can trust her now."

I did not like to discuss Gilbertine, even with Dorothy, so I said nothing. But she was too full of her theme to stop. I think she wished to unburden her mind once and for ever of all that had disturbed it.

"Our aunt's death," she continued, "will be a sort of emancipation for her. I don't think you, or any one out of our immediate household, can realise the control which Aunt Hannah exerted over every one who came within her daily influence. It would have been the same had she occupied a dependent position instead of being the wealthy autocrat she was. In her cold nature dwelt an imperiousness which no one could withstand. You know how her friends, some of them as rich and influential as herself, bowed to her will and submitted to her interference. What, then, could you expect from two poor girls entirely dependent upon her for everything they enjoyed? Gilbertine, with all her spirit, could not face Aunt Hannah's frown, while I studied to have no wishes. Had this been otherwise, had we found a friend instead of a tyrant in the woman who took us into her home, Gilbertine might have gained more control over her feelings. It was the necessity she felt of smothering her natural impulses, and of maintaining in the house and before the world an appearance of satisfaction in her position as bride-elect, which caused her to fall into such extremes of despondency and deep despair. Her self-respect was shocked. She felt she was a living lie, and hated herself in consequence.

"You may think I did wrong not to tell her of your affection for myself, especially after what you whispered into my ear that night at the theatre. I did do wrong; I see it now. She was really a stronger woman than I thought, and we might all have been saved the horrors which have befallen us had I acted with more firmness at that time. But I was weak and frightened. I held you back and let her go on deceiving herself, which meant deceiving Mr. Sinclair, too. I thought, when she found herself really married and settled in her own home, she would find it easier to forget, and that soon, perhaps very soon, all this would seem like a troubled dream to her. And there was reason for this hope on my part. She showed a woman's natural interest in her outfit and the plans for her new house, but when she heard you were to be Mr. Sinclair's best man every feminine instinct within her rebelled, and it was with difficulty she could prevent herself from breaking out into a loud 'No!' in face of aunt and lover. From this moment on her state of mind grew desperate. In the parlour, at the theatre, she was the brilliant girl whom all admired and many envied; but in my little room at night she would bury her face in my lap and talk of death, till I moved in a constant atmosphere of dread. Yet, because she looked gay and laughed, I turned a like face to the world and laughed also. We felt it was expected of us, and the very nervous tension we were under made these ebullitions easy. But I did not laugh so much after coming here. One night I found her out of her bed long after every one else had retired for the night. Next morning Mr. Beaton told a dream—I hope it was a dream—but it frightened me. Then came that moment when Mr. Sinclair displayed the amethyst box and explained with such a nonchalant air how a drop from the little flask inside would kill a person. A toy, but so deadly! I felt the thrill which shot like lightning through her, and made up my mind she should never have the opportunity of touching that box. And that is why I stole into the library, took it down and hid it in my hair. I never thought to look inside; I did not pause to think that it was the flask and not the box she wanted, and consequently felt convinced of her safety so long as I kept the latter successfully concealed in my hair. You know the rest."

Yes, I knew it. How she opened the box in her room and found it empty. How she flew to Gilbertine's room, and, finding the door unlocked, looked in, and saw Miss Lane lying there asleep, but no Gilbertine. How her alarm grew at this, and how, forgetting that her cousin often stole to her room by means of the connecting balcony, she had wandered over the house in the hope of coming upon Gilbertine in one of the downstairs rooms. How her mind misgave her before she had entered the great hall, and how she turned back only to hear that awful scream go up as she was setting foot upon the spiral stair. I had heard it all before, and could imagine her terror and dismay; and why she found it impossible to proceed any further, but clung to the stair-rail, half alive and half dead, till she was found there by those seeking her, and taken up to her aunt's room. But she never told me, and I do not yet know, what her thoughts or feelings were when, instead of seeing her cousin outstretched in death on the bed they led her to, she beheld the lifeless figure of her aunt. The reserve she maintained on this point has always been respected by me. Let it continue to be so.

When, therefore, she said, "You know the rest," I took her in my arms and gave her my first kiss. Then I softly released her, and by tacit consent we each went our way for that day.

Mine took me into the hall below, which was all alive with the hum of departing guests. Beaton was among them, and as he stepped out on the porch I gave him a parting hand-clasp, and quietly whispered:

"When all dark things are made light, you will find that there was both more and less to your dream than you were inclined to make out."

He bowed, and that was the last word which ever passed between us on this topic.

But what chiefly impressed me in connection with this afternoon's events was the short talk I had with Sinclair. I fear I forced this talk, but I could not let the dreary day settle into still drearier night without making clear to him a point which, in the new position he held toward Gilbertine, if not toward myself, might seem to be involved in some doubt. When, therefore, the opportunity came, I accosted him with these words:

"It is not a very propitious time for me to intrude my personal affairs upon you, but I feel as if I should like you to know that the clouds have been cleared away between Dorothy and myself, and that some day we expect to marry."

He gave me the earnest look of a man who has recovered his one friend. Then he grasped my hand warmly, saying, with something like his old fervour:

"You deserve all the happiness that awaits you. Mine is gone; but if I can regain it I will. Trust me for that, Worthington."

The coroner, who had seen much of life and human nature, managed with much discretion the inquest he felt bound to hold. Mrs. Lansing was found to have come to her death by a meddlesome interference with one of her niece's wedding trinkets; and, as every one acquainted with Mrs. Lansing knew her to be quite capable of such an act of malicious folly, the verdict was duly accepted, and the real heart of this tragedy closed for ever from every human eye.

As we were leaving Newport Sinclair stepped up to me.

"I have reason to know," said he, "that Mrs. Lansing's bequests will be a surprise, not only to her nieces, but to the world at large. Let me advise you to announce your engagement before reaching New York."

I followed his advice, and in a few days understood why it had been given. All the vast property owned by this woman had been left to Dorothy. Gilbertine had been cut off without a cent.

We never knew Mrs. Lansing's reason for this act. Gilbertine had always been considered her favourite, and, had the will been a late one, it would have been generally thought that she had left her thus unprovided for solely in consideration of the great match which she expected her to make. But the will was dated back several years—long before Gilbertine had met Mr. Sinclair, long before either niece had come to live with Mrs. Lansing in New York. Had it always been the latter's wish, then, to enrich the one and slight the other? It would seem so; but why should the slighted one have been Gilbertine?

The only explanation I ever heard given was the partiality which Mrs. Lansing felt for Dorothy's mother, or, rather, her lack of affection for Gilbertine's. Whether or not this is the true one, the discrimination she showed in her will put poor Gilbertine in a very unfortunate position. At least, it would have done so if Sinclair, with an adroitness worthy of his love, had not proved to her that a break at this time in their supposed relations would reflect most seriously upon his disinterestedness, and thus secured for himself opportunities for urging his suit which ended, as such opportunities often do, in a renewal of their engagement. But this time with mutual love as its basis. This was evident to any one who saw them together. But how the magic was wrought—how this hard-to-be-won heart learned at last its true allegiance I did not know till later, and then it was told me by Gilbertine herself.

I had been married for some months and she for some weeks, when one evening chance threw us together. Instantly, and as if she had waited for this hour, she turned upon me with the beautiful smile which has been hers ever since her new happiness came to her, and said:

"You once gave me some very good advice, Mr. Worthington; but it was not that which led me to realise Mr. Sinclair's affection. It was a short conversation which passed between us on the day my aunt's will was read. Do you remember my turning to speak to him the moment after that word all fell from the lawyer's lips?"

"Yes, Mrs. Sinclair."

Alas! did I not! It was one of the most poignant memories of my life. The look she gave him and the look he gave her! Indeed, I did remember.

"It was to ask him one question—a question to which misfortune only could have given so much weight. Had my aunt taken him into her confidence? Had he known that I had no place in her will? His answer was very simple; a single word, 'Always.' But after that do I need to say why I am a wife—why I am his wife?"

Was it a spectre?

For days I could not answer this question. I am no believer in spiritual manifestations, yet—But let me tell my story.

I was lodging with my wife on the first floor of a house in Twenty-seventh Street. I had taken the apartments for three months, and we had already lived in them two and found them sufficiently comfortable. The back room we used as a bedroom, and as we received but few friends, the two great leaves of old mahogany connecting the rooms, usually stood wide open.

One morning, my wife being ill, I left her lying in bed and stepped into the parlour preparatory to going out for breakfast. It was late—nine o'clock probably—and I was hastening to leave, when I heard a sound behind me—or did I merely feel a presence?—and, turning, saw a strange and totally unknown woman coming toward me from my wife's room.

As I had just left that room, and as there was no other way of entrance save through a door we always kept locked, I was so overpowered by my astonishment that I never thought of speaking or moving until she had passed me. Then I found voice, and calling out "Madam!" endeavoured to stop her.

But the madam, if madam she was, passed on as quietly, as mechanically even, as if I had not raised my voice, and before I could grasp the fact that she was melting from before me flitted through the hall to the front door and so out, leaving behind on the palm of my hand the "feel" of her wool dress, which I had just managed to touch.

Not understanding her or myself or the strange thrill awakened by this contact, I tore open the front door and looked out, expecting, of course, to see her on the steps or on the sidewalk in front. But there was no one of her appearance visible, and I came back questioning whether I was the victim of a hallucination or just an everyday fool. To satisfy myself on this important question I looked about for the hallboy, with the intention of asking him if he had seen any such person go out, but that young and inconsequent scamp was missing from his post as usual and there was no one within sight to appeal to.

There was nothing to do but to re-enter my rooms, where my attention was immediately arrested by the sight of my wife sitting up in bed and surveying me with a look of unmistakable astonishment.

"Who was that woman?" she asked. "And how came she in here?"

So she had seen her too.

"What woman, Lydia? I have not let in any woman. Did you think there was a woman in this room?"

"Not in that room," she answered hoarsely, "but in this one. I saw her just now passing through the folding doors. Wilbur, I am frightened. See how my hands shake. Do you think I am sick enough to imagine things?"

I knew she was not, but I did not say so. I thought it would be better for her to think herself under some such delusion.

"You were dozing," said I. "If you had seen a woman here you could tell me how she looked."

"And I can," my wife broke in excitedly. "She was like the ghosts we read of, only that her dress and the veil or drapery she wore were all grey. Didn't you see her? You must have seen her. She went right by you—a grey woman, all grey; a lady, Wilbur, and slightly lame. Could I have dreamed all that?"

"You must have!" I protested, shaking the door leading directly into the hall so she might see it was locked, and even showing her the key to it lying in its accustomed place behind the bureau cushion. Yet I was in no satisfied condition myself, for she had described with the greatest accuracy the very person I had myself seen. Had we been alike the victims of a spiritual manifestation?

This was Tuesday. On Friday my question seemed to receive an answer. I had been downtown, as usual, and on returning found a crowd assembled in front of my lodging-house. A woman had been run over and was being carried into our rooms. In the glimpse I caught of her I saw that she was middle-aged and was wrapped in a long black cloak. Later this cloak fell off, as her hat had done long before, and I perceived that her dress was black and decent.

She was laid on our bed and every attention paid her. But she had been grievously injured about the head and gradually but surely sank before our eyes. Suddenly she roused and gave a look about her. It was a remarkable one—a look of recognition and almost of delight. Then she raised one hand and, pointing with a significant gesture into the empty space before her, sank back and died.

It was a sudden ending, and, anxious to see its effect upon my wife, who was standing on the other side of the bed, I glanced her way with some misgiving. She showed more feeling than I had anticipated. Indeed her countenance was a study, and when, under the influence of my scrutiny, she glanced my way, I saw that something of deeper import than this unexpected death in our rooms lay at the bottom of her uneasy look.

What that was I was soon to know, for catching up from amid the folds of the woman's grey-lined cloak a long grey veil which had fallen at the bedside, she disposed it softly about the woman's face, darting me a look full of significance.

"You remember the vision I had the morning when I was sick?" she whispered softly in my ear.

I nodded, secretly thrilled to my very heart's core.

"Well, it was a vision of this woman. If she were living and on her feet and wrapped, as I have shown you, in this veil, you would behold a living picture of the person I saw passing out of this room that morning."

"I shall not dispute you," I answered. Alas! I had myself perceived the likeness the instant the veil had fallen about the pinched but handsome features!

"A forewarning," whispered my wife; "a forewarning of what has this day happened under our roof. It was a wraith we saw. Wilbur, I shall not spend another night in these rooms."

And we did not. I was as anxious to leave as she was. Yet I am not a superstitious man. As proof of it, after the first effect of these events had left me I began to question my first impressions and feel tolerably ashamed of my past credulity. Though the phenomenon we had observed could not to all appearance be explained by any natural hypothesis; though I had seen, and my wife had seen, a strange woman suddenly become visible in a room which a moment before had held no one but ourselves, and into which no live woman could have entered without our knowledge, something—was it my natural good sense?—recoiled before a supernatural explanation of this, and I found myself forced to believe that our first visitor had been as real as the last; in other words, the same woman.

But could I prove it? Could the seemingly impossible be made possible and the unexplainable receive a solution satisfying to a rational mind? I determined to make an effort to accomplish this, if only to relieve the mind of my wife, who had not recovered her equanimity as readily as myself.

Starting with the assumption above mentioned—that the woman who had died in our presence was the same who had previously found an unexplainable entrance into our rooms—I first inquired if the black cloak lined with grey did not offer a solution to some of my previous difficulties. It was a long cloak, enveloping her completely. When worn with the black side out she would present an inconspicuous appearance, but with the grey side out and the effect of this heightened by a long grey veil hung over her hat, she would look like the grey lady I had first seen. Now, a cloak can be turned in an instant, and if she had chosen to do this in flitting through my door I would naturally find only a sedate, black-clothed woman passing up the street, when, rousing from the apathy into which her appearance had thrown me, I rushed to the front door and looked out. Had I seen such a woman? I seemed to remember that I had.

Thus much, then, was satisfactory, but to account for her entrance into our rooms was not so easy. Had she slipped by me in coming in as she had on going out? The parlour door was open, for I had been out to get the paper. Could she have glided in by me unperceived and thus found her way into the bedroom from which I afterward saw her issue? No, for I had stood facing the front hall door all the time. Through the bedroom door, then? But that was, as I have said, locked. Here, then, was a mystery; but it was one worth solving.

My first step was to recall all that I had heard of the actual woman who had been buried from our rooms. Her name, as ascertained in the cheap boarding-house to which she was traced, was Helmuth, and she was, so far as any one knew, without friends or relatives in the city. To those who saw her daily she was a harmless, slightly demented woman with money enough to live above want, but not enough to warrant her boasting talk about the rich things she was going to buy some day and the beautiful presents she would soon be in a position to give away. The money found on her person was sufficient to bury her, but no papers were in her possession nor any letters calculated to throw light upon her past life.

Her lameness had been caused by paralysis, but the date of her attack was not known.

Finding no clue in this to what I wished to learn, I went back to our old rooms, which had not been let since our departure, and sought for one there, and, strangely enough, found it. I thought I knew everything there was to be known about the apartment we had lived in two months, but one little fact had escaped me which, under the scrutiny that I now gave it, became apparent. This was simply that the key which opened the hall door of the bedroom and which we had seldom if ever used was not as old a key as that of the corresponding door in the parlour, and this fact, small as it was, led me to make inquiries.

The result was that I learned something about the couple who had preceded us in the use of these rooms. They were of middle age and of great personal elegance but uncertain pay, the husband being nothing more nor less than a professional gambler. Their name was L'Hommedieu.

When I first heard of them I thought that Mrs. L'Hommedieu might be the Mrs. Helmuth in whose history I was so interested, but from all I could learn she was a very different sort of person. Mrs. L'Hommedieu was gay, dashing, and capable of making a show out of flimsy silk a shopgirl would hesitate to wear. Yet she looked distinguished and wore her cheap jewelry with more grace than many a woman her diamonds. I would, consequently, have dropped this inquiry if some one had not remarked upon her having had a paralytic stroke after leaving the house. This, together with the fact that the key to the rear door, which I had found replaced by a new one, had been taken away by her and never returned, connected her so indubitably with my mysterious visitor that I resolved to pursue my investigations into Mrs. L'Hommedieu's past.

For this purpose I sought out a quaint little maiden lady living on the top floor who, I was told, knew more about the L'Hommedieus than any one in the building. Miss Winterburn, whose acquaintance I had failed to make while residing in the house, was a fluttering, eager, affable person whose one delight was, as I soon found, to talk about the L'Hommedieus. Of the story she related I give as much of it as possible in her own words.

"I was never their equal," said she, "but Mrs. L'Hommedieu was lonely, and, having no friends in town, was good enough to admit me to her parlour now and then and even to allow me to accompany her to the theatre when her husband was away on one of his mysterious visits. I never liked Mr. L'Hommedieu, but I did like her. She was so different from me, and, when I first knew her, so gay and so full of conversation. But after a while she changed and was either feverishly cheerful or morbidly sad, so that my visits caused me more pain than pleasure. The reason for these changes in her was patent to everybody. Though her husband was a handsome man, he was as unprincipled as he was unfortunate. He gambled. This she once admitted to me, and while at long intervals he met with some luck he more often returned dispirited and with that hungry, ravaging look you expect to see in a wolf cheated of its prey.

"I used to be afraid he would strike her after some one of these disappointments, but I do not think he ever did. She had a determined character of her own, and there have been times when I have thought he was as much afraid of her as she was of him. I became sure of this after one night. Mrs. L'Hommedieu and myself were having a little supper together in the front parlour you have so lately occupied. It was a very ordinary supper, for the L'Hommedieus' purse had run low, and Mrs. L'Hommedieu was not the woman to spend much at any time on her eating. It was palatable, however, and I would have enjoyed it greatly, if Mrs. L'Hommedieu had shown more appetite. But she ate scarcely anything and seemed very anxious and unhappy, though she laughed now and then with sudden gusts of mirth too hysterical to be real. It was not late, and yet we were both very much surprised when there came a knock at the door, followed by the entrance of a visitor.

"Mrs. L'Hommedieu, who was always la grande dame, rose without apparent embarrassment to meet the gentleman who entered, though I knew she could not help but feel keenly the niggardly appearance of the board she left with such grace. The stranger—he was certainly a stranger; this I could see by the formality of her manner—was a gentleman of urbane bearing and a general air of prosperity.

"I remember every word that passed.

"'My name is Lafarge,' said he. 'I am, or rather have been, under great obligations to your husband, and I have come to discharge my debt. Is he at home?'

"Mrs. L'Hommedieu's eye, which had sparkled at his name, dropped suddenly as he put the final question.

"'I am sorry,' she returned after a moment of embarrassment, 'but my husband is very seldom home evenings. If you will come about noon some day—'

"'Thank you,' said he, with a bright smile, 'but I will finish my business now and with you, seeing that Mr. L'Hommedieu is not at home. Years ago—I am sure you have heard your husband mention my name—I borrowed quite a sum of money from him, which I have never paid. You recall the amount, no doubt?'

"'I have heard Mr. L'Hommedieu say it was a thousand dollars,' she replied, with a sudden fluttering of her hands indicative of great excitement.

"'That is the sum,' he allowed, either not noticing me or thinking me too insignificant to be considered. 'I regret to have kept him so long out of it, but I have not forgotten to add the interest in making out this statement of my indebtedness, and if you will look over this paper and acknowledge its correctness I will leave the equivalent of my debt here and now, for I sail for Europe to-morrow morning and wish to have all my affairs in order before leaving.'

"Mrs. L'Hommedieu, who looked ready to faint from excess of feeling, summoned up her whole strength, looking so beautiful as she did so that one forgot the ribbons on her sleeves were no longer fresh and that the silk dress she wore hung in the very limpest of folds.

"'I am obliged to you,' she said in a tone from which she strove in vain to suppress all eagerness. 'And if I can speak for Mr. L'Hommedieu he will be as grateful for your remembrance of us as for the money you so kindly offer to return to him.'

"The stranger bowed low and took out a folded paper, which he handed to her. He was not deceived, I am sure, by her grand airs, and knew as well as I did that no woman ever stood in greater need of money. But nothing in his manner betrayed this knowledge.

"'It is a bond I give you,' he now explained. 'As you will see, it has coupons attached to it which you can cash at any time. It will prove as valuable to you as so much ready money and possibly more convenient.'

"And with just this hint, which I took as significant of his complete understanding of her position, he took her receipt and politely left the house.

"Once alone with me, who am nobody, her joy had full vent. I have never seen any one so lost in delight as she was for a few minutes. To have this money thrust upon her just at a moment when actual want seemed staring her in the face was too much of a relief for her to conceal either the misery she had been under or the satisfaction she now enjoyed. Under the gush of her emotions her whole history came out, but as you have often heard the like I will not repeat it, especially as it was all contained in the cry with which a little later she thrust the bond into my hand.

"'He must not see it! He must not! It would go like all the rest, and I should again be left without a cent. Take it and keep it, for I have no means of concealing it here. He is too suspicious.'

"But this was asking more than I was willing to grant. Seeing how I felt, she took the paper back and concealed it in her bosom with a look I had rather not have seen. 'You will not charge yourself with such a responsibility,' said she. 'But I can trust you not to tell him?'

"'Yes,' I nodded, feeling sick of the whole business.

"'Then—' But here the door was violently flung open and Mr. L'Hommedieu burst into the room in a state of as much excitement as his wife, only his was the excitement of desperation.

"'Gone! Gone!' he cried, ignoring me as completely as Mr. Lafarge had done. 'Not a dollar left; not even my studs! See!' And he pointed to his shirt-front hanging apart in a way I would never have looked for in this reckless but fastidious gentleman. 'Yet if I had had a dollar more or even a ring worth a dollar or so, I might have—Theresa, have you any money at all? A coin now might save us.'

"Mrs. L'Hommedieu, who had turned alarmingly pale, drew up her fine figure and resolutely confronted him. 'No!' said she, and shifting her gaze she turned it meaningly upon me.

"He misunderstood this movement. Thinking it simply a reminder of my presence, he turned, with his false but impressive show of courtesy, and made me a low bow. Then he forgot me utterly again, and, facing his wife, growled out:

"'Where are you going to get breakfast then? You don't look like a woman who expects to starve!'

"It was a fatal remark, for, do what she would, she could not prevent a slight smile of disdain, and, seeing it, he kept his eye riveted on her face till her uneasiness became manifest. Instantly his suspicion took form, and, surveying her still more fixedly, he espied a corner of the precious envelope protruding slightly above her corsage. To snatch it out, open it, and realise its value was the work of a moment. Her cry of dismay and his shout of triumph rang out simultaneously, and never have I seen such an ebullition of opposing passions as I was made witness to as his hand closed over this small fortune and their staring eyes met in the moral struggle they had now entered upon for its ultimate possession.

"She was the first to speak. 'It was given to me, it was meant for me. If I keep it both of us will profit by it, but if you—'

"He did not wait for her to finish. 'Where did you get it?' he cried. 'I can break the bank with what I can raise on this bond at the club. Darraugh's in town. You know what that means. Luck's in the air, and with a hundred dollars—But I've no time to talk. I came for a dollar, a fifty-cent piece, a dime even, and go back with a bond worth—'

"But she was already between him and the door. 'You will never carry that bond out of this house,' she whispered in the tone which goes further than a cry. 'I have not held it in my hand to see it follow every other good thing I have had in life. I will not, Henry. Take that bond and sink it as you have all the rest and I fall at your feet a dead woman. I will never survive the destruction of my last hope.'

"He was cowed—for a moment, that is; she looked so superb and so determined. Then all that was mean and despicable in his thinly veneered nature came to the surface, and, springing forward with an oath, he was about to push her aside, when, without the moving of a finger on her part, he reeled back, recovered himself, caught at a chair, missed it, and fell heavily to the floor.

"'My God, I thank thee!' was the exclamation with which she broke from the trance of terror into which she had been thrown by his sudden attempt to pass her; and without a glance at his face, which to me looked like the face of a dead man, she tore the paper from his hand and stood looking about her with a wild and searching gaze, in the desperate hope that somehow the walls would open and offer her a safe place of concealment for the precious sheet of paper.

"Meanwhile I had crept near the prostrate man. He was breathing, but was perfectly unconscious.

"'Don't you mean to do something for him?' I asked. 'He may die.'

"She met my question with the dazed air of one suddenly awakened. 'No, he'll not die; but he'll not come to for some minutes, and this must be hidden first. But where? where? I cannot trust it on my person or in any place a man like him would search. I must devise some means—ah!'

"With this final exclamation she had dashed into the other room. I did not see where she went—I did not want to—but I soon realised she was working somewhere in a desperate hurry. I could hear her breath coming in quick, short pants as I bent over her husband, waiting for him to rouse and hating my inaction even while I succumbed to it.

"Suddenly she was back in the parlour again, and to my surprise passed immediately to the little table in the corner where we had sat at supper. We had had for our simple refreshment that homeliest of all dishes, boiled milk thickened with flour. There was still some left in a bowl, and taking this away with her she called back hoarsely:

"'Pray that he does not come to till I have finished. It will be the best prayer you ever made.'

"She told me afterward that he was subject to these attacks and that she had long ceased to be alarmed by them. But to me the sight of that man lying there so helpless was horrible, and, though I hated him and pitied her, I scarcely knew what to wish. While battling with my desire to run and the feeling of loyalty which held me kneeling at that man's side, I heard her speak again, this time in an even and slightly hard tone: 'Now you may dash a glass of cold water in his face. I am prepared to meet him now. Happily his memory fails after these attacks. I may succeed in making him believe that the bond he saw was one of his fancies.'

"'Had you not better throw the water yourself?' I suggested, getting up and meeting her eye very quietly.

"She looked at me in wonder, then moved calmly to the table, took the glass, and dashed a few drops of water into her husband's face. Instantly he began to stir, seeing which I arose without haste, but without any unnecessary delay, and quickly took my leave. I could bear no more that night.

"Next morning I awoke in a fright. I had dreamed that he had come to my room in search of the bond. But it was only her knock at the door and her voice asking if she might enter at this early hour. It was such a relief I gladly let her in, and she entered with her best air and flung herself on my little lounge with the hysterical cry:

"'He has sent me up. I told him I ought not to intrude at such an inconvenient hour; that you would not have had your breakfast.' (How carelessly she spoke! How hard she tried to keep the hungry note out of her voice!) 'But he insisted on my coming up. I know why. He searched me before I left the room, and now he wants to search the room itself.'

"'Then he did remember?' I began.

"'Yes, he remembers now. I saw it in his eyes as soon as he awoke. But he will not find the bond. That is safe, and some day when I have escaped his vigilance long enough to get it back again I will use it so as to make him comfortable as well as myself. I am not a selfish woman.'

"I did not think she was, and felt pity for her, and so after dressing and making her a cup of tea, I sat down with her, and we chatted for an hour or so quite comfortably. Then she grew so restless and consulted the clock so often that I tried to soothe her by remarking that it was not an easy task he had set himself, at which she laughed in a mysterious way, but failed to grow less anxious till our suspense was cut short by the appearance of the janitor with a message from Mr. L'Hommedieu.

"'Mr. L'Hommedieu's compliments,' said he, 'and he hopes Mrs. L'Hommedieu will make herself comfortable and not think of coming down. He is doing everything that is necessary and will soon be through. You can rest quite easy, ma'am.'

"'What does he mean?' marvelled the poor woman as the janitor disappeared. 'Is he spending all this time ransacking the rooms? I wish I dared disobey him. I wish I dared go down.'

"But her courage was not equal to an open disregard of his wishes, and she had to subdue her impatience and wait for a summons that did not come till near two o'clock. Then Mr. L'Hommedieu himself appeared with her hat and mantle on his arm.

"'My dear,' said he as she rose, haggard with excitement, to meet him, 'I have brought your wraps with me that you may go directly from here to our new home. Shall I assist you to put them on? You do not look as well as usual, and that is why I have undertaken this thing all myself—to save you, my dear; to save you each and every exertion.'

"I had flung out my arms to catch her, for I thought she was going to faint, but she did not, though I think it would have been better for her if she had.

"'We are going to leave this house?' she asked, speaking very slowly and with a studied lack of emotion that imposed upon nobody.

"'I have said so,' he smiled. 'The dray has already taken away the half of our effects, and the rest will follow at Mrs. Latimer's convenience.'

"'Ah, I understand!' she replied, with a gasp of relief significant of her fear that by some super-human cunning he had found the bond she thought so safely concealed. 'I was wondering how Mrs. Latimer came to allow us to leave.' (I tell you they always talked as if I were not present.) 'Our goods are left as a surety, it seems.'

"'Half of our goods,' he blandly corrected. 'Would it interest you to know which half?'

"The cunning of this insinuation was matched by the imperturbable shrug with which she replied, 'So a bed has been allowed us and some clothes I am satisfied,' at which he bit his lips, vexed at her self-control and his own failure to break it.

"'You have not asked where we are going,' he observed, as with apparent solicitude he threw her mantle over her shoulders.

"The air of lassitude with which she replied bespoke her feeling on that point. 'I have little curiosity,' she said. 'You know I can be happy anywhere.' And, turning toward me, she moved her lips in a way I interpreted to mean: 'Go below with me. See me out.'

"'Say what you have to say to Miss Winterburn aloud,' he drily suggested.

"'I have nothing to say to Miss Winterburn but thanks,' was her cold reply, belied, however, by the trembling of her fingers as she essayed to fit on her gloves.

"'And those I will receive below!' I cried, with affected gaiety. 'I am going down with you to the door.' And resolutely ignoring his frown I tripped down before them. On the last stair I felt her steps lagging. Instantly I seemed to comprehend what was required of me, and, rushing forward, I entered the front parlour. He followed close behind me, for how could he know I was not in collusion with her to regain the bond? This gave her one minute by herself in the rear, and in that minute she secured the key which would give her future access to the spot where her treasure lay hidden.

"The rest of the story I must give you mainly from hearsay. You must understand by this time what Mr. L'Hommedieu's scheme was in moving so suddenly. He knew that it would be impossible for him, by the most minute and continuous watchfulness, to prevent his wife from recovering the bond while they continued to inhabit the rooms in which, notwithstanding his failure to find it, he had reason to believe it still lay concealed. But once in other quarters it would be comparatively easy for him to subject her to a surveillance which not only would prevent her from returning to this house without his knowledge, but would lead her to give away her secret by the very natural necessity she would be under of going to the exact spot where her treasure lay hid.

"It was a cunning plot and showed him to be as able as he was unscrupulous. How it worked I will now proceed to tell you. It must have been the next afternoon that the janitor came running up to me—I suppose he had learned by this time that I had more than ordinary interest in these people—to say that Mrs. L'Hommedieu had been in the house and had been so frightened by a man who had followed her that she had fainted dead away on the floor. Would I go down to her?

"I had rather have gone anywhere else, unless it was to prison; but duty cannot be shirked, and I followed the man down. But we were too late. Mrs. L'Hommedieu had recovered and gone away, and the person who had frightened her was also gone, and only the hallboy remained to give any explanations.

"This was what he had to say:

"'The man it was who went first. As soon as the lady fell he skipped out. I don't think he meant no good here—'

"'Did she drop here in the hall?' I asked, unable to restrain my intense anxiety.

"'Oh, no, ma'am! They was in the back room yonder, which she got in somehow. The man followed her in, sneaking and sneaking like an eel or a cop, and she fell right against—'

"'Don't tell me where!' I cried. 'I don't want to know where!' And I was about to return upstairs when I heard a quick, sharp voice behind me and realised that Mr. L'Hommedieu had come in and was having some dispute with the janitor.

"Common prudence led me to listen. He wanted, as was very natural, to enter the room where his wife had just been surprised, but the janitor, alarmed by the foregoing very irregular proceedings, was disposed to deny his right to do so.

"'The furniture is held as a surety,' said he, 'and I have orders—'

"But Mr. L'Hommedieu had a spare dollar, and before many minutes had elapsed I heard him go into that room and close the door. Of the next ten minutes and the suspense I felt I need not speak. When he came out again, he looked as if the ground would not hold him.

"'I have done some mischief, I fear,' he airily said as he passed the janitor. 'But I'll pay for it. Don't worry. I'll pay for it and the rent, too, to-morrow. You may tell Mrs. Latimer so.' And he was gone, leaving us all agape in the hallway.

"A minute later we all crept to that room and looked in. Now that he had got the bond I for one was determined to know where she had hid it. There was no mistaking the spot. A single glance was enough to show us the paper ripped off from a portion of the wall, revealing a narrow gap behind the baseboard large enough to hold the bond. It was near—"

"Wait!" I put in as I remembered where the so-called Mrs. Helmuth had pointed just before she died. "Wasn't it at the left of the large folding doors and midway to the wall?"

"How came you to know?" she asked. "Did Mrs. Latimer tell you?" But as I did not answer she soon took up the thread of her narrative again, and, sighing softly, said:

"The next day came and went, but no L'Hommedieu appeared; another, and I began to grow seriously uneasy; a third, and a dreadful thing happened. Late in the afternoon Mrs. L'Hommedieu, dressed very oddly, came sliding in at the front door, and with an appealing smile at the hallboy, who wished but dared not ask her for the key which made these visits possible, glided by to her old rooms, and, finding the door unlocked, went softly in. Her appearance is worth description, for it shows the pitiful efforts she made at disguise, in the hope, I suppose, of escaping the surveillance she was evidently conscious of being under. She was in the habit of wearing on cool days a black circular with a grey lining. This she had turned inside out so that the gray was uppermost; while over her neat black bonnet she had flung a long veil, also grey, which not only hid her face, but gave her appearance an eccentric look as different as possible from her usual aspect. The hallboy, who had never seen her save in showy black or bright colours, said she looked like a ghost in the daytime, but it was all done for a purpose, I am sure, and to escape the attention of the man who had followed her before. Alas, he might have followed her this time without addition to her suffering! Scarcely had she entered the room where her treasure had been left than she saw the torn paper and gaping baseboard, and, uttering a cry so piercing it found its way even to the stolid heart of the hallboy, she tottered back into the hall, where she fell into the arms of her husband, who had followed her in from the street in a state of frenzy almost equal to her own.

"The janitor, who that minute appeared on the stairway, says that he never saw two such faces. They looked at each other and were speechless. He was the first to hang his head.

"'It is gone, Henry,' she whispered, 'It is gone. You have taken it.'

"He did not answer.

"'And it is lost! You have risked it, and it is lost!'

"He uttered a groan. 'You should have given it to me that night. There was luck in the air then. Now the devil is in the cards and—'

"Her arms went up with a shriek. 'My curse be upon you, Henry L'Hommedieu!' And whether it was the look with which she uttered this imprecation, or whether there was some latent love left in his heart for this long-suffering and once beautiful woman, he shrank at her words, and, stumbling like a man in the darkness, uttered a heart-rending groan, and rushed from the house. We never saw him again.

"As for her, she fell this time under a paralytic attack which robbed her of her faculties. She was taken to a hospital, where I frequently visited her, but either from grief or the effect of her attack she did not know me, nor did she ever recognise any of us again. Mrs. Latimer, who is a just woman, sold her furniture and, after paying herself out of the proceeds, gave the remainder to the hospital nurses for the use of Mrs. L'Hommedieu, so that when she left them she had something with which to start life anew. But where she went or how she managed to get along in her enfeebled condition I do not know. I never heard of her again."

"Then you did not see the woman who died in these rooms?" I asked.

The effect of these words was magical and led to mutual explanations. She had not seen that woman, having encountered all the sorrow she wished to in that room. Nor was there any one else in the house at this time likely to recognise Mrs. L'Hommedieu, the janitor and hallboy both being new and Mrs. Latimer one of those proprietors who are only seen on rent day. For the rest, Mrs. L'Hommedieu's defective memory, which had led her to haunt the house and room where the bond had once been hidden, accounted not only for her first visit, but the last, which had ended so fatally. The cunning she showed in turning her cloak and flinging a veil over her hat was the cunning of a partially clouded mind. It was a reminiscence of the morning when her terrible misfortune occurred. My habit of taking the key out of the lock of that unused door made the use of her own key possible, and her fear of being followed caused her to lock the door behind her. My wife, who must have fallen into a doze on my leaving her, did not see her enter, but detected her just as she was trying to escape through the folding doors. My presence in the parlour probably added to her embarrassment, and she fled, turning her cloak as she did so.

How simple it seemed now that we knew the facts; but how obscure, and, to all appearance, unexplainable, before the clue was given to the mystery!

THE THIEF

"And now, if you have all seen the coin and sufficiently admired it, you may pass it back. I make a point of never leaving it off the shelf for more than fifteen minutes."

The half dozen or more guests seated about the board of the genial speaker, glanced casually at each other as though expecting to see the object mentioned immediately produced.

But no coin appeared.

"I have other amusements waiting," suggested their host, with a smile in which even his wife could detect no signs of impatience. "Now let Robert put it back into the cabinet."

Robert was the butler.

Blank looks, negative gestures, but still no coin.

"Perhaps it is in somebody's lap," timidly ventured one of the younger women. "It doesn't seem to be on the table."

Immediately all the ladies began lifting their napkins and shaking out the gloves which lay under them, in an effort to relieve their own embarrassment and that of the gentlemen who had not even so simple a resource as this at their command.

"It can't be lost," protested Mr. Sedgwick, with an air of perfect confidence. "I saw it but a minute ago in somebody's hand. Darrow, you had it; what did you do with it?"

"Passed it along."

"Well, well, it must be under somebody's plate or doily." And he began to move about his own and such dishes as were within reach of his hand.

Each guest imitated him, lifting glasses and turning over spoons till Mr. Sedgwick himself bade them desist. "It's slipped to the floor," he nonchalantly concluded. "A toast to the ladies, and we will give Robert the chance of looking for it."

As they drank this toast, his apparently careless, but quietly astute, glance took in each countenance about him. The coin was very valuable and its loss would be keenly felt by him. Had it slipped from the table some one's eye would have perceived it, some hand would have followed it. Only a minute or two before, the attention of the whole party had been concentrated upon it. Darrow had held it up for all to see, while he discoursed upon its history. He would take Darrow aside at the first opportunity and ask him—But—it! how could he do that? These were his intimate friends. He knew them well, more than well, with one exception, and he—Well, he was the handsomest of the lot and the most debonair and agreeable. A little more gay than usual to-night, possibly a trifle too gay, considering that a man of Mr. Blake's social weight and business standing sat at the board; but not to be suspected, no, not to be suspected, even if he was the next man after Darrow and had betrayed something like confusion when the eyes of the whole table turned his way at the former's simple statement of "I passed it on." Robert would find the coin; he was a fool to doubt it; and if Robert did not, why, he would simply have to pocket his chagrin, and not let a triviality like this throw a shadow over his hospitality.

All this, while he genially lifted his glass and proposed the health of the ladies. The constraint of the preceding moment was removed by his manner, and a dozen jests caused as many merry laughs. Then he pushed back his chair.

"And now, some music!" he cheerfully cried, as with lingering glances and some further pokings about of the table furniture, the various guests left their places and followed him into the adjoining room.

But the ladies were too nervous and the gentlemen not sufficiently sure of their voices to undertake the entertainment of the rest at a moment of such acknowledged suspense; and notwithstanding the exertions of their host and his quiet but much discomfited wife, it soon became apparent that but one thought engrossed them all, and that any attempt at conversation must prove futile so long as the curtains between the two rooms remained open and they could see Robert on his hands and knees searching the floor and shoving aside the rugs.

Darrow, who was Mr. Sedgwick's brother-in-law and almost as much at home in the house as Sedgwick himself, made a move to draw these curtains, but something in his relative's face stopped him and he desisted with some laughing remark which did not attract enough attention, even, to elicit any response.

"I hope his eyesight is good," murmured one of the young girls, edging a trifle forward. "Mayn't I help him look? They say at home that I am the only one in the house who can find anything."

Mr. Sedgwick smiled indulgently at the speaker, (a round-faced, round-eyed, merry-hearted girl whom in days gone by he had dandled on his knees), but answered quite quickly for him:

"Robert will find it if it is there." Then, distressed at this involuntary disclosure of his thought, added in his whole-hearted way: "It's such a little thing, and the room is so big and a round object rolls unexpectedly far, you know. Well, have you got it?" he eagerly demanded, as the butler finally showed himself in the door.

"No, sir; and it's not in the dining-room. I have cleared the table and thoroughly searched the floor."

Mr. Sedgwick knew that he had. He had no doubts about Robert. Robert had been in his employ for years and had often handled his coins and, at his order, sometimes shown them.

"Very well," said he, "we'll not bother about it any more to-night; you may draw the curtains."

But here the clear, almost strident voice of the youngest man of the party interposed.

"Wait a minute," said he. "This especial coin is the great treasure of Mr. Sedgwick's valuable collection. It is unique in this country, and not only worth a great deal of money, but cannot be duplicated at any cost. There are only three of its stamp in the world. Shall we let the matter pass, then, as though it were of small importance? I feel that we cannot; that we are, in a measure, responsible for its disappearance. Mr. Sedgwick handed it to us to look at, and while it was going through our hands it vanished. What must he think? What has he every right to think? I need not put it into words; you know what you would think, what you could not help but think, if the object were yours and it was lost in this way. Gentlemen—I leave the ladies entirely out of this—I do not propose that he shall have further opportunity to associate me with this very natural doubt. I demand the privilege of emptying my pockets here and now, before any of us have left his presence. I am a connoisseur in coins myself and consequently find it imperative to take the initiative in this matter. As I propose to spare the ladies, let us step back into the dining-room. Mr. Sedgwick, pray don't deny me; I'm thoroughly in earnest, I assure you."

The astonishment created by this audacious proposition was so great, and the feeling it occasioned so intense, that for an instant all stood speechless. Young Hammersley was a millionaire himself, and generous to a fault, as all knew. Under no circumstances would any one even suspect him of appropriating anything, great or small, to which he had not a perfect right. Nor was he likely to imagine for a moment that any one would. That he could make such a proposition then, based upon any such plea, argued a definite suspicion in some other quarter, which could not pass unrecognised. In vain Mr. Sedgwick raised his voice in frank and decided protest, two of the gentlemen had already made a quick move toward Robert, who still stood, stupefied by the situation, with his hand on the cord which controlled the curtains.

"He is quite right," remarked one of these, as he passed into the dining-room. "I shouldn't sleep a wink to-night if this question remained unsettled." The other, the oldest man present, the financier of whose standing and highly esteemed character I have already spoken, said nothing, but followed in a way to show that his mind was equally made up.

The position in which Mr. Sedgwick found himself placed was far from enviable. With a glance at the two remaining gentlemen, he turned towards the ladies now standing in a close group at the other end of the room. One of them was his wife, and he quivered internally as he noted the deep red of her distressed countenance. But it was the others he addressed, singling out, with the rare courtesy which was his by nature, the one comparative stranger, Darrow's niece, a Rochester girl, who could not be finding this, her first party in Boston, very amusing.

"I hope you will appreciate the dilemma in which I have been placed by these gentlemen," he began, "and will pardon—"

But here he noticed that she was not in the least attending; her eyes were on the handsome figure of Hugh Clifford, her uncle's neighbour at table, who in company with Mr. Hammersley was still hesitating in the doorway. As Mr. Sedgwick stopped his useless talk, the two passed in and the sound of her fluttering breath as she finally turned a listening ear his way, caused him to falter as he repeated his assurances and begged her indulgence.

She answered with some conventional phrase which he forgot while crossing the room. But the remembrance of her slight satin-robed figure, drawn up in an attitude whose carelessness was totally belied by the anxiety of her half-averted glance, followed him into the presence of the four men awaiting him. Four? I should say five, for Robert was still there, though in a corner by himself, ready, no doubt, to share any attempt which the others might make to prove their innocence.

"The ladies will await us in the music-room," announced the host on entering; and then paused, disconcerted by the picture suddenly disclosed to his eye. On one side stood the two who had entered first, with their eyes fixed in open sternness on young Clifford, who, quite alone on the rug, faced them with a countenance of such pronounced pallor that there seemed to be nothing else in the room. As his features were singularly regular and his almost perfect mouth accentuated by a smile as set as his figure was immobile, the effect was so startling that not only Mr. Sedgwick, but every other person present, no doubt, wished that the plough had never turned the furrow which had brought this wretched coin to light.

However, the affair had gone too far now for retreat, as was shown by Mr. Blake, the elderly financier whom all were ready to recognise as the chief guest there. With an apologetic glance at Mr. Hammersley, the impetuous young millionaire who had first proposed this embarrassing procedure, he advanced to an empty side-table, and began, in a quiet, business-like way, to lay on it the contents of his various pockets. As the pile rose, the silence grew, the act in itself was so simple, the motive actuating it so serious and out of accord with the standing of the company and the nature of the occasion. When all was done, he stepped up to Mr. Sedgwick, with his arms raised and held out from his body.

"Now accommodate me," said he, "by running your hands up and down my chest. I have a secret pocket there which should be empty at this time."

Mr. Sedgwick, fascinated by his look, did as he was bid, reporting shortly:

"You are quite correct. I find nothing there."

Mr. Blake stepped back. As he did so, every eye, suddenly released from his imposing figure, flashed towards the immovable Clifford, to find him still absorbed by the action and attitude of the man who had just undergone what to him doubtless appeared a degrading ordeal. Pale before, he was absolutely livid now, though otherwise unchanged. To break the force of what appeared to be an open, if involuntary, self-betrayal, another guest stepped forward; but no sooner had he raised his hand to his vest-pocket than Clifford moved, and in a high, strident voice totally unlike his usual tones remarked:

"This is all—all—very interesting and commendable, no doubt. But for such a procedure to be of any real value it should be entered into by all. Gentlemen"—his rigidity was all gone now and so was his pallor—"I am unwilling to submit myself to what, in my eyes, is an act of unnecessary humiliation. Our word should be enough. I have not the coin—" Stopped by the absolute silence, he cast a distressed look into the faces about him, till it reached that of Mr. Sedgwick, where it lingered, in an appeal to which that gentleman, out of his great heart, instantly responded.

"One should take the word of the gentleman he invites to his house. We will excuse you, and excuse all the others from the unnecessary ceremony which Mr. Blake has been good enough to initiate."

But this show of favour was not to the mind of the last-mentioned gentleman, and met with instant reproof.

"Not so fast, Sedgwick. I am the oldest man here and I did not feel it was enough simply to state that this coin was not on my person. As to the question of humiliation, it strikes me that humiliation would lie, in this instance, in a refusal for which no better excuse can be given than the purely egotistical one of personal pride."

At this attack, the fine head of Clifford rose, and Darrow, remembering the girl within, felt instinctively grateful that she was not here to note the effect it gave to his person.

"I regret to differ," said he. "To me no humiliation could equal that of demonstrating in this open manner the fact of one's not being a thief."

Mr. Blake gravely surveyed him. For some reason the issue seemed no longer to lie between Clifford and the actual loser of the coin, but between him and his fellow guest, this uncompromising banker.

"A thief!" repeated the young man, in an indescribable tone full of bitterness and scorn.

Mr. Blake remained unmoved; he was a just man but strict, hard to himself, hard to others. But he was not entirely without heart. Suddenly his expression lightened. A certain possible explanation of the other's attitude had entered his mind.

"Young men sometimes have reasons for their susceptibilities which the old forget. If you have such—if you carry a photograph, believe that we have no interest in pictures of any sort to-night and certainly would fail to recognise them."

A smile of disdain flickered across the young man's lip. Evidently it was no discovery of this kind that he feared.

"I carry no photographs," said he; and, bowing low to his host, he added in a measured tone which but poorly hid his profound agitation, "I regret to have interfered in the slightest way with the pleasure of the evening. If you will be so good as to make my excuses to the ladies, I will withdraw from a presence upon which I have made so poor an impression."

Mr. Sedgwick prized his coin and despised deceit, but he could not let a guest leave him in this manner. Instinctively he held out his hand. Proudly young Clifford dropped his own into it; but the lack of mutual confidence was felt and the contact was a cold one. Half regretting his impulsive attempt at courtesy, Mr. Sedgwick drew back, and Clifford was already at the door leading into the hall, when Hammersley, who by his indiscreet proposition had made all this trouble for him, sprang forward and caught him by the arm.

"Don't go," he whispered. "You're done for if you leave like this. I—I was a brute to propose such an asinine thing, but having done so I am bound to see you out of the difficulty. Come into the adjoining room—there is nobody there at present—and we will empty our pockets together and find this lost article if we can. I may have pocketed it myself, in a fit of abstraction."

Did the other hesitate? Some thought so; but, if he did, it was but momentarily.

"I cannot," he muttered; "think what you will of me, but let me go." And dashing open the door he disappeared from their sight just as light steps and the rustle of skirts were heard again in the adjoining room.

"There are the ladies. What shall we say to them?" queried Sedgwick, stepping slowly towards the intervening curtains.

"Tell them the truth," enjoined Mr. Blake, as he hastily repocketed his own belongings. "Why should a handsome devil like that be treated with any more consideration than another? He has a secret if he hasn't a coin. Let them know this. It may save some one a future heartache."

The last sentence was muttered, but Mr. Sedgwick heard it. Perhaps that was why his first movement on entering the adjoining room was to cross over to the cabinet and shut and lock the heavily panelled door which had been left standing open. At all events, the action drew general attention and caused an instant silence, broken the next minute by an ardent cry:

"So your search was futile?"

It came from the lady least known, the interesting young stranger whose personality had made so vivid an impression upon him.

"Quite so," he answered, hastily facing her with an attempted smile. "The gentlemen decided not to carry matters to the length first proposed. The object was not worth it. I approved their decision. This was meant for a joyous occasion. Why mar it by unnecessary unpleasantness?"

She had given him her full attention while he was speaking, but her eye wandered away the moment he had finished and rested searchingly on the other gentlemen. Evidently she missed a face she had expected to find there, for her colour changed and she drew back behind the other ladies with the light, unmusical laugh women sometimes use to hide a secret emotion.

It brought Mr. Darrow forward.

"Some were not willing to subject themselves to what they considered an unnecessary humiliation," he curtly remarked. "Mr. Clifford—"

"There! let us drop it," put in his brother-in-law. "I've lost my coin and that's the end of it. I don't intend to have the evening spoiled for a thing like that. Music! ladies, music and a jolly air! No more dumps." And with as hearty a laugh as he could command in face of the sombre looks he encountered on every side, he led the way back into the music-room.

Once there the women seemed to recover their spirits; that is, such as remained. One had disappeared. A door opened from this room into the main hall and through this a certain young lady had vanished before the others had had time to group themselves about the piano. We know who this lady was; possibly, we know, too, why her hostess did not follow her.

Meanwhile, Mr. Clifford had gone upstairs for his coat, and was lingering there, the prey of some very bitter reflections. Though he had encountered nobody on the stairs, and neither heard nor saw any one in the halls, he felt confident that he was not unwatched. He remembered the look on the butler's face as he tore himself away from Hammersley's restraining hand, and he knew what that fellow thought and also was quite able to guess what that fellow would do, if his suspicions were farther awakened. This conviction brought an odd and not very open smile to his face, as he finally turned to descend the one flight which separated him from the front door he was so ardently desirous of closing behind him for ever.

A moment and he would be down; but the steps were many and seemed to multiply indefinitely as he sped below. Should his departure be noted, and some one advance to detain him! He fancied he heard a rustle in the open space under the stairs. Were any one to step forth, Robert or—With a start, he paused and clutched the banister. Some one had stepped forth; a woman! The swish of her skirts was unmistakable. He felt the chill of a new dread. Never in his short but triumphant career had he met coldness or disapproval in the eye of a woman. Was he to encounter it now? If so, it would go hard with him. He trembled as he turned his head to see which of the four it was. If it should prove to be his hostess—But it was not she; it was Darrow's young friend, the pretty inconsequent girl he had chatted with at the dinner-table, and afterwards completely forgotten in the events which had centred all his thoughts upon himself. And she was standing there, waiting for him! He would have to pass her,—notice her,—speak.

But when the encounter occurred and their eyes met, he failed to find in hers any sign of the disapproval he feared, but instead a gentle womanly interest which he might interpret deeply, or otherwise, according to the measure of his need.

That need seemed to be a deep one at this instant, for his countenance softened perceptibly as he took her quietly extended hand.

"Good-night," she said; "I am just going myself," and with an entrancing smile of perfect friendliness, she fluttered past him up the stairs.

It was the one and only greeting which his sick heart could have sustained without flinching. Just this friendly farewell of one acquaintance to another, as though no change had taken place in his relations to society and the world. And she was a woman and not a thoughtless girl! Staring after her slight, elegant figure, slowly ascending the stair, he forgot to return her cordial greeting. What delicacy, and yet what character there was in the poise of her spirited head! He felt his breath fail him, in his anxiety for another glance from her eye, for some sign, however small, that she had carried the thought of him up those few, quickly-mounted steps. Would he get it? She is at the bend of the stair; she pauses—turns, a nod,—and she is gone.

With an impetuous gesture, he dashed from the house.

In the drawing-room the noise of the closing door was heard, and a change at once took place in the attitude and expression of all present. The young millionaire approached Mr. Sedgwick and confidentially remarked:

"There goes your precious coin. I'm sure of it. I even think I can tell the exact place in which it is hidden. His hand went to his left coat-pocket once too often."

"That's right. I noticed the action also," chimed in Mr. Darrow, who had stepped up, unobserved. "And I noticed something else. His whole appearance altered from the moment this coin came on the scene. An indefinable half-eager, half-furtive look crept into his eye as he saw it passed from hand to hand. I remember it now, though it didn't make much impression upon me at the time."

"And I remember another thing," supplemented Hammersley in his anxiety to set himself straight with these men of whose entire approval he was not quite sure. "He raised his napkin to his mouth very frequently during the meal and held it there longer than is usual, too. Once he caught me looking at him, and for a moment he flushed scarlet, then he broke out with one of his witty remarks and I had to laugh like everybody else. If I am not mistaken, his napkin was up and his right hand working behind it, about the time Mr. Sedgwick requested the return of his coin."

"The idiot! Hadn't he sense enough to know that such a loss wouldn't pass unquestioned? The gem of the collection; known all over the country, and he's not even a connoisseur."

"No; I've never even heard him mention numismatics."

"Mr. Darrow spoke of its value. Perhaps that was what tempted him. I know that Clifford's been rather down on his luck lately."

"He? Well, he don't look it. There isn't one of us so well set up. Pardon me, Mr. Hammersley, you understand what I mean. He perhaps relies a little bit too much on his fine clothes."

"He needn't. His face is his fortune—all the one he's got, I hear it said. He had a pretty income from Consolidated Silver, but that's gone up and left him in what you call difficulties. If he has debts besides—"

But here Mr. Darrow was called off. His niece wanted to see him for one minute in the hall. When he came back it was to make his adieu and hers. She had been taken suddenly indisposed and his duty was to see her immediately home. This broke up the party, and amid general protestations the various guests were taking their leave when the whole action was stopped by a smothered cry from the dining-room, and the precipitate entrance of Robert, asking for Mr. Sedgwick.

"What's up? What's happened?" demanded that gentleman, hurriedly advancing towards the agitated butler.

"Found!" he exclaimed, holding up the coin between his thumb and forefinger. "It was standing straight up between two leaves of the table. It tumbled and fell to the floor as Luke and I were taking them out."

Silence which could be felt for a moment. Then each man turned and surveyed his neighbour, while the women's voices rose in little cries that were almost hysterical.

"I knew that it would be found, and found here," came from the hallway in rich, resonant tones. "Uncle, do not hurry; I am feeling better," followed in unconscious naïveté, as the young girl stepped in, showing a countenance in which were small signs of indisposition or even of depressed spirits.

Mr. Darrow, with a smile of sympathetic understanding, joined the others now crowding about the butler.

"I noticed the crack between these two leaves when I pushed about the plates and dishes," he was saying. "But I never thought of looking in it for the missing coin. I'm sure I'm very sorry that I didn't."

Mr. Darrow, to whom these words had recalled a circumstance he had otherwise completely forgotten, anxiously remarked: "That must have happened shortly after it left my hand. I recall now that the lady sitting between me and Clifford gave it a twirl which sent it spinning over the bare table-top. I don't think she realised the action. She was listening—we all were—to a flow of bright repartee going on below us, and failed to follow the movements of the coin. Otherwise, she would have spoken. But what a marvel that it should have reached that crack in just the position to fall in!"

"It wouldn't happen again, not if we spun it there for a month of Sundays."

"But Mr. Clifford!" put in an agitated voice.

"Yes, it has been rather hard on him. But he shouldn't have such keen sensibilities. If he had emptied out his pockets cheerfully and at the first intimation, none of this unpleasantness would have happened. Mr. Sedgwick, I congratulate you upon the recovery of this valuable coin, and am quite ready to offer my services if you wish to make Mr. Clifford immediately acquainted with Robert's discovery."

"Thank you, but I will perform that duty myself," was Mr. Sedgwick's quiet rejoinder, as he unlocked the door of his cabinet and carefully restored the coin to its proper place.

When he faced back, he found his guests on the point of leaving. Only one gave signs of any intention of lingering. This was the elderly financier who had shown such stern resolve in his treatment of Mr. Clifford's so-called sensibilities. He had confided his wife to the care of Mr. Darrow, and now met Mr. Sedgwick with this remark:

"I'm going to ask a favour of you. If, as you have intimated, it is your intention to visit Mr. Clifford to-night, I should like to go with you. I don't understand this young man and his unaccountable attitude in this matter, and it is very important that I should. Have you any objection to my company? My motor is at the door, and we can settle the affair in twenty minutes."

"None," returned his host, a little surprised, however, at the request. "His pride does seem a little out of place, but he was among comparative strangers, and seemed to feel his honour greatly impugned by Hammersley's unfortunate proposition. I'm sorry way down to the ground for what has occurred, and cannot carry him our apologies too soon."

"No, you cannot," retorted the other shortly. And so seriously did he utter this that no time was lost by Mr. Sedgwick, and as soon as they could get into their coats, they were in the motor and on their way to the young man's apartment.

Their experience began at the door. A man was lolling there who told them that Mr. Clifford had changed his quarters; where he did not know. But upon the production of a five-dollar bill, he remembered enough about it to give them a number and street where possibly they might find him. In a rush, they hastened there; only to hear the same story from the sleepy elevator boy anticipating his last trip up for the night.

"Mr. Clifford left a week ago; he didn't tell me where he was going."

Nevertheless the boy knew; that they saw, and another but smaller bill came into requisition and awoke his sleepy memory.

The street and number which he gave made the two well-to-do men stare. But they said nothing, though the looks they cast back at the second-rate quarters they were leaving, so far below the elegant apartment house they had visited first, were sufficiently expressive. The scale of descent from luxury to positive discomfort was proving a rapid one and prepared them for the dismal, ill-cared-for, altogether repulsive doorway before which they halted next. No attendant waited here; not even an elevator boy; the latter for the good reason that there was no elevator. An uninviting flight of stairs was before them; and on the few doors within sight a simple card showed the name of the occupant.

Mr. Sedgwick glanced at his companion.

"Shall we go up?" he asked.

Mr. Blake nodded. "We'll find him," said he, "if it takes all night."

"Surely he cannot have sunk lower than this."

"Remembering his get-up I do not think so. Yet who knows? Some mystery lies back of his whole conduct. Dining in your home, with this to come back to! I don't wonder—"

But here a thought struck him. Pausing with his foot on the stair, he turned a flushed countenance towards Mr. Sedgwick. "I've an idea," said he. "Perhaps—" He whispered the rest.

Mr. Sedgwick stared and shook his shoulders. "Possibly," said he, flushing slightly in his turn. Then, as they proceeded up, "I feel like a brute, anyway. A sorry night's business all through, unless the end proves better than the beginning."

"We'll start from the top. Something tells me that we shall find him close under the roof. Can you read the names by such a light?"

"Barely; but I have matches."

And now there might have been witnessed by any chance home-comer the curious sight of two extremely well-dressed men pottering through the attic hall of this decaying old domicile, reading the cards on the doors by means of a lighted match.

And vainly. On none of the cards could be seen the name they sought.

"We're on the wrong track," protested Mr. Blake. "No use keeping this up," but found himself stopped, when about to turn away, by a gesture of Sedgwick's.

"There's a light under the door you see there untagged," said he. "I'm going to knock."

He did so. There was a sound within and then utter silence.

He knocked again. A man's step was heard approaching the door, then again the silence.

Mr. Sedgwick made a third essay, and then the door was suddenly pulled inward and in the gap they saw the handsome face and graceful figure of the young man they had so lately encountered amid palatial surroundings. But how changed! how openly miserable! and when he saw who his guests were, how proudly defiant of their opinion and presence.

"You have found the coin," he quietly remarked. "I appreciate your courtesy in coming here to inform me of it. Will not that answer, without further conversation? I am on the point of retiring and—and—"

Even the hardihood of a very visible despair gave way for an instant as he met Mr. Sedgwick's eye. In the break which followed, the older man spoke.

"Pardon us, but we have come thus far with a double purpose. First, to tender our apologies, which you have been good enough to accept; secondly, to ask, in no spirit of curiosity, I assure you, a question that I seem to see answered, but which I should be glad to hear confirmed by your lips. May we not come in?"

The question was put with a rare smile such as sometimes was seen on this hard-grained handler of millions, and the young man, seeing it, faltered back, leaving the way open for them to enter. The next minute he seemed to regret the impulse, for backing against a miserable table they saw there, he drew himself up with an air as nearly hostile as one of his nature could assume.

"I know of no question," said he, "which I feel at this very late hour inclined to answer. A man who has been tracked as I must have been for you to find me here, is hardly in a mood to explain his poverty or the mad desire for former luxuries which took him to the house of one friendly enough, he thought, to accept his presence without inquiry as to the place he lived in or the nature or number of the reverses which had brought him to such a place as this."

"I do not—believe me—" faltered Mr. Sedgwick, greatly embarrassed and distressed. In spite of the young man's attempt to hide the contents of the table, he had seen the two objects lying there—a piece of bread or roll, and a half-cocked revolver.

Mr. Blake had seen them, too, and at once took the word out of his companion's mouth.

"You mistake us," he said coldly, "as well as the nature of our errand. We are here from no motive of curiosity, as I have before said, nor from any other which might offend or distress you. We—or rather I am here on business. I have a position to offer to an intelligent, upright, enterprising young man. Your name has been given me. It was given me before this dinner, to which I went—if Mr. Sedgwick will pardon my plain speaking—chiefly for the purpose of making your acquaintance. The result was what you know, and possibly now you can understand my anxiety to see you exonerate yourself from the doubts you yourself raised by your attitude of resistance to the proposition made by that head-long, but well-meaning, young man of many millions, Mr. Hammersley. I wanted to find in you the honourable characteristics necessary to the man who is to draw an eight thousand dollars a year salary under my eye. I still want to do this. If then you are willing to make this whole thing plain to me—for it is not plain—not wholly plain, Mr. Clifford—then you will find in me a friend such as few young fellows can boast of, for I like you—I will say that—and where I like—"

The gesture with which he ended the sentence was almost superfluous, in face of the change which had taken place in the aspect of the man he addressed. Wonder, doubt, hope, and again incredulity were lost at last in a recognition of the other's kindly intentions toward himself, and the prospects which they opened out before him. With a shame-faced look, and yet with a manly acceptance of his own humiliation that was not displeasing to his visitors, he turned about and pointing to the morsel of bread lying on the table before them, he said to Mr. Sedgwick:

"Do you recognise that? It is from your table, and—and—it is not the only piece I had hidden in my pockets. I had not eaten in twenty-four hours when I sat down to dinner this evening. I had no prospect of another morsel for to-morrow and—and—I was afraid of eating my fill—there were ladies—and so—and so—"

They did not let him finish. In a flash they had both taken in the room. Not an article which could be spared was anywhere visible. His dress-suit was all that remained to him of former ease and luxury. That he had retained, possibly for just such opportunities as had given him a dinner to-night. Mr. Blake understood at last, and his iron lip trembled.

"Have you no friends?" he asked. "Was it necessary to go hungry?"

"Could I ask alms or borrow what I could not pay? It was a position I was after, and positions do not come at call. Sometimes they come without it," he smiled with the dawning of his old-time grace on his handsome face, "but I find that one can see his resources go, dollar by dollar, and finally, cent by cent, in the search for employment no one considers necessary to a man like me. Perhaps if I had had less pride, had been willing to take you or any one else into my confidence, I might not have sunk to these depths of humiliation; but I had not the confidence in men which this last half hour has given me, and I went blundering on, hiding my needs and hoping against hope for some sort of result to my efforts. This pistol is not mine. I did borrow this, but I did not mean to use it, unless nature reached the point where it could stand no more. I thought the time had come to-night when I left your house, Mr. Sedgwick, suspected of theft. It seemed the last straw; but—but—a woman's look has held me back. I hesitated and—now you know the whole," said he; "that is, if you can understand why it was more possible for me to brave the contumely of such a suspicion than to open my pockets and disclose the crusts I had hidden there."

"I can understand," said Mr. Sedgwick; "but the opportunity you have given us for doing so must not be shared by others. We will undertake your justification, but it must be made in our own way and after the most careful consideration; eh, Mr. Blake?"

"Most assuredly; and if Mr. Clifford will present himself at my office early in the morning, we will first breakfast and then talk business."

Young Clifford could only hold out his hand, but when, his two friends gone, he sat in contemplation of his changed prospects, one word and one only left his lips, uttered in every inflection of tenderness, hope, and joy. "Edith! Edith! Edith!"

It was the name of the sweet young girl who had shown her faith in him at the moment when his heart was lowest and despair at its culmination.

THE HOUSE IN THE MIST

I

AN OPEN DOOR

It was a night to drive any man indoors. Not only was the darkness impenetrable, but the raw mist enveloping hill and valley made the open road anything but desirable to a belated wayfarer like myself.

Being young, untrammelled, and naturally indifferent to danger, I was not averse to adventure; and having my fortune to make, was always on the lookout for El Dorado, which to ardent souls lies ever beyond the next turning. Consequently, when I saw a light shimmering through the mist at my right, I resolved to make for it and the shelter it so opportunely offered.

But I did not realise then, as I do now, that shelter does not necessarily imply refuge, or I might not have undertaken this adventure with so light a heart. Yet who knows? The impulses of an unfettered spirit lean toward daring, and youth, as I have said, seeks the strange, the unknown, and sometimes the terrible.

My path towards this light was by no means an easy one. After confused wanderings through tangled hedges, and a struggle with obstacles of whose nature I received the most curious impression in the surrounding murk, I arrived in front of a long, low building, which, to my astonishment, I found standing with doors and windows open to the pervading mist, save for one square casement, through which the light shone from a row of candles placed on a long mahogany table.

The quiet and seeming emptiness of this odd and picturesque building made me pause. I am not much affected by visible danger, but this silent room, with its air of sinister expectancy, struck me most unpleasantly, and I was about to reconsider my first impulse and withdraw again to the road, when a second look thrown back upon the comfortable interior I was leaving convinced me of my folly, and sent me straight toward the door which stood so invitingly open.

But half-way up the path my progress was again stayed by the sight of a man issuing from the house I had so rashly looked upon as devoid of all human presence. He seemed in haste, and at the moment my eye first fell on him was engaged in replacing his watch in his pocket.

But he did not shut the door behind him, which I thought odd, especially as his final glance had been a backward one, and seemed to take in all the appointments of the place he was so hurriedly leaving.

As we met he raised his hat. This likewise struck me as peculiar, for the deference he displayed was more marked than that usually bestowed on strangers, while his lack of surprise at an encounter more or less startling in such a mist, was calculated to puzzle an ordinary man like myself. Indeed, he was so little impressed by my presence there that he was for passing me without a word or any other hint of good-fellowship save the bow of which I have spoken. But this did not suit me. I was hungry, cold, and eager for creature comforts, and the house before me gave forth, not only heat, but a savoury odour which in itself was an invitation hard to ignore. I therefore accosted the man.

"Will bed and supper be provided for me here?" I asked. "I am tired out with a long tramp over the hills, and hungry enough to pay anything in reason—"

I stopped, for the man had disappeared. He had not paused at my appeal, and the mist had swallowed him. But at the break in my sentence his voice came back in good-natured tones, and I heard:

"Supper will be ready at nine, and there are beds for all. Enter, sir; you are the first to arrive, but the others cannot be far behind."

A queer greeting certainly. But when I strove to question him as to its meaning, his voice returned to me from such a distance that I doubted if my words had reached him any more than his answer had reached me.

"Well," thought I, "it isn't as if a lodging had been denied me. He invited me to enter, and enter I will."

The house, to which I now naturally directed a glance of much more careful scrutiny than before, was no ordinary farm-building, but a rambling old mansion, made conspicuously larger here and there by jutting porches and more than one convenient lean-to. Though furnished, warmed, and lighted with candles, as I have previously described, it had about it an air of disuse which made me feel myself an intruder, in spite of the welcome I had received. But I was not in a position to stand upon ceremony, and ere long I found myself inside the great room and before the blazing logs whose glow had lighted up the doorway and added its own attraction to the other allurements of the inviting place.

Though the open door made a draught which was anything but pleasant, I did not feel like closing it, and was astonished to observe the effect of the mist through the square thus left open to the night. It was not an agreeable one, and, instinctively turning my back upon that quarter of the room, I let my eyes roam over the wainscoted walls and the odd pieces of furniture which gave such an air of old-fashioned richness to the place. As nothing of the kind had ever fallen under my eyes before, I would have thoroughly enjoyed this opportunity of gratifying my taste for the curious and the beautiful, if the quaint old chairs I saw standing about me on every side had not all been empty. But the solitude of the place, so much more oppressive than the solitude of the road I had left, struck cold to my heart, and I missed the cheer rightfully belonging to such attractive surroundings. Suddenly I bethought me of the many other apartments likely to be found in so spacious a dwelling, and, going to the nearest door, I opened it and called out for the master of the house. But only an echo came back, and returning to the fire, I sat down before the cheering blaze, in quiet acceptance of a situation too lonely for comfort, yet not without a certain piquant interest for a man of free mind and adventurous disposition like myself.

After all, if supper was to be served at nine, some one must be expected to eat it; I should surely not be left much longer without companions.

Meanwhile ample amusement awaited me in the contemplation of a picture which, next to the large fireplace, was the most prominent object in the room. This picture was a portrait, and a remarkable one. The countenance it portrayed was both characteristic and forcible, and so interested me that in studying it I quite forgot both hunger and weariness. Indeed its effect upon me was such that, after gazing at it uninterruptedly for a few minutes, I discovered that its various features—the narrow eyes in which a hint of craft gave a strange gleam to their native intelligence; the steadfast chin, strong as the rock of the hills I had wearily tramped all day; the cunning wrinkles which yet did not interfere with a latent great-heartedness that made the face as attractive as it was puzzling—had so established themselves in my mind that I continued to see them before me whichever way I turned, and even found it impossible to shake off their influence after I had resolutely set my mind in another direction by endeavouring to recall what I knew of the town into which I had strayed.

I had come from Scranton, and was now, according to my best judgment, in one of those rural districts of Western Pennsylvania which breed such strange and sturdy characters. But of this special neighbourhood, its inhabitants, and its industries, I knew nothing, nor was I likely to become acquainted with it so long as I remained in the solitude I have described.

But these impressions and these thoughts—if thoughts they were—presently received a check. A loud "Halloo!" rose from somewhere in the mist, followed by a string of muttered imprecations, which convinced me that the person now attempting to approach the house was encountering some of the many difficulties which had beset me in the same undertaking a few minutes before.

I therefore raised my voice and shouted out, "Here! This way!" after which I sat still and awaited developments.

There was a huge clock in one of the corners, whose loud tick filled up every interval of silence. By this clock it was just ten minutes to eight when two gentlemen—I should say men, and coarse men at that—crossed the open threshold and entered the house.

Their appearance was more or less noteworthy—unpleasantly so, I am obliged to add. One was red-faced and obese; the other was tall, thin, and wiry, and showed as many seams in his face as a blighted apple. Neither of the two had anything to recommend him either in appearance or address, save a certain veneer of polite assumption as transparent as it was offensive. As I listened to the forced sallies of the one and the hollow laugh of the other, I was glad that I was large of frame and strong of arm, and used to all kinds of men and—brutes.

As these two newcomers seemed no more astonished at my presence than the man I had met at the gate, I checked the question which instinctively rose to my lips, and with a simple bow—responded to by a more or less familiar nod from either—accepted the situation with all the sang-froid the occasion seemed to demand. Perhaps this was wise, perhaps it was not; there was little opportunity to judge, for the start they both gave as they encountered the eyes of the picture before mentioned drew my attention to a consideration of the different ways in which men, however similar in other respects, express sudden and unlooked-for emotion. The big man simply allowed his astonishment, dread, or whatever the feeling was which moved him, to ooze forth in a cold and deathly perspiration which robbed his cheeks of colour, and cast a bluish shadow over his narrow and retreating temples; while the thin and waspish man, caught in the same trap (for trap I saw it was), shouted aloud in his ill-timed mirth, the false and cruel character of which would have made me shudder, if all expression of feeling on my part had not been held in check by the interest I immediately experienced in the display of open bravado with which, in another moment, these two tried to carry off their mutual embarrassment.

"Good likeness, eh?" laughed the seamy-faced man. "Quite an idea that! Makes him one of us again! Well, he's welcome—in oils. Can't say much to us from canvas, eh?" And the rafters above him vibrated, as his violent efforts at joviality went up in loud and louder assertion from his thin throat.

A nudge from the other's elbow stopped him, and I saw them both cast half-lowering, half-inquisitive glances in my direction.

"One of the Witherspoon boys?" queried one.

"Perhaps," snarled the other. "I never saw but one of them. There are five, aren't there? Eustace believed in marrying off his gals young."

"Damn him, yes! And he'd have married them off younger if he had known how numbers were going to count some day among the Westonhaughs." And he laughed again in a way I should certainly have felt it my business to resent if my indignation, as well as the ill-timed allusions which had called it forth, had not been put to an end by a fresh arrival through the veiling mist which hung like a shroud at the doorway.

This time it was for me to experience a shock of something like fear. Yet the personage who called up this unlooked-for sensation in my naturally hardy nature was old, and to all appearance harmless from disability, if not from good-will. His form was bent over upon itself like a bow; and only from the glances he shot from his upturned eyes was the fact made evident that a redoubtable nature, full of force and malignity, had just brought its quota of evil into a room already overflowing with dangerous and menacing passions.

As this old wretch, either from the feebleness of age or from the infirmity I have mentioned, had great difficulty in walking, he had brought with him a small boy, whose business it was to direct his tottering steps as best he could.

But once settled in his chair, he drove away this boy with his pointed oak stick, and with some harsh words about caring for the horse and being in time in the morning, he sent him out into the mist. As this little shivering and pathetic figure vanished, the old man drew with gasp and haw a number of deep breaths, which shook his bent back, and did their share, no doubt, in restoring his own disturbed circulation. Then, with a sinister twist which brought his pointed chin and twinkling eyes again into view, he remarked:

"Haven't ye a word for kinsman Luke, you two? It isn't often I get out among ye. Shakee, nephew! Shakee, Hector! And now, who's the boy in the window? My eyes aren't what they used to be, but he don't seem to favour the Westonhaughs overmuch. One of Salmon's four grandchildren, think 'e? Or a shoot from Eustace's gnarled old trunk? His gals all married Americans, and one of them, I've been told, was a yellow-haired giant like this fellow."

At this description, pointed directly toward me, I was about to venture a response on my own account, when my attention, as well as theirs, was freshly attracted by a loud "Whoa!" at the gate, followed by the hasty but assured entrance of a dapper, wizen, but perfectly preserved little old gentleman with a bag in his hand.

Looking askance with eyes that were like two beads, first at the two men, who were now elbowing each other for the best place before the fire, and next at the revolting figure in the chair, he bestowed his greeting, which consisted of an elaborate bow, not on them, but upon the picture hanging so conspicuously on the open wall before him; and then, taking me within the scope of his quick, circling glance, cried out with an assumption of great cordiality:

"Good-evening, gentlemen; good-evening one, good-evening all. Nothing like being on the tick. I'm sorry the night has turned out so badly. Some may find it too thick for travel. That would be bad, eh? very bad—for them."

As none of the men he openly addressed saw fit to answer, save by the hitch of a shoulder or a leer quickly suppressed, I kept silent also. But this reticence, marked as it was, did not seem to offend the newcomer. Shaking the wet from the umbrella he held, he stood the dripping article up in a corner, and then came and placed his feet on the fender. To do this he had to crowd between the two men already occupying the best part of the hearth. But he showed no concern at incommoding them, and bore their cross looks and threatening gestures with professional equanimity.

"You know me?" he now unexpectedly snapped, bestowing another look over his shoulder at that oppressive figure in the chair. (Did I say that I had risen when the latter sat?) "I'm no Westonhaugh, I; nor yet a Witherspoon nor a Clapsaddle. I'm only Smead, the lawyer—Mr. Anthony Westonhaugh's lawyer," he repeated, with another glance of recognition in the direction of the picture. "I drew up his last will and testament, and, until all of his wishes have been duly carried out, am entitled by the terms of that will to be regarded both legally and socially as his representative. This you all know, but it is my way to make everything clear as I proceed. A lawyer's trick, no doubt. I do not pretend to be entirely exempt from such."

A grumble from the large man, who seemed to have been disturbed in some absorbing calculation he was carrying on, mingled with a few muttered words of forced acknowledgment from the restless old sinner in the chair, made it unnecessary for me to reply, even if the last comer had given me the opportunity.

"It's getting late!" he cried, with an easy garrulity rather amusing under the circumstances. "Two more trains came in as I left the depot. If old Phil was on hand with his waggon, several more members of this interesting family may be here before the clock strikes; if not, the assemblage is like to be small. Too small," I heard him grumble a minute after, under his breath.

"I wish it were a matter of one," spoke up the big man, striking his breast in a way to make it perfectly apparent whom he meant by that word one. And having (if I may judge by the mingled laugh and growl of his companions) thus shown his hand both figuratively and literally, he relapsed into the calculation which seemed to absorb all of his unoccupied moments.

"Generous, very!" commented the lawyer in a murmur which was more than audible. "Pity that sentiments of such broad benevolence should go unrewarded."

This, because at that very instant wheels were heard in front, also a jangle of voices, in some controversy about fares, which promised anything but a pleasing addition to the already none too desirable company.

"I suppose that's Sister Janet," snarled out the one addressed as Hector. There was no love in his voice, despite the relationship hinted at, and I awaited the entrance of this woman with some curiosity.

But her appearance, heralded by many a puff and pant which the damp air exaggerated in a prodigious way, did not seem to warrant the interest I had shown in it. As she stepped into the room I saw only a big frowsy woman, who had attempted to make a show with a new silk dress and a hat in the latest fashion, but who had lamentably failed owing to the slouchiness of her figure and some misadventure, by which her hat had been set awry on her head and her usual complacency destroyed. Later, I noted that her down-looking eyes had a false twinkle in them, and that, commonplace as she looked, she was one to steer clear of in times of necessity and distress.

She, too, evidently expected to find the door open and people assembled, but she had not anticipated being confronted by the portrait on the wall, and cringed in an unpleasant way as she stumbled by it into one of the ill-lighted corners.

The old man, who had doubtless caught the rustle of her dress as she passed him, emitted one short sentence.

"Almost late," said he.

Her answer was a sputter of words.

"It's the fault of that driver," she complained. "If he had taken one drop more at the half-way house I might really not have got here at all. That would not have inconvenienced you. But oh! what a grudge I would have owed that skinflint brother of ours"—here she shook her fist at the picture—"for making our good luck depend upon our arrival within two short strokes of the clock!"

"There are several to come yet," blandly observed the lawyer. But before the words were well out of his mouth we all became aware of a new presence—a woman, whose sombre grace and quiet bearing gave distinction to her unobtrusive entrance, and caused a feeling of something like awe to follow the first sight of her cold features and deep, heavily-fringed eyes. But this soon passed in the more human sentiment awakened by the soft pleading which infused her gaze with a touching femininity. She wore a long loose garment, which fell without a fold from chin to foot, and in her arms she seemed to carry something.

Never before had I seen so beautiful a woman. As I was contemplating her, with respect but yet with a masculine intentness I could not quite suppress, two or three other persons came in. And now I began to notice that the eyes of all these people turned mainly one way, and that was toward the clock. Another small circumstance likewise drew my attention. Whenever any one entered—and there were one or two additional arrivals during the five minutes preceding the striking of the hour—a frown settled for an instant on every brow, giving to each and all a similar look, for the interpretation of which I lacked the key. Yet not on every brow either. There was one which remained undisturbed, and showed only a grand patience.

As the hands of the big clock neared the point of eight a furtive smile appeared on more than one face; and when the hour rang out a sigh of satisfaction swept through the room, to which the little old lawyer responded with a worldly-wise grunt as he moved from his place and proceeded to the door.

This he had scarcely shut when a chorus of voices rose from without. Three or four lingerers had pushed their way as far as the gate, only to see the door of the house shut in their faces.

"Too late!" growled old man Luke from between the locks of his long beard.

"Too late!" shrieked the woman who had come so near being late herself.

"Too late!" smoothly acquiesced the lawyer, locking and bolting the door with a deft and assured hand.

But the four or five persons who thus found themselves barred out did not accept without a struggle the decision of the more fortunate ones assembled within. More than one hand began pounding on the door, and we could hear cries of: "The train was behind time!" "Your clock is fast!" "You are cheating us; you want it all for yourselves!" "We will have the law on you!" and other bitter adjurations unintelligible to me from my ignorance of the circumstances which called them forth.

But the wary old lawyer simply shook his head and answered nothing; whereat a murmur of gratification rose from within, and a howl of almost frenzied dismay from without, which latter presently received point from a startling vision which now appeared at the casement where the lights burned. A man's face looked in, and behind it, that of a woman, so wild and maddened by some sort of heart-break that I found my sympathies aroused in spite of the glare of evil passions which made both of these countenances something less than human.

But the lawyer met the stare of these four eyes with a quiet chuckle, which found its echo in the ill-advised mirth of those about him; and moving over to the window where they still peered in, he drew together the two heavy shutters which hitherto had stood back against the wall, and, fastening them with a bar, shut out the sight of this despair, if he could not shut out the protests which ever and anon were shouted through the keyhole.

Meanwhile, one form had sat through this whole incident without a gesture; and on the quiet brow, from which I could not keep my eyes, no shadows appeared save the perpetual one of native melancholy, which was at once the source of its attraction and the secret of its power.

Into what sort of gathering had I stumbled? And why did I prefer to await developments rather than ask the simplest question of any one about me?

Meantime the lawyer had proceeded to make certain preparations. With the help of one or two willing hands he had drawn the great table into the middle of the room, and, having seen the candles restored to their places, began to open his small bag and take from it a roll of paper and several flat documents. Laying the latter in the centre of the table and slowly unrolling the former, he consulted, with his foxy eyes, the faces surrounding him, and smiled with secret malevolence, as he noted that every chair and every form was turned away from the picture before which he had bent with such obvious courtesy on entering. I alone stood erect, and this possibly was why a gleam of curiosity was noticeable in his glance, as he ended his scrutiny of my countenance and bent his gaze again upon the paper he held.

"Heavens!" thought I. "What shall I answer this man if he asks me why I continued to remain in a spot where I have so little business?"

The impulse came to go. But such was the effect of this strange convocation of persons, at night and in a mist which was itself a nightmare, that I failed to take action and remained riveted to my place, while Mr. Smead consulted his roll and finally asked in a business-like tone, quite unlike his previous sarcastic speech, the names of those whom he had the pleasure of seeing before him.

The old man in the chair spoke up first.

"Luke Westonhaugh," he announced.

"Very good!" responded the lawyer.

"Hector Westonhaugh," came from the thin man.

A nod and a look toward the next.

"John Westonhaugh."

"Nephew?" asked the lawyer.

"Yes."

"Go on, and be quick; supper will be ready at nine."

"Eunice Westonhaugh," spoke up a soft voice.

I felt my heart bound as if some inner echo responded to that name.

"Daughter of whom?"

"Hudson Westonhaugh," she gently faltered. "My father is dead—died last night. I am his only heir."

A grumble of dissatisfaction and a glint of unrelieved hate came from the doubled-up figure, whose malevolence had so revolted me.

But the lawyer was not to be shaken.

"Very good! It is fortunate you trusted your feet rather than the train. And now you? What is your name?"

He was looking, not at me, as I had at first feared, but at the man next to me, a slim but slippery youth, whose small red eyes made me shudder.

"William Witherspoon."

"Barbara's son?"

"Yes."

"Where are your brothers?"

"One of them, I think, is outside"—here he laughed—"the other is—sick."

The way he uttered this word made me set him down as one to be especially wary of when he smiled. But then, I had already passed judgment on him at my first view.

"And you, madam?"—this to the large, dowdy woman with the uncertain eye, a contrast to the young and melancholy Eunice.

"Janet Clapsaddle," she replied, waddling hungrily forward and getting unpleasantly near the speaker, for he moved off as she approached, and took his stand in the clear space at the head of the table.

"Very well, Mistress Clapsaddle. You were a Westonhaugh, I believe?"

"You believe, sneak-faced hypocrite that you are!" she blurted out. "I don't understand your lawyer ways. I like plain speaking myself. Don't you know me, and Luke and Hector, and—and most of us, indeed, except that puny, white-faced girl yonder, whom, having been brought up on the other side of the Ridge, we have none of us seen since she was a screaming baby in Hildegarde's arms. And the young gentleman over there"—here she indicated me—"who shows so little likeness to the rest of the family, he will have to make his connection to us pretty plain before we shall feel like acknowledging him, either as the son of one of Eustace's girls, or a chip from Brother Salmon's hard old block."

As this caused all eyes to turn upon me, even hers, I smiled as I stepped forward. The lawyer did not return that smile.

"What is your name?" he asked shortly and sharply, as if he distrusted me.

"Hugh Austin," was my quiet reply.

"There is no such name on the list," snapped old Smead, with an authoritative gesture toward those who seemed anxious to enter a protest.

"Probably not," I returned, "for I am not a Witherspoon, a Westonhaugh, nor yet a Clapsaddle. I am merely a chance wayfarer passing through the town on my way West. I thought this house was a tavern, or at least a place I could lodge in. The man I met in the doorway told me as much, and so I am here. If my company is not agreeable, or if you wish this room to yourselves, let me go into the kitchen. I promise not to meddle with the supper, hungry as I am. Or perhaps you wish me to join the crowd outside; it seems to be increasing."

"No, no," came from all parts of the room. "Don't let the door be opened. Nothing could keep Lemuel and his crowd out if they once got foot over the threshold."

The lawyer rubbed his chin. He seemed to be in some sort of quandary. First he scrutinised me from under his shaggy brows with a sharp gleam of suspicion; then his features softened, and, with a side-glance at the young woman who called herself Eunice (perhaps, because she was worth looking at, perhaps because she had partly risen at my words), he slipped toward a door I had before observed in the wainscoting on the left of the mantelpiece, and softly opened it upon what looked like a narrow staircase.

"We cannot let you go out," said he; "and we cannot let you have a finger in our viands before the hour comes for serving them; so if you will be so good as to follow this staircase to the top, you will find it ends in a room comfortable enough for the wayfarer you call yourself. In that room you can rest till the way is clear for you to continue your travels. Better we cannot do for you. This house is not a tavern, but the somewhat valuable property of—" He turned with a bow and smile, as every one there drew a deep breath; but no one ventured to end that sentence.

I would have given all my future prospects (which, by the way, were not very great) to remain in that room. The oddity of the situation; the mystery of the occurrence; the suspense I saw in every face; the eagerness of the cries I heard redoubled from time to time outside; the malevolence but poorly disguised in the old lawyer's countenance; and, above all, the presence of that noble-looking woman, which was the one off-set to the general tone of villainy with which the room was charged, filled me with curiosity, if I might call it by no other name, that made my acquiescence in the demand thus made upon me positively heroic. But there seemed no other course for me to follow, and with a last lingering glance at the genial fire and a quick look about me, which, happily, encountered hers, I stooped my head to suit the low and narrow doorway opened for my accommodation, and instantly found myself in darkness. The door had been immediately closed by the lawyer's impatient hand.

II

WITH MY EAR TO THE WAINSCOTING

No move more unwise could have been made by the old lawyer—that is, if his intention had been to rid himself of an unwelcome witness. For, finding myself thrust thus suddenly from the scene, I naturally stood still instead of mounting the stairs, and, by standing still, discovered that though shut from sight, I was not from sound. Distinctly through the panel of the door, which was much thinner, no doubt, than the old fox imagined, I heard one of the men present shout out:

"Well, that makes the number less by one!"

The murmur which followed this remark came plainly to my ears, and, greatly rejoicing over what I considered my good luck, I settled myself on the lowest step of the stairs in the hope of catching some word which would reveal to me the mystery of this scene.

It was not long in coming. Old Smead had now his audience before him in good shape, and his next words were of a character to make evident the purpose of this meeting.

"Heirs of Anthony Westonhaugh, deceased," he began in a sing-song voice strangely unmusical, "I congratulate you upon your good fortune at being at this especial moment on the inner rather than outer side of your amiable relative's front-door. His will, which you have assembled to hear read, is well known to you. By it his whole property—not so large as some of you might wish, but yet a goodly property for farmers like yourselves—is to be divided this night, share and share alike, among such of his relatives as have found it convenient to be present here between the strokes of half-past seven and eight. If some of our friends have failed us through sloth, sickness, or the misfortune of mistaking the road, they have our sympathy, but they cannot have his dollars."

"Cannot have his dollars!" echoed a rasping voice which from its smothered sound probably came from the bearded lips of the old reprobate in the chair.

The lawyer waited for one or two other repetitions of this phrase (a phrase which, for some unimaginable reason, seemed to give him an odd sort of pleasure), then he went on with greater distinctness and a certain sly emphasis, chilling in effect, but very professional:

"Ladies and gentlemen, shall I read this will?"

"No, no! The division! the division! Tell us what we are to have!" rose in a shout about him.

There was a pause. I could imagine the sharp eyes of the lawyer travelling from face to face as each thus gave voice to his cupidity, and the thin curl of his lips as he remarked in a low, tantalising way:

"There was more in the old man's clutches than you think."

A gasp of greed shook the partition against which my ear was pressed. Some one must have backed up against the wainscoting since my departure from the room. I found myself wondering which of them it was. Meantime old Smead was having his say, with the smoothness of a man who perfectly understands what is required of him.

"Mr. Westonhaugh would not have put you to so much trouble or had you wait so long if he had not expected to reward you amply. There are shares in this bag which are worth thousands instead of hundreds. Now, now stop that! Hands off! hands off! There are calculations to make first. How many of you are there? Count yourselves up."

"Nine!" called out a voice with such rapacious eagerness that the word was almost unintelligible.

"Nine." How slowly the old knave spoke! What pleasure he seemed to take in the suspense he purposely made as exasperating as possible!

"Well, if each one gets his share, he may count himself richer by two hundred thousand dollars than when he came in here to-night."

Two hundred thousand dollars! They had expected no more than thirty. Surprise made them speechless—that is, for a moment; then a pandemonium of hurrahs, shrieks, and loud-voiced enthusiasm made the room ring till wonder seized them again, and a sudden silence fell, through which I caught a far-off wail of grief from the disappointed ones without, which, heard in the dark and narrow place in which I was confined, had a peculiarly weird and desolate effect.

Perhaps it likewise was heard by some of the fortunate ones within! Perhaps one head, to mark which, in this moment of universal elation, I would have given a year from my life, turned toward the dark without, in recognition of the despair thus piteously voiced; but if so, no token of the same came to me, and I could but hope that she had shown by some such movement the natural sympathy of her sex.

Meanwhile the lawyer was addressing the company in his smoothest and most sarcastic tones.

"Mr. Westonhaugh was a wise man—a very wise man," he droned. "He foresaw what your pleasure would be, and left a letter for you. But before I read it, before I invite you to the board he ordered to be spread for you in honour of this happy occasion, there is one appeal he bade me make to those I should find assembled here. As you know, he was not personally acquainted with all the children and grandchildren of his many brothers and sisters. Salmon's sons, for instance, were perfect strangers to him, and all those boys and girls of the Evans's branch have never been long enough this side of the mountains for him to know their names, much less their temper or their lives. Yet his heirs—or such was his wish, his great wish—must be honest men, righteous in their dealings, and of stainless lives. If, therefore, any one among you feels that, for reasons he need not state, he has no right to accept his share of Anthony Westonhaugh's bounty, then that person is requested to withdraw before this letter to his heirs is read."

Withdraw? Was the man a fool? Withdraw? These cormorants! these suckers of blood! these harpies and vultures! I laughed as I imagined sneaking Hector, malicious Luke, or brutal John responding to this naïve appeal, and then found myself wondering why no echo of my mirth came from the men themselves. They must have seen much more plainly than I did the ludicrousness of their weak old kinsman's demand; yet Luke was still, Hector was still, and even John and the three or four others I have mentioned gave forth no audible token of disdain or surprise. I was asking myself what sentiment of awe or fear restrained these selfish souls, when I became conscious of a movement within, which presently resolved itself into a departing footstep.

Some conscience there had been awakened. Some one was crossing the floor toward the door. Who? I waited in anxious expectancy for the word which was to enlighten me. Happily it came soon, and from the old lawyer's lips.

"You do not feel yourself worthy?" he queried, in tones I had not heard from him before. "Why? What have you done that you should forego an inheritance to which these others feel themselves honestly entitled?"

The voice which answered gave both my mind and heart a shock. It was she who had risen at this call— she, the only true-faced person there!

Anxiously I listened for her reply. Alas! it was one of action rather than speech. As I afterwards heard, she simply opened her long cloak and showed a little infant slumbering in her arms.

"This is my reason," said she. "I have sinned in the eyes of the world, therefore I cannot take my share of Uncle Anthony's money. I did not know he exacted an unblemished record from those he expected to enrich, or I would not have come."

The sob which followed these last words showed at what a cost she thus renounced a fortune of which she, of all present, perhaps, stood in the greatest need; but there was no lingering in her step, and to me, who understood her fault only through the faint sound of infantile wailing which accompanied her departure, there was a nobility in her action which raised her in an instant to an almost ideal height of unselfish virtue.

Perhaps they felt this, too. Perhaps even these hardened men and the more than hardened woman whose presence was in itself a blight, recognised heroism when they saw it; for when the lawyer, with a certain obvious reluctance, laid his hand on the bolts of the door with the remark, "This is not my work, you know; I am but following out instructions very minutely given me," the smothered growls and grunts which rose in reply lacked the venom which had been infused into all their previous comments.

"I think our friends out there are far enough withdrawn by this time for us to hazard the opening of the door," the lawyer now remarked. "Madam, I hope you will speedily find your way to some comfortable shelter."

Then the door opened, and after a moment closed again in a silence which at least was respectful. Yet I warrant there was not a soul remaining who had not already figured in his mind to what extent his own fortune had been increased by the failure of one of their number to inherit.

As for me, my whole interest in the affair was at an end, and I was only anxious to find my way to where this desolate woman faced the mist with her unfed baby in her arms.

III

A LIFE DRAMA

But, to reach this wanderer, it was first necessary for me to escape from the house. This proved simple enough. The upstairs room toward which I rushed had a window overlooking one of the many lean-tos already mentioned. The window was fastened, but I had little difficulty in unlocking it or in finding my way to the ground from the top of the lean-to. But once again on terra-firma, I discovered that the mist was now so thick that it had all the effect of a fog at sea. It was icy cold as well, and clung to me so closely that I presently began to shudder most violently, and, strong man though I was, wish myself back in the little attic bedroom from which I had climbed in search of one in more unhappy case than myself.

But these feelings did not cause me to return. If I found the night cold, she must find it biting. If desolation oppressed my naturally hopeful spirit, must it not be more overwhelming yet to one whose memories were sad and whose future was doubtful? And the child! What infant could live in an air like this? Edging away from the house, I called out her name, but no answer came back. The persons whom we had heard flitting in restless longing about the house a few moments before had left in rage, and she, possibly, with them. Yet I could not imagine her joining herself to people of their stamp. There had been a solitariness in her aspect which seemed to forbid any such companionship. Whatever her story, at least she had nothing in common with the two ill-favoured persons whose faces I had seen looking in at the casement. No; I should find her alone, but where? Certainly the ring of mist, surrounding me at that moment, offered me little prospect of finding her anywhere, either easily or soon.

Again I raised my voice, and again I failed to meet with response. Then, fearing to leave the house lest I should be quite lost amid the fences and brush lying between it and the road, I began to feel my way along the walls, calling softly now, instead of loudly, so anxious was I not to miss any chance of carrying comfort, if not succour, to the woman I was seeking. But the night gave back no sound, and when I came to the open door of a shed I welcomed the refuge it offered, and stepped in. I was, of course, confronted by darkness—a different darkness from that without, blanket-like and impenetrable. But when after a moment of intense listening I heard a soft sound as of weariful breathing, I was seized anew by hope, and, feeling in my pocket for my matchbox, I made a light and looked around.

My intuitions had not deceived me: she was there. Sitting on the floor with her cheek pressed against the wall, she revealed to my eager scrutiny only the outlines of her pure, pale profile; but in those outlines and on those pure, pale features I saw such an abandonment of hope, mingled with such quiet endurance, that my whole soul melted before it, and it was with difficulty I managed to say:

"Pardon! I do not wish to intrude; but I am shut out of the house also, and the night is raw and cold. Can I do nothing for your comfort or for—for the child's?"

She turned toward me, and I saw the faintest gleam of pleasure tremble in the sombre stillness of her face, and then the match went out in my hand, and we were again in complete darkness. But the little wail, which at the same instant rose from between her arms, filled up the pause as her sweet "Hush!" filled my heart.

"I am used to the cold," came in another moment from the place where she crouched. "It is the child—she is hungry; and I—I walked here—feeling, hoping that, as my father's heir, I might partake in some slight measure of Uncle Anthony's money. Though my father cast me out before he died, and I have neither home nor money, I do not complain. I forfeited all when—" Another wail, another gentle "Hush!" then silence.

I lit another match. "Look in my face!" I prayed. "I am a stranger, and you would be showing only proper prudence not to trust me. But I overheard your words when you withdrew from the room where your fortune lay; and I honour you, madam. If food can be got for your little one, I will get it."

I caught sight of the convulsive clasp with which she drew to her breast the tiny bundle she held; then darkness fell again.

"A little bread," she entreated; "a little milk—ah, baby, baby, hush!"

"But where can I get it?" I cried. "They are at table inside. I hear them shouting over their good cheer. But perhaps there are neighbours near by. Do you know?"

"There are no neighbours," she replied. "What is got must be got here. I know a way to the kitchen; I used to visit Uncle Anthony when a little child. If you have the courage—"

I laughed. This token of confidence seemed to reassure her. I heard her move; possibly she stood up.

"In the further corner of this shed," said she, "there used to be a trap, connecting this floor with an underground passage-way. A ladder stood against the trap, and the small cellar at the foot communicated by means of an iron-bound door with the large one under the house. Eighteen years ago the wood of that door was old; now it should be rotten. If you have the strength—"

"I will make the effort and see," said I. "But when I am in the cellar, what then?"

"Follow the wall to the right; you will come to a stone staircase. As this staircase has no railing, be careful in ascending it. At the top you will find a door; it leads into a pantry adjoining the kitchen. Some one will be in that pantry. Some one will give you a bite for the child, and when she is quieted and the sun has risen I will go away. It is my duty to do so. My uncle was always upright, if cold. He was perfectly justified in exacting rectitude in his heirs."

I might have rejoined by asking if she detected rectitude in the faces of the greedy throng she had left behind her with the guardian of this estate, but I did not; I was too intent upon following out her directions. Lighting another match, I sought the trap. Alas! it was burdened with a pile of sticks and rubbish which looked as if they had lain there for years. As these had to be removed in total darkness, it took me some time. But once this débris had been scattered and thrown aside, I had no difficulty in finding the trap, and, as the ladder was still there, I was soon on the cellar-bottom. When, by the reassuring shout I gave, she knew that I had advanced thus far, she spoke, and her voice had a soft and thrilling sound.

"Don't forget your own needs," she said. "We two are not so hungry that we cannot wait for you to take a mouthful. I will sing to the baby. Good-bye."

These ten minutes we had spent together had made us friends. The warmth, the strength which this discovery brought, gave to my arm a force that made that old oak door go down before me in three vigorous pushes.

Had the eight fortunate ones above not been indulging in a noisy celebration of their good luck, they must have heard the clatter of this door when it fell. But good eating, good drink, and the prospect of an immediate fortune far beyond their wildest dreams, made all ears deaf, and no pause occurred in the shouts of laughter and the hum of good-fellowship which sifted down between the beams supporting the house above my head. Consequently, little or no courage was required for the completion of my adventure; and before long I came upon the staircase and the door leading from its top into the pantry. The next minute I was in front of that door.

But here a surprise awaited me. The noise, which had hitherto been loud, now became deafening, and I realised that, contrary to Eunice Westonhaugh's expectation, the supper had been spread in the kitchen, and that I was likely to run amuck of the whole despicable crowd in any effort I might make to get a bite for the famished baby.

I therefore naturally hesitated to push open the door, fearing to draw attention to myself; and when I did succeed in lifting the latch and making a small crack, I was so astonished by the sudden lull in the general babble that I drew hastily back and was for descending the stairs in sudden retreat.

But I was prevented from carrying out this cowardly impulse by catching the sound of the lawyer's voice, addressing the assembled guests.

"You have eaten and you have drunk," he was saying; "you are therefore ready for the final toast. Brothers, nephews—heirs all of Anthony Westonhaugh, I rise to propose the name of your generous benefactor, who, if spirits walk this earth, must certainly be with us to-night."

A grumble from more than one throat and an uneasy hitch from such shoulders as I could see through my narrow vantage-hole testified to the rather doubtful pleasure with which this suggestion was received. But the lawyer's tones lost none of their animation, as he went on to say:

"The bottle, from which your glasses are to be replenished for this final draught, he has himself provided. So anxious was he that it should be of the very best and altogether worthy of the occasion it is to celebrate, that he gave into my charge, almost with his dying breath, this key, telling me that it would unlock a cupboard here in which he had placed a bottle of wine of the very rarest vintage. This is the key, and yonder, if I do not mistake, is the cupboard."

They had already quaffed a dozen toasts. Perhaps this was why they accepted this proposition in a sort of panting silence, which remained unbroken while the lawyer crossed the floor, unlocked the cupboard, and brought out before them a bottle which he held up before their eyes with a simulated glee almost saturnine.

"Isn't that a bottle to make your eyes dance? The very cobwebs on it are eloquent. And see! look at this label. Tokay, friends—real Tokay! Mow many of you ever had the opportunity of drinking real Tokay before?"

A long deep sigh from a half-dozen throats, in which some strong but hitherto repressed passion, totally incomprehensible to me, found sudden vent, rose in one simultaneous sound from about that table, and I heard one jocular voice sing out:

"Pass it around, Smead! I'll drink to Uncle Anthony out of that bottle till there isn't a drop left to tell what was in it!"

But the lawyer was in no hurry.

"You have forgotten the letter, for the hearing of which you are called together. Mr. Anthony Westonhaugh left behind him a letter. The time is now come for reading it."

As I heard these words, and realised that the final toast was to be delayed, and that some few moments must yet elapse before the room would be cleared and an opportunity given me for obtaining what I needed for the famishing mother and child, I felt such impatience with the fact, and so much anxiety as to the condition of those I had left behind me, that I questioned whether it would not be better for me to return to them empty-handed than to leave them so long without the comfort of my presence, when the fascination of the scene again seized me, and I found myself lingering to mark its conclusion with an avidity which can only be explained by my sudden and intense consciousness of what it all might mean to her whose witness I had thus inadvertently become.

The careful lawyer began by quoting the injunction with which this letter had been put in his hands. "'When they are warm with food and wine, but not too warm'—thus his adjuration ran—'then let them hear my first and only words to them.' I know you are eager for these words. Folk so honest, so convinced of their own purity and uprightness that they can stand unmoved while the youngest and most helpless among them withdraws her claim to wealth and independence rather than share an unmerited bounty—such folk, I say, must be eager, must be anxious, to know why they have been made the legatees of so great a fortune under the easy conditions and amid such slight restrictions as have been imposed upon them by their munificent kinsman."

"I had rather go on drinking toasts," babbled one thick voice.

"I had rather finish my figuring," growled another, in whose grating tones no echo remained of Hector Westonhaugh's formerly honeyed voice. "I am making out a list of stock—"

"Blast your stock—that is, if you mean horses and cows!" screamed a third. "I'm going in for city life. With less money than we have got, Andreas Amsberger got to be Alderman—"

"Alderman!" sneered the whole pack; and the tumult became general. "If more of us had been sick," called out one, "or if Uncle Luke, say, had tripped into the ditch instead of on the edge of it, the fellows who came safe through might have had anything they wanted, even to the governorship of the State, or—or—"

"Silence!" came in commanding tones from the lawyer, who had begun to let his disgust appear, perhaps because he held under his thumb the bottle upon which all eyes were now lovingly centred—so lovingly, indeed, that I ventured to increase in the smallest perceptible degree the crack by means of which I was myself an interested, if unseen, participator in this scene.

A sight of Smead, and a partial glimpse of old Luke's covetous profile, rewarded this small act of daring on my part. The lawyer was standing; all the rest were sitting. Perhaps he alone retained sufficient steadiness to stand, for I observed by the control he exercised over this herd of self-seekers that he had not touched the cup which had so freely gone about among the others. The woman was hidden from me, but the change in her voice, when by any chance I heard it, convinced me that she had not disdained the toasts drunk by her brothers and nephews.

"Silence!" the lawyer reiterated, "or I will smash this bottle on the hearth!" He raised it in one threatening hand, and every man there seemed to tremble, while old Luke put out his long fingers with an entreaty that ill became them. "You want to hear the letter?" old Smead called out. "I thought so."

Putting the bottle down again, but still keeping one hand upon it, he drew a folded paper from his breast. "This," said he, "contains the final injunctions of Anthony Westonhaugh. You will listen, all of you—listen till I am done—or I will not only smash this bottle before your eyes, but I will keep forever buried in my breast the whereabouts of certain drafts and bonds in which, as his heirs, you possess the greatest interest. Nobody but myself knows where these papers can be found."

Whether this was so, or whether the threat was an empty one, thrown out by this subtle old schemer for the purpose of safeguarding his life from their possible hate and impatience, it answered his end with these semi-intoxicated men, and secured him the silence he demanded. Breaking open the seal of the envelope he held, he showed them the folded sheet which it contained with the remark:

"I have had nothing to do with the writing of this letter. It is in Mr. Westonhaugh's own hand, and he was not even so good as to communicate to me the nature of its contents. I was bidden to read it to such as should be here assembled under the provisos mentioned in his will; and as you are now in a condition to listen, I will proceed with my task as required."

This was my time for leaving, but a certain brooding terror, latent in the air, held me chained to the spot, listening with my ears, but receiving the full sense of what was read from the expression of old

Luke's face, which was probably more plainly visible to me than to those who sat beside him. For, being bent almost into a bow, as I have said, his forehead came within an inch of touching his plate, and one had to look under his arms, as I did, to catch the workings of his evil mouth, as old Smead gave forth, in his professional sing-song, the following words from his departed client:

"'Brothers, nephews, and heirs! Though the earth has lain upon my breast a month, I am with you here to-night.'"

A snort from old Luke's snarling lips, and a stir—not a comfortable one—in the jostling crowd, whose shaking arms and clawing hands I could see projecting here and there over the board.

"'My presence at this feast—a presence which, if unseen, cannot be unfelt, may bring you more pain than pleasure. But if so, it matters little. You are my natural heirs, and I have left you my money. Why, when so little love has characterised our intercourse, must be evident to such of my brothers as can recall their youth and the promise our father exacted from us on the day we set foot in this new land.

"'There were nine of us in those days—Luke, Salmon, Barbara, Hector, Eustace, Janet, Hudson, William, and myself—and all save one were promising, in appearance at least. But our father knew his offspring, and when we stood, an alien and miserable band in front of Castle Garden, at the foot of the great city whose immensity struck terror to our hearts, he drew all our hands together and made us swear by the soul of our mother, whose body we had left in the sea, that we would keep the bond of brotherhood intact, and share with mutual confidence whatever good fortune this untried country might hold in store for us. You were strong, and your voices rang out loudly. Mine was faint, for I was weak—so weak that my hand had to be held in place by my sister Barbara. But my oath has never lost its hold upon my heart, while yours—answer how you have kept it, Luke; or you, Janet; or you, Hector, of the smooth tongue and vicious heart; or you, or you, who, from one stock, recognise but one law—the law of cold-blooded selfishness, which seeks its own in face of all oaths and at the cost of another man's heart-break.

"'This I say to such as know my story. But lest there be one amongst you who has not heard from parent or uncle the true tale of him who has brought you all under one roof to-night, I will repeat it here in words, that no man may fail to understand why I remembered my oath through life and beyond death, yet stand above you an accusing spirit while you quaff me toasts and count the gains my justice divides among you.

"'I, as you all remember, was the weak one—the ne'er-do-weel. When all of you were grown and had homes of your own, I still remained under the family roof-tree, fed by our father's bounty and looking to our father's justice for that share of his savings which he had promised to all alike. When he died it came to me as it came to you; but I had married before that day—married, not, like the rest of you, for what a wife could bring, but for sentiment and true passion. This, in my case, meant a loving wife, but a frail one; and while we lived a little while on the patrimony left us, it was far too small to support us long without some aid from our own hands; and our hands were feeble and could not work. And so we fell into debt for rent and, ere long, for the commonest necessities of life. In vain I struggled to redeem myself; the time of my prosperity had not come, and I only sank deeper and deeper into debt, and finally into indigence. A baby came. Our landlord was kind, and allowed us to stay for two weeks under the roof for whose protection we could not pay; but at the end of that time we were asked to leave, and I found myself on the road with a dying wife, a wailing infant, no money in my purse, and no power in my arm to earn any. Then, when heart and hope were both failing, I recalled that ancient oath and the six prosperous homes scattered up and down the very highway on which I stood. I could not leave my wife; the fever was in her veins, and she could not bear me out of her sight; so I put her on a horse, which a kind old neighbour was willing to lend me, and holding her up with one hand, guided the horse with the other to the home of my brother Luke. He was a straight enough fellow in those days—physically, I mean—and he looked able and strong that morning, as he stood in the open doorway of his house, gazing down at us as we halted before him in the roadway. But his temper had grown greedy with the accumulation of a few dollars, and he shook his head as he closed his door, saying he remembered no oath, and that spenders must expect to be beggars.

"'Struck to the heart by a rebuff which meant prolongation of the suffering I saw in my dear wife's eyes, I stretched up and kissed her where she sat half fainting on the horse; then I moved on. I came to Barbara's home next. She had been a little mother to me once—that is, she had fed and dressed me, and doled out blows and caresses, and taught me to read and sing. But Barbara in her father's home and without fortune was not the Barbara I saw on the threshold of the little cottage she called her own. She heard my story; looked in the face of my wife, and turned her back. She had no place for idle folk in her little house; if we would work she would feed us; but we must earn our supper or go hungry to bed. I felt the trembling of my wife's frame where she leaned against my arm, and kissing her again, led her on to Salmon's. Luke, Hector, Janet, have you heard him tell of that vision at his gateway, twenty-five years ago? He is not amongst you. For twelve years he has lain beside our father in the churchyard, but his sons may be here, for they were ever alert when gold was in sight or a full glass to be drained. Ask them, ask John, whom I saw skulking behind his cousins at the garden fence that day, what it was they saw as I drew rein under the great tree which shadowed their father's doorstep.

"'The sunshine had been pitiless that morning, and the head, for whose rest in some loving shelter I would have bartered soul and body, had fallen sidewise till it lay on my arm. Pressed to her breast was our infant, whose little wail struck in pitifully as Salmon called out, "What's to do here to-day?" Do you remember it, lads? Or how you all laughed, little and great, when I asked for a few weeks' stay under my brother's roof till we could all get well and go about our tasks again? I remember. I, who am writing these words from the very mouth of the tomb, I remember; but I did not curse you. I only rode on to the next. The way ran uphill now; and the sun which, since our last stop, had been under a cloud, came out and blistered my wife's cheeks, already burning red with fever. But I pressed my lips upon them, and led her on. With each rebuff I gave her a kiss; and her smile, as her head pressed harder and harder upon my arm, now exerting all its strength to support her, grew almost divine. But it vanished at my nephew Lemuel's.

"'He was shearing sheep, and could give no time to company; and when late in the day I drew rein at Janet's, and she said she was going to have a dance, and could not look after sick folk, the pallid lips failed to return my despairing embrace; and in the terror which this brought me I went down in the gathering twilight into the deep valley where William raised his sheep, and reckoned day by day the increase among his pigs. Oh, the chill of that descent! Oh, the gloom of the gathering shadows! As we neared the bottom, and I heard a far-off voice shout out a hoarse command, some instinct made me reach up for the last time and bestow that faithful kiss, which was at once her consolation and my prayer. My lips were cold with the terror of my soul, but they were not so cold as the cheek they touched, and, shrieking in my misery and need, I fell before William where he halted by the horse-trough and—He was always a hard man, was William, and it was a shock to him, no doubt, to see us standing in our anguish and necessity before him; but he raised the whip in his hand, and when it fell my arm fell with it, and she slipped from my grasp to the ground and lay in a heap in the roadway.

"'He was ashamed next minute, and pointed to the house nearby. But I did not carry her in, and she died in the roadway. Do you remember it, Luke? Do you remember it, Lemuel?

"'But it is not of this that I complain at this hour, nor is it for this I ask you to drink the toast I have prepared for you.'"

The looks, the writhings of old Luke and such others as I could now see through the widening crack my hands unconsciously made in the doorway, told me that the rack was at work in this room so lately given up to revelry. Yet the mutterings, which from time to time came to my ears from one sullen lip or another, did not rise into frightened imprecation or even into any assertion of sorrow or contrition. It seemed as if some suspense common to all held them speechless, if not dumbly apprehensive; and while the lawyer said nothing in recognition of this, he could not have been quite blind to it, for he bestowed one curious glance around the table before he proceeded with old Anthony's words.

Those words had now become short, sharp, and accusatory.

"'My child lived, and what remained to me of human passion and longing centred in his frail existence. I managed to earn enough for his eating and housing, and in time I was almost happy again. This was while our existence was a struggle; but when, with the discovery of latent powers in my own mind, I began to find my place in the world and to earn money, then your sudden interest in my boy taught me a new lesson in human selfishness, but not as yet new fears. My nature was not one to grasp ideas of evil, and the remembrance of that oath still remained to make me lenient toward you.

"'I let him see you; not much, not often, but yet often enough for him to realise that he had uncles and cousins, or, if you like it better, kindred. And how did you repay this confidence on my part? What hand had ye in the removal of this small barrier to the fortune my own poor health warranted you in looking upon even in those early days as your own? To others' eyes it may appear none; to mine, ye are one and all his murderers as certainly as all of you were the murderers of the good physician hastening to his aid. For his illness was not a mortal one. He would have been saved if the doctor had reached him; but a precipice swallowed that good Samaritan, and only I of all who looked upon the footprints which harrowed up the road at this dangerous point knew whose shoes would fit those marks. God's providence, it was called, and I let it pass for such; but it was a providence which cost me my boy and made you my heirs.'"

Silence, as sullen in character as the men who found themselves thus openly impeached, had for some minutes now replaced the muttered complaints which had accompanied the first portion of this denunciatory letter. As the lawyer stopped to cast them another of those strange looks, a gleam from old Luke's sidewise eyes startled the man next him, who, shrugging a shoulder, passed the underhanded look on, till it had circled the board and stopped with the man sitting opposite the crooked sinner who had started it.

I began to have a wholesome dread of them all, and was astonished to see the lawyer drop his hand from the bottle, which to some degree offered itself as a possible weapon. But he knew his audience better than I did. Though the bottle was now free for any man's taking, not a hand trembled toward it, nor was a single glass held out.

The lawyer, with an evil smile, went on with his relentless client's story.

"'Ye had killed my wife; ye had killed my son; but this was not enough. Being lonesome in my great house, which was as much too large for me as my fortune was, I had taken a child to replace the boy I had lost. Remembering the cold blood running in the veins of those nearest me, I chose a boy from alien stock, and for a while knew contentment again. But as he developed and my affections strengthened, the possibility of all my money going his way roused my brothers and sisters from the complacency they had enjoyed since their road to fortune had been secured by my son's death, and one day—can you recall it, Hudson? Can you recall it, Lemuel?—the boy was brought in from the mill, and laid at my feet dead! He had stumbled amongst the great belts, but whose was the voice which, with the loud "Halloo!" had startled him? Can you say, Luke? Can you say, John? I can say, in whose ear it was whispered that three, if not more of you were seen moving among the machinery that fatal morning.

"'Again God's providence was said to have visited my house; and again ye were my heirs.'"

"Stop there!" broke in the harsh voice of Luke, who was gradually growing livid under his long grey locks.

"Lies! lies!" shrieked Hector, gathering courage from his brother.

"Cut it all and give us the drink!" snarled one of the younger men, who was less under the effect of liquor than the rest.

But a trembling voice muttered "Hush!" and the lawyer, whose eye had grown steely under these comments, took advantage of the sudden silence which had followed this last objurgation, and went steadily on:

"'Some men would have made a will and denounced you. I made a will, but did not denounce you. I am no breaker of oaths. More than this, I learned a new trick. I, who hated all subtlety, and looked upon craft as the favourite weapon of the devil, learned to smile with my lips while my heart was burning with hatred. Perhaps this was why you all began to smile, too, and joke me about certain losses I had sustained, by which you meant the gains which had come to me. That these gains were many times greater than you realised added to the sting of this good-fellowship, but I held my peace, and you began to have confidence in a good-nature which nothing could shake. You even gave me a supper.'"

A supper!

What was there in these words to cause every man there to stop in whatever movement he was making, and stare with wide-open eyes intently at the reader? He had spoken quietly; he had not even looked up; but the silence which for some minutes back had begun to reign over that tumultuous gathering now became breathless, and the seams in Hector's cheeks deepened to a bluish criss-cross.

"'You remember that supper?'"

As the word rang out again I threw wide the door. I might have stalked openly into their circle; not a man there would have noticed me.

"'It was a memorable occasion,'" the lawyer read on, with stoical impassiveness. "'There was not a brother lacking. Luke, and Hudson, and William, and Hector, and Eustace's boys, as well as Eustace himself; Janet too, and Salmon's Lemuel, and Barbara's son, who, even if his mother had gone the way of all flesh, had so trained her black brood in the love of the things of this world that I scarcely missed her when I looked about among you all for the eight sturdy brothers and sisters who had joined in one clasp and one oath under the eye of a true-hearted immigrant, our father. What I did miss was one true eye lifted to my glance; but I did not show that I missed it. And so our peace was made, and we separated, you to wait for your inheritance, and I for the death which was to secure it to you. For when the cup passed round that night you each dropped into it a tear of repentance, and tears make bitter drinking. I sickened as I quaffed, and was never myself again, as you know. Do you understand me, you cruel, crafty ones?"'

Did they not! Heads quaking, throats gasping, teeth chattering—no longer sitting—all risen, all looking with wild eyes for the door—was it not apparent that they understood, and only waited for one more word to break away and flee the accursed house?

But that word lingered. Old Smead had now grown pale himself, and read with difficulty the lines which were to end this frightful scene. As I saw the red gleam of terror shine out from his small eyes, I wondered if he had been but the blind tool of his implacable client, and was as ignorant as those before him of what was to follow this heavy arraignment. The dread with which he finally proceeded was too marked for me to doubt the truth of this surmise. This is what he found himself forced to read:

"'There was a bottle reserved for me. It had a green label on it—'"

A shriek from every one there and a hurried look up and down at the bottles standing on the table.

"'A green label,'" the lawyer repeated, "'and it made a goodly appearance as it was set down before me. But you had no liking for wine with a green label on the bottle. One by one you refused it, and when I rose to quaff my final glass alone, every eye before me fell and did not lift again until the glass was drained. I did not notice this then, but I see it all now, just as I hear again the excuses you gave for not filling your glasses as the bottle went round. One had drunk enough; one suffered from qualms brought on by an unaccustomed indulgence in oysters; one felt that wine good enough for me was too good for him, and so on, and so on. Not one to show frank eyes and drink with me as I was ready to drink with him! Why? Because one and all of you knew what was in that cup, and would not risk an inheritance so nearly within your grasp.'"

"Lies! lies!" again shrieked the raucous voice of Luke, smothered by terror; while oaths, shouts, imprecations, rang out in horrid tumult from one end of the table to the other, till the lawyer's face, over which a startling change was rapidly passing, drew the whole crowd forward again in awful fascination, till they clung, speechless, arm in arm, shoulder propping shoulder, while he gasped out in dismay equal to their own these last fatal words:

"'That was at your board, my brothers; now you are at mine. You have eaten my viands, drunk of my cup; and now, through the mouth of the one man who has been true to me because therein lies his advantage, I offer you a final glass. Will you drink it? I drank yours. By that old-time oath which binds us to share each other's fortune, I ask you to share this cup with me. You will not?'"

"No, no, no!" shouted one after another.

"'Then,'" the inexorable voice went on, a voice which to these miserable souls was no longer that of the lawyer, but an issue from the grave they had themselves dug for Anthony Westonhaugh, "'know that your abstinence comes too late; that you have already drunk the toast destined to end your lives. The bottle which you must have missed from that board of yours has been offered you again. A label is easily changed, and—Luke, John, Hector, I know you all so well—that bottle has been greedily emptied by you; and while I, who sipped sparingly, lived three weeks, you, who have drunk deep, have not three hours before you, possibly not three minutes.'"

Oh, the wail of those lost souls as this last sentence issued in a final pant of horror from the lawyer's quaking lips! Shrieks—howls—prayers for mercy—groans deep enough to make the hair rise—and curses, at sound of which I shut my ears in horror, only to open them again in dread, as, with one simultaneous impulse, they flung themselves upon the lawyer, who, foreseeing this rush, had backed up against the wall.

He tried to stem the tide.

"I knew nothing of the poisoning," he protested. "That was not my reason for declining to drink. I wished to preserve my senses—to carry out my client's wishes. As God lives, I did not know he meant to carry his revenge so far. Mercy! mer—"

But the hands which clutched him were the hands of murderers, and the lawyer's puny figure could not stand up against the avalanche of human terror, relentless fury, and mad vengeance which now rolled in upon it. As I bounded to his relief he turned his ghastly face upon me. But the way between us was blocked, and I was preparing myself to see him sink before my eyes when an unearthly shriek rose from behind us, and every living soul in that mass of struggling humanity paused, set and staring, with stiffened limbs and eyes fixed, not on him, not on me, but on one of their own number—the only woman amongst them, Janet Clapsaddle—who, with clutching hands clawing her breast, was reeling in solitary agony in her place beside the board. As they looked she fell, and lay with upturned face and staring eyes, in whose glassy depths the ill-fated ones who watched her could see mirrored their own impending doom.

It was an awful moment. A groan, in which was concentrated the despair of seven miserable souls, rose from that petrified band; then, man by man, they separated and fell back, showing on each weak or wicked face the particular passion which had driven them into crime and made them the victims of this wholesale revenge. There had been some sort of bond between them till the vision of death rose before each shrinking soul. Shoulder to shoulder in crime, they fell apart as their doom approached, and rushing, shrieking, each man for himself, they one and all sought to escape by doors, windows, or any outlet which promised release from this fatal spot. One rushed by me—I do not know which one—and I felt as if a flame from hell had licked me, his breath was so hot and the moans he uttered so like the curses we imagine to blister the lips of the lost. None of them saw me; they did not even detect the sliding form of the lawyer crawling away before them to some place of egress of which they had no knowledge; and, convinced that in this scene of death I could play no part worthy of her who awaited me, I too rushed away, and, seeking my old path through the cellar, sought her side, where she still crouched in patient waiting against the dismal wall.

IV

THE FINAL SHOCK

Her baby had fallen asleep. I knew this by the faint, low sweetness of her croon; and, shuddering with the horrors I had witnessed—horrors which acquired a double force from the contrast presented by the peace of this quiet spot and the hallowing influence of the sleeping infant—I threw myself down in the darkness at her feet, gasping out:

"Oh, thank God and your uncle's seeming harshness that you have escaped the doom which has overtaken those others! You and your babe are still alive; while they—"

"What of them? What has happened to them? You are breathless, trembling; you have brought no bread—"

"No, no. Food in this house means death. Your relatives gave food and wine to your uncle at a supper; he, though now in his grave, has returned the same to them. There was a bottle—"

I stopped, appalled. A shriek, muffled by distance but quivering with the same note of death I had heard before, had gone up again from the other side of the wall against which we were leaning.

"Oh!" she gasped, "and my father was at that supper! my father, who died last night cursing the day he was born! We are an accursed race! I have known it all my life. Perhaps that was why I mistook passion for love. And my baby—O God, have mercy! God, have mercy!"

The plaintiveness of that cry, the awesomeness of what I had seen—of what was going on at that moment almost within the reach of our arms—the darkness, the desolation of our two souls, affected me as I had never been affected in my whole life before. In the concentrated experience of the last two hours I seemed to have lived years under this woman's eyes; to know her as I did my own heart; to love her as I did my own soul. No growth of feeling ever brought the ecstasy of that moment's inspiration. With no sense of doing anything strange, with no fear of being misunderstood, I reached out my hand, and, touching hers where it lay clasped about her infant, I said:

"We are two poor wayfarers. A rough road loses half its difficulties when trodden by two. Shall we, then, fare on together—you, I, and the little child?"

She gave a sob; there was sorrow, longing, grief, hope in its thrilling, low sound. As I recognised the latter emotion I drew her to my breast. The child did not separate us.

"We shall be happy," I murmured, and her sigh seemed to answer a delicious "Yes," when suddenly there came a shock to the partition against which we leaned, and, starting from my clasp, she cried:

"Our duty is in there. Shall we think of ourselves, or even of each other, while these men, all relatives of mine, are dying on the other side of this wall?"

Seizing my hand, she dragged me to the trap; but here I took the lead and helped her down the ladder. When I had her safely on the floor at the foot she passed in front of me again; but once up the steps and in front of the kitchen door I thrust her behind me, for one glance into the room beyond had convinced me it was no place for her.

But she would not be held back. She crowded forward beside me, and together we looked upon the wreck within. It was a never-to-be-forgotten scene. The demon that was in those men had driven them to demolish furniture, dishes, everything. In one heap lay what, an hour before, had been an inviting board surrounded by rollicking and greedy guests. But it was not upon this overthrow we stopped to look. It was upon something that mingled with it, dominated it, and made of this chaos only a setting to awful death. Janet's face, in all its natural hideousness and depravity, looked up from the floor beside this heap; and farther on, lay the twisted figure of him they called Hector, with something more than the seams of greedy longing round his wide-staring eyes and icy temples. Two in this room! and on the threshold of the one beyond a moaning third, who sank into eternal silence as we approached; and before the fireplace in the great room a horrible crescent that had once been aged Luke, upon whom we had no sooner turned our backs than we caught glimpses here and there of other prostrate forms which moved once under our eyes and then moved no more.

One only still stood upright, and he was the man whose obtrusive figure and sordid expression had so revolted me in the beginning. There was no colour now in his flabby and heavily fallen cheeks. The eyes, in whose false sheen I had seen so much of evil, were glazed now, and his big and burly frame shook the door it pressed against. He was staring at a small slip of paper he held, and, from his anxious looks, appeared to miss something which neither of us had power to supply. It was a spectacle to make devils rejoice and mortals fly aghast. But Eunice had a spirit like an angel, and, drawing near him, she said:

"Is there anything I can do for you, Cousin John?"

He started, looked at her with the same blank gaze he had hitherto cast at the wall, then some words formed on his working lips, and we heard:

"I cannot reckon; I was never good at figures. But if Luke is gone, and William, and Hector, and Barbara's boy, and Janet, how much does that leave for me?"

He was answered almost the moment he spoke, but it was by other tongues, and in another world than this. As his body fell forward I tore open the door before which he had been standing, and, lifting the almost fainting Eunice in my arms, I carried her out into the night. As I did so I caught a final glimpse of the pictured face I had found it so hard to understand a couple of hours before. I understood it now.

A surprise awaited us as we turned toward the gate. The mist had lifted, and a keen but not unpleasant wind was driving from the north. Borne on it we heard voices. The village had emptied itself, probably at the alarm given by the lawyer, and it was these good men and women whose approach we heard. As we had nothing to fear from them we went forward to meet them. As we did so three crouching figures rose from some bushes we passed and ran scurrying before us through the gateway. They were the late-comers who had shown such despair at being shut out from this fatal house, and who probably were not yet acquainted with the doom they had escaped.

There were lanterns in the hands of some of the men who now approached. As we stopped before them these lanterns were held up, and by the light they gave we saw, first, the lawyer's frightened face, then the visages of two men who seemed to be persons of some authority.

"What news?" faltered the lawyer, seeing by our faces that we knew the worst.

"Bad," I returned; "the poison had lost none of its virulence by being mixed so long with the wine."

"How many?" asked the man on his right anxiously.

"Eight," was my solemn reply.

"There were but eight," faltered the lawyer; "that means, then, all?"

"All," I repeated.

A murmur of horror rose, swelled, then died out in tumult as the crowd swept on past us.

For a moment we stood watching these people; saw them pause before the door we had left open behind us, then rush in, leaving a wail of terror on the shuddering midnight air. When all was quiet again, Eunice laid her hand upon my arm.

"Where shall we go?" she asked despairingly. "I do not know of a house that will open to me."

The answer to her question came from other lips than mine.

"I do not know one that will not," spoke up a voice behind our backs. "Your withdrawal from the circle of heirs did not take from you your rightful claim to an inheritance which, according to your uncle's will, could be forfeited only by a failure to arrive at the place of distribution within the hour set by the testator. As I see the matter now, this appeal to the honesty of the persons so collected was a test by which my unhappy client strove to save from the general fate such members of his miserable family as fully recognised their sin and were truly repentant."

It was Lawyer Smead. He had lingered behind the others to tell her this. She was, then, no outcast, but rich, very rich; how rich I dared not acknowledge to myself, lest a remembrance of the man who was the last to perish in that house of death should return to make this calculation hateful. It was a blow which struck deep—deeper than any either of us had sustained that night. As we came to realise it, I stepped slowly back, leaving her standing erect and tall in the middle of the roadway, with her baby in her arms. But not for long; soon she was close at my side murmuring softly:

"Two wayfarers still! Only, the road will be more difficult and the need of companionship greater. Shall we fare on together, you, I—and the little child?"

Anna Katharine Green – A Concise Bibliography

The Leavenworth Case (1878)
A Strange Disappearance (1880)
The Sword of Damocles: A Story of New York Life (1881)
The Defence of the Bride, and other Poems (1882)
X Y Z: A Detective Story (1883)
Hand and Ring (1883)
The Mill Mystery (1886)
7 to 12: A Detective Story (1887)
Risifi's Daughter, A Drama (1887)
Behind Closed Doors (1888)

Forsaken Inn (1890)
A Matter of Millions (1891)
The Old Stone House and Other Stories (1891)
Cynthia Wakeham's Money (1892)
Marked "Personal" (1893)
Miss Hurd: An Enigma (1894)
The Doctor, His Wife, and the Clock (1895)
Doctor Izard (1895)
That Affair Next Door (1897)
Lost Man's Lane: A Second Episode in the Life of Amelia Butterworth (1898)
Agatha Webb (1899)
The Circular Study (1900)
A Difficult Problem (1900)
One of my Sons (1901)
The Filigree Ball: Being a Full and True Account of the Solution of the Mystery Concerning the Jeffrey-Moore Affair (1903)
The Amethyst Box (1905)
The House in the Mist (1905)
The Millionaire Baby (1905)
The Chief Legatee' (1906)
The Woman in the Alcove (1906)
The Mayor's Wife (1907)
The House of the Whispering Pines (1910)
Three Thousand Dollars (1910)
Initials Only (1911)
Masterpieces of Mystery (1913)
Dark Hollow (1914)
The Golden Slipper, and Other Problems for Violet Strange (1915)
To the Minute; Scarlet and Black: Two Tales of Life's Perplexities (1916)
The Mystery of the Hasty Arrow (1917)
The Step on the Stair (1923)